I0589192

Love, Death
and Revolution

Mochtar Lubis
Translated from the Indonesian by
Stefanny Irawan

Dalang Publishing

Love, Death and Revolution
Originally published as *Maut dan Cinta* in 1977 by Penerbit Pustaka Jaya,
    Jakarta, Indonesia
5th printing by Yayasan Obor, Jakarta, Indonesia (ISBN 979-461-127-1)
Copyright © 1993 Mochtar Lubis
Translation copyright © 2015 Stefanny Irawan

Cover design: Herfitrisna Yulianti Asnar
Book design: Son Do
Editor: Elizabeth Ridley
Indonesian literary advisors: Manneke Budiman and Muhammad Taufiqurrohman

Dalang Publishing LLC
San Mateo, CA
www.dalangpublishing.com
dalangpublishing@gmail.com

ISBN: 978-0-9836273-5-7
Library of Congress number: 2015938550

LOVE, DEATH AND REVOLUTION

Dedication

The first English-language edition of this book is lovingly and respectfully dedicated to the memory of Anwar Rawy (1927–2014), an Indonesian in the true sense of the word. His acceptance and guidance have been a beacon on my long journey home.

> *Semoga semangat perjuangan para pahlawan dan pejuang selalu berkobar dalam hati masing-masing orang Indonesia.*

> *May the spirit of the warriors of the revolution always fill the hearts of the Indonesian people.*

Lian Gouw
Publisher

I could not possibly have felt anything but honored when I was asked to translate the work of one of Indonesia's legendary literary figures.

I read and learned about Mochtar Lubis in my Indonesian language class as early as primary school. In middle school my teacher introduced me to one of Lubis' widely acclaimed novels, *Harimau! Harimau! (Tiger! Tiger!)* and I remember regarding him as a compelling writer with a distinct voice. Working on *Love, Death and Revolution* reminded me of my first impression about him.

As I worked on Mochtar Lubis' biography for this publication, I read more about his life and I realized this novel is his recollection of life in relationship to his beloved nation.

Through the main character, Sadeli, Lubis explores and raises valid and difficult questions regarding idealism, power, corruption, humanity, justice, loyalty, compassion, and love. Considering the book was originally published in 1977, I am surprised how closely the narrative echoes Indonesia's ongoing concerns. Lubis, through his critical thinking and sharp analysis, has managed to distill a set of profound and ever-relevant topics worth pondering.

As a translator, I believe every book I work on hones my skills. *Love, Death and Revolution* is the second historical novel I have translated for Dalang Publishing, where I have learned that translating historical novels calls for research to ensure historical accuracy within the work. I thank Lian Gouw for working with me and insisting I check the historical facts. While it was taxing at times, I realize it is a necessary, even mandatory, step in the process of publishing accurate historical fiction. I also thank Elizabeth Ridley, Dalang's savvy and patient editor, for doing her magic on the manuscript.

Although this novel will resonate most deeply with Indonesians, the universal issues it explores make it an important addition to every bookshelf, including, I hope, your own.

Stefanny Irawan
April 2015

Southeast Asia
N
W E
S
China
Hong Kong
Macao
Thailand
Bangkok
South China Sea
Riau Islands
Singapore
Sumatra
Biliton Bangka
Islands
Indonesia
Indian Ocean
Java

Sumatra

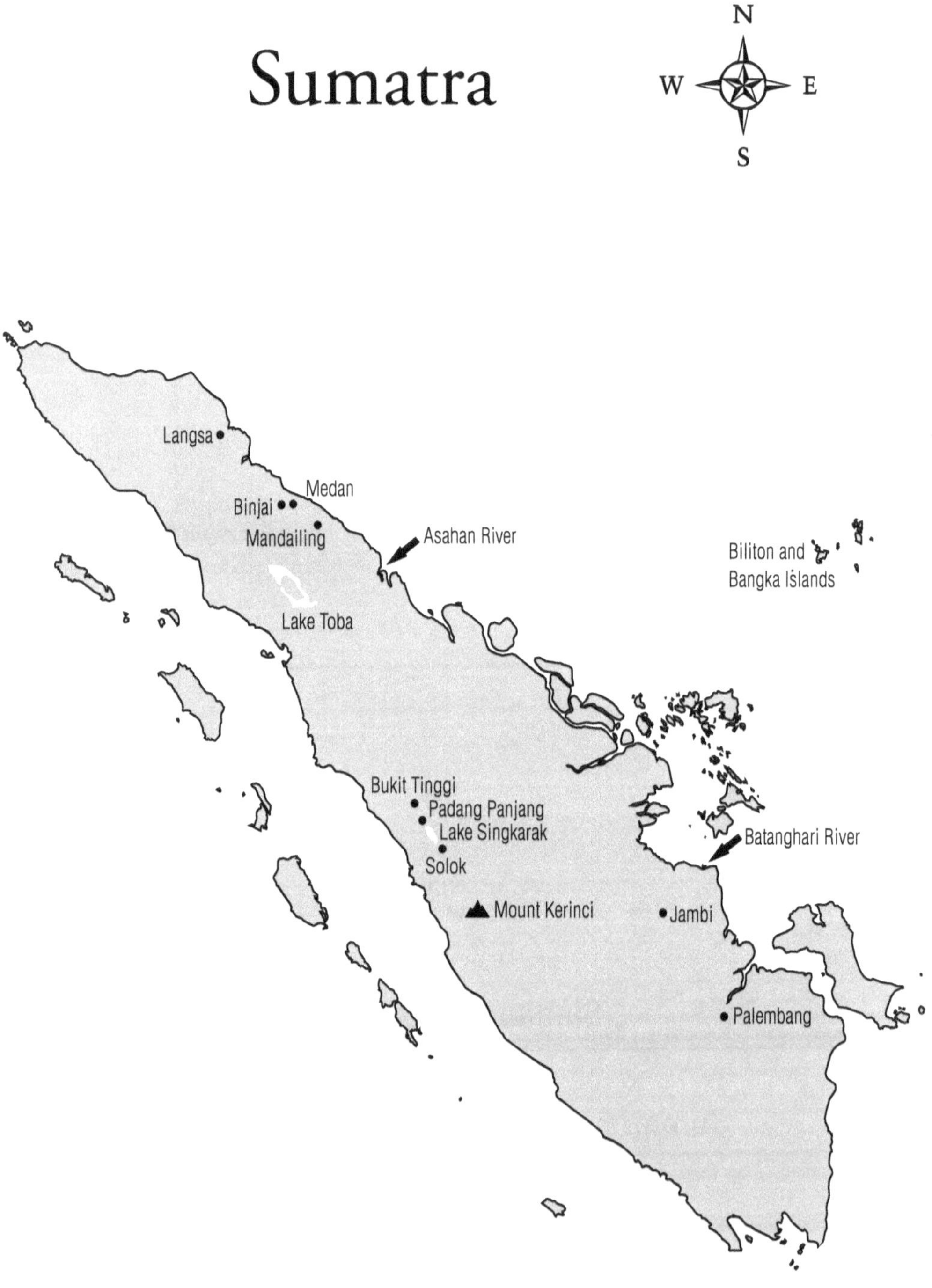
N
W
E
S
Langsa
Medan
Binjai
Mandailing
Asahan River
Biliton and
Bangka Islands
Lake Toba
Bukit Tinggi
Padang Panjang
Lake Singkarak
Solok
Batanghari River
Mount Kerinci
Jambi
Palembang

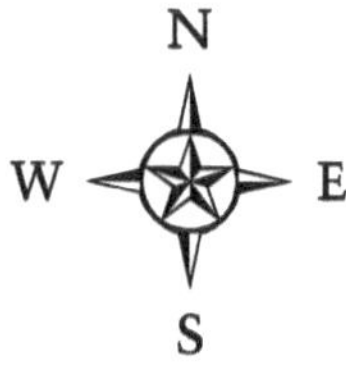

Java

N
W E
S

Jakarta
Semarang
Tuban
Magelang
Kaliurang
Solo
Madiun
Yogyakarta

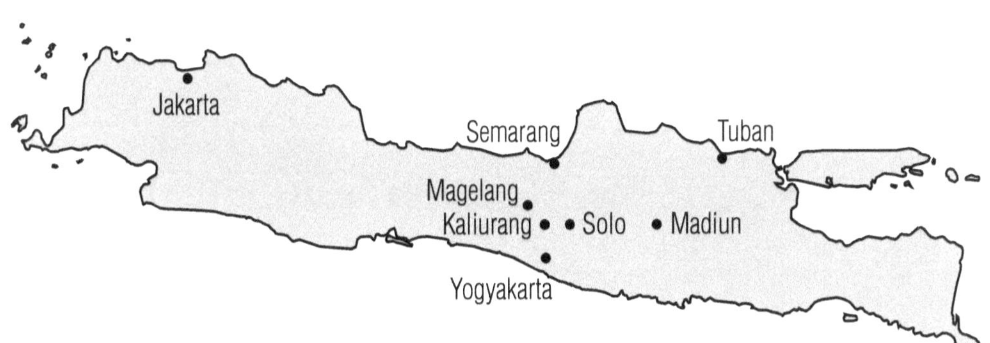

LOVE, DEATH AND REVOLUTION

Chapter 1

Early 1947

The dark sky above the ocean thinned in the east as dawn began to break. The wind was still strong and the waves were big but not big enough to disturb their journey.

Sadeli lay on the deck of the Bugis ship near the main mast. The wind filled the large sail. His whole body seemed to be on alert. From his toes to the back of his head, and his hands resting on the wooden deck, he felt everything through the thin *pandan* mat underneath him. He felt every rocking movement the waves caused. He felt the depth of the ocean beneath those waves. He felt the lap of the earth on the ocean's floor.

He heard every single sound the ship made: the screeching at the top of each mast, the scraping of the lines, the flapping of the sails, the creaking from the lower deck, to the squeaking of the heavy steering wheel at the stern. He also heard the caws of seagulls flying by, welcoming the sunrise.

He smelled the fragrant coffee from the galley and the savory smell of barbequed salted fish.

Sadeli smiled as he listened to Wan A Lang. The old and overweight captain complained that his coffee needed more sugar. It reminded Sadeli of the ship's cargo. The 80-ton *Sri Mulia* carried sugar from Tuban, a port in East Java, to Singapore, where the sugar had to be sold. The proceeds of the sale were to finance the struggle for Indonesia's independence. The money was to be used to buy guns, gunpowder, and medicines, and finance the overseas activities of the two-year-old republic.

They had left Tuban eleven days ago.

Sadeli was a major in the Indonesian National Army's intelligence. He was thirty-three years old, born in 1914 in Semarang into the family of a regent's assistant. His mother raised him to be religious, while his father made sure he would be an independent adult. His father never wanted any of his children to become a civil servant like him. He often said to Sadeli and his younger sisters and brothers, "Let me be the only East Indies' civil servant in this family. You'd better study so you can stand on your own two feet. Be a merchant, a doctor, a successful modern farmer, anything but a civil servant."

Sadeli was the oldest of three boys and two girls. As far as he could remember, his childhood had never been marred by violence from a father or neglect by a mother. Both of his parents died from lack of medicine for their illness during the Japanese occupation. He always thought of them fondly and lovingly. He also had a loving relationship with his sisters and brothers. His sisters were married and had many children, while one brother became a doctor and the other was a governor's assistant in Sumatra.

Sadeli smiled, recalling his father's warning about working as a civil servant. Surely his father referred to holding such a position with the Dutch East Indies' government and not the sovereign and independent Republic of Indonesia.

Light-hearted, humorous, frank, and helpful, Sadeli was a simple man. He easily liked and trusted someone he just met. His ambition to become a teacher stemmed from his desire to teach his fellow Indonesians to think independently, and free themselves from the ignorance the Dutch colonizers imposed on them.

While Sadeli attended the Hollands Indische Kweekschool—a teacher training school for native Indonesians during the Dutch colonization—in Bandung, he had been drawn to the national movement. The writings of Indonesian leaders like Hatta, Syahrir, Soekarno, Dr. Soetomo, and Dewantoro influenced him greatly. Multatuli's novel, *Saijah and Adinda,* also affected him deeply.

He increased his knowledge in history, politics, and literature by reading any type of books on the topics he could get his hands on. The more he read, the more determined he became to devote his life to the independence of his nation.

Sadeli vowed to stay single until his nation achieved independence. He trained his body to stay fit and strong, always poised to perform any necessary tough job to achieve the goal. To keep in shape, he engaged in all kinds of sports; he played tennis and soccer, swam and lifted weights. He intentionally prepared himself, physically and mentally, to become a true Indonesian warrior.

When he contemplated what kind of a person an Indonesian warrior might be, he conjured the great knights and warriors of the past centuries. The Dutch history lessons during his primary school years brought to mind Admiral Piet Hein, the governors Daendels and Jan Pieterzoon Coen, whom he hated, then Sir Francis Drake, Walter Raleigh, Saladin, Richard the Lionheart, Charlemagne, El Cid of Spain, the Muslim knights in Spain, Alexander the Great, Hannibal, Caesar, Siegfried, Odysseus, Gatotkaca, Hanuman, Rama, Arjuna, Diponegoro, Tuanku Imam Bonjol, and the heroes of Aceh who died fighting the Dutch.

Sadeli thought a knight should be fair. Always honest and faithful, he should be a defender of truth and justice who fights against cruelty, supporting the weak and oppressed. He would respect and protect women, guard and love children. Sadeli imagined a knight to be healthy, strong, and agile, have mercy for his fallen enemy and be forgiving.

A knight, to Sadeli, represented the perfection of good human traits and, among all knights, the Indonesian knight was the best. Thus was the perfect picture of a knight Sadeli had formed when he was between seventeen and twenty years old.

During those teenage years he often dreamed of donning armor and a steel helmet, holding a long sword in his right hand and a shield in his left. He dreamed of riding a horse on a stunning saddle, being the leader of a cavalry sporting colorful flags, and of the sunlight shining on his armor and helmet bearing beautiful feathers. He dreamed of the cheering crowd, the music of war trumpets and drums, the sound of galloping horses, and the sonorous war cry slicing the air.

In his dreams, he fought the battle at Agincourt and joined Richard the Lionheart seizing Darussalam, yet he was also with Saladin warding off the Crusaders' attack. He was the first person who set foot at the valley of Istanbul when Mehmed the Conqueror invaded Europe. He was one of the Turkish knights who besieged Vienna, a member of the Arabian cavalry conquering Spain and attacking France. He joined Marco Polo's team exploring from Venice to Cathay. He was Kublai Khan's general. He was also a knight to Harun al-Rashid.

He conquered Xerxes and traveled to India with Alexander the Great. He disliked Napoleon even though he admired his work as a commander. He thought highly of Mustafa Kemal. He was among the Anglo Saxons pioneering North America and continuing westward. But he had greater respect for the Native Americans who fought them: Sitting Bull and Crazy Horse.

He hated Cortez. He was wholeheartedly on King Montezuma's side. He was interested in Washington and Lafayette. He imagined himself as Captain Blood, Scaramouche, Sisingamangaraja, Teuku Umar, and Diponegoro.

Whenever Sadeli recalled his dreams about these exalted knights, he smiled to himself. He recalled the Japanese occupation of Indonesia during World War II, when he joined the training for a *Chudancho*, company commander, because the one for a *Daidancho*, battalion commander, was already full. Many of his opinions about a true knight's behavior changed during that time. The first one to go, and how easily so, was his commitment to celibacy.

Sadeli remembered the evening when his friends dared him to share a bed with a woman in a locked room. They bet on a pack of Koa, a popular but very hard to get brand of cigarettes during Japan's occupation, that he would lose his virginity.

As Sadeli entered the room with great confidence, his friends immediately locked the door from outside and said they would be back in an hour. The woman lying on the bed smiled at him. Under a sheer pink kimono, her small round breasts and her lean figure challenged Sadeli's innocence.

Apparently his friends had briefed her about their bet with him. She patted the place next to her and invited him to sit down. He had never been that close to a woman with no one else in the room. Although he remained calm, something strange started to stir in his subconscious. It felt like fear, but the fear urged him to meet the challenge.

Sadeli walked with confidence to the bed and took a seat. The young woman sat up and inched next to him. Brushing her breasts against his arm, she aroused the tiger below his waist. When she took his hand and placed it over her breast, the tiger roared. It sat up straight, and sniffed the scent of his approaching prey. He had a difficult time taming the beast. Suddenly his blood rushed and his body started to tremble. The tiger crouched. Its long tail lowered close to the ground, every muscle in that stout body contracted, it roared and jumped its prey.

The woman giggled as she pulled him into an embrace that brought him to lie on the bed.

When his friends knocked on the door an hour later, Sadeli remained quiet. He didn't want to leave the warm-bodied woman just yet. The woman told them to leave. His friends laughed and moved away from the door.

The next day, he paid what he owed them from the bet, plus another pack of Kao. His friends laughed and wanted to hear about his experience, but he had only scoffed, "Two packs of Kao should serve as an elaborated report."

His friends seemed satisfied with his answer. They broke into laughter and slapped his shoulder, hard. They didn't know Sadeli felt he had reached a new level in his life.

The young woman had let him into a secret he had no access to before. He had been a little surprised by this because his friends had told him they felt disgusted after sex, even with their own wives. One of them said, "I want to kick her far, far away."

Sadeli felt completely different. Zainab had filled him with love. The young woman had enriched him with something beautiful and intimate, something that only the union of a woman and a man could create. Later, Sadeli would know other women, but he was never able to forget Zainab, his first.

Sadeli also recalled the revolution after Indonesia proclaimed its independence on August 17, 1945. His thoughts drifted back to the battle to overtake a Japanese armory on the outskirts of Bandung. They expected they would be able to do it peacefully, but the Japanese broke their promise. The Japanese received orders to surrender their weaponry only to the Allies who were expected to land soon on Java.

Sadeli and his battalion attacked the Japanese headquarters at two in the morning. The Japanese were taken by surprise and failed to launch any effective counterattack.

Sadeli's unit took over the command center in no time. They killed the Japanese using all the assassination techniques they had once learned from the Japanese. All of their hatred and vengeance toward the viciousness shown by the Japanese during their occupation exploded during those wee hours of the morning. Each shot and stab was a payback for every insult, slap, kick, or rape that Indonesian women had endured. It was also for every cruelty experienced by Indonesian forced laborers who were tricked and blackmailed, then buried on the numerous islands in the Pacific Ocean and across Southeast Asia. The ambush on the Japanese headquarters was Sadeli's first killing.

During his training with the Japanese military, Sadeli had often wondered if he would have the mettle to kill someone. He wondered how he would feel afterwards. For him, human beings held their own sanctity among all God's creatures. Humans were not on the same level as a chicken or a water buffalo. Humans were unique in this universe. Humans think, speak in different languages, and can tell the difference between right and wrong. Humans have instinct, but they also use their logic. Humans, according to Freud, are sexually driven beings, but also have a conscience.

All of that led Sadeli to believe that humans deserved respect as individuals. A person's happiness and freedom were a matter of value and dignity and should never be controlled by the state or other authority, or a dictator like Hitler. Cultured and civilized humans should avoid using violence to solve the problems they have with one another and even among nations. Slavery and colonization must be vigorously opposed.

Sadeli was convinced that violence, be it a war or in other forms, was the most primitive way to solve a problem. He was certain that violence was not a permanent solution to make the Japanese army surrender their weaponry in peace.

At first, Captain Tanaka, the Japanese commander in charge of surrendering, welcomed Sadeli's request and promised to have the weapons ready for pickup at six that evening. However, when Lieutenant Abu showed up at six with an old truck, the Japanese captured him. Fortunately, one of the lieutenant's men who waited in the truck was able to escape and report back to Sadeli.

Without much debating with his conscience on whether it was necessary to kill a person, Sadeli decided to attack. He used the logic of the revolution. Indonesian people could only obtain their independence if they were willing to fight and, when necessary, to sacrifice their lives. Only through independence could the people of Indonesia reclaim their dignity, honor, and values that had been disgraced and trampled all this time by the Dutch and Japanese.

The whites had always thought of the browns, blacks, or yellows as lower-class humans who were inferior when it came to dignity, intelligence, conscience, moral, self-worth, and honor.

Sadeli was also convinced that the values, dignity, and honor of the Indonesian people he tried to recover were those of the new Indonesians—those who mastered science, who were fair, who dealt with other nations with integrity, who used their conscience and intelligence to unlock the secrets of the universe; Indonesians who believed in and loved their God, who respected women and loved children along with other of God's creatures; Indonesians who were true to themselves and society, who had self-esteem; but were neither boastful, proud, nor arrogant, who wanted to foster good relationships with others and share in freedom, peace, prosperity, and happiness.

That was Sadeli's dream for his people. And for that, he was willing to kill and be killed that night. Indeed, he came face-to-face with death soon enough after his unit reached the Japanese command post.

Holding a gun, Sadeli ran into the building. He wanted to threaten and force Captain Tanaka to surrender and order his soldiers to stop resisting. A few of his men followed him while others split up to find the Japanese soldiers. Sadeli kicked the door to Captain Tanaka's office open and was about to walk in when he noticed Tanaka look at something behind him. Sadeli quickly stepped aside and turned. A samurai sliced the air where he had stood before.

Sadeli fired without thinking. He heard the captain's aide moan and the clinking of his sword as he dropped to the tile floor. Sadeli turned and shifted his pistol's aim on Captain Tanaka. He was surprised when the captain laid his sword on the table and walked across the room. After he bellowed through the open window his command to surrender, the captain turned to Sadeli. He bowed and said, "These headquarters are yours now, Captain. Please tell your men not to kill my soldiers who surrendered."

Sadeli issued the order and one of his men rushed outside to relay it to the others.

Soon, all gunshots and battle noises stopped. Captain Tanaka picked up his sword, put it inside its sheath, and handed it to Sadeli.

"Where's Abu?" Sadeli asked.

At that moment, Lieutenant Abu barged in and raged, "There he is, the treacherous Japanese dog. Kill him!"

Sadeli held Abu back and said, "Calm down. Lead your men to collect all the weapons. Round up all the Japanese soldiers in the yard and be on guard."

Lieutenant Abu saluted and left.

Sadeli turned to Tanaka again. "Captain, you broke your promise to me. Why?"

"I received an order not to surrender our weapons. The leaders of the Allied Forces gave that command to the Japanese leaders. I was only obeying the order."

"But at least you should have known better than to capture Lieutenant Abu," Sadeli said.

Captain Tanaka remained silent.

Sadeli wondered what should be done to Captain Tanaka and his men. He had heard that in some other similar situations, the mob had killed all the Japanese soldiers since they no longer could hold back their rage over all the cruelty the Japanese had imposed on the Indonesian people. Sadeli had no desire to do that.

Our revolution, he thought, *is the revolution for human freedom and honor. We're not animals going berserk, blinded by our fury. We have to preserve our humanity, even during war.*

Captain Tanaka looked nervously at Sadeli.

"Can you tell me why you surrendered? I thought Japanese warriors have the spirit of *Bushido,* of never giving up? They would rather die than…" Sadeli smiled.

"Are you, Sadeli, an Indonesian warrior, laughing at your defeated opponent?" Tanaka countered.

"I'm sorry, Captain Tanaka," Sadeli said. "I was just curious."

Captain Tanaka held Sadeli's eyes for a while. And for the first time Sadeli saw fear in the captain's eyes. Tanaka exhibited the fear of a human in the face of impending death.

"I don't want to die," Tanaka said. "My wife and four children are waiting for me to come home. You shouldn't believe the Japanese propaganda about fighting to the death. Some Japanese do want to live. For me, the war is over."

Sadeli rose and said, "And for me, it has just begun. You and all your men will leave and join the rest of your infantry in Bandung first thing in the morning. You will relinquish all your weapons to us." He saluted and left the room.

That was the beginning of the revolution for Sadeli—one pitch-black night filled with gunshots. He witnessed bullets taking human life and was surprised that the killing of Japanese soldiers didn't bother him at all. *Is it that easy to take a human life?* he wondered.

Sadeli wouldn't even have been on the deck of this ship with a secret mission if he had not run into Colonel Suroso, a friend he met during his military training, three months after that night.

"Hello, Professor." The colonel used a nickname friends had given Sadeli due to his love of philosophy and circulating philosophy books. "The intelligence agency needs your knowledge, especially your proficiency in foreign languages."

Sadeli was indeed known as someone who loved learning other languages. Not only did he know Dutch, English, French, German, and Japanese, he was also good in Chinese.

At first he didn't want to leave his battalion. He thought that having reached the rank of major after having been promoted from captain was sufficient. Besides, he led a battalion he very much cared about. He dreamed of grand battles and glorious victories and was eager to try some of his war strategies and endurance training.

However, Colonel Suroso convinced Sadeli that he could serve their revolution for independence better as an intelligence agent than as a commander on the battlefield. "Remember," Suroso said, "we have more than two million Chinese in this country, yet we don't know anything about where they stand regarding our country's independence. After World War II, Russia, the motherland of Communism, emerged as a world power on par with the United States. In China, a struggle for power is happening between the Communists led by Mao Zedong and the nationalist Kuomintang under Chiang Kai-shek. If the Communists win, then all of Asia, or even the entire world, will be facing a threat from Communism. The goal of our revolution is to free our nation from foreign domination, which has been feeding on the blood and marrow of our people. Communism is an international movement to conquer the world. It is a foreign power that will also try to pull the wool over our eyes and rule over our nation. From now on, we must carefully calculate every possibility and closely monitor the development in this world, especially in Asia. We must stay alert and be on our toes. The revolution of this republic is like a newborn baby. We must take every necessary step to protect and save it from both internal and external enemies." Suroso paused for moment, then added, "Being a commander on the battlefield may bring you reputation and fame, but we are fighting a different battle, clandestine, out of sight. Our major achievements will have to stay secret. I can only tell you, we need you. Badly."

Sadeli didn't need much time to think. He accepted the colonel's challenge. He resigned as a commander of his battalion and moved to Yogyakarta, to work for the intelligence agency headquarters under Colonel Suroso.

Sadeli soon found the work of an intelligence agent intriguing. It challenged his brain, his analytical skills, and his intuition to draw conclusions and develop new thoughts. It was as if he had to think further ahead, more deeply and keenly. He couldn't just trust matters to be the way they appeared. Instead, he had to check things from every angle and find the right meaning among the many he encountered. Being a secret agent forced him to say goodbye to his dream of being a perfect knight. Fighting openly, for instance, was strongly prohibited for a secret agent. Instead, a secret agent held firmly to tactics like maneuvers to fool the enemy, indirect approaches, attacks from behind, pulling from below, stabbing from the side, and wearing numerous masks. The tiniest negligence could mean death, capture, defeat, or disaster. Little by little, Sadeli adjusted his life and soul to this kind of a fight. Then one day, Colonel Suroso summoned him to a villa in Kaliurang for a very important secret mission.

Secret agent Umar Yunus had been sent to Singapore six months ago. He went undercover, as a merchant. The agency had sent him to sell sugar so he could fund their revolution abroad in the areas of diplomatic relations and propaganda as well as to buy medicines, weaponry, radios, and other things for the Indonesian Republic. Now they had good reason to believe that he might have betrayed the revolution.

Other than a couple shipments of medicine and weapons, Umar Yunus had never sent anything else. He always claimed the transactions were not finished yet. In fact, regarding the 500 tons of sugar shipped two months ago, he said the Chinese had tricked him and he was trying to get the sugar back. No one had heard from him since. A report stated that he had bought a big house in Singapore. He supposedly lived there lavishly with his Chinese mistress on the money he made from the sugar sale.

According to Colonel Suroso, Captain Umar Yunus was accountable for around half a million SGD. Sadeli's job was to investigate the matter and take any necessary steps to recover the money for the revolution. The colonel said Sadeli was authorized to kill Captain Umar Yunus, if necessary. Another mission for Sadeli was to establish international naval and air routes to Sumatra and Java.

Major Sadeli went undercover to Singapore as a merchant. He was to sell the sugar that the ship carried and use the money to fund his operation. Before he set sail, he had to go through naval navigation training and learn a little about sailing.

On Sadeli's departure from Tuban, Colonel Suroso came to see him. The colonel shook his hand and said, "You know the importance of this mission. I'll pray for you. Have a safe trip."

With just one thousand SGD bills printed before World War II in his wallet, Sadeli the merchant boarded the Sri Mulia. Captain Wan A Lang had his men ready. The sugar was loaded. Everything was good to go. That was twelve days ago. Now, they were to reach Singapore's port by tomorrow morning or noon.

The atmosphere on the ship had changed. Gone was the tension felt during the last few days. They were more at ease now. A British corvette had stopped them four days ago and searched the ship and the cargo, but then let them pass.

When a crewmember told Sadeli he had been worried the British would detain the ship and arrest the crew, Sadeli said, "Why would they do that? We come to Singapore to trade; we're bringing a commodity they need. The British are merchants themselves." Sadeli then told the sailor that the British had a strong passion for trading and described how they set the industrial revolution in motion. Sadeli often went the extra mile when answering a question from a crewmember in a conversation. His training to become a teacher had taught him the skill to explain things. And as of the third day of the journey, the entire crew and Captain Wan A Lang called Sadeli, "Professor."

Once, a sailor brought him a flying fish. The fish had flown so high that it fell and landed on the deck. The crew asked Sadeli how a fish could fly.

Sadeli's explanation went on to include Darwin's evolution theory. As he reached the part about humans descending from simian-like creatures, some of the crew yelled out their disagreement and anger.

"How can it be, Professor?" they said, "Our religion says we come from Adam and Eve. God created Adam and Eve. That's outrageous. What's the name of the man who said we come from apes?"

Sadeli laughed and explained theories about the origins of the earth, animals, the sea, the moon, and the sun. He had no idea how well his audience understood him. All he knew was they never stopped questioning him about different topics.

He ended his explanation about Darwin's evolution theory with humor, saying, "Indeed, we must believe in our religion's teaching about God creating Adam and Eve. But couldn't Adam and Eve have taken form as a single cell when God created them? And only after hundreds of years of evolution humans developed into the form we know today?"

Again, the crew disagreed and Sadeli laughed.

Sadeli's favorite time was at night when the ship moved fast while the sea was calm and thousands of stars decorated the clear sky. At times like this, everyone gathered on the deck at the stern and took turns telling stories of ghosts and demons, witch doctors and spells, cemeteries and *keris*, the sacred blade.

There was always a debate because Sadeli intentionally created some skepticism. He was not superstitious, but could see how his countrymen still held on to it with conviction.

"You don't believe in *kebal*—people who possess a certain kind of magic that makes them immune from things that can wound them, Professor?"

"No," Sadeli said, "If it's indeed true, bring that person to me. I'm sure I'll be able to hurt him by pricking him with just a safety pin."

The crew went on to tell the story of a kebal witch doctor who was bulletproof as well as sword-proof.

"If such a thing really exists," Sadeli said, "how could the Dutch colonize us for hundreds of years? Surely we could have won all the battles. In fact, our people would be able to conquer the whole world."

The crew who believed in kebal couldn't give him any explanation. Sadeli said that the first and foremost meaning of independence for Indonesians was freedom from other nations' power. Indonesians must become a self-governing nation. This meant more than merely replacing the Dutch at the high levels of government with Indonesians. That was not the point. Independence meant changes in the people's lives and welfare. Independence also meant that everyone was equal, had the same rights and obligations. Not a single person, family, or group should have privileges over others. It also meant that all Indonesians had to be free from starvation, ignorance, fear, and colonization from anyone. A child of a pedicab driver should have the same opportunities as a child of a minister, general, or president. Anyone who was diligent, talented, and smart, should have the chance to become a doctor or engineer, or even become a minister, general, or president. Independence meant there was no longer an upper class. Royalty, be it by blood or by wealth, would lose its supremacy. The people would hold the highest power and be free to choose their leaders. Basically, independence was about the guarantee of everyone's freedom of choice. The only limitation to one's freedom of choice would be the prohibition to harm others or the greater public good.

"For example, you, Abdul," Sadeli turned to the mate next to him, "cannot take Kayang's wife because that means you are violating Kayang's rights."

"That all sounds very nice, Professor," Wan A Lang interjected, "but who can guarantee everything goes that way? What if there are some selfish leaders who want to have it all and oppress others?"

Sadeli was pleased with the captain's response. He said, "The guarantor is us. Me, you, Captain, Abu, Kayang, all of us, we are the people. Every one of us needs to be aware of the people's freedom and authority and always be prepared to defend them. If there are leaders or government officials who violate people's freedom and rights, all of us must fight them. That's why we have our constitution and law. Everyone, from the clerks and farmers to the ministers, generals, and president, has to obey and uphold the constitution and law."

"Wow, independence does sound nice, *Pak*," Abu said.

"But it also brings great responsibility," Sadeli answered.

"How so?"

"We have to take good care of ourselves now. Think about it. Our nation is behind in so many things. To be able to compete with the developed countries, we need tens of thousands of doctors, engineers, and experts in farming, fishing, electricity, communication, machinery, and other fields of knowledge. We have to learn to make iron, aluminum, lamps, radios, ships, cars, planes, guns, cannons, torpedoes, clothes, medicines, and thousands of other things we need. Our country needs a police force, an army and navy. We need to add many more schools at all levels. We have to educate hundreds of thousands of teachers in so many fields. We must build roads, bridges, factories, and power plants, just like we must improve the housing and healthcare for the people. We are required to create equal welfare for all, by restoring the life of our farmers, workers, fishermen, civil officials, and the people in general. All of that calls for government officials who are smart, diligent, honest, and willing to dedicate their lives to their nation. Hard work awaits us all and we must do our very best. If we do that while preserving our unity as a nation, then after ten or fifteen years, God willing, we'll harvest the sweet fruit of our labor and our children will enjoy the sweetness of freedom."

"What if we fail?" someone asked.

The question caught Sadeli off guard and stumped him for a short while. He could not imagine the possibility of his nation falling apart, of corrupt leaders who wouldn't dedicate their lives to the good of the nation but instead would satisfy their own hunger for power, corrupt the people's money, live lavishly while lording over the poor, and thus bring down the constitution and the law.

"We won't," he said firmly. "It doesn't make sense for our leaders who are now living modestly and have proven their willingness to sacrifice everything for our independence to later betray our revolution. If they do so, they'll betray their own selves. No, my brothers, don't you worry. Believe in the sincerity of our leaders. Even more so because we are living in the age of freedom. We're not the only nation seizing our independence.

"The dawn of independence has broken all over Asia, like in the Philippines and India. Everyone is fighting for their freedom. The dominance of the whites over the blacks in Africa will also come to an end. Countries in Arabia will break free from the shackles of foreign power. The colonizers who are members of the Allied Forces will have no choice but to implement the war slogan they used in their propaganda against Germany, Italy, and Japan. However, we still face a tough struggle. It seems the Dutch think that the concept of independence only applies to them and not to us. But we will certainly win, as we move with the current of history," Sadeli said.

When anyone asked him about Indonesia's natural resources, Sadeli responded enthusiastically. "Seriously," he said, "God blesses our soil with His never-ending grace. We have sunshine throughout the year to give life to humans, animals, and plants. We have no winter, or other similar problems like they do in Europe, North America, and Japan. From the coastal areas to the mountaintops, our land is fertile. Almost have every type of plant and animal can live here. In the future, we will produce so much rice and other food products that hunger won't exist anymore. Our children will be stronger and taller than us because they will be fed better. We will have a surplus of meat and fish. The sea surrounding our country is so rich that it attracts the Japanese and Chinese fishermen. Sugar, coffee, tea, coconut, rubber, plants that contain etheric oils like eucalyptus and lemongrass, different types of exotic flowers and orchids, nutmeg, cloves, coconut, basically everything that the world needs we can produce. Our earth contains minerals like iron, oil, coal, nickel, aluminum, manganese, asbestos, gold, silver, diamonds, and other precious stones. Our rivers and lakes can produce very strong electricity. Independence is the key for us to mine all this natural wealth and create evenly distributed welfare for every Indonesian instead of just a powerful few. Our slogan should say, "prosperously independent and independently prosperous."

Everyone clapped when Sadeli finished. His passion ignited a similar feeling inside his listeners' hearts. Even the old Wan A Lang was fascinated and enticed.

"Thank God," he said solemnly, "we have our independence and, like you said, great leaders. But I may not experience the benefits of our revolution," he ended with a hint of regret.

"How old are you, Sir?" Sadeli asked.

"Over fifty," the captain answered.

"If God's willing, you will taste the fruit of our independence," Sadeli said. He looked around. Some of the crew were still in their twenties, but some were over forty. He added, "God willing, we'll all live long enough to enjoy the result of our freedom."

"How can you be so sure?"

"Because I believe in the righteousness of our fight for freedom and in the calculations of how things will progress. Although the Dutch stubbornly still want to rule over us, most nations in the world sympathize with our struggle for independence. The Western countries with colonies are now devastated by World War II. Their people lost their spirit in the war. They don't want to see any of their sons die in other new wars. They just want to rebuild their welfare that the war has wrecked. And for that, they need massive help from the United States, the only Western country that managed to come out of the war in one piece. However, the Americans no longer want to help Holland, Britain, or France in the wars against their colonies to restore their power there. Besides, the Soviet Union now emerges as a new superpower, something the Western countries need to pay close attention to. We can't expect much from the Soviets because their foreign policy is based on international Communism, meaning they will help only if the Communists gain more influence and power. We must say no to Communism because it's against the dreams of our independence. However, we can actually benefit from this fight between the Communist countries and the West."

"Why should we reject the Communists?" Wan A Lang asked. "I once had an uncle whom the Dutch exiled in Boven-Digoel, where he died. They said he was a Communist, but he told us before the Dutch arrested him that he was actually fighting for our country's independence."

Sadeli smiled. "The Dutch regarded all our revolutionaries as Communists. Soekarno, they said, was a Communist, and so were Sutan Syahrir and Hatta. We must reject Communism for several important reasons. First of all, their goal conflicts with ours. Communism will not enable us to be fully independent; instead, we will be bound to Moscow because Communists all over the world acknowledge Moscow as their leader.

"Next, Communists also do not uphold freedom and human rights. In Communist countries, the laborers are severely oppressed. Laborers in capitalist countries like the United States, France, and Britain have a better fate. They have the right to go on strike, to move, or quit whenever they want. When workers in Communist countries do that, they will be shot, thrown in jail, or exiled to do forced labor. Farmers pretty much have the same fate as the laborers. They no longer own their land; the country does, and they are simply workers on those farmlands. They no longer have a choice of the crops they plant or cattle they raise. The ruling Communists make all the decisions.

"Although Communists seem to have a noble goal, in reality, they have to use violence to force their doctrine upon the people. Their theories about the bourgeoisie and the class struggle can't justify a dictatorship and cruel oppression over other groups. So, in order to stay in power, the Communists have to oppress the laboring class themselves. They must get rid of the laborers' and farmers' rights because they can't afford any rivalry. Since the Communists took over the Soviet Union, the country has become a clear example of how Communism oppresses and eliminates human rights, honor, and freedom. We have no use for the Communists and Communism. They will only bring a huge problem to our people. That's why we need to oppose them and throw them out of our country."

Sadeli had a hard time elaborating on his explanation of how some of the good parts of Marx's findings and analysis on society could be used productively rather than simply adopted blindly.

"The 19th-century capitalist society illustrated by Marx has changed a lot," Sadeli continued. "The workers now hold great power. In fact, in the United States, they almost have the same power as the middle class. We, in Indonesia, don't have landlords in the same sense they do in Egypt, Iran, or other countries. We also don't have the capitalists. So, having almost no class struggle, it's easier for us to create and implement social justice. With honesty, wisdom, hard work, and principled leaders who serve as role models for modest living, plus the natural wealth we have, we should be able to create a society with equally distributed welfare. As long as our leaders don't become drunk on the power they have, God willing, this independence will realize the dreams tens of generations before us always wished for after hundreds of years of suffering under the oppression of the colonialists."

"Amen," Wan A Lang responded in earnest.

As Sadeli lay on the deck that morning, he recalled the days in this journey so far. His blood rushed through his body. He wanted to jump, sing, and dance on this deck, then give everyone on board a hug. He was ecstatic because he was alive during the time of revolution. He played an active role in that revolution, and took part in creating the new history of the world. He turned the tide for his people and by doing so also made a difference for the rest of mankind. He imagined great opportunities awaited his nation after they secured their independence. Deep inside, Sadeli was certain that the independence of his people had to be meaningful to the rest of the world.

Sadeli said a prayer before he took a deep breath, and filled his lungs with the fresh morning air in the middle of the ocean. He struggled to hold back his wish to jump up and fill the air with his shouts of joy.

He was determined to fight until they won, even if this fight for their freedom would cost him his life.

Sadeli envisioned highways and railways crisscrossing the islands of Indonesia, ships sailing through its seas, fishermen busy catching fish, tractors clearing the forest, factory machines roaring, and Indonesians busy mining their natural wealth, while the air trembled from hundreds of airplanes, and young generations flocked to schools. What a beautiful dream of freedom he had. The golden dream filled his heart.

Sadeli remembered friends who died in different types of battles. They did not seize weapons from the Japanese but fought the British. These men died in Bekasi, Tangerang, Semarang, Surabaya, and other places throughout the country. He remembered the poem Sofyan recited when they buried dear friends near Sukabumi, friends who fell defending their country against British troops:

> *Sleep, sleep now, dear friends,*
> *we cry over the absence of your laughter,*
> *but we won't forget what we owe you.*
> *Until our motherland, my friends,*
> *lies in freedom's embrace,*
> *Sleep, dear friends, sleep.*

Major Sadeli could not contain his feelings any longer. He sprang to his feet and shouted his happiness to be alive. He danced and sang on the deck. At first, the crew was a little surprised, but then they found his joy contagious and joined him in his song and dance.

Wan A Lang just shook his head. In all his years as captain, this was the first time that such a performance happened on his ship. "Revolution," he thought as he twisted the tip of his moustache.

Chapter 2

Sadeli sat on the porch of a house on a street behind Orchard Road. He waited for Umar Yunus, the Indonesian secret agent in Singapore. Sadeli had already sold the sugar and used the money to buy radio interception equipment and crates of medicines needed in Indonesia. In post-war Singapore, some items were available in bulk while others were scarce. Rice, for example, was rationed in restaurants. People were only allowed to order one small portion. Second helpings were not allowed.

However, weapons like rifles, machine guns, and even canons, were freely offered. Mercenaries from around the world, without much conscience, roamed the country looking to make easy money. One Englishman and a few Chinese men offered Sadeli a cache of Japanese weaponry stored in some secluded coastal area in Serawak. The load was cheap, only a thousand US dollars. He simply needed to pick it up by boat.

A Frenchman, Colonel Jean Lafittre from the French Foreign Legion, who deserted rather than go to war in Indochina, offered his services in the revolution against the Dutch. He requested ten thousand US dollars cash up front and two thousand US dollar per month afterward. He told Sadeli he was a behind-enemy-line sabotage agent. It had been his main duty during World War II in North Africa and Europe. He was always parachuted in far behind the enemy line.

He had fought in the battles against Rommel in North Africa, Sicily, Italy, France, The Netherlands, and Germany itself. He presented an idea of leading a small Indonesian sabotage team to attack the Dutch airports and destroy bridges, armories, radio stations, and other important installations. "I want to help your people to seize your independence," he told Sadeli.

"I'm happy to hear that," Sadeli said, "but you're asking too much."

"*Mais, merde de Dieu*! Isn't my life worth anything to you?"

"Sure," Sadeli said, "but not that much."

Then the French colonel changed his tactic. After further bargaining on the price of his life, he finally realized that Sadeli didn't have any intention of hiring a mercenary to fight Indonesian's revolution.

"We're willing to accept help from anyone in any kind of form and we'll pay the right price," Sadeli said, "but we're not looking for any hired soldiers. We have enough Indonesian men who are prepared to make the utmost sacrifice for their nation's freedom."

Major Sadeli noticed that everything could be bought in Singapore as long as someone was willing to pay. The British turned a blind eye to all the trades, including the black market. They wanted Singapore to quickly recover its position as the trading center of Southeast Asia.

Indonesians who came to Singapore were left alone, but placed under tight surveillance. Sadeli knew he was being watched. He spotted British secret agents following him a couple of times. One morning, a week after his arrival in Singapore, he decided to trick the agents who shadowed him. He managed to suddenly come face-to-face with the agent, a middle-aged Chinese in civilian clothes.

"You," Sadeli said, "tell your boss I want to talk to him. I'm tired of you shadowing me. You know where I'm staying." He turned his back to the agent and walked away. When he turned around after a few steps, the man was headed in a different direction.

The next morning, the phone in Sadeli's room rang. He picked up the receiver. "Hello?"

"Good morning," a cheerful voiced answered him in English at the other end of the line. "May I please speak to Mr. Sadeli?"

Sadeli hesitated for a moment. The English pronunciation of his name, *Sadelai,* had thrown him off. He responded, "Yes, yes, speaking."

"I'm sorry to bother you this early. I was wondering if you'd like to drop by my office. Any time before noon is good. I'm Inspector Hawkins. I received your message last night." Hawkins let out a tiny chuckle.

"Oh right, very well, Inspector Hawkins. I'll meet you around ten. Thank you." Sadeli also chuckled.

"Thank you, Sir!"

Sadeli carefully put the phone down and smiled. When, a couple of hours later, he presented his card to the office clerk and said he would like to meet Inspector Hawkins, the inspector immediately came to welcome him.

"Good morning, Mr. Sadeli. Thank you for coming. Please come in." They shook hands and Inspector Hawkins led the way to his office. He offered Sadeli a seat and a cigarette and asked if Sadeli wanted something to drink.

Sadeli declined. He had just eaten breakfast before he left his hotel.

The inspector lit his cigarette, took a drag, and slowly exhaled through his nose as he drew a bead on Sadeli.

Such blue eyes, Sadeli thought.

"Major Sadeli, you wanted to talk to me?" the inspector suddenly asked.

Sadeli was able to control his surprise. He knew there was no way to keep his identity from the British intelligence but had not expected to be exposed this quickly. He smiled and decided to lay his cards on the table. "Did you have to mention my rank?"

They spent a few moments observing each other. The Englishman took stock of the rather tall, well-built Indonesian with sleek black hair. His honest face and strong gaze reflected his courage; a pair of quite full lips indicated a sense of humor and controlled sensuality. *Had his skin been fair and his hair red, he would have looked like O'Connor, especially if his nose was a little sharper.* Hawkins remembered an army buddy, Captain O'Connor, a cheerful and brave Irishman who died from shrapnel from the Germans' mortar that hit him in the battle at the Rhine.

Sadeli took in the tall, lean Brit who was around his age. The little smile that never left softened his sharp gaze. Sadeli was sure he could have a heart-to-heart with this British inspector. "I'm happy we can be honest with each other," he said. "I came to assure you that my presence in Singapore is neither a danger nor a threat to your city, Sir."

Inspector Hawkins smiled and said, "You have very keen eyes. Our men are normally invisible to those whom they shadow. However, it's our job to stay on guard. Your country is at war with the Dutch and we often have Dutch troops passing through Singapore. In fact, there's a barrack here to house the Dutch who were enslaved in Thailand and Burma during the war. We can't let your people attack them here."

Sadeli chuckled. "Ah, if that's what you're worried about, rest assured. I'm not here to attack the Dutch or their barracks, although we know that they conduct military training there and later send the people to fight the war in Indonesia."

The inspector held up his hands.

"I know this is a matter that those of much higher rank deal with," Sadeli said, "and it's pointless for us to discuss. That's fine. But you should know why I'm here. I'm here to assure the success of our revolution. I'm here to sell sugar. My people need the money from the sale to fund our fight both nationally and internationally. We need to explain to the world why we're fighting against the Dutch.

"Do you remember Winston Churchill's speech when he asked the British to stand on the front line fighting the German Nazi? Ah, surely you were in that war yourself, fighting against Hitler, who wished to conquer and enslave all of Europe. The same thing that drove the British, French, Dutch, Belgians, Americans, Russians, Yugoslavians, Greeks, and many others to fight until death now drives my people to fight for our independence. We are hoping for at least your understanding, if not help, in our fight. My people want an independent life the way the British do.

"Just like you fought against Hitler colonizing your country, we oppose the Dutch. You want to be free from hunger, so do we. You wish to be free from oppression, so do we. You want to have the freedom of religion and speech; the same goes for us. You demand a guarantee for freedom and human rights, we ask for the same thing.

"My people are no different from you who want to live in peace, justice, and prosperity. Those dreams brought me to Singapore. Are you, the one who comes from the country considered to be the birthplace of the parliamentary system, going to give me a hard time?"

The inspector looked at Sadeli carefully. Sadeli's words left a deep impression on him. He suddenly said, "You spoke very well and convincingly. Officially, the British government wishes not to meddle in the problems your country has with Holland. Our government has an open door policy in Singapore for every legal trading activity, because Singapore's life depends on it. Personally, I'm very sympathetic towards your nation's struggle for independence. I was among the British troops that made the first landing in Jakarta. I was still a captain at that time.

"I truly regret what happened in Surabaya and killed Brigadier General Mallaby. It was our mistake. The Dutch's effort to reclaim their colony was really none of our business. The British army was assigned to disarm the Japanese army and establish peace. There were a lot of misunderstandings within the Allied Forces. We can now say that if only the peacekeeping had been left to your government, we could have avoided much trouble. But it wasn't an easy call that time.

"You know that Holland is a member of the Allied Forces, so it's impossible for the rest of the members to acknowledge your independence without some kind of negotiation with the Dutch. But the tide of history is on your side. The end of World War II brings us to the century of freedom for mankind. The people in my own country have had a major shift in their way of thinking. The misery we were exposed to during the war has led to a demand for a new world order which can better guarantee peace and humanity." The inspector extended his hand.

They shook hands and Sadeli said, "I'm glad I came to meet you."

"I'm sorry for tailing you. We have to keep an eye on Communism," the inspector replied.

"Already?" Sadeli asked.

The inspector smiled and pointed to the world map on the wall behind his desk. "That was the world map before the war. Much has to be changed. Look at Eastern Europe. The war against the German Nazi and military fascist Japan is over, but there's a new kind of war going on right now, the one without bombs or canons. It's between Communism and democracy at the ideological level. Perhaps you don't completely agree." He smiled again, then finished, "Or, to be precise, it's between the Soviets and the Western world. The Russians have forced a Communist government upon countries they occupied, from those in Eastern Europe to East Germany, where the Red Army rules.

"Nations that love freedom and human rights now have to be on alert for the big new problem: aggressive international Communism. In China, under the leadership of Mao Zedong and with help from the Soviets, the Communists will seize power in the whole country. Overseas, millions of Chinese live in other Asian countries and there's the question of their loyalty towards the countries they live in, your country included. We're facing the same problem."

"I thank you, Sir," Sadeli said, "and I hope more and more British officials will think like you do. Now, if you'd excuse me."

Inspector Hawkins quickly rose and shook Sadeli's hand. "If I can be of any help," he said, "you know where to find me."

Hawkins walked Sadeli to the door. When Sadeli was about to step out of the room, he held Sadeli's arm. He smiled and said, "I'm sure you'll be cautious in dealing with individuals who present themselves as salesmen of weapons that once belonged to the Japanese."

Sadeli returned his smile and said, "You know I didn't come here to buy weapons."

"Oh yes, I know, I know." Before he let Sadeli leave, Hawkins said, "There are many bona fide merchants in Singapore."

"Oh yes, I know. Thank you, Sir." Sadeli chuckled.

Later, when Sadeli sat alone in a restaurant with a glass of cold beer, he carefully went over his whole conversation with Hawkins. His training and experience as a secret agent had taught him not to trust first impressions. The enemy was also capable of putting on an act. He wondered how Hawkins knew he was a major. He had assumed the identity of a merchant here. Perhaps someone of the crew knew who he really was and a British secret agent had retrieved the information. Agents surely roamed around the port.

While the British in Singapore knew his true identity, Sadeli concluded from his conversation with Hawkins that they were fine with having him around as long as he limited his activities to trading. Hawkins had been quite frank when warning him not to attack the Dutch in Singapore. Sadeli smiled. No one at the intelligence headquarters in Yogyakarta had even thought about, let alone mentioned, that before his departure to Singapore. It probably would be good to report the information to Yogyakarta so they could consider the pros and cons for Indonesia's revolution. At face value, he saw more cons than pros. A direct attack by Indonesian sabotage units on British territory would anger the British and create another enemy for Indonesia. It would make it even harder for Indonesia to conduct future trading in Singapore. The best thing to do was to observe the Dutch activities in Singapore and immediately report to Yogyakarta. Good radio communication was imperative.

Sadeli remembered his meeting with Ali Nurdin two days after he touched shore in Singapore. Ali was a journalist from a national news agency in Jakarta who had lived in Singapore for a month. He was around thirty years old, thin, a little short, with dark skin and curly hair. He was on his own mission of creating a network with the international press to introduce Indonesia's struggle for independence to the world. Sadeli remembered Ali saying, "The news agency only let me leave if I financed the assignment myself. They don't have the money to pay for my living here."

It turned out that Ali Nurdin had been working hard. He stayed in a house of a *Melayu* family from Sumatra who had lived in Singapore for generations. He had established a network with the newspaper, *Utusan Melayu*, some Melayu youth organizations, journalists from the *Straits Times*, the Chinese newspapers, and journalists from other news agencies who worked in Singapore.

"I'm starting to realize how important money is in this foreign land," he told Sadeli. "It's different than in our country. In Indonesia, we can work without needing money. Everyone is willing to help us. Here, I need to put aside funds for networking. I've been dealing with these journalists. They always like to go out. I can't be their guest all the time. It'll be embarrassing. I'll ruin the good relationship if I always have them pay. I want to publish some kind of monthly newsletter here and elsewhere abroad about our revolution, but it's still just a plan because I don't have the money."

"Then how do you manage?" Sadeli wanted to know more.

"Oh, a friend in Jakarta gave me a few pounds of oxidized silver from Yogyakarta," Ali said, "and I've been selling that bit by bit."

"What if that runs out?"

"Well then I have to find a job. I'll be a coolie if necessary," Ali said with conviction.

"Why don't you try asking Umar Yunus for help?"

"The Umar Yunus sent here to sell sugar for our revolution?" Ali sounded bitter. "That would be totally pointless. I went there and so did other Indonesians, but he wouldn't help any of us. He ignores the order from Yogyakarta to help our fight here. He's extremely stingy. In fact, he has earned himself a bad reputation among Indonesians who live here and those who sympathize with our revolution."

"A bad reputation? In what way?"

"Many people say he's corrupt. He lives a very extravagant life. Did you go to his house?"

Sadeli shook his head and Ali continued, "No? It's extremely grand. It's huge. He has two cars and he lives openly with his Chinese mistress."

"What else do people say about him?" Sadeli probed.

"Oh, I heard he sells sugar below market price here, and if he buys stuff for the Republic, he marks up the price and keeps the difference. That's how he became so rich. People say he met his mistress on the dance floor of the Cathay Hotel."

***

"Good morning, Mr. Sadeli," a gentle female voice greeted him. Somewhat startled, Sadeli raised his head. He had not heard her approach. He quickly rose and shook hands with the slender Chinese woman standing in front of him. She was young, no more than twenty-one or two. He could easily look down at the top of her head and found the part of her black, shoulder-length hair. The shape of her breasts was visible in the tight, light blue outfit she wore.

"I'm Rita Lee."

"A great pleasure, Miss Lee." Sadeli bowed a bit in respect and looked at her face. She had a smooth face, almond eyes with long eyelashes, a delicate fine nose, and a pair of small yet full lips. Rita Lee was a beautiful Chinese woman. She looked like a doll, Sadeli thought.

"Please come in. Mr. Umar Yunus is waiting for you," she invited him inside.

Sadeli watched her smooth, fair legs show and disappear in the high side slit of her *cheongsam* as she walked. She walked like a cat. Her graceful movements hid her actual strength. He thought she could be dangerous because he also sensed her strong sex appeal. It was in her gaze, her gentle yet alluring voice, her hidden smile, and the way she glided when she walked.

She led him through a luxuriously furnished living and dining room. Vases of fresh flowers were on the tables. He had the impression that both rooms were intentionally lavishly decorated.

Umar Yunus sat at the breakfast table on the spacious back porch. He quickly rose to welcome him. Sadeli wondered, *Why didn't he meet me outside? Did he send the young woman to seduce me?* Sadeli had never met Captain Umar Yunus. He wondered if the man knew his identity as he approached Umar Yunus and shook his hand.

"Oh, Mr. Sadeli, forgive me for not welcoming you out there. Have a seat and let's have breakfast."

They sat down and Sadeli saw four plates, glasses, coffee cups, spoons, knives, and forks on the table. At the center was a long porcelain plate with nicely sliced white bread. In a big bowl were apples, pears, and grapes. A rattan basket was filled with California navel oranges. He also saw a porcelain cream pitcher, a sugar bowl, coffee and chocolate tins, finely sliced smoked beef, three different kinds of cheese, various jams, salt and pepper shakers, Worcestershire sauce, and Tabasco. *How different from dining tables in Indonesia,* Sadeli thought.

Sadeli said that he had already eaten.

Rita Lee came in with boiled eggs in a small bowl. "Sorry," she turned to Sadeli as she put the egg in an egg cup next to Umar Yunus' plate, "these are soft-boiled. Perhaps Mr. Sadeli prefers hard-boiled eggs?"

Before Sadeli could respond, Umar Yunus said, "That's fine, Rita. Mr. Sadeli had his breakfast. Please make him some coffee." He turned to Sadeli and said, "Or perhaps you prefer orange juice, grape, or pineapple? Please choose whatever you like."

"Coffee with a little cream and this apple are good enough for me." Sadeli still hadn't had enough apples since he arrived in Singapore. Apples, pears, and grapes had not been available in Indonesia during the Japanese occupation. He felt the warmth of Rita's body as she bent over his right side to serve him.

"One or two?" As Rita reached for the sugar her scent wafted around Sadeli.

"Just one, please. Thank you." Sadeli peeled his apple.

"Why didn't you come to see me as soon as you arrived?"

Sadeli noticed Umar Yunus did not waste any time before he attacked. Sadeli had not yet decided whether to reveal his true identity to Umar Yunus immediately. He had gathered a lot of information about the man, not just from Indonesians but also from Chinese merchants who did business with Indonesia.

Sadeli realized his front as a big sugar merchant from Java made it easy to create a network with anyone in Singapore. Every big shop welcomed him. Three banks had solicited his business. A few big trading companies suggested they close the deal on buying however much sugar Sadeli could bring to Singapore. They also wanted to buy rubber, dried coconut, cloves, cinnamon, pepper, coffee, and tea and were willing to pay an advance in the form of goods, weapons, or money.

For the last ten days, Sadeli had been working hard on establishing networks, gathering information, checking and identifying which merchants were bona fide and which gave grand promises but were only after his money. He also managed to get important intelligence reports on Dutch activities in Singapore, including the sailing schedules of their ships.

He thought it was important to have a few trained agents in Singapore to deal with the Dutch. They would report on the Dutch equipment and ship routes and create networks with the harbor labor unions, not just as informants, but as sabotage units for the Dutch ships and airplanes when necessary. Sadeli had also suggested these agents would establish contacts with unions of hotel workers, taxi drivers, and people within the British intelligence. A lot had to be done. Sadeli was quite confident about asking Ali Nurdin to work as an intelligence agent aside from his job as a journalist. Besides, being a journalist was the best disguise for a secret agent. A secret radio communication system was needed between Singapore, Sumatra, and Java.

Sadeli sensed that most Chinese in Singapore were merchants who aimed for big profits. J.C. Kwan Tok, a big merchant he was introduced to, offered him a speedboat, which was a naval ship that had been remodeled into a freighter. The vessel came with a crew and could be used to transport anything from Indonesia. Kwan Tok asked for a seventy percent share of the profit.

Sadeli gasped, then said he would think about it. Next, he had to painstakingly refuse the Chinese billionaire's invitation to go dancing.

"There are many pretty girls. You can choose any of them," Kwan Tok tried to persuade him.

Sadeli managed to refuse the invitation, but knew that if he really wanted to enter their world, he eventually had to behave like them. Soon it would be his turn to wine and dine them and take them dancing. He had to move out of his hotel room and live in a respectable house. It would be difficult to establish his reputation in Singapore's business circles if he kept living in a hotel. Sadeli decided to postpone revealing his identity to Umar Yunus.

There were many aspects related to a merchant's position that might resemble corrupt acts, but were actually inevitable parts of the lifestyle and should be treated as business costs. Unless, of course, Umar Yunus really had sold the sugar under the market price, reported even less to Yogyakarta, and kept the difference for private use. However, this required evidence; the invoices, for instance, needed checking. Sadeli's training and experience had taught him to differentiate between appearance and reality.

As Sadeli's attention returned to the present, he smiled at Umar Yunus sitting across the table and said, "Forgive me. I intended to come see you as soon as I arrived, but the salt water wet some of my sugar, so I had to oversee the unloading process and try to sell it as soon as possible."

"How much are you asking for a pound?" Umar Yunus' facial expression and tone told Sadeli that he actually knew the price already. He told Umar Yunus how much he had sold the sugar for.

"Good for you. That's better than what I got three months ago and it makes perfect sense. We've had no sugar shipments from Java for two months. So the price is higher now." Umar Yunus then asked, "How long do you plan to stay here?"

"I'm not sure," Sadeli replied, "It depends on the opportunities I find here. As you know, I'm here partly on official business, representing the Ministry of Economy and Welfare to sell sugar and other crops."

"You surely know who I really am," Umar Yunus suddenly blurted.

Hmm, is he going to play the authority card? Sadeli thought and smiled secretly.

"Yes, someone told me about your position here before I left. I'll be glad to work with you."

"Do you have your papers with you?" Umar Yunus sounded confident. It seemed that some of his earlier doubt was gone. Lately, he was always suspicious about newcomers, especially those who came from Yogyakarta.

Sadeli took an envelope from his jacket's inside pocket.

Umar Yunus read the letters bearing official stamps. The contents seemed to banish his last doubt about Sadeli. He smiled as he put the letters back into the envelope and returned it to Sadeli.

He then started to eat heartily. He took a couple slices of bread and buttered them heavily. Next he added a piece of cheese and a little jam and picked up the conversation. He said, "Now, tell me how things are back home. How's Yogya, Solo? I'm always homesick. If it were up to me, I would rather stay there, fighting with the people, raising our weapons together. But here…" With a sweeping gesture he waved at the spacious yard full of beautiful flowers, at the extravagant furniture on the porch, including Rita Lee, who cooked something on a small electric stove at the end of the porch, the tantalizing food on the table, the house, the two cars in the driveway, and all of Singapore, which had started to recover from the effects of the war, ready to provide fun and pleasure for anyone brave and smart enough to claim it. "Here we lose the spirit of the revolution. We lose the camaraderie, unity, and the passion of the revolution," he complained, regretfully.

Sadeli wondered if Umar Yunus was putting on an act, but he went on telling Umar Yunus about the progress the country had made in preparing its components.

"We have taken over Java and Sumatra, and we are creating a strong army in Bali. We already sent young men to Kalimantan, Sulawesi, Maluku, and other islands. People across the entire country are fighting against the Dutch, who are trying to make a comeback. We are preparing our national air force and navy, although, in my opinion, we'd better focus all of our resources, equipment, and weapons to create a strong and effective army. The old Japanese airplanes we have can no longer be used to fight the enemy's superior aircraft, and we have no naval fleet. It's better for our navy to concentrate on training their sailors for the time being instead of keeping them in the mountains."

"What's happening in Yogya?" Umar Yunus asked.

"Oh, it's so crowded. It's the center of everything, but it's lacking so many things right now, especially tires. Many cars can't be used because they have no tires. The price of tires is unbelievably high because they are smuggled in from cities occupied by the Allied Forces. We have enough medicine, radio equipment, and weapons for the infantry. However, we need new weapons to destroy the enemy's steel trains and tanks. We need the Allied Forces' bazookas. We have started printing newspaper on straw paper."

"Yes, those are the difficult things to do because our country has not received acknowledgement either de facto or de jure from the international world. We encounter a lot of problems here because we can't act as official representatives of the Republic of Indonesia," said Umar Yunus.

Sadeli said, "Things that can't be done officially must be carried out secretly."

"True, but it's sure risky," Umar Yunus replied. "For example, if a Dutch warship intercepts our cargo, we are on our own because our government can't report the Dutch to anyone. Also, if the British find the weapons we bought, they will arrest us and confiscate the weapons. There's no way our government can help."

"Yes," Sadeli said, never revealing what he actually thought.

"It's very difficult," Umar Yunus said and added, "People in Yogya often don't care about these things. They simply issue an order to send this amount of rifles, that amount of pistols, X amount of this and that medicine, this and that equipment. You know yourself those items are not yet available in large quantities on the open market, especially weapons. Every weapon is illegal. When we're late in filling our orders, we're branded incompetent."

Sadeli wondered if Umar Yunus was talking about him. He had become intrigued by this man. It was as if he dealt with a clever adversary who merely toyed with him, seeming to know who he really was and why he came to Singapore.

"Yes, yes, indeed," Sadeli said, "but Indonesia really needs all of those things. No matter how quickly we send them, it still feels slow there."

"Exactly," said Umar Yunus, "I just want them to understand the problems we have here. Tell me, how do our leaders rate our chance to be successful?"

"Oh everyone is confident about our victory. We will win. From President Soekarno to our soldiers, all share the same sentiment. In his speeches, President Soekarno always says he will lead the guerrilla against the Dutch himself. You should feel what it was like to be among our youths in the battles in Semarang, Tangerang, Surabaya, and many other places. It's like new Indonesians are being born. Both Pak Kromo and Pak Wongso who lived during the Dutch occupation are dead. And so is *Genjumin*, who kneeled in front of those midget Japs.

"Even if the Dutch return with cannons, airplanes, flame throwers, or even rockets, these new Indonesians have no fear. People may say they are fooled by witch doctors, and have no war strategy. That's true, but we have to see the raging spirit behind their daredevil acts. It's the spirit within them that makes them do all that. It's heroic. It's much more heroic than the British infantry attacking the Russian cannons in Balaclava, the battle that Tennyson sings about. The unit conducting the suicide mission came from a nation with hundreds of years of war history. They joined an army of such history.

"On the other hand, our youth, who attack the enemy tanks with only bamboo spears, are newly born Indonesians. Their heroic actions will shape our military tradition, a tradition of the new Indonesian warriors. Ah, our revolution for independence has shaken our people to the core. The colonial society that bound our people is shaken and its shackles are broken. Everything will change. The structure of our society will change, and we'll be free.

"Aren't you worried that some of our leaders may go astray?" Umar Yunus asked.

"Go astray?" Sadeli was a little surprised. "Oh, that's impossible. During this time of revolution, our nation is happy to have leaders who are dedicated to freedom, democracy, justice, truth, and God. Remember what *Bung* Karno, Bung Hatta, and Bung Syahrir said in their speeches. All of them are determined to defend democracy and freedom. It's impossible that any of them has any intention to go astray, get drunk on power, live lavishly, and gather wealth for their own sake. Look how modestly they live; their lives are not that much different from ours. I have frequented the presidential palace, the residences of Bung Hatta, Bung Syahrir, Bung Natsir, Amir Syarifuddin, General Sudirman, and many others. We're very lucky to have leaders like them."

"Please forgive me for asking," Umar Yunus said. "Your high-spirited speech is very convincing. I'll accept your information regarding our leaders' determination.

"Now what about the effects of the revolution on Indonesians? Is it a permanent change, or is it just a phenomenon, something caused by, let's just call it 'revolution fever'? What will happen after the fever is gone? Will the people return to their old passive selves, to their slow lifestyle, their surrendering to authority, and succumb to the strong with the animal-like traits we loathe? How can we be sure this revolution has really changed the Indonesian people and therefore has given birth to what you call new Indonesians? Could they just be Pak Kromo, *Genjumin*, or the *inlander* waiting to resurface? Take this experience as a little example.

"I know an Indonesian who hated the Japanese with all his might during their occupation. He hated their cockiness, the way they acted as if they were the great conquerors of this land. He hated their cruelty and the way they robbed our country and raped Indonesian women. The Japanese never took any responsibility for the torture and murder of tens of thousands of Indonesian *romushas* and *heihos,* whose bones are scattered as far as Burma, Malaya, Thailand, Formosa, Papua, and other islands in the Pacific we never even heard of. This Indonesian fellow vowed that when the time came, he would kill as many Japanese as he could, but guess what happened?

"When Japan surrendered, the head of the office, whom he hated the most and was at the top of his list, called him and gave him a house and everything inside it, a sedan, a large amount of yen, and his samurai.

"Do you know what my friend did? Instead of drawing the samurai and chopping the officer's head off, he hugged the much-hated man and they cried in each other's arms. That's how easy people have a change of heart. Even now, a lot of our people hate the Japanese. They should redeem themselves for what they did to us."

Sadeli was very interested in what Umar Yunus had just shared. He had actually been secretly wondering about the same thing, but did not dare to talk openly about it. A new sense of respect for Umar Yunus sprouted.

What if everything I believe in turns out to be wrong? Sadeli couldn't imagine that the issues Umar Yunus raised earlier would come true. He remembered how many of his friends proclaimed the birth of this new Indonesian in political discussions after the declaration of independence. These new Indonesians knew their worth; they had a free soul and mind, and intended to live as free people among mankind.

Sadeli wondered what would happen after they succeeded with this revolution and got rid of the colonizer. Would Indonesian people then bow to leaders who abused the revolution to gain their own power and privileges? Would the people yield, be as apathetic and helpless as they were during the Dutch and Japanese fascist military occupancy and, therefore, be easily pitted against one another by those heartless leaders? Would any of the leaders who were currently living a modest life and displayed great idealism in establishing the people's welfare and social justice disregard the fate of their people? Would any of them go astray, get drunk on power, or even have the heart to deceive their people through the use of empty slogans?

Sadeli couldn't accept that. His heart and mind refused to believe that. "I think that's a good question," he replied to Umar Yunus, "But I still believe our people have truly awakened from their hundreds of years of slumber. New Indonesians were indeed born. Perhaps not every Indonesian is a new Indonesian, but there are a lot of them. Their number is large enough to affect the course of our history, large enough to go beyond the limits of bloodline and ethnicity. They can push our nation's development to establish one nation, one national language, one motherland.

"Just look at them; they are the pioneers of the revolution. They stand in the front line; they are the knights brandishing their weapons. The revolution and the war for independence will forge them into the defenders of our freedom and dignity. They will be our future leaders, the cadets and soldiers in our military, our government officials, our journalists, our writers and artists. They will carry the torch to further our revolutionary dreams."

"Your words erase all my doubts about the future," said Umar Yunus, then added, "but there's one weakness in your description."

"What is it?" Sadeli grew curious. He leaned forward to take a State Express cigarette from the tin Umar Yunus held out to him.

"The description you gave," said Umar Yunus, "is that of a solid unit, an entity that encompasses and binds everything into one giant force to fight the enemy. What happens when the enemy is gone? What will happen to the large number of political parties we have? What about the armed groups that belonged to various elements of the society? What about the Sundanese, Javanese, Madurese, Balinese, Acehnese, Kalimantanese, Ambonese, Minahasanese, Buginese, and many others? No matter how hard we wish to get a global view of our unity, we need to be realistic. Our different backgrounds in religion, traditions, norms, economy, and culture create different ways of thinking. Won't that cause disintegrations? Won't the parties fight for power? It's even apparent now how our communal poverty can easily transform positions and power into means to collect wealth. How firmly can someone with power hold on to their principle of living modestly if the very power they have can easily provide a wealthy and lavish life? Power holds temptations. Never did we or our leaders have to deal with such temptations. I can't say they will all pass the test. We surely hope so, because if they don't, disasters await our country. How can we tell in advance how new Indonesians will behave when faced with temptation? Neither of us knows. Religious people would say only God does."

"I'm happy to hear you say all of that." Sadeli rested his eyes on Umar Yunus. The man had a sharp mind, and a healthy dose of cynicism. Sadeli always respected people who thought rationally, who had their own opinion, and were brave enough to voice it. Umar Yunus had unleashed a stream of thought that had been buried under his own conscience all this time.

"I can't say I disagree," Sadeli said, "Maybe my way of thinking is still clouded by the fervor and joy of the revolution; maybe I'm idealistic and romantic. Until twenty days ago, I lived, slept, ate, and dreamed in the middle of the revolution. You left our country earlier than I. After living in Singapore, where life is basically harder and involves neither romanticism nor idealism whatsoever, you must have formed a more objective view. I can agree on the dangers you mentioned."

Dear God, this man is more realistic than I am, Sadeli thought, and wondered if he indeed suffered from the revolution fever, which, as Umar Yunus said, made him see everything in a fancy and shiny light.

He looked at Umar Yunus with a dash of melancholy. The man appeared to be someone who had good intentions but had flaws that caused him to act against his conscience.

From his psychology books Sadeli had learned that many people with sharp minds and who could tell right from wrong, often have psychological flaws that make them inadvertently do something wrong.

Umar Yunus was actually just like him and millions of other Indonesians. Together they searched for their identity and tried to secure a new position in this world, among mankind.

"With our awareness of all the dangers you mentioned," Sadeli said, "we need to start thinking of ways to avoid them. We have to bring the armed groups together as one national army. The development of the army, navy, and air force must be done in such a way that instead of competing against one another, they will work closely together. We have to come up with an efficient combined chain of command.

"We can learn a lot from countries that were in World War II. We need to have a clear structure for our government institutions, parliament, both the constitutional and executive positions of the president, and also an independent judicial branch that is independent of either the executive or legislative branch. We can't just copy the Western parliament system, but we need to structure a government based on the real needs of our country.

"In my opinion, we need a presidential democracy to guarantee the leadership of our country for a period of time and thus, avoid crises in the cabinet due to competition among parties within the parliament. Besides The People's Representative Council, we should have a Senate that will develop local potentials. Other than that, we need to guarantee freedom of the press.

"Only free speech can become the true guardian of the society, stop misbehaving authority, keep the people's morality in check, and be the pulpit where the public voices their opinion. We saw how the Dutch restrained and oppressed the freedom of the press because they were afraid of that influential institution of democracy.

"We must also create the tradition for upholding the law. The law must apply to everyone without exception.

"Education is also important. We need more than formal education at school. We need personal education for our leaders so they will live a clean, modest life, and be polite and honest. I think their modesty, generosity, and selflessness will set a great example.

"We have to secure the tradition for *musyawarah*, a discussion to reach consensus, to resolve issues among us. We have to teach our people that force or violence is the most primitive way to solve problems among humans.

"Independent Indonesia should no longer have political exile areas like Boven-Digoel or other political prisons. Let's not do what the Dutch did, when they exiled Syahrir and Hatta, detained Soekarno in Sukamiskin, and captured thousands of our freedom fighters. Let there not be any manhunt of people with different religions or political views. The Communists are an exception, of course. We have to reject them because they're part of the international Communism movement."

"Ah, you and I are actually not that much different." Umar Yunus smiled. "The real difference between us is that you're looking at the situation through clear, bright glasses, while I am using rather dim ones."

Sadeli laughed. He suddenly felt happy. The conversation of this morning had lightened his heart and mind, which since his arrival in Singapore had been burdened by the problems of his job.

Umar Yunus was also happy. "Did you have a chance to look around the city?" he asked.

"No, I haven't had time."

"Well then, what if we, hmm…when will I have time?" Umar Yunus mumbled. After he thought for a few moments, he snapped his fingers and said, "What about the day after tomorrow? Sunday. We'll leave at eight in the morning. We'll go to Johor, have lunch there, and continue our conversation. I'll pick you up. Where are you staying? Adelphi Hotel? Very well, just wait in the lobby."

They went on to talk about business issues, difficulties with shipping, and how cautious they needed to be when presented with various forms of deception.

It was almost eleven thirty when Sadeli excused himself and apologized for taking so much of Umar Yunus' precious time. When he said goodbye to Rita Lee, she shook his hand and looked deep into his eyes while giving him a very beautiful smile.

After Sadeli left, Umar Yunus returned to his seat at the dining table. He spun an apple in his hand, thinking.

Rita Lee approached him from behind, held his shoulders, and caressed his head. "Is he the one?"

Umar Yunus patted her hand and shook his head. "I'm not sure yet," he said.

"Is there still danger?"

"I don't know."

"I didn't sense any danger coming from him. He seemed to be clean and honest."

"That's exactly why I'm not sure about him. He's too open for a secret agent. However, in this kind of business, you can't draw conclusions that easily."

"Please be careful, Johnny," Rita Lee whispered. She suddenly hugged him tightly before she moved to his lap. Her lips searched for his and she tightened her embrace. Her tongue roved inside his mouth, and he suddenly noticed her tremble. She ended her kiss and whispered in a shaky voice, "I'm scared. Will you always protect me?"

Umar Yunus recalled the first time they met and the story she told him a couple of weeks after.

Umar Yunus met Rita Lee at a dinner party and dance night hosted by Yueh Khow Kie, who was also known as Joe, a big-shot merchant who bought Umar Yunus' sugar the very first time he came to Singapore. From all the offers he received, Joe's was the highest. According to rumors, the forty-seven-year-old Joe had received a large inheritance when his father died before World War II. Joe had spent all that money on an extravagant lifestyle, trips to London, Paris, the Riviera, and Rome. By the time the war broke out, his wealth was gone, but during the Japanese occupation, he showed a remarkable skill in black market trading.

People speculated he was now even richer than before. People who knew him attributed his success to his reckless business practices. They said, "He was on the brink of poverty, but since he'd rather die than live in poverty, he took much bigger risks than other people."

Joe had never married. He was the one who introduced Umar Yunus to life behind the scenes in Singapore, the hidden life beyond the city's open face. It was a life no different from living in the wilderness. Only the strongest and the most cunning ones survived. And then there was the gang law. It was imperative to be loyal to one's pack to survive. Betrayal led to certain death.

Umar Yunus knew little to nothing about the division into various groups of the Chinese in Singapore in which some secret crime rings fed on other weaker groups. He soon learned that in the half-legal, half-black market, he had no other option but to deal with Chinese figures like Joe. The British merchants wanted to buy the sugar he brought, but refused to get involved in illegal transactions.

The ringing of the phone in the living room interrupted his thoughts and made Rita Lee jump off his lap as she rushed to answer it. He heard a melodious, "Hello," followed by conversation in Chinese. When he heard Rita mention the name *Suzie*, he knew the caller was the shopkeeper of the Mayflower, Rita's flower shop on Selegie Road.

Umar Yunus leaned back in his chair. His thoughts returned to the time he met Rita Lee. Joe and three other Chinese merchants had taken him out to dinner. Four young ladies accompanied them. Three were Chinese and the other was of mixed Chinese and British descent. Only the chair next to Umar Yunus was empty.

"Rita's late. She's for you, Johnny," Joe laughed, "Maybe her taxi broke down. She's never late."

Perhaps it was this small incident that made him pay more attention to Rita Lee that night. Rita Lee arrived after they had almost finished dinner. Blushing, she apologized profusely to Joe before taking her seat next to Umar Yunus. Joe introduced them to each other. She shook his hand and they locked eyes.

Umar Yunus was immediately attracted to Rita Lee. She was a pretty, petite, young woman with thick, black, shoulder-length hair and had a melodious voice, but what captured his heart was the hint of fear in her eyes.

They finished dinner, talked about everything happening in the world, and shared their experiences during the Japanese occupation. By then, they were able to joke about those horrible encounters.

Joe shared how he sold a supply of medicine he had stolen from a hospital storage room guarded by the Japanese. Umar Yunus told them how Indonesians during the war liked to say they ate pants, shirts, or a chair, meaning they had to sell those items to buy food. He told a story about a policeman on patrol and a pregnant woman.

"The policeman pointed at the woman's big belly and asked, 'When are you due?'

"She answered, 'Fifteen pounds.' Turned out the woman hid a sack of rice underneath her clothes."

They all broke into laughter.

After dinner, Joe drove them to the Cathay Hotel. They danced well into the night, and Umar Yunus drank a lot. Then, in the middle of a dance, he realized Joe and the others were gone.

"Hey," he asked Rita Lee, "where is everyone?"

"They all left," she said, "Do you still want to dance?"

"No. It's past midnight anyway. Let's go home," he said.

In the taxi, Umar Yunus took Rita Lee into his arms and whispered, "Come with me." She gave a small nod, and he gave the driver his address.

His hand trembled as he tried to fit his key into his front door. The whiskey he drank earlier started to affect him. "Hey, where's the keyhole?"

Rita Lee took the key and opened the door.

Inside, he took her hand and led her to the bedroom. "We're like thieves in the night," he whispered. Half-drunk, he laughed, "We're about to steal love." He was about to turn the bedroom light on, but she stopped him.

"No," she said and whispered, "Where's the restroom?"

He pointed to a door. Only the light from the street lamp came in through the blinds.

Umar Yunus whistled happily, undressed, and lay on the bed. He closed his eyes when the bathroom door opened and stayed that way when Rita Lee entered the bedroom. He sensed her presence near the bed, the rustle of the clothes as she undressed and unhooked her bra. He felt her coming closer to the bed before she softly said, "Hey, you."

Umar Yunus still kept his eyes closed. The whiskey he drank earlier called up lustful fantasies. He felt Rita Lee climb on the bed and press her body on his. At that moment, the passion he had been holding back during the last minutes turned into a wild, ferocious beast. It jumped on its prey, tore it apart, bit and smacked it to the ground over and over. He didn't even hear her screaming in agony, telling him no.

Quite some time afterward, when he lay detached from her, he thought he heard whimpers. At first he didn't recognize the sound. When he listened closer, he realized it was a woman crying. He wondered who it could be and then suddenly remembered. He opened his eyes and shot up. He was shocked to see Rita Lee sobbing. Even though she tried hard, she was unable to control her tears.

"Why? Why are you crying?" When he reached for her shoulder she jerked away as if frightened, and he pulled his hand back. He did not understand nor feel guilty. "Have I hurt you?" he asked softly and added, "I'm so sorry!"

Rita Lee didn't answer. Her sobbing subsided and he sat looking at her. When she finally stopped crying, he took her hand and said, "Tell me, Rita, why were you crying like that? I don't understand. Honestly. I didn't mean to hurt you. I…I…ah, I'm a beast for doing this to you. I didn't give it any thought. Forgive me."

Rita Lee by then had regained her control. "It's not your fault," she said. "It's I who needs to apologize. Women like me work to please men. I'm so embarrassed."

"Why did you cry like you were scared?" Umar Yunus asked.

Rita Lee didn't answer. Only after he kept on pushing, she said, "If a man takes sudden control of me like you did, I become frightened. Let me tell you what happened." She then told him a horrifying story that made him pity her and evoked a strong desire to protect her.

Rita Lee told him that she stayed with her mother in Malacca when she was seventeen. The Japanese captured her father, accusing him of involvement with an underground movement and being a British contact. Her mother then had to work for a few Japanese soldiers, taking care of their house and food. One day, her mother was sick, and she went to replace her mother at work. She was cleaning the bedroom around ten in the morning, when one of the soldiers who lived there returned. She didn't know why he came back early or why he was drunk. Perhaps it was his day off. When he saw her in his bedroom, he immediately hugged and kissed her. The harder she tried to break away, the more he tried to dominate her. Then his lust took over and he brutally raped her.

"I don't know what happened," she said, "I just remember I struggled to get away from him, fighting him with all my might, then there was this horrible pain and everything went dark as I became unconscious."

Umar Yunus felt an intense regret rise along with his great love for her.

"Please, don't talk any more about it," he whispered and put an arm around her shoulders, "I'm really sorry. Try to forget it."

"Be gentle to me," she said. "I think I'll be fine, then. I may even be able to enjoy it."

He held her and gently kissed her cheek as he whispered words of love that came from his heart. Rita Lee seemed to sense his truthfulness. She hugged him tighter and whispered, "You're so kind. You're a wonderful man." And he made love to her.

That night, both of them found the peace they were looking for, the mountain they longed to climb. They followed the path, going higher and higher, faster and faster, until they finally reached the peak. They fell asleep without uttering another sound until late into the morning.

Two months later, Umar Yunus asked Rita Lee to move in with him. And three months after that, he gave her the money from the sugar sales, meant to fund the revolution, to open the Mayflower, a florist, on Selegie Road. He told himself it was a good investment. He would be able to repay the money little by little with the profit from the florist, and the florist itself served as an investment for the revolution. It was only the certificate that registered Rita and him as co-owners of the store.

They never talked about marriage. Umar Yunus had told Rita Lee that back home in Yogyakarta he had a wife and three children. "Let's just wait until this fight for freedom is over," he said. "We simply can't think of marriage now because they can summon me home or transfer me somewhere else at any time."

Deep down, Umar Yunus had contemplated his options if he received such an order from Yogyakarta. He felt like he had found a new kind of peace and happiness with Rita. He felt like a real man for protecting her and giving her happiness. His sex life with her confirmed it further. He knew that he was man enough to bring her to orgasm. He never had that experience with his wife. He always finished earlier than she. This left her unsatisfied and annoyed and after a while, she started to ignore him.

Umar Yunus felt he had found himself with Rita. He did not see any reason why he should abandon this peaceful and happy island. He had the right to be happy and protect her from the dark world around them. For the moment, he did not want to think about his duty to his country, his people, the revolution, or his job. He put his inner voice aside. He didn't want to deal with those difficult issues yet. It wouldn't change them into something easier. He would deal with them when the time came.

Umar Yunus heard Rita's footsteps approaching from the living room. She kissed his cheek, and said, "That was Suzie. She said she has a new delivery boy. Mai Sung happened to be there, so I thought it would be a good idea to bring her along to the beach. She'll be good company for your friend, Mr. Sadeli. Who knows, he might find her attractive." She giggled, pleased with her idea.

Umar Yunus scratched the tip of his nose, thinking. Then he patted Rita's hand and said, "Maybe. We'll have nothing to lose even if he doesn't take the bait."

"So call and tell him we'll go swimming in the sea."

***

In his office on the fifth floor of the KPM Building, Joe, alias Yueh Khow Kie, had a business meeting with his staff. He hoped the Republic of Indonesia, which now had survived a year, would maintain its sovereignty. It turned out the British and Americans were not willing to give military aid to the Dutch to reclaim Indonesia. Countries that sympathized with the Netherlands were Belgium and France. However, Belgium had no army and could only help at a diplomatic level while France was involved in the Indochina war and, therefore, couldn't provide any military support. The Dutch themselves did not have enough resources to recolonize Indonesia. Perhaps they could reclaim the big cities and some adjacent areas, but the Indonesians would control most of the country because the Dutch didn't have a big enough army.

This created a great profitable business opportunity for merchants in Singapore. Indonesia could send sugar, tea, coffee, rubber, pepper, ethereal oils, peanuts, dried coconuts, and many other products. In return, the young republic needed vehicles, weapons, ships, engine parts, clothing, fabrics, medicine, radios, cars, and other items.

Chinese merchants in Singapore needed to unite and not fight over the selling and buying price. They had to conduct a meeting soon to reach an agreement. Joe mentioned names like Kwan Tok, Liem Goan, and J.P. Tek to be invited to this important meeting to protect their common interests. "And," he added, "don't forget to invite the newcomer, Mr. Sadeli, as soon as possible. He holds an important position in the Indonesian government. Invite him to lunch, and don't forget to invite some pretty ladies. This is an introduction lunch, not business."

"Who do you want?" asked his secretary.

"Well, Flora. She's beautiful and understands a lot of things since she went to college for a couple of years. And Clara...no, no, not Clara. It'll be too obvious. I was thinking someone smart, but sexier than Flora. Who could it be? Oh I know, Emily. Emily and Flora. Those two will do. Take care of it."

At that moment, their target, Major Sadeli, known as an officer in the Indonesian Ministry of Economy and Welfare, was at the dock. Wan A Lang would make his homeward journey that evening. Sadeli came to say goodbye, give him a few letters for Yogyakarta, and check whether his shipment of tires, medicine, and radios was on board.

"If the wind stays like this, God willing, we'll reach Tuban in two weeks at the latest," Wan A Lang said. "We'll miss you on our journey back."

"The same with me," Sadeli said, "you're all going home, leaving me alone here, but we'll meet again. Is everything set? Are the men ready?"

"Yes, yes," Wan A Lang said.

Sadeli shook hands with every one of the crew. Sadness filled him as he left the Sri Mulia. He turned around once to wave before he quickly left.

He needed to see Inspector Hawkins to check the credibility of some of his contacts. He took a taxi to Hawkins' office, where he received a warm welcome.

After Sadeli finished mentioning the names on his list, the British inspector looked at him and smiled.

"You work very fast," said the inspector.

"Our revolution can't wait," he replied.

The inspector rose and took out a thick folder from the safe behind his desk. "This is a confidential report," he said, "and I'll share it with you because I sympathize with your revolution. Let's see. Here it is. You asked me about John Osborne. A pilot, ex-Royal Air Force in fact, and he's now a private pilot for Tiger Airways. Hmm, he's a risk-taker but demands high pay. He has a criminal record. After the war, after he left the air force, he was reported to be smuggling cocaine from Burma to Macau.

"Kwan Tok. A large-scale merchant. We suspect he's linked to the Communists, but we have no evidence. You sold your sugar to him, didn't you?

"Hmm. J. P. Tek, a big merchant since before the Kuomintang war. He's pro-British, and is suspected to have some involvement in illegal transactions of weapons across Southeast Asia. Is he your man for weapons?

"Let's see, hmm, this French chap is a serious daredevil. He'd be willing to cut his mother's neck or sell his grandmother for ten cents. And this American rogue sells someone else's ships and airplanes and is willing to give you a test drive. This Chinese man will sell you the British port in Singapore in fifteen minutes if you believe in him."

The inspector wrote a number next to each name on Sadeli's list, zero for the untrustworthy, two for the seriously questionable, and five for fifty-fifty. So far he didn't write any tens. Joe only rated a six, and so did Kwan Tok.

Hawkins handed the list to Sadeli and returned the folder to the safe. After he locked the safe he took a seat and closely watched Sadeli check the list.

Out of around twenty names, nine received a zero. Sadeli smiled. The inspector's evaluation was not that much different from his own.

"You don't seem surprised." Hawkins offered Sadeli some 555 cigarettes in a tin.

"Hmm, true," Sadeli answered, "I'm just wondering why you gave Joe and Kwan Tok only a six. I would have given them each an eight, meaning they are a good risk."

"They have limitations," said the inspector, "When they reach their limits, which are their own goods and interests, they'll simply abandon other people."

"Right," Sadeli said. "I really thank you for this. But honestly, I don't understand why you're so willing to help me."

"Do you need to ask?" Hawkins smiled. "By helping you, I know your contacts and what you're doing. As long as it doesn't harm the British government in Singapore and Malaya, I'll stay out of it. You know that'll be my answer if my superior asks why I have such a good relationship with Major Sadeli from the Republic of Indonesia, right?"

Sadeli shrugged and said, "Your government doesn't need to worry about us doing anything here."

"We actually are worried. One day, the seed of freedom you planted in the Indonesian soil will cross the Strait of Malacca. In fact, the flame of freedom will ignite on all the continents where the oppressed still reside. Mr. Sadeli, I envy you. You stand with the progressive line of fighters. The future is yours. I, on the other hand, represent a power whose days are numbered. There'll soon be an end to the British Empire here and on the other side of the world. I can't actively assist you, but I can look the other way when needed. Trust me, not every Englishman is an evil capitalist conqueror."

He turned more serious when he said, "Sadeli, may I call you that? You can call me John; we're friends now. Let me tell you something, friend. Don't see every white man as an imperialist, a capitalist who sucks your land and people dry. I was a soldier defending humanity's freedom and honor against the Nazis. I love freedom. I wish your revolution all the best."

Sadeli stood and shook Hawkins' hand. He looked the inspector in the eye and said, "Can Major Sadeli of the Republic of Indonesia invite Inspector Hawkins in Singapore for lunch one of these days?"

"Inspector Hawkins would gladly accept the invitation," Hawkins said.

They laughed, happy for having reached this new understanding. They scheduled lunch on the following Tuesday.

Chapter 3

That Sunday, Sadeli waited in the lobby of his hotel for Umar Yunus to pick him up. He took a sip of coffee and flipped through his newspaper. At the end of the lobby stood a small shop selling all kinds of cigarettes and chocolate while functioning as a bureau de change as well. When Sadeli passed the shop earlier, the owner, an Indian, was cleaning his store. He said hello when Sadeli passed and asked about news from Indonesia. Sadeli said he knew just as much as the newspaper did. The Indian came closer and whispered, "I heard many Indian soldiers ran away and joined the Indonesians. I'm so proud of it."

Sadeli felt good. Last night he had created a basic intelligence network in Singapore and given the group their guidelines. He no longer felt alone. He had developed a small machine and it already went to work, gathering information, making contacts related to Dutch troops, people, airplanes, and ships, and watching Umar Yunus' activities, contracts, and maneuvers.

He now could focus on two other major matters, finding and creating international naval and air connections for Indonesia. He had already given all necessary instructions. While waiting for the reports to come in, he would do his part.

He looked up from his cup and saw Umar Yunus step into the lobby. He chuckled. His guerilla sense was still alert. He had sensed someone looking at him while he drank his coffee. He rose to greet Umar Yunus.

"Coffee?" he asked.

"Don't bother, had some at home," Umar Yunus said and they left the hotel.

Sadeli saw Rita Lee on the passenger side. He was about to get in the backseat when Umar Yunus said, "Let's just all sit in front."

Rita opened her door and Sadeli got in. Umar Yunus took his seat behind the wheel and Rita scooted over, closer to Sadeli, to give Umar Yunus more room. She wore shorts that exposed half of her thigh and a short-sleeved, low-cut blouse.

Sadeli felt the warmth of her body and her femininity—her freshness, her cleavage, and the scent of her perfume.

"We have to pick up Mai Sung first, Johnny," Rita said.

"Mai's Rita's friend," Umar Yunus explained, "she wanted to join us. You'll like her."

"She's very nice," Rita added.

It was a clear morning. The sun was still low in the east and the streets were pretty empty. Umar Yunus took the seaside streets, near the harbor. Sadeli noticed many freighters and warships. Most of them flew the British flag, some the American one. Then he spotted a warship with a red, white, and blue flag, the Dutch flag.

Sadeli didn't understand himself. Every time he saw that red, white, and blue, he felt an urge to tear off the blue and throw it far away. The combination of those three colors evoked hatred and rage inside him. The color combination reminded him of the crimes the Dutch had committed, the treacheries and killings, betrayals and rapes, the oppression and exploitation that they had exercised all over Indonesia. He remembered the *hongi tochten* in the Maluku, *cultuurstelsel* in Java, *kuli kontrak* or indentured servants, which was actually a hidden form of slavery, and the forced labor, Daendel's road across Java's northern coastal line that had claimed tens of thousands of lives during its construction, the Aceh war, the Paderi war, the rebellions led by Diponegoro, Sultan Hasanudin, and Pattimura; he remembered Boven-Digoel. And now, that tri-colored flag on the gray warship represented the imperialist who wanted to bury his sharp nails and fangs into the Indonesian's neck once again.

"A Dutch warship!" Sadeli exclaimed.

"Yes, they always stop here to load oil, water, groceries, and ex-KNIL—The Royal Netherlands East Indies Army—who are gathered here from Burma and Thailand." Umar Yunus stopped in front of a small apartment building on Orchard Road and honked twice.

A woman popped her head out from a window on the third floor and waved.

When a young lady came out of the main door of the building and walked toward them, Sadeli stepped out of the car and said, "Let me sit in the back."

The woman was around Rita's age. She wore sporty clothes, shorts, a half-buttoned shirt, and a pair of straw woven sandals. She carried a hat and a bag.

Rita Lee introduced them.

"Hello." Mai Sung gave Sadeli a strong handshake. "Hello, Rita. Hello, Johnny."

Sadeli held the door for Mai Sung then took a seat next to her.

"Did you get the chance to look around the city?" Mai Sung asked Sadeli as Umar Yunus drove away.

"Not really," he answered.

While Umar Yunus drove around the city, both women showed him some buildings and pointed out good restaurants. Sadeli didn't find post-war Singapore attractive. Everything was still in chaos. When they reached the Johor Strait, Mai Sung pointed at a huge iron pipe alongside the street.

"That's Singapore's lifeline," she said. "Water. Without water from Johor, Singapore will die of thirst."

Sadeli remembered the Japanese used that pipe to attack Singapore. While the British boasted about their formidable seaside fortress with big canons, the Japanese came through the back door.

"How was it here, during the Japanese occupation?" Sadeli asked.

"So-so. Just as tough as everywhere else," she said.

They didn't cross to Johor as Umar Yunus turned the car back to Singapore. "We should go for a swim at Joe's private beach," he said.

When they reached the shore, Umar Yunus drove into the driveway of a medium-sized house. The caretaker, an old Chinese man, greeted them. Apparently, he already knew Umar Yunus, Rita, and Mai Sung. "Mr. Joe is not around," he said.

"That's okay, we're just going to swim," said Umar Yunus. Joe had told him to go swimming whenever he visited and he often took Rita with him.

Tall, lush pine trees grew around the house. A well-tended lawn stretched across the property to the wall by the beach where a short flight of stairs led to the white sandy beach. The view was breathtaking. Small islands dotted the ocean's surface not too far from the shore.

"Fifteen miles away from this shoreline, Indonesian territory starts. Some of those islands belong to our country," Umar Yunus said.

They went into the house to change into their bathing suits.

Sadeli was the first one done. He stepped outside. A gentle sea breeze freshened the morning air. The sea was calm. Seagulls circled a few fishing boats. The wind carried the sound of a Latin song on the radio from a neighbor's yard.

Sadeli listened to the female singing voice and all of a sudden, he was overwhelmed by joy. He was euphoric. He jogged towards the wall, skipped down the steps, crossed the beach, and jumped into the water. He swam away from the shore with powerful, efficient strokes. He was a good and strong swimmer. After about fifty-five yards, he headed back to shore. He swam slowly. Cradled by the small waves, he floated on the open sea and was one with all the continents connected by the water that carried him. He felt humanity tied him to hundreds of millions of humans all around the world. Despite the differences in skin color, nationality, religion, and culture, human beings were inherently the same. Be it the Kubu tribe in the Sumatran jungle, or the Papuan in the Baliem Valley, the Pygmy in the Kalahari Desert in Africa, the Tibetan on the Himalayas, the American in the skyscrapers of New York, or the French who dined in the restaurant atop the Eiffel

Tower in Paris, humans were basically the same. What differentiated them were their courses of history, society, and culture.

Sadeli felt a strong unity with the earth, the world, and mankind. If the entire human race realized this, wars would be unnecessary, peace would reign over the earth, and people would live happily in brotherhood.

He felt peaceful in the cradle of the ocean. All the rampaging noises seemed so far away—the explosion of bombs and grenades, the rat-a-tat of machine guns, the war cry of the revolution, the cry of wounded soldiers—all the uproar he left behind only a few weeks ago.

For God's sake, he thought, angry at himself. He now understood why Umar Yunus lived in Singapore. Disguised as a merchant, he was able to live with his mistress in a big house. Under these different circumstances, completely detached from the revolution, the burning passion of the revolution fizzled pretty easily. What remained was a fiery discussion without really experiencing it, let alone implementing it.

Sadeli remembered his conversation with Umar Yunus about what would happen when their rebellion against the enemy was over and the leaders were in power. *Would the new situation weaken his dedication to the revolution? Would the saying 'power corrupts and absolute power corrupts absolutely' apply to them as well? Would their power provide a luxurious life, which then would ruin their pure dedication to the people's welfare?*

Now that he had experienced it himself, Sadeli knew the possibility would always be there. No human was made of steel. Everyone had a devil and an angel inside of him. If they allowed it, the devil would control them. And even if the angel were the one in control, they should always be on the lookout for the devil's sly attacks, which could appear at any time. He felt he had been too romantic or even naive in viewing life.

Sadeli snapped out of his thoughts when he heard Umar Yunus, Rita Lee, and Mai Sung's voices. He heard them jump into the water and their arms and legs splash, when, suddenly, a pair of hands grabbed his head and pushed him down into the water. To resurface, he had to turn around and catch the hands that held his head down.

He grabbed the shoulders he saw and pushed down. They wrestled for a while. When he ran out of breath, he pushed to the surface.

They came up nearly at the same time. Mai Sung squirted water from her mouth, laughing. He laughed too.

Umar Yunus and Rita called, "Let's race to the reef!" and pointed to a big black rock some forty yards from where they were.

"Let's," Sadeli replied.

Off they went. Umar Yunus and Rita swam fast, but they were no competition for Sadeli and Mai Sung, who swam powerfully and with great speed. Sadeli and Mai Sung easily won the race.

Sadeli climbed up the rock and offered his hand to help Mai Sung. When she held his hand and climbed up, he felt her young, toned, and strong body. She was taller and bigger than Rita and did not look like a fragile doll. Instead, her body was a reminder of the strong female farmers along the Yellow River. Her face was honest and joyful.

"You are indeed very strong," said Sadeli when they sat side by side, waiting for Umar Yunus and Rita. "You almost drowned me back there," he added.

Mai laughed. Her voice and laughter sounded different from Rita's. Mai's voice was a bit coarse and her laughter heavier. These facts pleased him.

"I intended to kill you but you were stronger," she laughed, then exclaimed, "Here come the lazy people!"

"You two swam like torpedoes," Umar Yunus complained.

"Oh Sadeli pulled me," Mai said. "He's very strong," she added and threw him a naughty glance.

"Oh, Mai's beauty pulled me like a magnet," Sadeli laughed.

They all joined in.

"Wow, this made me pretty tired." Umar Yunus inhaled deeply, and tried to steady his breathing. "I need to swim more," he added.

"That's what you get from living like a capitalist," Mai Sung teased.

Umar Yunus quickly turned to Sadeli. But Sadeli still stared across the open sea, even though he sensed that something stirred in Umar Yunus after Mai Sung finished her sentence.

"Hmm, do you know that Indonesians are starting to be very popular in Singapore? They look dashing and have a lot of money," Mai Sung continued.

"Nah, this one is not dashing and has no money," Sadeli said.

"No, no, you are. I like you very much," Mai Sung assured him.

"But I don't have money," Sadeli said.

"I don't need money," Mai Sung replied. Suddenly her words and her gaze meant a lot to Sadeli.

Tension filled the air. For a moment, Sadeli was at a loss for words.

"You are so kind, Mai Sung," he finally replied and smiled at her.

"Look!" Rita pointed at the ocean. The rumble of an airplane creased the air. An airplane flew along the coast. It flew so low that its belly almost touched the waves.

"Nuts," said Umar Yunus, "if the propellers hit the water even just a bit, he'll be doomed."

"Looks like he's a pro," Sadeli said.

The plane flew close to the rock and they could see the pilot inside the cockpit.

"Look!" Rita exclaimed again.

The pilot pulled the plane up; it climbed steeply up the sky, higher, higher, and higher still before it performed some stunts: outside loop, snap roll, inverted whip stall, inside-outside vertical eight, half roll up, half roll down, and some other maneuvers.

They all held their breath as they watched it.

Then suddenly the plane dived. It moved fast, almost vertical to the sea, faster, faster, toward the water. It got lower and lower, closer to the water at high speed. They all held their breath and wondered if the pilot would make it, when all of a sudden, the plane freed itself from the gravity force and moved away from death's hand, flying free.

The four of them let out a sigh of relief and Sadeli suddenly felt a burning sensation on his shoulder where Mai Sung had dug her nails in during the intense stunt.

Mai Sung looked at him, smiled a little, and said, "I'm sorry I hurt you." She then rubbed the red marks her nails had left on his shoulder.

"You're very strong." Sadeli laughed and looked at his left shoulder.

"That was an extremely skillful pilot," Umar Yunus said, "I'd like to know him and his life story. Surely, he experienced many wars in Europe or North Africa."

"Was that a Spitfire?" Sadeli asked.

"I think so," Umar Yunus replied.

"If only our national air force had such a plane." Sadeli wishfully remembered the ancient Japanese airplanes that Indonesian pilots flew. Those planes were even too old for a flying lesson, let alone a battle.

"Let's swim again," Mai Sung said and they all went back into the water.

Tired, they found a spot on the sand near the wall. The sun was high in the sky. Mai Sung spread out a big blanket and lay on it. Sadeli lay beside her. Lying there on the sand with the breeze blowing gently felt nice. Farther away, Umar Yunus and Rita Lee lay next to each other.

They were quiet for a short while, then Mai Sung said, "It's nice swimming here."

"Hmm," Sadeli answered lazily.

"The weather is wonderful," she said.

"Hmm," he said.

"Have you been here long?"

"No."

"Will you stay a while?"

"Don't know."

"There's a good movie playing at Cathay tonight."

"Hmm."

Mai Sung sat up and looked at Sadeli, who lay there with his eyes closed. She smiled at herself. She had given him a couple of obvious hints but he didn't seem to care. She now thought of a plan to make him pay more attention to her. She lay back down. Not long after, she said, "You're really quiet."

"Huh, what's that?" asked Sadeli, as if he were just awakened.

Mai laughed a little and said, "I was talking to you for about five minutes and your answers were just 'huh, huh, hmm.' I asked you to go to a movie tonight and you just said 'hmm.' What's on your mind?"

Sadeli opened his eyes and looked at her. "You know, Mai," he said, "you're a very attractive young lady." He had answered her question while concealing his thoughts. When he lay down after the swim, he figured out the solution for the problems in his job. He was able to choose the paths he had to take. His heart was full of joy for he knew what to do.

"Do you want to watch a movie at Cathay tonight?" he asked. "What time should I pick you up? We should have dinner and catch the last show."

"Speaking of eating, I'm hungry," she said. She sat up and called to Rita, "Hey, Rita, we're hungry."

Umar Yunus sat up and checked his watch inside Rita's basket. "Yes," he said, "it's almost twelve. Let's shower and change in the house."

While the two women used the bathroom, Sadeli sat down in front of the piano in the living room and opened its lid. Umar Yunus went to the back of the house, looking for the old caretaker to have him make them something cold to drink.

Sadeli softly played the "Serenata" by Toselli. He really enjoyed this song whenever he felt romantic.

After Rita and Mai were done, Sadeli and Umar Yunus took turns showering.

All dressed up, they went to the car. Inside the car, Umar Yunus said they should go to Johor for lunch, to a restaurant specializing in boiled crab.

Though small, the restaurant had a cozy atmosphere. "Ah, this is nice indeed," said Sadeli, leaning back in his chair.

Umar Yunus offered him a cigarette.

"This is a good place," Mai Sung said, "They stayed open during the Japanese occupation."

They ate and talked.

"Do you know why the crab here is so good?" Rita asked Sadeli.

He shook his head.

"The crab are still alive and fresh when put into a boiling pot, and they're only boiled for a short time," Mai Sung said.

"The secret," Rita added, "is in the delicious chili sauce."

"You talk like culinary experts," Sadeli said.

"Of course," Mai Sung said, "everything was hard to get during the Japanese occupation. We learned to make due with anything."

"Was it tough back then?" Sadeli asked.

"It was a horrible nightmare. My uncle was captured and killed by the Japanese. Ugh!" Mai Sung rushed the painful memory out of her mind.

"When people are in constant danger, they learn to live with it," Sadeli said. He went on telling them about the week of battle he experienced when death could strike at any second. "It was an eighteen-hour battle against a Gurkha troop. There were only fifty of us and they were about the same number. They had more weapons and experience. We needed to hold them to buy some time for our friends to empty a Japanese armory. It's a battle I'll never forget. We held our ground for as long as we could and only shot when we had to. We retreated when we were almost surrounded by the enemy. At first we always thought of and feared death. But since the battle went on for hours, we forgot to eat and, strangely, we forgot about death. Only when the battle was over and we left the empty armory for the Gurkhas did we realize how close we had been to death. Only thirty people survived. We had no idea of the number of casualties on the Gurkha's side, but we knew that without a Japanese Nambu machine gun, none of us would have lived."

"Yes, I know," said Mai Sung, "When people live in danger, they only live for the moment. They don't think or look too far ahead. That was how we lived during the Japanese occupation. We only thought about survival in terms of a day at a time. The strange thing is that I still feel that way even though the war is over. Take what you can from life right now, all the fun and joy. Who knows what tomorrow will bring. Tomorrow, the sun may not even rise."

"Ah," Sadeli interrupted her, "it's not nice to think that way. The sun will rise tomorrow. We need to know how to place the sun, the moon, and the stars in our heart."

"Aw, he speaks like a poet," Rita exclaimed.

"Though not a good one," Sadeli said.

"But it sounds beautiful." Mai Sung repeated, "The sun, the moon, and the stars in our heart. How romantic."

"I'm not a romantic person." Sadeli was a little embarrassed.

"Look, he's blushing." Mai Sung clapped happily.

"That's proof he's romantic," said Umar Yunus.

It was three in the afternoon when Umar Yunus drove Mai Sung to her apartment and Sadeli to his hotel.

"Thank you both very much," Sadeli said before they parted, "I had so much fun today." He waved and watched the car drive away long enough to see Rita Lee scoot over and lean into Umar Yunus. Sadeli suddenly felt lonely and wished the night would come faster so he would see Mai Sung again.

Mai Sung was all dressed up when Sadeli picked her up with a taxi at seven. She immediately opened her apartment door when he knocked.

"I saw you get out of the taxi," she said. "Come in."

She wore a tight cheongsam with high side slits. A black crystal necklace sparkled around her fair neck. She had put up her black hair.

"Wow, you're very beautiful," Sadeli remarked honestly.

"Thank you," she laughed, "Do you want anything to drink? Or should we just leave?"

"Let's just leave," he said, "The taxi's still waiting and I'm hungry. Where shall we eat?" He helped her put on her silk shawl and they left.

In the taxi, she asked him, "What are you in the mood for? European cuisine, Chinese, or Indian? I like all of them."

"You should choose because you know Singapore better."

Mai Sung took him to a small yet clean Chinese restaurant. "Duck is their specialty," she said.

Mai Sung spoke Mandarin to the restaurant's owner, who came to their table. After the owner left, she said to Sadeli, "I hope you like what I ordered: Peking duck, bird's nest soup, rice, and a little Chinese rum. Rum enhances our taste buds." She smiled at him.

They looked at the street outside the window. That small street was full of traffic. Restaurants lined up on both sides of the street. Duck, chicken, pork ribs, Chinese mustard, and garlic could be seen among the colors of fruit, lamps, clothes, and the dark shadows. Various scents and sounds rose from every part of the street. Everything rose to join the yellow and red lamplight. The smell of garlic, pork, shrimp, the sound of bells chiming, cars honking, the tick-tick-tick of the wooden instruments used by the hawkers, and the buzzing of conversations rose high to the stars in the sky. These were the signs of a crowded, lively city—a pulsing heat.

Sadeli felt his blood rush. His spirit burned and his eyes sparkled when he pointed at the street and said, "It's a flowing river of life. There are many like this in the world. Some meet and form a bigger river, others meet and clash. Humans have to learn how to manage the merging of the rivers of life peacefully."

Mai Sung gaped. She didn't understand what he meant.

Sadeli smiled. "Forgive me," he said, "Sometimes strange thoughts get into my head. Here comes our food, let's eat."

***

Inside the movie theater, Sadeli watched the silver screen. The film didn't interest him. It was a romance with the main character singing and dancing on rooftops in New York with stars in the background. It was boring, but Mai Sung seemed captivated. Since the theater lights went down, she had moved close to him and put her right hand on his.

Sadeli was more than happy to hold her hand while he leaned back in his chair and made plans for his mission. He was happy because he knew exactly what to do. Tomorrow he would receive the final report from Ali Nurdin regarding a few things he had asked him to do. Some of them were about the possibility of getting a speedboat, renting an airplane, and buying a bazooka, a type of antitank rocket launcher.

To each of Mai Sung's comments on the film, he only responded with, "Hmm. Yes. Huh, hmm?"

Inside the taxi on their way to Mai Sung's place, she put her head on his chest, let out a happy breath, and said, "You're so kind to me. I feel very happy today."

"So do I." Sadeli leaned over to kiss her cheek.

She looked up, pulled his face down, and kissed him passionately on the mouth. When the taxi pulled over in front of her building, she whispered, "Will you come up?"

Sadeli paid the taxi and they went into the building. She gave him her key as they climbed up the stairs. He opened the door to her apartment and she walked in, stopping by the doorway. She closed the door behind him, put her hands on his shoulders, and moved closer to him. He held her tightly and kissed her. They stood like that for a short while until she whispered with a hoarse voice, "Come."

Then, after a good while, on the bed inside her room, when the storm had died down, when their heartbeats had returned to normal, the lighting and thunder ceased, and the blazing fire was reduced to glowing embers, Sadeli looked at Mai Sung, who lay beside him with closed eyes, breathing steadily, a little smile on her lips. He took in her face, which turned softer in the dark, the curves of her body, and a mass of black hair on her pillow. Every time he had sex with a woman, he was always amazed at how this gentle being could bring out a storm, light a raging fire, cause a very strong earthquake, yet also invoke the gentlest feeling, a very strong love, and a profound passion all at the same time. She could bring out a man's best traits or his wild side.

How different was a woman's bedroom from a man's. Clothes, bras, and panties were neatly stacked on a chair. Everything in the room showed a woman lived there.

Sadeli sat up, reached into his jacket pocket for cigarettes and a lighter. When he lit one, Mai opened her eyes and said, "Light one for me."

He handed her his.

Mai Sung stroked his shoulder gently and whispered, "You're so strong." Then she took a long drag of the cigarette.

"You are very wonderful too," he said. Then he asked, "Mai?"

"Hmm."

"Do you like me?"

"Yes."

"Are we friends?"

"Yes."

"You won't lie to me?"

"No."

"Alright. Then tell me, what does Umar Yunus want to know about me that he asked you to be this nice to me?"

Mai sat up straight. Her eyes were wide open. "How do you know that?" she asked.

"Oh that's easy," he smiled, "So, it's true?"

"Yes," she answered after a few moments, and quickly added, "Please don't tell anyone I told you this. He's a powerful man around here with wealthy and prominent friends. He can make my job difficult. I'm scared."

"Scared?" Sadeli asked, surprised.

"Yes," Mai Sung said, "I work as a taxi girl at the dance club. If they're angry with me, no dance club will hire me. I'll lose that good job. Do you understand?"

Sadeli nodded. "Don't be afraid, Mai," he said, "You don't need to worry. Umar Yunus won't know. I promise." He thought, *Oh my God, is this how rampant fear has taken hold of the world? There are so many kinds of fear. We must erase fear from everyone's heart; it's a must.*

Sadeli asked, "Umar Yunus wants to know who I really am, right?"

Mai Sung nodded.

"Tell him, when he asks you tomorrow, I'm an officer of the Ministry of Economy and Welfare of Indonesia. I've been sent to establish a trading relationship with Singapore. Do you want to know more?"

"No," Mai Sung shook her head, then asked softly, "You're not angry at me?"

"No." Sadeli laughed.

"Are we still friends?"

"Yes." Sadeli took the cigarette Mai Sung held between her fingers and snuffed it into an ashtray on the chair. He pulled her to him and whispered, "Yes, we're still friends."

Mai giggled and then stretched her body and legs to meet Sadeli's and slipped into the embrace of their rushing blood and heated bodies. The world outside the window and the bedroom moved away, vanished. All that remained was the two of them. Unified.

Chapter 4

Sadeli listened closely to Ali Nurdin's report. He was happy.

It had been three days since he left Mai Sung's apartment at eight in the morning. Two more ships carrying sugar had docked at the port safely. His new instructions from Colonel Suroso were to quickly purchase radio interception equipment for an intelligence unit in North Sumatra. Bukit Tinggi and Yogyakarta needed airplanes right away due to a very urgent matter.

All his plans were set. Ali Nurdin had established contact with Tan Ciat Tong, a Chinese merchant who owned a well-running speedboat in Penang. Tan was willing to either rent or sell the boat. He could also find them the radio interceptor.

Sadeli thought the asking price was reasonable, but Ali Nurdin told him there was a risk to consider. The radio device was made in Britain. The guerilla troops were to use the devices in their fight against the Japanese, but before they could make use of the equipment, Japan surrendered. The ex-guerillas would now like to sell the equipment, but the British thought the devices still belonged to them and would surely impound them. Sadeli needed to have security in place.

Ali Nurdin also managed to purchase fifty automatic guns for the intelligence unit in North Sumatra. The problem here was that the Communists owned the weapons and they were under heavy surveillance by the British. This transaction therefore also required tight security.

"Why do they want to sell to us?" Sadeli asked.

"Oh, under the current circumstances they like to help us with our fight for freedom," said Ali Nurdin. "The Communists here are also getting ready to overthrow the British, but their position is a little difficult because most of them are Chinese. The Malayans are Muslims and not interested in Communism. When it's time for the Communists here to revolt, they'll easily get weapons from Thailand, Burma, and even China itself after the Communists gain power there."

"How do they know the Communists will win in China?"

"They not only know it, they're sure of it. They base their prediction on a factual calculation. Chinese Communist agents have been actively working here for a while. With Russia emerging as the other superpower besides America, the Communists have no doubt they will take over Asia in a short time. They'll start with China, then Indochina, the Philippines, Thailand, Burma, Malaya, Indonesia, and India. Africa is next on the list and so are the Latin American countries."

Sadeli nodded. *Indonesia has to pay attention to these possibilities*, he thought.

"I'm actually reluctant to do business with them," Ali Nurdin said.

"Don't feel that way," Sadeli said, "Although we know the Communists will eventually oppose the nationalists, and they want to conquer our country, we should not hesitate to do business with them if that means we can get what we need today. Please arrange a meeting for me with them. I have to inspect that radio equipment and the weapons. I also need to meet Tan Ciat Tong. He lives in Penang, but if I go there, it'll be easy for the British to figure out what we're up to. Can he come here? Or can I check the boat somewhere else? Perhaps he can bring his boat near Singapore and we take a boat to see it? I also need to meet the crew who will carry the radio equipment and weapons. We need to arm them as well, in case the Dutch chase our boat. Can you get all of that done in a week?"

Ali Nurdin thought for a moment. "I'll try," he said.

"Try to get it done as soon as possible," said Sadeli, "And be really careful. We're being closely watched, not only by the British but also by the Dutch. When we're done with this, I'm going to Bangkok. I received word that we're going to have the talk regarding the airplane rental there. A lot of American, British, and French pilots live there, and fly illegal drugs from North Burma and South China via Thailand to Macau. They also transport smuggled goods between the Philippines, Hong Kong, and other Asian regions."

Ali Nurdin's eyes lit up. He was filled with the spirit of revolution. His coming to Singapore now had a purpose since he could fully dedicate himself to the revolution that would bring freedom and justice to all Indonesians.

Ali Nurdin remembered how extremely poor he was when he worked as a journalist for *Pelita Bangsa*, a Jakarta-based newspaper, during the Dutch colonization before World War II. He only made ten rupiahs a month. As a high school graduate he could have made a lot more had he wanted to work for the Dutch.

However, he and many other journalists in Jakarta wanted to fight for their nation's rights for freedom and justice. There were months he wore patched pants to work and had to cover the big hole in the sole of his shoes with a thick wad of paper from the inside, and even the socks inside those shoes were full of holes. He went hungry when he ran out of money and couldn't borrow from the office because they simply had nothing to lend.

He remembered all that, the suffering of an Indonesian journalist during the fight for freedom of the press and his nation's independence.

It was not until the Japanese occupation that his life improved somewhat. The Japanese needed journalists. However, he soon resented writing fake propaganda that deceived his own people.

This led to his involvement in an underground movement against the Japanese. He went through times of fear and terror when the Kempeitai, the Japanese military police, arrested a few college students from the movement. None of those students confessed. They were released after being tortured.

Their stories were horrific. The Kempeitai used electric shocks on them and stubbed out burning cigarettes on their cheeks, chests, stomachs, and even their genitals. The Kempeitai also removed some of the students' nails and smashed their hands with a board. Some of the students were forced to drink water until they bloated and then their stomachs were stomped on. The students also witnessed the Japanese commit atrocities toward others, including women.

He spent years in the movement, and the constant threat of petrifying terror affected his health. Whenever he was under a lot of stress, his left eyelid would blink uncontrollably. The tick became his enduring reminder of the Japanese occupation.

Six months before Japan surrendered, he fell in love with the secretary at his newspaper agency. He was crazy about Nani. He was so madly in love with her that he didn't know whether he was dead or alive. The worst of the situation was that he didn't have the courage to express his love. He passed her house almost every night and stood for hours under a lush tree looking at her house. At that time Jakarta experienced a constant blackout for fear of airstrikes from the Allies and there was not much he could see on dark nights like that.

A month before Japan surrendered, the rumors that Japan would soon capitulate gave him courage to express his feelings to Nani.

To this date, he still cringed whenever he recalled that moment. They were in a *becak* on their way home from work. He purposely offered to take her home that day. He had done that many times before, but that day he was determined to tell her his feelings. They reached Pasar Senen, and the weather was burning hot. The becak driver pedaling behind them panted heavily.

Ali Nurdin said, "Nani, I love you. Will you marry me?"

Nani looked at him, amazed. Then she laughed, "You're joking."

"No, I'm serious. I've been in love with you for a long time. Will you marry me?"

Nani was surprised with the unexpected proposal in the scorching heat of the day. In her dreams, she had imagined the love of her life would propose to her under moonlight in the middle of a flower garden or by the shore where silvery waves crashed. Her romantic dreams never included a becak ride on a hot afternoon with a becak driver panting behind them. The situation struck her as very funny and she burst out laughing. She laughed even harder when Ali Nurdin's expression changed from surprised to embarrassed and he turned pink. She didn't hear him tell the driver to pull over. She only realized he had left when she noticed he was no longer next to her. Only then did she stop laughing and jumped out of the becak, calling for him. She shrugged when she could not find him and got back in the becak to continue her journey home. She had not meant to hurt his feelings.

Ali remembered how long he walked aimlessly that night. He didn't want to go home and felt he was the most unfortunate man on earth. Not only had Nani rejected him, she had laughed at him as well. He was embarrassed and sad. He didn't see any point in living; he'd be better off dead.

Around ten, when the streets were empty, he lay down on the asphalt in front of Nani's house. He wanted to be run over by a car and have Nani find his body in the morning. *She would know no one else but she had killed him. She might as well have choked him with her bare hands.* Filled with those bitter thoughts, he fell asleep lying on the street. He woke up near dawn, uninjured. He rose and hurried home with a mixed feeling of regret and relief. He didn't go to work for a couple of days.

When he returned to work, Nani acted as if nothing had happened. It was then that he vowed to be a prominent figure. He would do great things that would make people, including Nani, admire him. Nani would be proud of him, fall in love with him, and marry him.

Japan surrendered soon afterward and when Soekarno and Hatta proclaimed Indonesia's independence, he worked very hard to join the revolution. He participated in collecting weapons from the Japanese and he took part in establishing the national news agency.

He sensed the opportunities had opened up to engage in great undertakings, and decided to broaden the scope of his job to abroad. His first step was to go to Singapore. Before he left, he met with Nani and told her about his plans. He bravely told her he still loved her and if she felt the same about him, she would need to wait until he returned or until she heard of his death abroad.

He was completely taken by surprise and overjoyed when she suddenly hugged him and whispered not to go so they could be married, soon.

However, he stood by his decision and said that they had to wait. This was the time of struggle and sacrifice and she could not make him change his mind. They vowed to be faithful to each other and he left for Singapore.

Ali Nurdin now felt he was closer to reaching his goal. With financial help from Major Sadeli, he had an office at Rames Square. The name of his news agency, *Indonesian News Agency Nasional*, could be seen from afar. He provided news from Indonesia to the British, Malaya, and Chinese newspapers, as well as the foreign news agencies stationed in Singapore, such as Reuters, Agence France Presse, United Press, Associated Press, International News Service, and many more. Although he still couldn't cover all the business expenses, he started to derive some income from his journalistic work.

In a letter to Nani in Jakarta, Ali told her that he worked for Major Sadeli, and had become more deeply involved in the fight for the revolution. If he succeeded, he would have contributed significantly to the revolution and he would definitely move up in rank. He felt fortunate to be able to participate in the Indonesian Revolution.

***

Two days later, Sadeli sat across from Inspector Hawkins in a restaurant. They had finished lunch and were enjoying the relaxed and friendly atmosphere.

Inspector Hawkins said, "Let's drop formalities. As I mentioned last time, please call me John. We're friends now; at least I hope so."

Sadeli smiled and said, "Just call me Sadeli. It's hard to shorten my name. You could call me Sad, but in your language that means sorrow, and Eli sounds like a girl's name."

They both laughed.

"Ah, I'll call you Eddy, if I may," Hawkins said, "It's a nice compromise."

"Alright." Sadeli laughed. He had invited Hawkins for lunch like he promised last week. He really admired the British detectives in Singapore.

One of Tan Ciat Tong's men had picked him up last night. After they went in and out of taxis that drove through maze-like streets, and going in and out of so many houses to avoid being followed by a British spy, they reached a narrow, dark alley. Tan Ciat Tong's man asked that Sadeli be blindfolded. Sadeli was a little nervous when the man covered his eyes with a black handkerchief then held his hand and said, "Come."

Sadeli felt himself being guided into another alley before he was taken up a short flight of stairs. He heard a door being opened before he was led across a flat area, down some steps, across another flat area and up some steps again. A doorknob clicked as it turned and after they crossed another flat area, they stopped. He heard someone ask a question in Chinese and a door open. A man asked him to come in. After the door closed, the man took off Sadeli's blindfold.

Sadeli looked around the clean room. A middle-aged Chinese man dressed in typical Chinese clothes sat on a chair. He had a military demeanor and his eyes were focused on Sadeli. He rose and moved toward Sadeli with an extended hand.

"Welcome. I'm sorry you had to go through all the inconvenience to get here, but it was necessary for both your safety and ours," he said in fluent English.

He offered Sadeli a seat. After he said something in Chinese to the man who had escorted Sadeli, the man left.

"Do you prefer to get our business done quickly?"

Sadeli nodded.

"Forgive me, I can't offer you anything to eat or drink. Do you smoke?" He handed Sadeli a cigar box.

Sadeli declined.

The door opened and the man who had brought Sadeli there came in with a long package. He put the package on a table and carefully unwrapped it. The package held a new Bren gun.

The beautiful weapon still had the lubricated casing to keep it from rusting.

"You have fifty of these?" Sadeli's calm voice concealed his excitement.

The Chinese man nodded and said, "If you need more, we can find them for you."

"Will you lower your price?" Sadeli asked. "You need to remember this is very risky for us. After you deliver the goods, we still have the risk of getting caught by the British and, or, the Dutch," he added.

"There's always a risk in war," the Chinese man answered curtly.

"Lower your price by ten percent," Sadeli bargained.

"You pay cash in dollars?" the Chinese man asked.

"As soon as the goods arrive on the ship. I'll pay in Singapore dollars just like you asked for."

The Chinese man thought for a moment. Then he said, "Fine. When and where should we send the merchandise?"

"I'll let you know. What about the radio equipment?"

"It's not here. But you can see it tonight if you want."

Sadeli nodded.

The Chinese man said something to the other man before he stood and shook Sadeli's hand.

"If you are satisfied with the radio equipment and the price, let me know. He will take you to see it now."

Once again Sadeli was blindfolded. When his blindfold was removed, he stood in a small, dark alley. He didn't recognize the place.

They went along the alley until they reached a main street. A taxi was already waiting for them. They quickly got in.

The taxi drove them to a house by the beach. They got out of the taxi and walked through the yard to the beach. It was late into the night. All of a sudden, a voice greeted them. Sadeli's escort answered.

Sadeli saw a boat on the beach and two men waiting by it. They got on the boat and the two rowers pushed the boat to the water before they jumped into the boat. Sadeli noticed the fishing gear.

"If we run across the harbor police patrol, we're going fishing," his escort explained.

Although there was no moon that night, it was quite bright in the middle of the sea under a star-studded sky. About a mile from the shore, they pulled up alongside a big freighter. Sadeli's escort spoke to the people on the freighter, then signaled Sadeli to board the ship. The captain ushered them inside the cabin. He ordered a couple of mates to move a few sacks and remove some floorboards. He then lifted a medium-sized chest out of the hole. The chest contained a radio interceptor Sadeli could almost drool over. Indonesia badly needed the equipment. The device was brand new, and still inside its original packaging.

Sadeli signaled that he was done checking. They walked to the deck and jumped back on their boat to make their way back to shore.

"Do you want to return to your hotel? Or do you want to spend the night here? It's very late."

Sadeli checked his watch. It was almost two in the morning. He said, "Won't the British agent shadowing me be suspicious when he sees me come out of this house tomorrow?"

His escort laughed and said, "No, absolutely not. This house is a high-class brothel. A place Singapore's billionaires visit for pleasure. There are only three women here: one British, one French, and one Arabian." He winked and added, "My boss said you're our guest tonight."

Sadeli figured that for his own safety, he should spend the night and go back to the hotel tomorrow. He would let Inspector Hawkins believe he just returned from the brothel. "Fine," he said, "give me a room, but no ladies, please."

***

The next morning, Sadeli returned to the hotel. After he completed the trading documents, he called Inspector Hawkins to have lunch.

Sadeli was relieved. The only thing left to do was to ship the radio interceptor and the automatic guns back home. He really wanted his first operation to succeed.

Hawkins came around noon. While they ate, Sadeli asked him about Tan Ciat Tong.

Hawkins said softly, "Eddy, you'd better be careful with Tan Ciat Tong."

"Huh?" Sadeli was a little surprised.

Hawkins pretended he didn't notice Sadeli's reaction. While he cut the steak on his plate he added, "He'd be willing to slit his own grandmother's throat for profit."

"Ah, I'm not too interested in Tan Ciat Tong," Sadeli said.

"Good. That shows you're wise," said Hawkins, "Just remember he's a thirteen-headed snake. I don't want to see your head between his jaws."

"Thanks for your concern, John. I know how to handle a thirteen-headed snake and am not worried about Tan Ciat Tong. I'm more concerned about the Dutch intelligence."

"Hmm, you need to be careful with them too. They're active here. They're hoping we'll help them. For instance, if we tell them that on a certain night, a ship will set sail for Sumatra, there's an excellent chance they'll intercept that ship."

"But if the ship takes another course, it surely will escape their interception."

The inspector nodded and took a swig of his beer. He wiped his lips with the back of his hand and said, "Believe it or not, Eddy, post-war beer is never as good as the pre-war one. I've no clue why."

Sadeli raised his glass and drank. He imitated Hawkins when he said, "Hmm, I'm not sure about this. I never drank any European beer before the war, but for a revolutionary freedom fighter, this beer is great."

Inspector Hawkins laughed. He cut another piece off his steak and ate it before he said, "It's not easy, and I dare not say that I'm anti-

Dutch, or French, or Belgian, or others. What's happening in Britain is surely happening in other European countries. The thing is, there's no single Europe now. There's Western Europe and Eastern Europe. Besides, after the war, the relationships among nations are still seeking a new equilibrium. Although we have the United Nations, this process of creating new and balanced relationships is not finished. Stalin is high on victory in Moscow. He wants to expand his Moscow-centered Communist power. It seems China will fall to the Communists within a couple of years. There's Ho Chi Minh in Indochina, and he's a Communist. The French will make the same mistakes there as the Dutch did in Indonesia. We have intelligence reports on the Communists' activities in the Philippines, Thailand, Indonesia, our very own Malaya, Burma, and India. Aside from Communism, nationalism is getting stronger and stronger in Asia and Africa. On the other hand, say in Britain, people are tired of war. In post-war United States, many demand a quick demobilization of the troops. It's apparent from the massive protests by the American soldiers in the Philippines and Japan who want to return to their country as soon as possible. In Britain, the Conservatives, as represented by Churchill, actually want to bring back the golden era of the British Empire upon which the sun never sets. Churchill once said he did not become a prime minister to put an end to the British Empire. Yet, most of the British people are not interested in that kind of mindset. They no longer want to see their countrymen die in the forests of India, Burma, Malaya, and other parts of the world. Also, the Labour Party's influence is getting stronger. It supports the development of a just and equal society and independence for every nation within the British Empire. In the 1945 post-war election, it turned out the British voted for the Labour party and gave the power to Attlee. Their victory had a tremendous influence on the mindsets of the British and other European nations as well. Besides, you can't say the four pillars of freedom put forth by Roosevelt and Churchill—freedom from fear and hunger, freedom of religion and speech—don't have any effect on the people of Western Europe."

"Yes, I remember that," Sadeli said, "We also heard that during the Japanese occupation and it gave us hope that we would not need to raise arms to seize our independence from the Dutch. But look what happened."

"True. There's a great gap between the slogan and the implementation. Still, the people of Western Europe, including the Dutch, are prioritizing the redevelopment of their own devastated country. They feel a new relationship among men and nations is indeed needed so we can avoid wars.

"Many times, wars have proven to be an extremely costly way to solve problems among nations. In the last war, Europe suffered billions of dollars of loss and millions of casualties among both the military and civilians. There was unimaginable suffering, grief, and lives cut short. A staggering number of scientists, musicians, painters, writers, and dancers died in the Nazi gas chambers and under the bomb attacks launched by both sides. It's clear now that a condition within a certain country affects the condition in other countries.

"A nation can no longer live alone and disregard other nations. Technology has made this world smaller. Remember, it used to take longer than a year to travel to Indonesia. We had to sail around the Cape of Good Hope. Now it only takes a few days by plane, and if the plane uses jet engines like the German fighter jets during the last couple of months in World War II, then it'll take even less time to travel around the world.

"Eddy, I believe your revolution happens at precisely the right moment. The world's perspective is on your side. In an unstable world, those who have the courage to pursue their dreams will reach their goals. The world sympathizes with you. The war between the West and Communism benefits you. Don't be tempted to join a certain bloc."

"That's exactly our stand. We employ independent foreign politics, and are not aligned with any of the blocs. We want to independently and peacefully work with all nations. Domestically, we want to foster independence, democracy, and social welfare. We don't want to have any political concentration camps in our country like Boven-

Digoel during the Dutch time. We no longer want to have the police intelligence spy on our citizens, by reading and censoring their mail, or attend meetings like the colonial police did. We want to nurture a free, prosperous, peaceful, and harmonious society. We believe our country and our people have positive values to contribute to the international collaboration for the good of all mankind."

"Noble sentiments, Eddy, those are honorable ideals and lofty wishes. The question is how to make it happen. After your country has defeated Dutch imperialism, you will have to deal with all kinds of problems, and need to figure out how to implement all these goals and revolutionary slogans."

Inspector Hawkins suddenly turned his head toward the door and said, "That's Dr. Banerji, an Indian doctor. He's been here a long time and he's a good friend of mine. You'll like him. Let's ask him to join us." Hawkins waved at the doctor.

Sadeli followed Hawkins' gaze. A tall Indian man with a huge belly and a plump face with thick layers of chin sagging down his neck stood in the doorway. His fat cheeks made his eyes appear like slits.

"Hello, Inspector!" the man said cheerfully.

Sadeli was a little surprised to hear a shrill, thin voice coming from someone that big.

"This is Mr. Sadeli from the Republic of Indonesia."

Sadeli was happy with the doctor's firm handshake.

"Please join us," the inspector invited Banerji, "We're planning a world revolution and you, Doctor, should be the first member of our movement."

Dr. Banerji sat down and let out a long sigh. He seemed to be glad he no longer had to stand and hold up the weight of his body. "One day," he said, "my heart will stop working as I'm getting fatter and fatter by the day."

"Ah, your heart is as strong as mine. Don't think about it," replied Hawkins. "Well, what can I get you, Doc?"

"The usual."

"A tall glass of beer, please," Hawkins informed the waiter.

"I'm so happy to meet you, Sir." Dr. Banerji turned to Sadeli. "Your people and mine share a long historic connection. We too will free ourselves from British colonialism, although we hope to do it, if possible, peacefully. The British with their Labour Party take a more shrewd approach than the Dutch. But, never mind, we're at a crossroad now and those who can't understand the current of history will be left behind. We're at the threshold of the century of freedom. The atomic energy launched by humans from their secret network has shown its destructive force. Yet, it also contains the power to build the welfare of all mankind. Who knows, one day, with the help of science, it will also be the key to free humans from gravity. Thus, humans will be able to roam freely in space, among places they call home. Therefore, all nations must form a unity, must learn to live together, work peacefully together in their quest for freedom."

"Bravo! Bravo!" Hawkins clapped. "Am I wrong to say he's a revolutionist? With that brief but fiery speech, doesn't he deserve to be the third member of our revolutionary band?"

Sadeli nodded and smiled. "I absolutely agree with you, John. From now on, Dr. Banerji is a member of our pact. I'm so happy to hear he believes in the victory of my country's revolution."

"Yes, no need to worry about that," said the doctor, "instead we have to think about what to do after we seize our independence. How do we develop a free, just, prosperous, and happy society? Look at my country, India. We have extraordinary problems. We have hundreds of languages. And then the different religions, the conflict between the Muslims and Hindus alone, may divide the nation.

"Gandhi is old and his thoughts about the *Swadeshi*, self-sufficiency movement, don't receive unanimous support. Many people want India to spring forward and be a modern country. But in the Hindu society, caste is a major obstacle. Tens of millions of the pariahs must be set free from the shackles of their disgraced fate. There are so many centrifugal forces in India that can catapult our country and nation into thousands of pieces. Poverty and hunger have been parts of life in India for centuries. To foster a free, prosperous, peaceful, just, and law-abiding society is not easy.

"In the early stages, a great responsibility lies on the shoulders of our leaders. They have to set a personal example of how to live a good, honest, and clean life. They need to live like a knight who puts the people's needs above his own and works hard from sun up to sun down. We're lucky to have Gandhi, Nehru, and Narayan, but there are only a very few of them, and what will happen after they die? I'm wondering if you have similar problems in Indonesia?" Banerji asked Sadeli.

"Ah…" Sadeli hesitated for a moment. "I guess our problems are not as complicated. We're lucky to have a national language, Bahasa Indonesia, so the many regional languages are no longer a problem. The Sundanese and Javanese in Java have played a crucial role in the national unity.

"During the Japanese occupation, our nation developed greatly. We don't have the caste system, and the one in Bali is not as rigid as yours in India. We don't have powerful landlords like you have in your country. We also don't have religious conflicts. Indonesians are very tolerant when it comes to religion. A few tribes in Tapanuli, Sumatra, for instance, allow Christian men to marry Muslim women, and their children are free to choose their own religion.

"Now, we do have a problem with the Chinese, who are small in number compared to the national population, but are very powerful in the economic sector. Perhaps this can create problems in the future. But this is a small matter compared to, say, the problem with the Chinese in Malaya. We also have many tribes and ethnicities, but the problems this may cause can be overcome during the revolution. The national struggle in the revolution for independence can be a very strong bind for the nation. The leaders of our revolution also come from all kinds of ethnic groups. Besides, no ethnic group in Indonesia has the tendency to rule over other ethnic groups.

"We still have feudalism. It's important to eliminate the feudal spirit engrained in our people's soul. Especially in Java, the notion to obey authority is anchored in people's minds. In my opinion, it's even harder to free our people from ancient traditions and superstitions that grip the soul and can hinder advancement. Often, during a battle, our soldiers became very brave because they carried a talisman given by a witch doctor. They became overconfident and careless and then were killed by the enemy's bullet. Still, some continued to believe in the talisman and blamed their friend's death on something he had done wrong that annulled the talisman's power. The person's behavior had tainted the talisman and therefore it could no longer do its magic. So many superstitions need to be erased from our people's mind and soul, like the belief in witch doctors, sacred days and signs, and many others that only hold back our development.

"We're lucky to have leaders who set good personal examples for the people. They live a humble life, away from luxury, and they don't lust for money or women. We simply can't imagine any of them becoming power- or money-hungry, especially because they are patriots who withstood the tests of capture and exile by the Dutch. They won't betray the dreams for our nation's freedom, justice, and honor. They're the ones who demand and make sacrifices for our freedom and rights from the colonial Dutch. There's no way they will oppress these rights in the future."

"I admire your confidence in Indonesia's future," said Dr. Banerji, "If only I could be as confident in my own people's future, I would be very happy."

"Let's pray," said Inspector Hawkins, "that the remains of the Nazi gas chambers in Bergen-Belsen, Auschwitz, and the fascist Japan's vicious concentration camps serve as monuments in mankind's heart, reminding us to forever glorify human life and freedom."

"Yes, Yes!" Dr. Banerji and Sadeli responded simultaneously.

When they were about to part, Dr. Banerji handed his business card to Sadeli and said, "Drop by my place sometime. I'm normally at home after seven in the evening, but better call first. My wife and children would love to meet you. They're also eager to visit your country."

Inspector Hawkins offered Sadeli a ride back to the hotel, but Sadeli refused. He had to check the speedboat they would use to transport the radio interceptors and automatic guns to Sumatra.

Sadeli took a taxi to a shop. He said to the shopkeeper, "I have an appointment with Ms. Sue Liong. Is she in?"

After checking outside, the man nodded. "Come with me," he said, and Sadeli followed him to another room.

A plump, short, Chinese man immediately rose from a chair and shook Sadeli's hand as he introduced himself. "Welcome, Mr. Sadeli. I'm Tan Ciat Tong."

Sadeli sized him up. Unless his reputation had preceded him, he would not have come across as a dangerous opportunist who would slit his own grandmother's throat for profit. Tan looked about fifty, although it was certainly hard to correctly guess a person's age based solely on their looks. Perhaps he was younger, but indulgence had aged him.

Sadeli tried hard to dismiss the image created by the infamous stories about Tan Ciat Tong, but also found it difficult to trust the man. There was something sleazy about him. Sadeli almost regretted his decision to contact him. He had received offers for radio equipment and guns from a few other people, but their price had been higher. Tan Ciat Tong's price was lower, but it was clear that the risk was also greater.

Tan Ciat Tong offered Sadeli a seat and said, "I apologize for the way we have to meet. I'm sure you understand, it's for safety." He then said something in Chinese to the shopkeeper. Sadeli, who had been honing his Mandarin skills since he arrived in Singapore, followed their conversation with a blank expression on his face.

Tan Ciat Tong sent the man to check if some Singaporean had followed Sadeli. After a moment, the shopkeeper returned and reported everything was clear. Tan Ciat Tong sighed with relief. "Come," he said to Sadeli.

They all went out to the back of the store, through a dirty yard filled with used old chests. Some chickens scratched the ground. The shopkeeper opened a small door in the wall and stepped into a narrow alley. They walked along the alley, passing a Malayan kampong, until they reached a dirt road where a small Morris was parked. The driver, who stood under a lush tree, quickly moved to open the car door for them.

Ciat Tong asked Sadeli to take a seat in the back and then took the seat next to him. After they drove for about an hour, they came to a crossroad. They made a right and drove a little over three hundred yards on a bumpy, deserted road that took them deep into a forest before the car stopped.

Tan Ciat Tong got out of the car. Sadeli followed him. It was dusk and there was nothing but trees around them.

"We need to walk a little further," Tan Ciat Tong said.

A good place to commit a murder. Sadeli regretted not taking Inspector Hawkins' advice about carrying a gun at all times. The inspector had even offered to help him obtain the gun license.

Sadeli followed Tan Ciat Tong, who walked in front of him, carefully avoiding holes in the ground. After a few hundred yards, they suddenly came upon a riverbank where a boat was moored. Sadeli had never seen such a beautiful boat. Although it was a bit dirty, Sadeli thought it was a gorgeous vessel. Its sharp, streamlined bow made it look like it was ready to plow through the waves. The ship was made of iron. Some of its gray war paint had cracked and peeled off, and red, anti-rust paint spots appeared everywhere, making it look as if it had a skin full of scabies. The stern displayed the ship's new name: *Shalimar*. Sadeli smiled secretly. Shalimar meant protected by love, seeming in contrast with the boat itself. For a moment, he and Ciat Tong stood at the end of the gangplank. Then Ciat Tong formed a cone with his two hands and shouted, "Obiiiiiii!"

His voice echoed across the river, before being absorbed by the surrounding woods. After a moment, a head magically popped out of the ladder hole between the deck and the hull. Someone laughed and yelled something. Ciat Tong nodded and walked across the gangplank to board the ship. Sadeli followed him.

Meanwhile, Obi climbed on the deck. He was covered from head to toe in grease and held a big wrench in his right hand.

"Obi, the boat's mechanic," Ciat Tong explained.

Obi nodded and, grinning, showed his dirty hands.

Ciat Tong and Sadeli stood by the open trap door on the deck and looked at two big machines below. A few people looked up briefly from their work to greet Ciat Tong.

"Look," Ciat Tong said, "those are two airplane engines. They run on airplane fuel as well. If they are working properly, this boat can sail at least thirty knots per hour with a full load. In an emergency, it could probably go more than forty knots, but we never tried that. We're afraid the engines will blow and don't want to take that chance. Obi's a good mechanic. When the engines are clean, I'm sure it can compete with any boat. With thirty knots an hour, it will be easy to lose a Dutch or British warship." Tan Ciat Tong winked.

Sadeli saw that all the war equipment like the torpedo launcher and the heavy machine gun port were dismantled. "When can it set sail?" Sadeli asked as they went down the steps.

"In two days."

They checked the hull, and Sadeli found the boat to be in very good condition even though it looked ugly and dirty. After Sadeli finished his inspection, they returned to land. Further away from the boat, Sadeli turned to Ciat Tong and said, "Alright. This time, we'll rent your boat. Please have the boat ready in two days. I'll send six men to guard the cargo. The radio interceptors and guns will be delivered when the boat is out in the open sea. I'll tell you the exact time and location. Once the cargo is on board, you or your man will receive payment either in cash or a check from a Singapore bank."

"Cash is better, for safety reasons," Tan Ciat Tong said and added, "Why did you ask for delivery at sea? Wouldn't it be better here?"

"It's better at sea," Sadeli said and added, "For safety reasons, but my men can get on board here."

They walked back to the car via the narrow path.

Chapter 5

Two days later, the boat was ready at the agreed location, off a small island six miles from Johor. The cargo was to be delivered at midnight. All the preparations were complete. Sadeli only needed to issue the order to the leader of the operation to leave. Until that point, the leader was not aware of his involvement in the mission.

It was only five in the afternoon; there was still enough time to arrange everything. Sadeli had prepared his coded report for Colonel Suroso. He had also called Inspector Hawkins from a public phone, to tell him a ship smuggling guns would be leaving from Malacca.

Hawkins chuckled. Everything changed now that Sadeli had put his trust in him to divert the Dutch warships in the Singaporean waters. Sadeli had mentioned Palembang as the destination while the speedboat would actually head to Langsa in North Sumatra.

Ali Nurdin reported that the Dutch seemed to have gotten a whiff of their first operation. A Dutch corvette was seen patrolling outside the Singaporean waters during the past three days.

Sadeli looked at his watch. It was time to leave. He hailed a taxi in front of the hotel and gave the driver Umar Yunus' address.

When Sadeli knocked, Umar Yunus answered the door himself.

"Let's sit on the back porch; it's cooler there," Umar Yunus said.

"If possible, let's talk in your office," Sadeli replied and added, "so we won't be interrupted."

Umar Yunus threw Sadeli a curious glance. He began to feel worried as he ushered Sadeli to his office and offered him a seat at his desk.

Once seated, Sadeli took a small piece of paper from his pocket and simply said, "Read it carefully."

Umar Yunus turned a little pale and his hand shook when he reached for the document. When he finished reading, he dropped the paper on the table. As if he suddenly remembered his military training, he rose, stood at attention, and saluted. "Captain Umar Yunus, ready to serve."

Sadeli nodded, and told Umar Yunus to be seated.

"Major Sadeli. Mr. Sadeli," Umar Yunus stammered. After getting a hold of himself, he continued, "I had a feeling you worked for the intelligence service, and I was right. I'm sure you know everything by now." He stopped and rested his eyes on Sadeli.

Umar Yunus saw his world crumble around him: Rita Lee, his love, all his current dreams and those for the future, all his efforts, his investments into the future and his newfound happiness with Rita. He wondered if he should hand it all over to Major Sadeli, the representative of his country's revolution. He could still fight. He could refuse the order. He could refuse to hand over the money he had. He could defend his happiness with Rita.

Umar Yunus was overwhelmed with the flood of thoughts. Didn't he deserve to fully pursue happiness? Would it mean betrayal if he did so? Betrayal of his military oath, of his nation, of the revolution, and the freedom it fought for? Could he still be happy, even with Rita on his side, if he tainted his honor? He'd see the face of a traitor every time he looked into a mirror. Would he be able to live with a traitor's soul inside him?

Umar Yunus tried to imagine what it would be like to live in exile, cast away from his own land and people. He wondered if he could do it. He knew of a lot of people who lived and worked in a foreign land, like the many anti-fascist fighters from Spain, the anti-Communist Russians, and many others. They left their countries to fight for their countrymen's freedom. It was completely different from what he had done.

Umar Yunus suddenly resented Major Sadeli, who had forced him to evaluate all his actions.

"I want you to be ready at ten tonight to supervise a shipment of radio interceptors and guns to North Sumatra," Sadeli said.

Umar Yunus almost couldn't believe his ears. He wondered why Sadeli still trusted him with a crucial mission. "But…" Umar Yunus' voice was full of doubt.

"This is an extremely important mission and it must succeed," Sadeli said, and continued, "You're the only soldier I can use here. I know what you did and you know the consequences your deeds could have, but we're in the middle of a revolution. What you did it doesn't matter for now. It'll have to wait until you return. Carry out this order the best you can and we'll see about the rest."

Umar Yunus felt a sudden relief. The confrontation was postponed and he would have more time to think about what he should do. He quickly said, "Yes, Sir. I'll do my very best to execute the order."

Sadeli explained the operation to Umar Yunus. He warned Umar Yunus about the possibility of Tan Ciat Tong's betrayal, either at the time of payment or after the boat sailed. He told Umar Yunus about the six men he sent and secretly armed as a precaution. He also warned him about the danger of interception by a Dutch warship. He said, "Run, if they chase you, but if you can't run anymore, fight them the best you can. Use the Bren guns in the cargo, if necessary. Don't let the Dutch catch any of you because if they do, our entire operation here will be shut down. This is an extremely dangerous mission."

Sadeli then reminded Umar Yunus about the meeting time for that night before he left to give Umar Yunus some time to get ready.

Umar Yunus remained seated for a long time after Sadeli left. He wondered what he should do. He could still refuse the assignment. Betrayal was still possible. All the pros and cons came back to him. He massaged his temples, groaning.

"Dear God," he grumbled, "what should I do?" The element of danger in the mission made him anxious. He noted the contrast to the early days of the revolution when he and his friends looked death in the eye while singing a happy song.

"Oh Lord," he murmured, "I want to be brave again, the way I used to be. I want to be a warrior, strong like Major Sadeli, who doesn't have any excuses. Is my love for Rita Lee making me weak? Is wanting to preserve my happiness actually a weakness? Don't I have the right to make myself happy? Why did I use the revolution money for my own needs? Why didn't You make me strong like Major Sadeli?"

He didn't hear Rita Lee call him from outside. Nor did he hear her footsteps approaching, let alone her opening the door. He only raised his head when Rita Lee screamed his name.

Rita Lee was surprised to find Umar Yunus sitting at his desk with his head dropped into his hands.

"Are you sick, Johnny?" Rita Lee came closer.

Umar Yunus rose with a wan smile, and led her to their bedroom.

"No, I'm not sick," he said and lay down on the bed.

Rita sat down next to him and massaged his head.

"Sadeli was here," Umar Yunus said.

"So he's…?"

"Yes." Umar Yunus nodded.

Rita Lee turned pale. "What will he do? Does he know?"

"He knows."

"What will happen to us? What will happen to you?"

"He ordered me to leave tonight for an important mission. I'll be away for a week, ten days. I'll be back, after that."

"He won't do anything?"

"He said he'll deal with it after my return."

"Oh, Johnny," Rita hugged him tightly, "I'm scared. I really am. What will happen?" Her tears fell on his cheek and lips.

Rita's fear and vulnerability filled Umar Yunus with a new, strange sense of power. He had to be strong. The tenderness he felt for Rita Lee turned into a fierce urge to protect her from all the evil in this world, even from Major Sadeli.

"Oh Johnny, I don't want to lose you. I love you so."

Something in her voice moved him. That line, the 'I love you so,' usually a casual exchange between them, seemed to have a deeper meaning when she said it just now. His heart felt lighter. "Do you really love me, Rita?"

"Yes, yes, yes, I really, really, really love you. I can't live without you, Johnny," Rita sobbed.

Umar Yunus felt as if the bright shining sun entered his body and repelled the darkness that confusion and doubt cast earlier inside him. He suddenly realized he loved Rita in the same way that she loved him. "I love you too, Rita," he whispered and hugged her tightly. Then he made his decision and said softly, "Let's get married when I return. I'll finish this assignment first." He felt much better after making that decision and believed it set the course for his future.

Rita freed herself from his embrace. She leaned over him and said, "Do you mean it?"

He nodded and smiled.

Rita dropped herself on top of him and her tears wet both their cheeks. He tasted her salty tears on his lips and listened to her sobs, "Johnny, oh Johnny, I love you so. I'm so very happy. I'm crying because I'm happy."

It was a good while before he moved. He stretched and looked at his watch. Six thirty. He said, "Rita, I need to get ready. Pack me a small bag of clothes, soap, toothbrush, and stuff."

***

At ten o'clock sharp, Umar Yunus was already waiting for Sadeli at their rendezvous. He jumped into the small Morris as soon as it pulled up and the door opened.

They left the Singapore downtown area and drove until they reached a small fishing village. An outboard-motored boat and two people standing nearby waited for them at the beach.

"We need to be on guard from now on," Sadeli whispered as they got out of the car, which immediately left. "Are you carrying a gun?"

"An automatic."

"Good."

They crossed a dark grove of coconut trees. It was a good place for an ambush. Sadeli suddenly felt the weight of his money belt. He reached into his pocket and wrapped his fingers around a bulldog revolver.

"Tan Ciat Tong," Sadeli shouted the code when they reached the beach.

"Sadeli," someone answered.

The two Chinese men pushed the boat into the water. Sadeli and Umar Yunus jumped on board, followed by the two Chinese men. One went immediately to the stern and turned on the engine. It started with just one pull. The boat headed for the open water. It was a dark, moonless night. Only a few stars were out. Fog hung low above the dark water and the waves were pretty high.

They had sailed for about an hour when, through the darkness, Sadeli saw a dark, low object on the water. *The speedboat.* Beyond it was the dark outline of an island.

As they came closer, the man killed the engine and let the boat drift. The few pale stars were unable to illuminate the dark night, and the island in the middle of the dark sea looked like a ghost island against the dark horizon.

Finally the bow of their boat softly touched the side of the speedboat. The man at the bow called out and someone on the speedboat quickly replied and threw a rope. After they secured the rope to the bow, Sadeli and Umar Yunus went on board.

"Amir?" Sadeli called in the darkness. He took Amir and Umar Yunus to the empty bow of the speedboat and introduced the two to each other. "This is Amir. This is Captain Umar Yunus, your commander. Is everything ready? Are the others at their positions?"

"Yes, Sir," Amir answered.

"Weapons ready? Alright, return to your post," Sadeli ordered.

Sadeli then briefed Umar Yunus about what needed to be done in case Tan Ciat Tong betrayed them. He added, "The captain of the boat, although Tan Ciat Tong appointed him, has to obey you on this trip. You are the real captain of this boat."

"Where's that captain?" Umar Yunus asked.

"He'll come with Ciat Tong on the boat that carries the radio equipment and weapons." Sadeli checked his watch. It was so dark that he couldn't see a thing. Umar Yunus took a box of matches from his pocket and struck one over Sadeli's watch. Five minutes to midnight. The wind blew out the flame and for a moment Sadeli experienced a temporary blindness.

Both Sadeli and Umar Yunus kept their ears open for the sound of an oncoming boat, until Umar Yunus pointed at a black boat that moved slowly toward them. The fog and waves drowned out the sound of its machine.

"There they come."

Sadeli and Umar Yunus moved to the side of the boat where the approaching boat would stop. A few lines of rope were thrown at them by dark figures moving on the deck.

A few men jumped onto the speedboat and Sadeli recognized Ciat Tong as he came toward him.

"Mr. Sadeli." Ciat Tong stopped abruptly when he saw Umar Yunus. He clearly didn't expect to see Umar Yunus on the boat. "Well, you're here, Mr. Umar Yunus?" he asked.

"Mr. Umar Yunus is the head of this operation," Sadeli explained.

The men started to move crates to the speedboat.

"Don't you want to check?" Ciat Tong asked.

"Someone on board will," Sadeli said.

"Do you have the money?" Ciat Tong asked.

"Yes."

They stood in silence. Every now and then, they glanced around them. When the loading was done, Amir reported that everything was in order. Sadeli reached inside his jacket to retrieve the money pouch and handed it to Ciat Tong.

"It's all here?"

"Count it."

"Ah, no need. If it's less than agreed, I can always collect from you."

"No, it's best you count it and spare us from some misunderstanding," Sadeli insisted.

Ciat Tong called out for someone and gave him the money pouch. "Count it quickly," he said.

"Amir, go with him," Sadeli said.

They waited on the deck until Ciat Tong's man returned. "It's all there," he said and handed Ciat Tong the pouch.

Ciat Tong extended his hand to Sadeli. After they shook hands he turned to Umar Yunus and said, "Have a good trip, Mr. Yunus." Next he pointed a gun at them and said, "Sorry, gentlemen. Please get on the boat that will take you back to shore."

Ciat Tong had moved so fast that Umar Yunus and Sadeli were taken by surprise and didn't have time to draw their guns.

Sadeli said calmly, "You live up to your reputation."

"I hope you're not mad at me," Ciat Tong said, "This is the dog-eat-dog world we live in. Only the quick and strong survive!"

"What if I report you to the police?"

"Are you going to report that you bought illegal weapons that belong to the British?" Ciat Tong laughed.

Sadeli asked, "Are you really going to betray us?"

"Ah, this is no betrayal. This is business, gentlemen," Ciat Tong said.

"Too bad this will be the last time you do business with me." Sadeli pointed. "Look behind you. A tommy gun is ready to fire."

"You're lying."

"No, no," Sadeli said, "We came prepared. There are six armed men on this boat who are ready to sink your boat. You're in for a war."

Ciat Tong turned carefully without taking his eyes off either Sadeli or Umar Yunus. He laughed and pocketed his gun when he saw Sadeli had told the truth. Then he bowed at Sadeli and said, "My respect to you, Sir. I think it's best we postpone this battle on the Singaporean waters."

"Tell your boat to move!" Sadeli ordered.

Ciat Tong jumped into his boat and soon the engine was started and the ropes were drawn. Sadeli heaved a sigh of relief. When the boat moved away, he turned to Umar Yunus. "Now, on your way, Yunus."

Umar Yunus saluted him.

Sadeli asked, "Wait, did Ciat Tong leave his captain? Is the captain here?"

"In the hull, Sir."

"Call him up. We're set to sail."

Amir went down below deck and returned with the captain, who introduced himself as Captain Sow Chiu.

Sadeli told him Umar Yunus was the head of this operation and he had to obey all orders coming from Umar Yunus. Then Sadeli shook Umar Yunus' hand, waved at Amir and said, "Have a good trip. Godspeed. Merdeka!"

Umar Yunus answered, "Merdeka!"

Captain Sow Chiu ordered the men to turn on the engine. In an instant, the sound of the airplane engines shook the whole boat.

The two Chinese men waited for Sadeli on the outboard-motored boat. They untied the rope and pulled the engine cord once he was on board. The boat pulled away. The speedboat moved slowly at first, but as the engine roared louder, it picked up speed and plowed through the fog and dark ocean toward a black horizon.

As his own boat moved toward the shore, Sadeli watched the speedboat roar away and disappear. After the last droning of the engine dissolved into the night, Sadeli suddenly felt lonely.

Chapter 6

The BOAC airplane flew low over a tapestry of green patches alternated by silvery patches of water as it approached Bangkok. It was only 11 a.m. Everything looked wet, like it had just stopped raining. When the airplane tilted, the city of Bangkok glistened as the morning sun reflected off the golden stupas on Buddhist temples. Sadeli saw the wide Mekong River flow gently. A few big ships made their way down the river; a tanker that pulled a line of barges looked like a mother duck and ducklings in a pond. *Klongs* divided the city into some kind of grids. Houses rested on tall wooden stilts high above the water. Thousands of small boats were part of the scene.

The view disappeared as the airplane turned the other way and descended steadily. The plane flew lower and lower, like it was about to land, when Sadeli suddenly felt it pick up speed again. He knew airplanes decreased speed when they prepared to land, yet the speed of the ground, trees, and houses moving closer suggested the opposite.

The airplane's tires touched the runway smoothly. Then the engines roared louder as the plane moved slower, came to a complete halt, then turned and moved toward the gate.

Sadeli unbuckled his seatbelt and disembarked with the rest of the passengers.

The immigration staff only stamped Sadeli's travel documents, a piece of white paper issued by the Foreign Ministry of the Republic of Indonesia, without asking any questions.

A petite Thai stewardess then led them to the baggage claim area. Again, the inspection here was brief. Then the stewardess asked them to get on a bus.

The city was quite a distance from the airport. Sadeli was amazed how similar the Thai landscapes were to those in Indonesia, vast rice fields, coconut trees, wooden houses. Only the medium-sized Buddhist temples along the streets set them apart. Someone who sat next to Sadeli said, "You know, it'll be an important discovery if someone investigates how much national wealth has been spent to build temples like these in all Buddhist countries across Asia. Angkor Wat, for one, may eventually be the reason for the fall of the Khmer empire. Just like the construction of the pyramids in Egypt became a contributing factor to the fall of the Pharaoh's dynasty."

"That's an interesting thought," Sadeli said, "Were you here before the war?"

The Frenchman, who was in his fifties, nodded. "Yes, in Indochina. I'm on my way back to Saigon."

"Were you there during the Japanese occupation?"

"Thank goodness, no. I was in France. But our condition was just as bad under the Germans. They were vicious and cruel. I joined the *Maquis*," he said proudly.

Sadeli knew the Maquis were the French guerilla groups who fought against the Germans during the war. He suddenly wanted to check if the new progressive thinking had indeed traveled across Europe as far as Inspector Hawkins had said. He wanted to know if this Frenchman believed in the new theories or if he still held on to the old ideas practiced by most French colonialists.

"I'm Sadeli from Indonesia," Sadeli introduced himself.

"I'm Gaston d'Arlieu," the French man said, "Nice to meet you."

"What did you do in Indochina?" Sadeli asked.

"Plant rubber trees. I was the director of a rubber plantation owned by the Michelin company."

"And you are going back to the plantation?"

"Yes."

"What about Ho Chi Minh in Indochina? Will France acknowledge Indochina's independence?"

"Ah, ah, you misunderstand the relationship France has with its overseas regions. We have a completely different policy from the British, Dutch, or Portuguese. We practice cultural assimilation politics. We don't differentiate between skin colors or nations. The French parliament, for instance, has African descendants as members."

"But what if they still want their freedom? Didn't France, like the British, Dutch, and other imperialists, conquer other nations with force?"

"Ah yes, but France has an entirely different colonial doctrine. Why would they want to be free when they're the same as us French?"

"You know why. Weren't you a maquis yourself?"

"Ah, that's different; Monsieur Sadeli, you don't understand." Gaston d'Arlieu seemed puzzled.

Sadeli held back his annoyance. "Doesn't it occur to you that they may not want to be French and would rather be Indochinese?"

Gaston d'Arlieu looked at Sadeli in amazement. He obviously could not comprehend that there were people who wouldn't want to be French. "*Nom de Dieu,*" he exclaimed, "Why wouldn't they want to be French? Ha ha ha. You shouldn't believe the stories about Ho Chi Minh's guerrilla movement for independence. He's always been an anarchist, a Communist. Your people have the right to claim independence from the Dutch. The Netherlands is so small and your country is very big."

"Didn't your experience of the German occupation convince you how cruel colonization is?"

"Oh, the Nazis are something entirely different. They're not human. Hitler was an evil dictator with no humanity inside him. He ordered a massacre of six million Jews in Europe. The cruelties inflicted by the Gestapo are inhumane, unimaginable. They're perhaps even worse than the Japanese. At least the Japanese didn't build gas chambers and furnaces to kill people and then use the victims' hair, fat, and gold teeth to drive their war effort. Not to mention the way they tortured the prisoners by using electric shocks, ice water soaking, beating, terror, and using them as guinea pigs for the Nazis' experiments. *Non, non,* they are incomparable. *Vraiment, c'est très différent!"*

"Ah, I didn't mean to compare France with the German Nazis." Sadeli smiled and tried to calm him. "But what about the nations' dream of freedom as proclaimed by Churchill, Roosevelt, and General de Gaulle during World War II? Is freedom only for Europeans?"

"*Non, non, mon ami,*" exclaimed Gaston d'Arlieu, "don't get it wrong. Freedom is indeed for all nations who want it. *Absolument.* I agree. But, trust me in this, France is unique. It's far different from other colonial countries because its politics are completely different from the beginning."

"I'm not sure about that," Sadeli said, "Trust me, Monsieur, France will face the demand for independence from all its colonies."

"Ah, since we can't agree on anything from the start, can we agree to disagree?"

"Ah, sure, but don't forget what I said. I would like to meet you again after five years." Sadeli laughed.

The bus made its stop at the Strand Hotel and they both got off.

***

Night fell over Bangkok. After dinner, Sadeli headed to the Hawai Club, a nightclub on the second floor of a huge building. He didn't find Bangkok attractive. The Thai lettering on street names and the Chinese characters on shop signs in the Chinese parts of the city felt strange. The streets were packed with three-wheeled pedicabs. Unlike those in Indonesia, pedicab drivers in Bangkok sat in front of the passenger seat.

His taxi stopped in front of the Hawai Club. When Sadeli entered, he saw couples dancing the *ramwong,* which reminded him of a rooster running around chasing a hen. A pretty interesting dance. He sat down at an empty table and a waiter came quickly. Sadeli ordered a glass of cold beer. The hot weather in Bangkok made people thirsty all the time.

When the waiter returned with the beer, a young Thai woman in a tight black dress came along. She sat down and introduced herself. "I'm Darling. If you like to dance, I'll dance with you." She smiled, and showed her two gold teeth.

"What would you like to have?" Sadeli asked.

"Whisky, please," she said to the waiter.

Sadeli smiled. Going solo to a nightclub always meant buying drinks for the taxi girl. He knew she didn't ask for real whisky. The club made a lot of profit this way and paid her a commission.

Sadeli looked at Darling. She was slender and shapely but the life she lived would soon tax that toned body to its limit. In two or three years, she would lose it. Fatigue already creased the corners of her eyes and lips. Only the spark in her eyes showed her determination to get as much money as possible in the shortest amount of time.

"Hey, are you new here?" she asked. "I never saw you before. You're good looking. Are you Filipino?"

"No, I'm from…" Sadeli hesitated. He wondered if he should tell her that he came from Indonesia and decided against it. He didn't want to help the Dutch intelligence. He smiled and said, "I'm from Manila."

"Ah, I like new people." Darling took his hand. "Do you want to dance?"

"Will you teach me the ramwong?"

"Ah, the ramwong is so easy. Come."

Sadeli learned the steps quickly and Darling was pleased. The music changed to a foxtrot, and Darling asked, "Do you want to keep dancing?"

"Let's," he said.

After the dance, they went back to the table. She complimented him for dancing so well.

"Ah, that's because you're a good dancer yourself," he replied.

She looked pleased to hear that.

Sadeli called the waiter and ordered another whisky for her.

"This time bring me the real stuff," he said.

When the waiter returned, Sadeli sniffed the glass and took a sip before he handed it to Darling. "It's real whisky," he said.

"Oh, thank you very much. Oh dear, I don't even know your name."

"Mendoza." The Spanish name happened to cross his mind. He almost said Don Quixote, but that would have been too obvious.

"Mendoza. What a manly name!"

Darling drank her whisky and her eyes turned brighter. Her spirits clearly soared.

"Do you like me, Mendoza?"

"Of course, you're sweet."

"How long will you stay here?"

"A week or two. I'm on my way to Europe."

"My, you're going to Europe? What do you do?"

"I'm a businessman."

"Oh. I really want to go to Europe. Once an Italian promised to take me to Rome, but then his wife found out about us and he quietly left me."

"Europe after the war isn't that exciting. Everything's in ruins," Sadeli said.

"You're right."

"Darling, actually, I'm here to find a friend. An American. He's a private pilot called David Wayne. I heard he came here a lot. Do you know him?"

"David Wayne? The name doesn't ring a bell. Many American or British pilots come here, so I don't remember all of them. But if he comes here a lot, some of the other girls here will surely know him."

"Will you help me, Darling? Go and ask your friends where I can find him. I'll give you ten US dollars if you succeed."

Darling's eyes widened. "Ten American dollars?" she asked in disbelief. She was willing to spend the night with a man for ten dollars, and all she had to do now was to find the address of an American. "You promise?"

Sadeli pulled out his wallet and withdrew a ten-dollar bill. He folded it and put it under the whisky glass. He said, "For you if you come back with the info."

Darling rose and went to the taxi girls' lounge.

Sadeli remembered the information he had received from Joe in Singapore about David Wayne. David was a Texan, a pilot of a four-engine bomber aircraft in the war. The scuttlebutt was that he now provided an all-purpose flight service using a Dakota plane. He was a highly skilled and courageous pilot. Joe had whispered to Sadeli that David Wayne often smuggled drugs from Laos. He picked up the drugs from a remote mountain area in northern Laos and flew them to Thailand or somewhere on the beach of China near Macao.

Joe couldn't give Sadeli David Wayne's address. He only said the pilot was a regular at the Hawai Club in Bangkok.

That was what had brought Sadeli to Bangkok now, dancing the ramwong in the Hawai Club. *Many stories could be written about people like David Wayne,* he thought.

Stories about World War II were bound to emerge and he remembered the speedboat that carried Umar Yunus, his troops, and their cargo. *What had that boat and its crew gone through? Battles against the German fleet? Taking agents to the shores of countries that had fallen to the Germans?*

Sadeli snapped back to reality when Darling returned. Judging from the look on her face, he knew she didn't get the information he was after.

"Oh, so sorry, Mendoza," she said, "I asked around but no one knows his address."

"Do any of them know him?"

"Oh yes. Patty and Mary know him, but they don't know his current address. He likes to move from one hotel to another and from one house to another. He also likes to date different girls. Patty said he's dating Peggy now, a Chinese girl. I know where she lives."

"Will you take me there?"

"I can only leave after midnight."

"Okay, I'll wait for you." Sadeli danced and bought a couple rounds of whisky for her. When midnight came, Darling was half drunk. Sadeli was tired and soaked in perspiration. He wasn't used to dancing for hours.

They hailed a samlor and Darling gave the pedicab driver the address. They soon left the main road and drove through narrow alleys. Sadeli thought, *If this woman is taking me to a robbers' lair, I'm easy prey.*

It was 12:30 a.m. when the pedicab stopped in front of a wooden house on a small road. The house was dark and silent. Sadeli hesitated, wondering if he should knock. He wanted to know right away where David Wayne was. Perhaps David was scheduled to fly out the next morning, and if so, he had no idea how long he should wait for his return.

Darling had no hesitation at all. She got off the samlor and pulled Sadeli's hand. "Come on, Mendoza," she said, then asked, "Hey, what's your first name?"

"Louis," Sadeli said.

"Louis Mendoza. Such a manly name." She laughed and put her arm around his waist. She stumbled in front of the door and leaned on him. "Uh-oh, I'm drunk," she said and continued, "Hey, Louis, d'you want to hear a good song? I'm a good singer, you know. I won first place in singing back at school. You want to listen?" She sang a Thai children's song. When she finished, she looked at Sadeli. "You don't like it? Hmm, you want an American song? No? A Japanese song?" She sang "Sayonara."

When she got to the second verse, and before Sadeli could stop her, a window flung open and a woman yelled, "Hush, go away, you! Stop being noisy, people are sleeping."

Darling shouted happily, "Hey, hey, Louis, that's Peggy." She looked up at the window and continued to shout, "Peggy, Peggy. I want to talk to you."

The window closed. Darling let out a happy sigh and turned to Sadeli. She hugged and kissed him and said, "So that was Peggy. You happy now? I did a good job, right? I'm not drunk."

The front door opened and a young woman in her pajamas walked out. "Hush, Do," she said, "do you want to wake the whole neighborhood?"

Sadeli greeted the woman and apologized for disturbing her, but Darling interrupted and said, "Hey, Peggy, I got him from the club. Isn't he handsome?"

"Oh…" Sadeli started to object.

Darling caressed his cheek and put her arms around his waist. "He's Filipino," she said and added, "And he's so rich."

"Do, it's midnight. What do you want?"

"His name is Louis Mendoza." Darling was completely drunk now.

"You're drunk, Do. I'm going to bed." Peggy turned around to go back inside.

"Wait a moment, Miss Peggy." Sadeli placed a hand over Darling's mouth as she was about to say something. "Can you tell me where I can find David Wayne?"

"Oh right, Peggy, I just remembered," Darling managed to move Sadeli's hand from her mouth, "my friend here wants to meet David. Where is he now?"

"Ah, he left yesterday."

"When is he coming back?" Sadeli asked.

"He said a week from now at the earliest."

"Do you have his address?"

"He doesn't even know where to stay when he gets back," Peggy said.

"Will you tell Darling when he's back in Bangkok?"

Peggy nodded.

"Thank you very much." Sadeli took Darling's hand and led her back to their samlor. She yelled a few lines in Thai to Peggy and Peggy laughed.

In the samlor, Sadeli said, "I'm going to take you home. You're drunk. Here's your money." He gave her the ten-dollar bill.

"Oh thank you, Louis. Thank you. You're very nice." Darling gave her address to the samlor driver. She inched closer and leaned against him.

Darling startled and groggily smiled at him when Sadeli awakened her, and he had no choice but to help her out of the samlor and walk her to the door of her house. Darling took a key from her bag, but couldn't find the keyhole. Sadeli finally decided to take the key from her and opened the door.

Darling took Sadeli's hand and led him to her bedroom. She quickly dragged him to the bed, lay down, and pulled him on top of her. "Kiss me! Kiss me!" she said, before falling asleep.

Sadeli rose and for a moment looked at the young woman. *This isn't a good way to live.* Filled with pity, he quietly left the bedroom. He locked the front door from the outside and slipped the key through a gap under the door.

"To the Strand Hotel," he told the samlor driver.

***

It had been five days since Sadeli waited for David Wayne to return from wherever he had gone. Sadeli went to all the nightclubs in Bangkok, asked the question, and left a message. He did the same thing at the hotels there, to no avail. It was as if David Wayne had vanished into thin air. Sometimes, Sadeli wondered if David Wayne even existed. Joe, back in Singapore, just might have lied to him, as Peggy and the hotel clerks who said David ever stayed there also could have done.

As days went by, the existence of David Wayne seemed to become more dubious. On the other hand, Sadeli became more familiar with the city and met a lot of people. One day, when he was tired of checking one hotel after another, he went to the temple of the Emerald Buddha and was stunned to see the arts of architecture, sculpture, and decoration developed by the religion. The Buddha was serene and contemplative. Meanwhile, the temple was guarded by endless statues of giants with terrifying faces. The bright colors used on the statues were very stimulating.

Sadeli was looking at a terribly fearful statue when someone next to him said, "Isn't he a ferocious-looking fellow?"

Sadeli turned; he had to look all the way up since the man was extremely tall. He was a Caucasian dressed in a white sharkskin suit and a white shirt without a tie. He held his jacket in one hand and used the other to wipe his face with his handkerchief. With only thin gray hair on both sides of his head, the man was almost bald. Sadeli suddenly remembered Sydney Greenstreet, the British-born American actor. This man looked just like him. Sadeli smiled. "Yes," he said, "good thing he's just a statue," then added, "I'm sorry, but you remind me of Sydney Greenstreet, the movie star. Are you him? Or related to him?"

That man burst out laughing so hard the upper half of his body reeled backward. Sadeli worried the man would fall. His laughter started from his huge belly, rose into his throat, and exploded through his mouth. Sadeli was concerned he would have a heart attack. The man finally stopped laughing and wiped his face and eyes with his handkerchief.

"I'm sorry," Sadeli said.

"No, no, it's I who needs to apologize. You're the third person telling me that today, so I just couldn't help but laugh. To think I'm Sydney Greenstreet. My name's Derek Scott; just call me Derek." He offered his hand to Sadeli.

"Louis Mendoza."

"Mendoza, Mendoza. Where did I hear that name?" Derek Scott frowned. He closed one eye and peered at Sadeli.

"Ah, now I remember. Someone from the Grace Hotel said a Louis Mendoza from the Philippines was looking for David Wayne. He asked me if I knew where Dave was. Are you the man looking for Dave?"

Sadeli nodded, surprised.

"I'm Dave's friend," Derek said, "Why are you looking for him?" He noticed Sadeli hesitate and winked. "Oh, I see. The less people know, the better, right?" Derek burst into another spell of laughter that turned his face red.

After Derek stopped laughing, he wiped his face and said, "Mr. Mendoza, would you come visit me? I'll show you something that may be useful for your country. The Philippines, right?"

"Yes."

"I'll serve you a big bottle of cold beer."

"Let's go," Sadeli said and added, "Your mention of beer made me thirsty."

Derek Scott laughed again and this time Sadeli patted him on the back and told him to stop.

"I laugh too easily, Mr. Mendoza. Ah, may I call you Louis? It's easier."

"Sure, Derek."

"One day this laughter will kill me. Once, during the Japanese occupation, it almost got me killed." Derek walked Sadeli to a parked car on the street. After he started to drive, he continued his story. He and some other fellows, American OSS agents, were deployed to Thailand's remote areas to help Thailand's army in their guerrilla fight against the Japanese.

"Our contact was Pridi, the guerilla's commanding chief against the Japanese, while Phibul Songgram worked together with the Japanese at that time. After a few months, the news about my presence started to travel. The Japanese offered a big reward for the head of the 'Laughing Giant;' I was that 'Laughing Giant.' I wasn't very safe in the villages where we hid. As soon as I laughed, the villagers would know it was me the Japs were after. Finally our three-man group decided to take refuge in a general's house in Bangkok, right under those Japanese noses."

A moment later, the car moved across a wooden bridge above a fairly wide klong filled with houseboats. Derek nodded at the canoes. "Actually, Bangkok consists of two cities," he said, "The one on the ground and the other in the klongs like this."

They drove through an open gate and stopped in front of a big teak house. The resort-like house rested on heavy teak pillars. A wide set of stairs led to the porch. Clusters of blooming Vanda Miss Joaquim orchids hung from the pillars that lined the beautiful garden.

Derek Scott honked three times, two short beeps and then a long one. They got out of the car and walked to the porch. An old Chinese woman opened the door and welcomed Derek with a big, toothless smile.

"Hello, Amah." Derek greeted the old woman amicably and put his hand on her shoulder.

Sadeli wondered if he saw Amah stoop a little under the weight of Derek's thigh-sized hand.

They went into a beautifully furnished living room. A small bar stood at the end of the room.

"Straight to the bar, Louis." Derek placed two tall glasses on the bar and stooped to get two bottles of beer from the ice bucket under the bar. He briefly touched the bottles to his cheek. "Ice cold, very good." He poured the beer into the glass, where its foam quickly formed a head.

"Now, let's drink." Derek raised his glass.

The deliciously cold beer refreshed Sadeli as it ran down his throat.

"More?" Derek asked.

"No, thank you."

"Well now, let's go to the back."

Derek guided Sadeli to the back of the house. The backyard was dotted with small bungalows with open windows. As they came closer, Sadeli saw dozens of women spinning yarn and weaving cloths using simple wooden tools.

At the door of the first bungalow, a young Thai woman welcomed them. Sadeli gasped. The woman was beautiful.

"Sheila Scott, my wife," Derek introduced her.

"Louis Mendoza. I'm so happy to meet you, Ma'am."

Sheila smiled at him.

Derek said, "Louis Mendoza's from the Philippines. I want to show him the handmade Thai silk we're making. Maybe there's something he can emulate in his country."

Derek took Sadeli to see the spinning and dyeing processes. His wife excused herself to check on the weaving.

"This is a dying craft," Derek said, "quality has deteriorated and the colors fade. We're now rebuilding all of it. While we're using the traditional patterns to the fullest, we're adjusting our color patterns to the taste of the Americans and Europeans." Derek took Sadeli to the weaving bungalow.

Sadeli was amazed to see how skillful the women were.

Next to the weaving room was the drawing room where five people were at work. They drew patterns on a tie, a dress, a shirt, and a man's jacket.

"This silk cloth sells well in the United States," Derek said and continued, "We're also going to sell it in London, Paris, and Rome."

Sadeli remembered the Batak, Silungkang, Palembang, Bali, and Bugis woven cloths. They were as good as the Thai and could be developed to dominate the world market. *Later, after the revolution.* He promised himself to keep this in mind.

When Sadeli excused himself to return to the hotel, Derek said, "Louis, where can I find you when I hear that Dave's back?"

Sadeli's face turned red. He was embarrassed for having toyed with Derek. He was sure he could trust this man. "Derek," he said, "I'm not who you think I am. I'll explain to you later. When you hear from David Wayne, call the Strand Hotel and leave a message for Sadeli. Thank you. Give my regards to Mrs. Scott."

Sadeli crossed the bridge and went to look for a taxi.

Derek Scott stood on his porch for a long time. Puzzled, he gazed in the direction Sadeli had walked away. Then he suddenly slapped himself on his forehead and went back into the house.

***

Sadeli didn't hear any news for the next two days. He was getting tired of going to nightclubs, dancing with the taxi girls, and looking for information. On the third day, around five in the afternoon, the phone in his room rang.

"Mr. Sadeli?"

"Yes?"

"Ha ha, my good friend Louis Mendoza, alias Sadeli." Derek's booming voice almost broke the receiver against Sadeli's ear. "If you would come over at seven, you may have yourself some news."

"Thank you. I'll be there."

"Okay, so long."

Sadeli's heart pounded and he was quite happy when he put down the receiver. He wondered if his search would come to an end that night.

Sadeli arrived at Derek's house a little before seven. While he hesitated to knock on the door, Sheila Scott opened it.

"Louis Mendoza, come in. Derek is not here yet. He just called and wants you to wait."

"I'm sorry for coming too early." Sadeli checked his watch.

Sheila laughed. Her laughter was like music to his ear.

"Ten minutes isn't a big deal," she said and continued, "Come, let's go to my pavilion if you're going to wait."

A small path that wound through a garden full of trees led to a pretty pavilion full of huge glass windows located across the main building of the house. They entered a small gate and suddenly it was as if they were in a different world. A hedge of dense and blooming Miss Joaquim orchids separated the small garden in front of the pavilion from that of the main house. Tens of other kinds of orchids like the moth orchid, dendrobium, cattleya, and oncidium hung from pots and wooden posts. They bloomed beautifully and the various colors made Sadeli stop to marvel at the sight.

"Your orchids are truly stunning, Ma'am," he said.

"Please," she said, and touched his hand, "call me Sheila. Derek likes you and considers you a friend."

"He does? How can he know me that well while we only met once?"

"Oh, you don't know him but he knows you. He can size up a person just by looking at his face, his eyes, and talking to him for a short while. He wants to help you, Sadeli."

"Sadeli?"

Sheila laughed and lightly tapped Sadeli's cheek. "Derek investigated your identity right away."

Sadeli laughed. "I'm glad it didn't take him long."

"Oh!" Sheila suddenly exclaimed and hurried to a toppled pot. "That must be Grace again." She scowled, fixed the pot's position, and explained, "She's my naughty cat."

"Wow, look at this beautiful white cypripedium. It's spotless," Sadeli exclaimed.

"You like orchids?" Sheila asked. "I have some others." She grabbed Sadeli's hand. "Come," she said and led him to the door of the pavilion's bedroom. When she flipped some switches, hidden lights illuminated a group of blooming orchids.

"How beautiful," Sadeli whispered and unintentionally squeezed Sheila's hand. She squeezed back and he was suddenly aware of her sex appeal and the fact that they were alone. Her eyes waited for him when he turned. "You're the most beautiful orchid in this garden." He couldn't keep his heart from beating faster or his blood from rushing and heating his body.

Sheila's lips formed a peculiar smile. Her eyes brightened. She pressed her body against Sadeli and lifted her face. "Kiss me," she said.

Sadeli was torn. He thought of Derek and it occurred to him he would be betraying the man, but locking eyes with her made him forget all his morals and knighthood values. It was as if her eyes were a vortex that drained all of his strength and determination. He felt helpless.

"Come," she whispered and held him tightly.

Their lips locked and her tongue eagerly explored. Her breasts pressed hard against his chest as he mumbled his last lame defense, "What about your husband?"

"Don't worry. He won't be home till nine."

For the first time ever Sadeli experienced a woman like Sheila. The dim bedroom with only weak light coming through the curtains soon filled with panting and choked whispers. Clothing dropped to the floor. Sadeli was lost in the warm embrace of the fair-skinned young woman, her relentless attacks and moans. The air filled with ebbs and flows of passion; raging passion quickly replaced a peaceful moment. As the ember turned into a blazing fire, there were thunderbolts and lightning, earthquakes, and volcano eruptions.

Sadeli lost track of time. The wild starving tigress he just wrestled down was completely different from the Mrs. Derek Scott he had been introduced to only two days ago. Exhausted, he turned to the sleeping Sheila next to him. Her breathing was steady and a little smile curved her lips. He checked his watch, almost 8:30 p.m. He quickly went to the adjacent bathroom, got dressed, and then woke Sheila.

Without even opening her eyes, Sheila said, "Now you can wait in the main house. Ask Amah for something to drink."

Sadeli left. He wondered how he would face Derek as he walked through the garden to the main house and took a seat in the foyer. He decided to ask Colonel Suroso to terminate him if he failed his Bangkok mission because of this indiscretion. He was flipping through the pages of a magazine when Amah came with a glass of beer.

Sheila walked into the room a little before nine. She was dressed in Thai clothing and acted like nothing had happened between them earlier. She said, "Ah, Amah served you a beer already."

A few minutes later, a car honked. "That's Derek," Sheila said.

The car door slammed and footsteps came up the stairs. Then the door opened and Derek filled the entire frame. "Good evening, Sadeli," he called from the door.

Sadeli rose.

Sheila hurried to the door and hugged her husband. Derek held her and kissed her before he walked into the room.

"Oh, Dave. Hello, Pierre," Sheila welcomed the two men who stood behind Derek.

Here comes the man I've been looking for, Sadeli thought. *David Wayne. The pilot, the brave adventurer.* He had imagined David Wayne to be tall, dashing, and good looking and was disappointed when David Wayne turned out to be rather small, somewhat slim, and had thinning blond hair. His chin and mouth seemed tough compared to the gentle expression in his sunken eyes that exuded an impenetrable tranquility.

Derek introduced them. "Sadeli, David Wayne."

Both men shook hands. Sadeli happily noticed that David's voice matched his gentle yet confident expression.

Then Derek introduced Pierre de Koonig. Nearly as tall as Derek, Pierre was more muscular. He had a thick moustache and held a cigar between his lips.

Sadeli detected his French accent and asked, "*Vous êtes Français?*"

Pleasantly surprised, Pierre replied in French. He told Sadeli he came from Alsace, a French region that bordered Germany, and although his name sounded German, he was actually a full-blooded Frenchman. "*Je suis très fier d'être un Français. J'ai combattu les Boches.*"

"Stop him, Dave!" Derek lifted his arms in mock protest.

Pierre laughed. "I'm sorry, my friends, especially you, Sheila, *ma jolie orchidée.*" He turned to Sadeli and said, "In this savage part of the world, I never have a chance to speak the cultured French language, and the barbaric English language ruins one's tongue. I'm simply overjoyed when I meet another cultured person who speaks French."

They all laughed, and Derek herded everyone to the bar. "I know what Dave and Pierre want," he said, "what about you, Sadeli? Are you sticking to your beer or will you try the Sheila cocktail by Derek Scott?"

Sadeli thought he detected something in Derek's eyes, but the man's voice was level. Sadeli concealed his surprise and said, "Fine. Fix me that cocktail. It must be amazing."

"And you, my dear?" Derek turned to his wife.

Sheila said, "Pardon me, gentlemen, but I have to excuse myself. You're about to enter into a negotiation and I have to finish the design the weavers need tomorrow. I'm so happy Dave and Pierre returned safely and Sadeli is finally able to meet you two. Have a good evening." She stood on her toes and Derek stooped to kiss her. She then waved at them and left.

"Well then," Derek said, "let's have a seat and talk."

"Very well," Sadeli opened the discussion, "let me start by apologizing to Derek for having kept this information from him. I'm Major Sadeli from the Republic of Indonesia's intelligence service."

Sadeli looked around the circle. Derek smiled; David Wayne and Pierre de Koonig looked at him calmly.

Sadeli continued, "I don't think I need to explain my country's struggle for freedom. You gentlemen can get that from the newspapers. I'm here to find David Wayne." He turned to David Wayne and continued, "I heard in Singapore, Sir, that you're a skillful and highly experienced pilot. My country needs to establish an international airline connection as well as a domestic one between Java and Sumatra, right away. We'll pay your regular price."

"Pricing is easy," Derek said, "The three of us are partners in Lotus Flights Inc., aircraft rental. We just need to factor in the fuel, plane insurance, war risk, crew insurance, and other easy-to-tally elements. But whether a flight will happen, that's Dave and Pierre's call. They're the ones who fly and they have their own considerations, which are often noncommercial. It's actually a weird way for entrepreneurs to operate, but that's the way they are and, strangely, I agree with them."

Pierre yawned and said, "Oh dear, I'm so sleepy. I'll go with whatever you say, Dave. Please, excuse me, gentlemen." He leaned back and was asleep a few moments later. His face turned gentler as he slept.

"Why do you want to be independent?" David Wayne asked out of the blue.

Sadeli threw a rather puzzled look at David and Derek. They calmly waited.

"Must you ask, Sir?" Sadeli replied.

Derek said, "Please, drop the formalities. Just call them Dave and Pierre."

"Must you ask?" Sadeli repeated and continued, "We want to live like ordinary human beings, independent and free. We want to be our own masters, not some other nations' slaves, or our own slaves, for that matter. We want to be free people who decide our own fate. We want to be treated equal to the rest of the free nations."

Sadeli recounted the cruelties of Dutch colonialism and the rebellions against the Dutch across the archipelago, in Sumatra, Kalimantan, Java, Bali, Lombok, Sulawesi, and Maluku. He shared with them how the Dutch had exploited the Indonesians for hundreds of years through the forced labor system.

"It's that indentured servitude system that enabled the Dutch to start the rubber, tea, coffee, coconut, tobacco, and other types of plantations all over Indonesia. It actually was just slavery in disguise because the coolies placed in Sumatra from Java, for example, hardly ever returned. Their life on the plantation was arranged in such a way that they were trapped in endless debts to the plantation. Those who escaped were hunted down like criminals and whipped the way the Americans used to whip their African slaves."

Sadeli then went on to explain how Japan had deceived the Indonesians with their fake Great East Asia slogan. He told them about the hundreds of thousands of murdered *romusha* in the Pacific, Thailand, and Burma.

"Aren't we entitled to our independence? Don't we, who fought against the colonialist for generations and painted mankind's history with our blood and bones, deserve acknowledgment and help from the world? This is our struggle; this is the quest for the freedom of the Indonesian people. Will you help us, Dave?"

David gave Sadeli a thoughtful look and said, "Listening to you, I'm inclined to help, but before I make my decision, I'd like to look further into the truth of your struggle. Don't get me wrong; I need to do this for myself.

"I'm also looking for the truth. I went to seminary to become a priest, but when World War II broke out, I joined the military and trained to be a jet fighter pilot. My war experiences made me doubt the truth of my religion's teachings about God's wisdom or His forgiving and loving nature.

"After I watched the Nazis viciously wipe out six million Jews in the gas chambers, my heart rebelled against the Catholic doctrine that punishes the Jews for killing the Son of God. Is the Catholic curse any different from what the Nazis did to the Jews? Why did God let human viciousness become the red-hot iron that branded the names of Belsen, Auschwitz, and Leningrad, where nine hundred thousand out of a population of three million died? During the German occupation, four thousand people died every day of starvation. In Stalingrad, hundreds of thousands more Russians died. The Allied Forces dropped incendiary bombs on Dresden.

"Those bombs turned people into burning torches that were impossible to extinguish. People could jump into the water but once they came out of the water and the phosphor was once again in contact with the air, the fire would rage back on, burning their skin to the bone. Their choices were limited to either burn to death on land or die freezing in the water. Countless others died on the battlefields of Yugoslavia, Italy, France, North Africa, Asia, the Pacific, Southeast Asia, and also in the air and at sea. The total casualties for both civilians and military personnel during the war came to forty-five, forty-six million, give or take a million.

"The war has just ended but we already see the world in a tense situation. The members of the Allied Forces are now against one another. Will we let the world fall into World War III? Will we let the atomic war break out and probably end all life on earth? Must we accept this as the inevitable fate of human beings? Which side is right? Who is right?

"You may wonder why I want to engage in the illegal transport of drugs if I have this take on the world. I do it because I want to know and see all the ugly facets of human life. Only by knowing the furthest extent of human crime, hypocrisy, and viciousness can we seek the truth and maybe recognize it as such.

"What is truth? Is it God? What or who is God? What do we live for? Can humans do more than merely exist? Instead, can we try to rise above our present stage of morality and obtain higher values of humanity? Can humanity grow and surpass the development of technology and science? If our culture cannot keep up with the technology, for example, wouldn't it be like giving a child something that he or she cannot control and thus create chaos?

"Is there any substance of God in a human being? Is it God who creates humans or is it the other way around? People used to be content with worshiping a tree, or cow, or the sun and the moon.

In fact, people made certain animals their god, like the cat in Egypt, snake in Greece, and cow in India. Then people worshipped statues.

"When they were not satisfied, the prophets who proclaimed they had received a divine message from God appeared. We started to have Judaism, Christianity, and Islam. India gave birth to Buddhism. People worship their own Gods around the world.

"Do humans make everything up? Where is the truth?

"Once, I was this pious man who surrendered himself completely to God, but at another time, I didn't believe in God at all. I went through that exercise to find the truth. I know one thing for sure: it's not enough to simply believe in God or to perform religious ceremonies. We have to live and implement the truth, but what is truth in life? How should we embrace the truth? Can you explain that to me, Sadeli? Can you end my search? Do you have the answers to my questions?"

Sadeli and David locked eyes. Moved by David's deep soul-searching, Sadeli responded in a rather trembling voice, "I don't know," and added, "Who can tell? Everyone must know what truth is for themselves, and even with that, there's a chance they won't know it for the rest of their lives.

"What is the truth? What is important to us right now is our struggle for independence and our dreams of what we want to achieve once we get our freedom, our dreams for humanity. We're certain that we're one with God in our struggle. Is this truth? I'll say *yes* without the slightest doubt now, but what about five or ten years from now? Who knows? We can only try. Of course, simply believing in God is not enough. People must live with and in the truth. God is present in all aspects of human life. The God essence covers, enters, and immerses the entire universe.

"Can humans achieve the level where they unite with God? No one knows. People can only do their best to find it. You're looking for it, Dave, and so am I. We all are. Let's look for it together. Let's help one another to find it. We're presented with many avenues. Which one is the best? Should we tirelessly keep looking? Or can we think of a better way?

"I once had the same questions you have now. How should mankind eventually coexist? How do we create peace, collaboration, and understanding among nations? How do we build a new world with freedom, justice, and equality? What are a nation's responsibilities for the communal survival of mankind? How does an individual carry his or her personal responsibilities towards others? What about the power of nationalism, Communism, socialism, religion, and internationalism?

"Does the currently emerging nationalism in Asia, Africa, and Latin America contribute to mankind's relationship, or is it a destructive force instead? Is there any chance for this nationalism to dangerously grow into a narrow-minded one or evolve into chauvinism, jingoism, and xenophobia? Due to technical improvement we live in an increasingly smaller world.

"America and Asia or Africa are connected within seconds via the radio and within hours by airplane. What happens if a country can influence life in many other countries? In the current situation, doesn't the pre-World-War nationalism become obsolete and in fact turn into a threat to human safety? Shouldn't a good nationalist now be a good internationalist as well? Someone who always thinks about the needs of the international world aside from those of his or her own country?

"If we want to have a new internationalism, what would it be? Surely not the Communist one, since that only means the slavery of the world under one totalitarian system. Marxism, as implemented by the Communist, has failed to bring freedom for mankind.

"Unlike cattle, humans need more than having their stomachs filled. Besides being free from starvation, humans must be free to think too. They must have the freedom to choose. For me, that's the essence of human freedom. To hold one's own fate in one's hand means to take part in the God substance. This is also a truth, and people should use it as the foundation to achieve the glory of developing a just, prosperous, and happy society.

"In my opinion, it is not important to create a socialist society. For example, the Communists worship Marxism as something scientific. But is that so? Isn't Marxism actually just a social theory based on a certain philosophy, which is also a mixture of what Marx learned from Engels, Feuerbach's materialism, and Hegel's dialectic? Marx only built his theory focusing on the production system.

"What about the distribution system, which is just as important in the life of a society? We must be pragmatic. We must do whichever is best for meeting the demand of the nation's independence, prosperity, happiness, and justice. Limiting ourselves to a certain dogma or doctrine means enslaving ourselves, and it will eventually lead to abolishing humans' rights for freedom. We must be patient in nurturing high-value culture, and plant the tradition of democracy and lawful freedom. How do we establish nations based on law supremacy and not power? Is it even possible? How?"

David's face showed his excitement. He looked at Derek, Pierre, and Sadeli individually. "What do you think about religion?" he asked.

"What do you mean by religion?" Sadeli became impatient. While the topic of their conversation was exciting, the most important thing was still to find a skillful pilot to help the Indonesian revolution for independence. David was the pilot they needed, but he preferred to talk about truth and religion.

"Ah, let's take the conventional religions, which people have embraced for hundreds of years, Christianity, Islam, Buddhism, and others," David said.

"Dear God, you want to talk about all human problems in one night while no one has been able to solve any of them for thousands of years?" Sadeli sputtered, somewhat desperate. "Do you know what I really want you to do?"

David gave him a big smile and said, "Fly to Indonesia tonight."

Sadeli shrugged and gave in. *Fine,* he thought, *if it takes an all-night debate to enlist David, our revolution pilot, then I, Sadeli, a major in the intelligence force of the Indonesian Republic, will bear it.*

David said, "Just think about it, why should I help your revolution? For money? I can make good or even better money here, and with less risk. Your people's revolution needs to have the values, hopes, and promises that can wake the world and grab its attention. That's why I ask what you need independence for. What do you think about human dignity? And about justice, law, social justice, the freedom of mankind, religion, and a new world order?

"Will you, after you gain independence, go back to the golden era of Sriwijaya and Majapahit? Ah, you're surprised that I know the history of your country. I studied the history of this part of the world before I came here. You surely know a nation's independence and sovereignty don't guarantee the freedom of its people.

"Look at China, and Germany with its Hitler, Italy with its Mussolini, Japan with its militarism. People are oppressed in those countries, and whoever refuses the official doctrine is hunted, captured, tortured, imprisoned, put into a political prisoner camp, and finally lands in the gas chamber and furnace. Does your independence also mean building political prisoner camps, gas chambers, and furnaces? Will Indonesia hunt down, capture, and torture those who are against its official doctrine?"

Sadeli sprang to his feet. He was angry and offended. His voice trembled when he said, "You're insulting us, Dave. You're crazy to think we, Indonesians who condemn imperialism and the persecution of one nation by another, will do that. Our entire revolution is to fight against and wipe out all the crimes you mentioned. Damn you, David Wayne."

David calmly asked Sadeli to sit down. "Your anger proves your sincerity, but how can you guarantee your nation is free from people who wish to be another Himmler, or any other sadistic, power-hungry figure? Do you think only Germany, Italy, Japan, or Russia has that sort of a bastard?"

"It won't happen in my country," Sadeli said with certainty, "We love freedom too much. We've been oppressed and insulted for too long. The entire nation will stand against anyone who wants to be a dictator."

"Are you absolutely sure?"

"Absolutely."

"You haven't witnessed the evil side of power destroy and poison a person's soul. It also happens to those who have good intentions and noble dreams at the beginning."

"But what you're afraid of can't possibly happen in my country. Really, all of our leaders are willing to die for freedom and democracy. Our revolution is based on democracy. We want democracy. We are against all forms of totalitarianism."

"If power can't corrupt your soul, what about wealth? Isn't it possible for the wish of good living and luxury to threaten your idealism in such a way that you forget about the fight for social justice and evenly distributed welfare for the people? Isn't it possible that you will be so busy with acquiring your own wealth that you completely neglect your suffering people?"

The statement enraged Sadeli even more. He told David how modest the leaders of Indonesia's revolution lived and, to his knowledge, no one had abused their power to enrich themselves.

"Ah, that doesn't prove anything," David said, "What is there to steal in the middle of this revolution? Later, after you win the revolution, when business has been revived, when economic activities grow, and foreign entrepreneurs come flocking, that's when your determination will be put to a test. How much will a single signature of someone in power cost? A hundred, a thousand, a million dollars?"

Sadeli was about to get angry again, but David raised his hand and said, "Wait, don't be upset. What I just said happened in my country and many others as well. In my country, they can prosecute things like that. There are legal procedures for that. Have you thought about these possibilities?"

Sadeli suddenly remembered Captain Umar Yunus. *Dear God,* he thought and said, "Our civil servants have a tradition of being honest. Even a mere ten-cent difference could cause a problem during the colonial time."

"That's not a guarantee. They would be punished if they stole from the Dutch, but they were basically used as a tool to oppress your people. They won't be of much use for the independent Indonesian government, because their souls have been corrupted by the Dutch colonial system and the Japanese plundering system," David said.

"Oh, but we can create a new tradition of dedication to the general public."

"How do you want to build the economy of your country? How will you develop the tradition of democracy? How do you guarantee human dignity? How do you nurture the nation?"

"D'you think I'm an all-knowing and all-wise person?" Sadeli asked. "I'm just a major, and those are all problems our leaders have to solve."

"You're a part of the revolution leadership for your nation," David said, "and you must also think about these kinds of problems."

"If you really want to know all about that, why don't you just go and see for yourself?" Sadeli was irritated. "Come to Indonesia and meet everyone there: farmers, workers, students, soldiers, generals, ministers, the president, a woman, anyone. Just take one flight and check things out. Only after that will we negotiate a contract. I can't answer all your questions. If I knew all the answers, I wouldn't be sitting here. I'd be king of the world."

"Even so, everyone must think about this. In this era, humans have more obligations and responsibilities," David said.

Sadeli lost track of time during his discussion with David. Sometimes Derek's voice and Pierre's light snore interrupted them. He felt like he was in some sort of a long, cruel nightmare. David asked him question after question and he answered. Sometimes his answers were short, sometimes elaborated. Sometimes he spoke in anger; sometimes he was full of excitement.

When it was David's turn to talk, he told Sadeli the story of his life. Once he mentioned the name of the woman he loved, who left him when he was at war. Sadeli heard names like Gandhi, Lenin, Marx, Feuerbach, Spinoza, Thoreau, Lincoln, Jefferson, Lao-tse, Roosevelt, Churchill, Malraux, African Americans in the U.S., Richard Wright, Silone, and many others.

"So you see, throughout the centuries there are people in this world who think about the fate and wellbeing of mankind. We must care, that's what is important. We must never be indifferent."

"So will you fly to Indonesia?"

"Of course. Did you doubt it?"

Sadeli was surprised. Then, he suddenly understood and said, "Oh, I'm so happy. We'll go and look together. We'll look for people anywhere in this world who care about other people's fate, who think and work for the sake of all mankind. Our revolution demands we stop using outdated beliefs. We're the heirs of the world's culture."

"Bravo!" Pierre de Koonig opened his eyes.

Sadeli startled. A grandfather clock in the corner of the room struck. It was five in the morning.

"Dear God, we've been talking all night," Sadeli exclaimed and rose.

"We'll arrange the flight later," David said, "Our Dakota needs a little fixing."

"I must return to the hotel," Sadeli said.

Although Sadeli was sleepy, he was happy for finally having found the pilot he had been looking for. He had to do so many things now that this was settled.

Derek walked him to the street, and when they reached the bridge, Derek held him by the shoulder and said, "I thank you for being so kind to Sheila. Now you know that she's ill, please always be gentle to her. She's a wonderful artist. Come and see her orchids again. I haven't been able to help her for a while."

Sadeli gave a small nod and walked away. He turned around at the end of the street and saw Derek's large frame standing alone in the middle of the bridge, wrapped in what seemed to be intense loneliness.

Only when Sadeli reached his hotel room did he understand what Derek meant by "now you know that she's ill." His body was covered with red scratch and bite marks. His skin was even broken in some places. As he applied Mercurochrome to his wounds, he couldn't stop thinking about the secret of Sheila and Derek's relationship. He figured that if Sheila did this with him, she might also do it with the gentle David, the giant Pierre, and who knows who else. He had thought Sheila, the starving lioness, strange. Now that he knew, he couldn't imagine coming back to marvel at Sheila Scott's orchids.

Chapter 7

It had been two days since Sadeli returned to Singapore. Umar Yunus returned from Sumatra bringing valuable cargo. The weapons and radio interceptors had reached their destination point safely. Also, three boats carrying sugar had docked in Singapore.

Sadeli was very happy. He had arranged David's maiden flight with great care. He made secret radio contact with Colonel Suroso and contacted the Indonesian Air Force. He had wanted to join this flight, but Colonel Suroso ordered him to stay put and wait for the next order.

Now Sadeli was simply waiting for the maiden flight to take off. They had chosen Bangkok-Singapore-Jambi-Lampung-Yogyakarta as the route, and the plane would fly along Java's southern coastline. Sadeli would send Ali Nurdin on the flight not just to carry a message for Colonel Suroso, but also to write an article for publication.

Ali Nurdin suggested inviting a couple of foreign journalists on the flight. It would be beneficial for their revolution in terms of international propaganda. Sadeli sent a telegram to Yogyakarta, asking for approval. A shipment of much-needed medicine was ready to be loaded on David's airplane. Doctor Banerji had donated some medicine, and other Indians living in Singapore had also made contributions.

Ali Nurdin had done his job very well. Indonesia had the attention and support from people in Singapore and Malaya. The red and white colors of the Indonesian flag were very popular.

The only problem left for Sadeli was how to handle Umar Yunus' case. Umar Yunus' bookkeeping turned out to be inaccurate. Based on the audit, there was about half a million Singapore dollars missing. Since he returned from Sumatra, Umar Yunus seemed somewhat distracted and after Sadeli's audit he became even tenser.

At first, Sadeli told Umar Yunus to return the half million dollars and in exchange he would ask Colonel Suroso not to prosecute him. Sadeli also suggested Umar Yunus resign from the intelligence service.

Umar Yunus had turned pale and said, "What will happen to me? You're so cruel."

"In my opinion, this is the best way for all of us," Sadeli said calmly and added, "Don't forget, we're still in the middle of a revolution. Under revolution law you will receive the death penalty."

Umar Yunus' face paled further. "How can I pay back half a million dollars?"

"You still have the florist, the car, and the house that are partly under your name and partly under Rita's. You can sell all the jewelry you gave her."

"No, not that," Umar Yunus' voice trembled, "Have mercy on Rita. I don't have the heart to take things away from her. You don't understand; you've never been in love. You're cruel. You're nothing but a tool of the revolution!"

Sadeli shrugged and said, "Think about it. Don't be angry at me or even consider me an enemy. I'm just carrying out an order. Consider this: you're having fun here using the revolution's money while there are soldiers back home who have to die because of the lack of medical supplies. Who knows, if that money…"

"Stop!" Umar Yunus interrupted and covered his ears. "You're mean. Didn't I perform the task you gave me? Shouldn't you take that into consideration? Haven't I been loyal to the revolution since the Proclamation Day on August 17, 1945? I admit I made a mistake.

Can't the revolution forgive me? Are the revolution, Colonel Suroso, and you all heartless robots?"

"Our revolution is a revolution of freedom for all humans. The spirit of our revolution is love for mankind. I didn't come with the order to kill you, did I? Didn't I give you a way out?"

"You came and ruined my happiness. Believe me, I've never been as happy as I am with Rita. Will you destroy that? Does your duty allow you to destroy the lives of two people?"

Sadeli sighed. He wondered how he could make Umar Yunus understand his utmost responsibility. Since his experience in Bangkok with Sheila, Derek, David, and Pierre, Sadeli did not take human emotions lightly. Perhaps Umar Yunus did love Rita with the profound love between a man and woman that he had never felt. A love so great it appeared to have a Godly quality someone would die for. Sadeli wondered if he had the right to ruin such an exceptional love. He reasoned that if people found such kind of love, they needed to nurture and protect it, but he was unable to pinpoint the difference between this love and its surrogate.

Sadeli decided to be patient in dealing with Umar Yunus. He didn't want this to become a scandal in Singapore. It would undoubtedly hurt Indonesia's reputation and the Dutch would definitely use it for their propaganda. He couldn't afford for that to happen. He warned Umar Yunus, "You're still a captain in the Intelligence Service of the Indonesian Republic, and you must obey all orders given."

Sadeli didn't want to ask for new orders from Colonel Suroso regarding Umar Yunus. The colonel had given him full authority to take any necessary action.

When Umar Yunus asked for a week to think about everything, Sadeli agreed right away. He also needed time to think about his decision. He was not the cruel person Umar Yunus accused him of being, but he had a heavy responsibility, obligation, and trust to bear. He couldn't let Umar Yunus off the hook for stealing that much money from the revolution. He asked himself if he should take Umar Yunus' love for Rita and Rita's life into consideration. His sense of responsibility toward the revolution told him not to.

The revolution for freedom was most important. Everything else had to give way to it. Personal interests, love, and happiness had to yield. It would be impossible to seize freedom without total dedication to the revolution. Umar Yunus had betrayed the revolution by putting his own happiness above the safety of the revolution and didn't deserve any special consideration. Sadeli sighed. He now realized how difficult it was to find the right path.

He picked up the phone and asked for Inspector Hawkins' office. He was happy to hear the inspector's voice on the other end. "It's Sadeli. I just came from Bangkok," he said, "How are you? How are things here? What's new?"

"Ah, welcome back! Your friends are very upset. They've been waiting for their flower delivery, but it never showed up. When can we meet for lunch? You know I owe you one."

"Alright, I'll call you tomorrow or the day after. I've been quite busy lately."

"Okay, be careful. Someone had a bad experience a few nights ago and wants revenge."

"Thank you and goodbye." Sadeli put down the receiver and chuckled. The inspector undoubtedly referred to Tan Ciat Tong. He noted that Hawkins really knew everything that happened on this island. He had no concerns about dealing with Tan Ciat Tong, but was glad he wasn't alone on this mission.

Ali Nurdin had done a good job and proved himself to be a talented intelligence agent. Sadeli had given him some intelligence training and told him to read books on the science of intelligence maneuvers. Ali's unit, as small as it might be, operated efficiently. Now they could mobilize the dockworkers to hold a protest rally against the Dutch vessels at any time. With better funding, Sadeli hoped they would be able to boycott the Dutch ships one day.

Five days later, Sadeli received a coded telegram from Colonel Suroso ordering him to buy radio interceptors and weapons to be shipped to Riau. Considering its large population of Chinese people with questionable loyalty, the Republic wanted to reinforce the intelligence unit and troops in that area. Moreover, the Riau Islands were very close to Singapore and played a significant role.

Colonel Suroso had ordered Sadeli to take the speedboat, check out the area, and report to Yogyakarta as soon as possible. Then he had to return to his post in Singapore and wait for the next order.

David Wayne and Pierre de Koonig would soon fly to Indonesia. Sadeli worked day and night on the preparation of the flight. He had to purchase the radio interceptors and weapons. He needed to buy the items from someone else, through a third party. He could ask a member of his organization to serve as the go-between and be on constant alert throughout the process. He had to always remember three things: safety, safety, safety.

After a few busy days passed, Sadeli realized Umar Yunus hadn't shown up for days. When Sadeli phoned him he was told that Umar Yunus was not home. He was about to find out more about Umar Yunus' strange behavior, when a wire from Bangkok arrived. *Tomorrow at eleven – David.* Sadeli put his concerns about Umar Yunus aside to focus his attention on the more pressing matter at hand.

Sadeli was so excited, he completely forgot about Umar Yunus. He told Ali Nurdin to get three foreign journalists ready for the trip: one from the International News Service, one from Reuters, and the other from the Associated Press. They also had to inform the local newspapers in Sumatra.

The next morning, long before eleven, Sadeli and Ali Nurdin were already at Changi airport, waiting. Soon, the three foreign journalists joined them. They were ready for the maiden flight.

At a little past eleven, the loudspeaker announced the Dakota plane from Lotus Flights Inc. was about to land. Sadeli's heart pounded as he watched the yellowish-gray plane descend and make a smooth landing. *Now the air connection with my country is established,* Sadeli thought happily, as if the plane was actually his.

After David Wayne and Pierre de Koonig exited the immigration room, Sadeli couldn't hold back his excitement and shook their hands vigorously. "You can just fly out after this. I'll have the cargo loaded right away. And you have four passengers," he said and introduced them to Ali Nurdin and the three journalists.

An hour later, the Dakota took off. "Godspeed," Sadeli wished as the plane disappeared into the clouds.

***

Umar Yunus held Rita's hand as they lay on their bed that night. "We need to talk, Rita," he said.

"Yes, Johnny."

"You know that Sadeli is my commander. He's a major in the intelligence service."

"Yes, you told me."

"He went through my bookkeeping and found half a million dollars missing."

Rita, shocked, sat up straight. She took Umar Yunus' shoulder and said, "That much?"

"Yes. The money belonged to the Indonesian Republic. I used some of it to open the florist, some to buy you gifts, the car, et cetera."

"And now he wants it back?"

"Yes, I have to return the half a million dollars."

Rita gave him a scrutinizing look. "What can he do to you?"

"Here? Nothing."

She sighed, relieved. "Then he can't harm us."

"Legally, he can't."

"Then why are you worried? Don't you love me?"

Umar Yunus held Rita tightly. "I love you, Rita. You're my joy. But not returning the money, would that be right?"

"Of course. Oh Johnny, you don't know what it means to be poor in this country. No one will help us. It wasn't until I met you that I knew what it meant to be free from poverty, from fear, uncertainty, and looming starvation. We now have the capital to build our life. Using what we have, we can start anew. I'll work real hard to develop the florist, Johnny. Oh, I also plan to sell some orchid seeds and gardening tools. With a little capital, we can buy some land in the suburbs and start an orchid garden." Her excitement and joy were infectious.

"Do you love me? Will you be with me through good and bad times?"

"Yes. Oh, Johnny, do you still doubt me? Let's get married, Johnny."

Umar Yunus lost all his doubt in Rita's embrace. He decided to resign from the intelligence service, send a divorce letter to his wife in Indonesia, and live in Singapore. Hundreds of Indonesians had emigrated to Singapore and Malaya before him. He would inform Major Sadeli of his decisions. Only then would he feel at peace.

Chapter 8

When, two days ago, Umar Yunus told him he wanted to resign from the Secret Service without paying his debt, Sadeli made his decision to kidnap him.

That night, the Shalimar speedboat was ready to sail. The weapons and radio interceptors were all on board. The only thing left was to kidnap Umar Yunus. Sadeli ordered two of his agents to do the job. He had decided to kidnap Umar Yunus and bring him back to Sumatra for trial. Based on his transgression, Sadeli knew what fate awaited Umar Yunus. Sadeli hardened himself. He knew such violation called for punishment if they wanted to keep order.

The night enveloped the shore. Sadeli grew tense. He checked his watch; it was almost eleven. If everything had gone well, Umar Yunus should be detained on the boat by now.

***

The night was pitch-black. A strong wind drove the big rolling waves, thunder rumbled, and lightning flashed on the horizon when Sadeli reached the Shalimar.

"We've a storm ahead," Captain Sow Chiu greeted Sadeli on the deck.

Amir, the head guard, reported that Umar Yunus was downstairs, in the cabin. Sadeli nodded and signaled the captain. The engine immediately roared to life and the boat forged forward strongly, riding the waves through the dark night. Meanwhile, the storm rumbled above and around them, poised to hit.

Sadeli stood with Captain Sow Chiu on the bridge. They were surrounded by the darkness of the ocean and unable to see a thing. Singapore had disappeared from the horizon and now the rain started to fall, harder and harder. The waves looked like a herd of black horses, whipped by thunder and lightning, their white manes draping their necks as they ran. The boat tilted left and right, bobbed up and down, but still moved steadily forward. The kerosene lamp was the only light they had.

Sadeli decided to go downstairs to check on Umar Yunus. He climbed down the steps, opened a cabin door, and signaled Amir, who was on guard, to leave.

Umar Yunus lay on the bed. Looking pale and tense, he didn't even try to sit up when Sadeli entered. The floor, wall, and the cell door shook from the engine's rapid movement. A black cloth covered the porthole. It was hot in the cabin.

Sadeli said, "I'm sorry I had to do this. I wish you'd come voluntarily."

"I'm not a goat that meekly obeys when herded to the slaughterhouse," Umar Yunus replied.

"If you were willing to pay back the half million dollars, you wouldn't have to go through this. Can't you understand that as a soldier and fighter of the revolution, I don't have a choice?"

"Why do you ask? To soothe your conscience? You ordered your men to kidnap me in the middle of the street. Your tricks are just as cunning as those of the Chicago bandits."

"I hope you'll understand."

"I understand that you've ruined the happiness Rita and I found in our love. You're the one who doesn't understand, Sadeli. You're the blind one. Your heart is frozen."

Sadeli drew a deep breath as he walked to the door. He threw Umar Yunus another look before he stepped out, closed the door, and walked back to the bridge.

In the cabin, Umar Yunus stared at the ceiling. His thoughts penetrated the storm and wandered to Rita. She would be all alone and must be worried sick by now since he had not come home.

In the meantime, a Dutch corvette also rode the waves through the stormy night. It was on its regular patrol, still pretty far from where they were. Its radar circled, searching the dark night. The captain, a veteran from the sea battle in the North Atlantic, had only recently been assigned to these tropical waters.

Captain Sow Chiu and Sadeli were having coffee when suddenly a crewmember at the stern yelled and pointed to the east.

A black, pointy ship slowly took shape in the midst of light rain. The waves were still strong and the wind blew hard. Sadeli peered through the telescope. He wished it was a British corvette, but there was no mistaking the tri-colored flag. Soon, the light on the corvette started blinking, ordering them to stop.

"Can we lose them?" Sadeli asked.

Captain Sow Chiu laughed. He issued an order to the engine room, and suddenly the engine made a different noise as it let out a frightening roar. A giant hand seemed to pull the boat forward between the parting waves.

The Dutch corvette sent a warning shot that hit the water far behind them and sent a splash high into the air.

The Shalimar ignored all communication and quickly created a big gap between itself and the corvette. Soon the corvette was only a small dot far away and no longer fired at them. The Shalimar was obviously faster.

Sadeli anxiously searched for the shoreline. Sow Chiu said it wouldn't be far. Suddenly, the coastline appeared, but even before he could congratulate Captain Sow Chiu, one of the engines coughed, sputtered, and then died completely. They dropped speed in no time.

Captain Sow Chiu spoke to his crew in the engine room. "The left engine is broken," he told Sadeli, "We must go on shore and hide behind the small islands of mangrove scattered along the shore and surrounded by narrow, winding, saltwater sloughs. Looking down from the air, any ship venturing into the mangrove forest won't make it back out unless the captain knows the area like the back of his hand."

Captain Sow Chiu took over the wheel and ordered them to reduce their speed when the ship reached a rather shallow part of the shore water. A few hundred yards from the beach, Sadeli saw the line of mangrove forest along the shoreline.

He also saw the Dutch corvette approach rapidly. His heart started to pound. The Shalimar moved too slowly. The corvette would catch up to them before they could take cover behind the mangroves. The Dutch navy would confiscate the ship and its cargo and would arrest everyone on board. *Colonel Suroso. What would the colonel say about his failure?*

Suddenly a cannon was heard a hundred yards behind Shalimar. Sadeli was relieved when their ship moved faster with just one engine. They were out of the shallow part and lurched forward along the curve before disappearing into the mangrove forest. In the last few hundred yards, the river grew narrower so that its surface was almost covered by the mangrove leaves. Captain Sow Chiu ordered the crew to drop anchor and kill the engine. Silence instantly wrapped around them. But it was not for long.

The corvette had reached the mouth of the estuary the Shalimar had entered. It was too big to go any farther. The captain ordered his crew to open full fire in the direction of the Shalimar.

Cannonballs dropped all around Sadeli's ship. Some hit the water only dozens of yards away. After a short while, the direction of the shots changed and moved away from them.

Sadeli drew a deep breath. "Can we fix the engine?" he asked Captain Sow Chiu.

"We always bring the necessary spare parts. Obi and his men are already working on it."

Sadeli called Amir and said, "Order some men to cover the ship with branches and leaves. I'm afraid the corvette will get an airplane to look for us. And bring Umar Yunus here."

A few moments later, Amir was back on the deck with Umar Yunus. Sadeli told Amir to prepare four Bren guns with enough ammo. He also ordered them to lower a small lifeboat they had on the deck into the water.

He turned to Umar Yunus and said, "Umar Yunus, we have an emergency. Follow my orders. I'm reinstating you as captain. We have to hold the enemy if the Dutch send an armed lifeboat after us. I'll be with three other men behind the shrubs near the estuary and ambush them. Take two men armed with a Bren and a rifle and position yourselves half a mile from the ship. If a plane comes looking for us, lure it to your post with some shots. If I'm under attack and need help, I'll call you. I'll fire two quick shots, pause, then another two. You're in command if I die. Now take the rubber raft and go."

Amir lined his men up on the deck. Sadeli looked at every one of them. Including himself and Umar Yusuf, there were only eight of them. He had given Amir, a young, stout man, the rank of sergeant. Amir was reliable and courageous. Darwis, Yahya, Mukmin, Idrus, and Syafei had undergone firearm training during the Japanese occupation, but had never gone to war. There were eight men to hold back a Dutch corvette.

This is crazy. Sadeli suppressed a chuckle. He said, "Darwis and Yahya, go with Pak Umar Yunus. Take a rifle and a Bren." He ordered Amir to be ready on the small lifeboat and turned to Captain Sow Chiu. "How long does Obi think it'll take to fix the engine?"

"At least four or five hours," the captain answered.

Sadeli checked his watch. It was six thirty in the morning. "That means they'll finish by noon. By then, the Dutch plane may get here and then we can only leave when it's dark. Is there any other way out from here?"

"Yes, but we have to sail across a shallow part. We must unload the cargo before we can cross."

"Where does this channel lead to?"

"An estuary, half a mile away from this one."

Sadeli thought for a moment. "Is there any kampong nearby?"

"Yes, a small fishing village."

"Does anyone know how to get there?"

"One of the sailors does."

"Alright." Sadeli wrote an order on a small notepad and handed it to Amir. "Here, hand this written order to the village chief. I want every adult man of that kampong to come here as fast as they can."

Amir seemed disappointed not to be joining the looming battle, but he saluted and carried on with a rifle slung across his shoulder.

"Watch it when you're about to enter the village," Sadeli called after him and added, "Take care. Don't forget to watch for planes."

Sadeli turned to the captain. "Sow Chiu, once the villagers arrive, move the ship to the shallow part of the river. Unload the cargo, sail the ship past the shallow water, and reload. Don't forget to watch for danger coming from above."

Then Sadeli climbed into the lifeboat. They were now left with the four of them and three Bren guns.

"No more weapons?" Sadeli asked.

"Still in the case," Idrus replied.

"Take one and some ammo."

Idrus ran to get the gun and the ammunition.

Sadeli waited for him, impatiently. As soon as Idrus came back, they took off. Mukmin and Syafei rowed while Sadeli steered the boat. Captain Sow Chiu's telescope still hung around his neck.

They approached a bend carefully, and kept the boat close to the bank. Idrus' Bren gun was at the ready. Right before the bend, they stopped the boat under the mangrove trees. Sadeli reached for a big branch above his head and climbed into the tree.

He was able to see the sea from his lookout. The Dutch corvette still patrolled the mouth of the estuary. Every now and then they fired their cannon at the shore. The rain had stopped and the morning sun lit the clear sky. The wind had died down and the waves were calmer.

Sadeli lifted the telescope to his eyes. The corvette appeared bigger and he was able to see the activities on deck. His heart beat faster. It appeared the men on deck prepared a lifeboat full of armed soldiers to look for them.

Sadeli climbed back down to the lifeboat. He ordered Idrus and Syafei to go on shore and position the Bren gun in a good spot. "Don't shoot before they are really close. Shoot the helmsman first," he said, "Mukmin and I will bring the other two Brens and place a sterling gun closer to the estuary. We're going to let them pass. Shoot them when they're close to you. The sterling will greet them when they retreat."

Sadeli suddenly thought of another scenario: *what if the Dutch convoy kept going and found their helpless ship at the shallow part of the river?* He was reluctant to send Mukmin away to guard the ship. They were already severely outnumbered.

Finally, he decided to take the risk. With Mukmin he rowed the lifeboat across the river and hid it, covered by branches and leaves, underneath the mangroves. Sadeli climbed up the mangrove, looked through his telescope, and scouted the sea. He saw the corvette had come closer to the estuary, and, in fact, the Dutch had launched a lifeboat. He counted twelve people in green marine uniforms with automatic guns.

Sadeli signaled to Idrus and Syafei that their enemies were coming before he quickly climbed back down and took his position, some sixty feet from Mukmin. Together they waited.

Sadeli suddenly realized how quiet the mangrove forest around him was. The dark brown water in front of him didn't seem to flow at all. A few brown birds flew from branch to branch in the trees nearby. Some two yards away from him, a snake made its way across the mud before it disappeared into the water. Sadeli remembered his dream of leading a major battle like General Patton or Montgomery. He faced one now, but he only had eight men.

Sadeli's thoughts returned to Umar Yunus. This would be a perfect time for him to escape. However, there weren't many places he would be able to go. The Sumatra coastal line was terribly vast and uninhabited. Only if he found a fishing village could he get back to Singapore by boat.

Thoughts ran through Sadeli's mind as he tried to concentrate on the coming battle. He remembered his mother, his father, and his sisters and brothers. He remembered Zainab. His first woman. *Where would she be now?* He recalled her young and sensual body and sighed. How quickly everything went by. And here he was, lying in the mud, in the middle of a mangrove forest holding an untested Bren, and waiting for death to come hitchhiking on the Dutch lifeboat. He realized how sweet life had been. Now, a bullet might end his life in an instant. No more Zainab for him.

Sadeli forced the dark thoughts out of his mind. He looked at Mukmin, who stared at the river bend where they expected the Dutch boat to appear.

Sadeli wondered what Mukmin, Idrus, and Syafei were thinking. He knew very little about them, about their lives, their hearts, dreams, and hopes. *What motivated them to fight?* He wondered if they understood the bigger meaning of the Indonesian revolution, which was to uphold the values and dignity of mankind. Did they understand that man couldn't live from rice alone, that humans had their basic rights, and the freedom to choose? Did they understand that establishing a nation was just a means and not a goal, and that the most important thing was happiness for mankind?

Sadeli startled, listening closely. A new sound disturbed the surrounding serenity. It was the rhythmic sound of a lifeboat's motor.

All of a sudden, some kind of calmness entered Sadeli's heart. He signaled across the river with his handkerchief. A wave of a handkerchief answered him before it disappeared into the greens. The noise of the motor grew louder. Sadeli looked at his watch. Seven fifty. The Dutch didn't waste any time in attacking them.

Suddenly, a lifeboat's bow appeared around the river bend. It moved slowly. All the marines huddled low. Only the tops of their steel helmets were visible. The helmsman was the only one who sat straight, and thus appeared taller than the rest.

The lifeboat passed, and Sadeli began to count: one, two, three, four, five—he checked his watch; thirty seconds had passed. Idrus and Syafei should have been firing by now—one, two, three, four, five, how time seemed to crawl. *Now.* Sadeli shouted in his heart, and in the next second, the noise from Idrus and Syafei's Brens tore the silence. Sadeli saw a bullet hit the water. It had been fired too low.

But then the shooter quickly adjusted his aim and now the bullets hit the boat.

Suddenly the helmsman slumped over, but the person sitting next to him quickly took over the wheel. Now the Dutch marines shot back at the two Brens.

The helmsman turned the boat around to head back to the estuary. They continued their fire as he cranked up the speed. Everything happened quickly and now the lifeboat headed back to the bend at full speed.

Sadeli signaled Mukmin, who carried a rifle. Mukmin nodded. Sadeli started to shoot. He aimed a little above the boat's side, looking for a target among the soldiers who hid underneath their steel helmets.

The marines shot back at Sadeli. The bullets swished by, shattering branches and leaves. Then the lifeboat disappeared behind the bend.

Idrus and Syafei cheered from across the river. Sadeli was happy. He turned to Mukmin, who threw him a wide grin.

Sadeli signaled Mukmin to return to their lifeboat while he climbed up the mangrove. He looked through his telescope and found the Dutch lifeboat at the mouth of the estuary. He saw the victims of his gunshots lying in the boat. He quickly climbed down and jumped into their lifeboat. They both rowed the boat quickly across the river to pick up Idrus and Syafei.

"As soon as their boat reaches the corvette and reports, they'll shower this spot with their cannons. We have to move fast," Sadeli said.

Idrus and Syafei jumped into the boat and they rowed upstream.

"How many casualties?" Syafei asked.

"I saw three people down," Sadeli responded. "I don't know how many are wounded. You guys shot expertly. Whose Bren hit the water at the start?"

"Mine, Sir." Syafei sounded a little embarrassed.

"But you quickly recovered. Still, remember, an accurate first shot is crucial. It can be the difference between winning and losing."

Fifteen minutes later, the corvette's cannons began shooting like crazy. Bullets rained systematically along both sides of the river from the bend to beyond the ambush spot. Cannons roared, deafening. The sound tore the air. Cannonballs uprooted the mangroves and shrapnel cut through the bark and leaves. The earth shook as if giants beat their war drums and stomped their feet. Death hovered in the air. It swung its giant sword and laughed viciously.

Sadeli felt as if cold fingers reached inside his chest and ripped him apart, pulled at his heart, stomach, feet, hands, mind, head, and face. Cold sweat broke out and drenched him.

Even when the spray of bullets quieted, Sadeli still worried. He feared the Dutch would resume shooting and they did. Bullets came and went. They came closer and they went away, over and over – Ratatatata! Dzzzingg! Ratatatatatatat!

The noise tore the air and the shells launched water, mud, branches, and leaves high up in the air before they all rained back down to earth.

Those Dutch are really pissed off. The thought calmed Sadeli. He looked at Mukmin, Idrus, and Syafei, who sank their bodies deep into the mud, except for their eyes, noses, and mouths. Sadeli was glad to see they held their weapons above their heads to keep them dry. He gave them a thumbs-up and laughed when their white teeth showed in their mud-covered faces. It reminded him of comedians in old American movies who painted their faces black.

The giants' drum and war cry slowly ebbed. The earth stopped trembling. The air, no longer shredded by noise, became whole again and by the river, everything was quiet once more.

Sadeli checked his watch. Eight thirty. He hoped everyone on the ship had kept on working despite the noise of the vicious battle. He wondered how Umar Yunus, Darwis, and Yahya were doing and ordered his men to check their weapons and ammo. Unless the enemy returned with two, three, or four lifeboats, they probably would be fine. He had yet to figure out what to do if their airplane showed up.

He suddenly was hungry and took some crackers from his pocket. He always carried those crackers with him on every mission. "Did you eat?" he asked.

"No," they said, but they also had some crackers and chocolate in their pockets. In fact, Syafei brought hot coffee in the flask he carried on his belt.

While they ate, Sadeli said, "We must get back immediately. The enemy will be back in no time to see if they destroyed our barricade. They'll seize our ship and the cargo and capture, perhaps even kill, us all. We must fight them courageously yet with extreme caution. Our resources are very limited. If only we had a bazooka." He drew a long sigh.

"We have dynamite on the ship, Sir," Mukmin said. "The captain likes to bring dynamite to catch fish in the rivers by the sea."

Sadeli thought hard for a moment. He could tie some TNT sticks together, give it a short fuse, and throw it at the enemy's lifeboat. It was extremely dangerous, but if he had to hold back the enemy, he had to try that. He said, "Good. Mukmin, take Idrus and Syafei across to find a good ambush spot, then quickly go to the ship. Bring me as many dynamite sticks, detonators, fuses, and ropes as you can. Also some medium-size cans. I'll wait for you here. Hurry!"

Sadeli nervously watched their lifeboat cross to the other side of the river. Then Mukmin rowed alone to the ship.

Suddenly, Sadeli heard two Bren shots in the distance, quickly followed by other automatic gunshots. *Dear God,* he thought, *it's Umar, Darwis, and Yahya. Did the Dutch airplane arrive?* He rose and listened for any sound of an airplane.

The shooting continued and grew fiercer, then decreased and stopped. Sadeli still couldn't hear any airplane sound. He checked his watch; fifteen minutes had passed. Mukmin should have returned by now.

As if answering his thought, Mukmin appeared, rowing quickly. He made a quick stop at Idrus and Syafei's ambush spot and gave them something, then quickly headed for Sadeli.

Together they pulled the lifeboat underneath the mangrove before they covered it with branches and leaves.

"I have extra ammo, food, and drink, Sir," Mukmin said. "Pak Umar was attacked but he managed to send the enemy back. The engine repair is going fast too. The captain said they hope to finish before twelve. Sergeant Amir and the crew haven't returned yet. The captain said they'll be back at twelve at the earliest."

Sadeli looked at his watch. A little past nine. He said, "Go eat first."

Sadeli quickly assembled the dynamite. He packed the sticks into the cans, placed the detonator and the fuse, and filled the remaining empty space with dirt for a firmer pack. He then stacked the cans carefully on a dry surface. He held each can to estimate its weight. He wouldn't be able to throw a can to the middle of the river, but if his men across the river shot at the enemy's lifeboat and forced them to sail closer to his side of the river, he might be able to throw some into their boat with a little luck.

Sadeli climbed up the mangrove to scout the sea, but other, taller trees blocked his view. He climbed back down and said to Mukmin, "Go back to the ship and tell the captain to immediately unload once Sergeant Amir returns. Have them hide the cargo in the waterways around the area. We won't be able to hold back the Dutch for too long if they return with a greater taskforce. Hurry!"

Mukmin cleared the leaves that camouflaged their boat and rowed back to the ship.

Sadeli wiped the sweat off his forehead. The sun was high in the eastern sky, and it was getting hotter. Sadeli was trying to pick up any sound of an airplane when he suddenly remembered his God. "Dear God," he prayed, "please protect and save us all. Give us victory today because we fight for freedom and the truth." Sadeli looked at his watch. Five minutes. Ten. Fifteen. Mukmin should have returned by now. Suddenly cannonballs whizzed through the air, and the noise of a bombardment filled the forest once more.

"They've come," Sadeli said to himself. He dropped to the ground and worried. If one of the bullets hit the dynamite cans, they would all blow up and erase him from the face of the earth. And even without the cans, he would have the same fate if a cannonball exploded near his head.

The shower of cannonballs sought them out. It came closer then pulled away. All of a sudden, Mukmin appeared in the middle of the river while deadly cannonballs exploded alongside the riverbanks.

Sadeli gasped. "The fool. What a fool." Sadeli cursed under his breath. *Why doesn't he take cover?* he wondered, then filled with admiration. *Oh, how brave you are. You're a hero, a knight. You defy death to return to us, to return to your fighting ground. Dear God.*

A cannonball landed in the river. It created a tall water pillar that sent water everywhere and rocked the lifeboat with the waves it caused. Sadeli was relieved when he saw Mukmin still rowing strongly after the water pillar dissolved.

Go away, go somewhere else! Sadeli silently exclaimed. "Why don't you take cover?" he questioned as fierce automatic gunfire opened behind the bend. Waves of gunshots tore through the mangrove forest.

Sadeli jumped to his feet in the heat of the shooting and shouted, "Come on, Min. Hurry." He watched the bend and at the same time, kept an eye on Mukmin, who rowed hard and jumped on the bank, next to him.

Sadeli was flat on the ground, ready with his Bren. The enemy's lifeboat was upon them and opened fire, aiming at both riverbanks. The next second, another enemy boat, some fifty yards behind the first one, surprised him.

Sadeli signaled Idrus and Syafei, showing them two fingers and pointing at himself, indicating he would shoot at the second boat while they should take care of the first.

Sadeli let the first boat pass. It continued firing like mad. A few moments later, the second boat came closer. Sadeli carefully aimed his Bren. Suddenly, two Brens across the river roared and sent bullets flying to the first boat.

The second boat changed its course and steered closer to Sadeli's side to help the first boat.

Sadeli grinned. He estimated the distance between him and the enemy's boat and reached for one of the dynamite cans. He checked the distance before he lit the fuse, then calculated the time, to match the speed of the burning fuse with the distance to the boat, before he drew his arm far back and flung the can toward the boat.

He immediately dropped back to the ground and fired at the boat with his Bren. A second later, the dynamite exploded in the air next to the lifeboat. Sadeli jumped to his feet, lit the fuse of another can, waited, and hurled the can, then dropped to the ground and resumed shooting. Everything happened incredibly fast.

The second dynamite explosion was very close to the boat. Sadeli saw some people collapse. Someone was thrown into the air and fell into the water. It was as if a gigantic force had hit the boat and tipped it on its side. After the boat steadied itself, it turned around.

The first boat quickly came toward the second boat. It threw a rope and quickly towed it toward the ocean. Both boats continued their fire until they vanished behind the river bend.

Sadeli sprang to his feet and said, "We must move away from here fast." He was surprised when he turned and saw Mukmin lying on the ground with blood on the side of his dirty shirt.

"Oh no, you're hit, Min." Sadeli squatted by Mukmin to check his pulse. Mukmin's heartbeat was strong. The wound turned out to be just a flesh wound and there were no broken bones. Sadeli covered the bullet hole with his handkerchief and carried Mukmin to their boat. He loaded the remaining two dynamite cans, the Bren gun, and the rifle, then rowed quickly across the river.

Syafei already waited by the bank. He looked at Mukmin lying in the boat and said, "Idrus was shot too. In the shoulder."

Sadeli jumped out of the boat to help Syafei carry Idrus into the boat.

"It was an automatic and the bullet went through," Syafei said.

Idrus writhed in pain. He was pale from the loss of blood.

After loading the remaining Brens into the boat, Sadeli and Syafei rowed with all their might while listening carefully for any airplane noise.

Sadeli checked his watch. It was past nine thirty. He didn't see the Shalimar and became anxious. He wondered if they finished the engine repair and if Captain Sow Chiu had sailed across the shallow water. He rowed faster.

After a while, he found the Shalimar about half a mile from its earlier spot, a few river bends away. He only spotted it when he was really close.

Many people helped move Mukmin and Idrus to the speedboat. Captain Sow Chiu immediately tended to their wounds. He said, "The engine's almost done. It's sooner than Obi expected. One of the cylinders was broken, but we had a spare. I moved the ship here during the bombardment. I was worried we'd get hit."

"Syafei and I must return to hold them back," said Sadeli. "When the fishermen come, and there's no enemy plane, unload the cargo and sail the ship across the shallow water. Tell the fishermen to hide their ships from the airplane's view. Syafei, get more ammo for the Bren."

When everything was ready, Sadeli said, "Now it's just the two of us, Syafei. Let's each take one riverside."

Sadeli dropped Syafei on the bank before a river bend. He slapped Syafei on the shoulder and said, "Perhaps they won't try another attack. They may want to wait for the airplane. Be careful."

Sadeli rowed across and looked for a good spot. After he hid his boat, he took a seat under a mangrove tree. He leaned against the trunk and waited; waited, and waited.

Silence fell over the mangrove forest once more. Time crept along, and Sadeli's mind started to wander. He remembered the strange conversation he had with David Wayne while Pierre de Koonig snored and Derek Scott nodded in agreement. He remembered Sheila Scott, the beautiful woman who was ill, who was charming yet frightening. He remembered Inspector John Hawkins. Dr. Banerji. Then Rita. And Mai Sung, her tempting, warm body. He somewhat regretted not paying her another visit after their movie night out. He only met her that one time and then had been too busy to bother with her. *Would she think I just disappeared? Maybe she thought I was mad at her.* He remembered Umar Yunus, then Idrus and Mukmin. He remembered Colonel Suroso, the head of the intelligence service. He recalled his father, mother, sisters and brothers. He recalled his friends. He remembered his past life.

He recalled David Wayne's story about the sixty million people who died around the world during World War II. He pondered on how cruel humans were to one another. Even the most vicious tiger couldn't cause that many victims. And now he experienced that himself.

He didn't know the Dutch captain. Neither did he know any of the Dutch soldiers who had attacked them. He didn't hold any grudge against them. Yet here, in a mangrove forest, they mercilessly tried to kill one another. He wondered what kind of power sent young Dutch men all the way across the ocean to kill in this unknown mangrove forest. *What could possibly be that evil and cruel?* He was curious if David Wayne would be able to explain this to him other than with the usual information about colonialism, imperialism, capitalism, and other theories. Meanwhile, in another place, under different circumstances, those Dutch young men were ordinary, civilized people who might become his good friends. *Who turned them into beasts here?*

Sadeli thought of Idrus, Yahya, and Darwis, who were of Malayan descent, unlike Syafei, Umar, and Mukmin, who were Indonesians. *Why were the three Malayan young men willing to fight and die for Indonesia's independence? Was it because they came from the same ancestors and it was their common lineage talking?*

What did David Wayne try to find with his truth? Did people always have to pay such a high price to perfect their humanity? Was it necessary to destroy so many souls, and so many values, which were impossible to account for in statistics?

Now, those who won the war in Europe, who defeated the Nazi and the fascist, forgot about their own fight against human cruelty and instead focused on killing others.

Sadeli concluded that humans were very complicated. Some people renounced their faith in the merciful God for what they saw happening in this world. They wondered how this God let so much cruelty happen throughout human history, continuing from century to century. On the other hand, if people believed in the loving and just God, should they accept what happens as His mysterious way, which as humans they would never be able to comprehend?

Should they stumble, fall, get up, and then do it all over again? Or did God plant the seed of light within each human, and all one had to do was look inside oneself? This would give humans the power to determine their own fate, be it for something better or worse.

People could believe in God and still hold their fate in their own hands. If this was the case, then fighting would have a meaning. People would believe mankind's fate was not determined by laws and powers beyond those of mankind. People could believe and hope to change their tragic fate.

Sadeli realized they had a very long way to go. He had been very naïve with his romantic notion of knighthood. In the real world, there was a very fine line between a hero and a coward.

The knights of his dreams were now blurry. He faced a new reality. The evolution of humans shows how humans lived on their own in the era of the Peking Man and Solo Man. Then, after a painful process, thousands of years later emerged what we recognize as nations.

Could people nowadays leave the confines of nation and nationality and become free men, members of the whole of mankind? Could the United Nations, conceived from the bloodshed of World War II, open the path to that? Could this be what David Wayne was looking for? Could there be a basic instinct within oneself to kill and suppress another person?

Sadeli was snapped back into reality when someone called his name. He lifted his head and saw Amir standing in a boat rowed by another person. Sadeli was pleased. This meant the fishermen had finally arrived. He looked at his watch. Eleven thirty. *How fast time passes*. He rose and waved. The rower saw Sadeli's signal and quickly navigated the boat toward him.

Sergeant Amir jumped out of the boat carrying a Bren and ammo. "The villagers are here. There are only twenty of them," he said, "The engine is done, and they have started unloading the cargo."

Sadeli slapped Amir's shoulder. *Now there's hope to get out of this trap.* He ordered the rower to return to the ship and help out. Then he and Amir sat down, leaning against a mangrove tree.

"How are Idrus and Mukmin doing?" Sadeli asked.

"They're pretty calm now. They're just wounded."

"Did you see Pak Umar Yunus?"

"No, Sir. We went through different creeks. Really, you'll get lost here if you don't know your way. There are just too many creeks crisscrossing one another. The fishing village is very small. There are only dozens of houses there, but they were quick to help. The awareness of our revolution had reached their village already. They said the Dutch sea patrol often stops by for inspection, but the Dutch leave them alone. There's no police in the area. They actually don't have a village chief either. They live as one family and mind their own business. I wonder how they learned about our revolution."

"They must go to places to sell their fish and heard there that Indonesia had proclaimed its independence."

"Was there a big battle here, Sir?" Amir's voice was filled with regret for having been sent to the village and thus missing the whole battle.

"Yes. The Dutch attacked three times. Twice here, and once at Umar Yunus' location. Mukmin and Idrus were shot in the second battle. I don't know what happened to Umar, Darwis, and Yahya. The Dutch also showered the forest with their cannonballs. It was a massive attack. Luckily they only hit the mangroves."

"Yes, we heard the rumbling noise from afar." Amir looked at Sadeli, his hero, in admiration. His eyes were filled with a burning desire to be in a battle.

"Syafei is right across." Sadeli pointed and added, "He's alone now. Hopefully the enemy airplane won't show up before our ship moves to a new place."

They waited. And waited.

Amir took a pack of cigarettes out of his pocket and looked at Sadeli for permission. Sadeli nodded and reached out for one.

Sadeli lit his cigarette and enjoyed the pleasant aroma of Virginia tobacco. He noticed his muscles and nerves had loosened up a bit. Moments earlier they were so tense they resembled a tight violin string on the verge of snapping.

The cigarette smoke slowly spiraled and disappeared among the leaves. Sadeli and Amir sat in silence with their own thoughts and memories. Suddenly Sadeli remembered Umar Yunus. He wondered if it would be right to simply turn him in to the military court like he planned initially if the man had fought courageously and faithfully. Sadeli felt he had to consider and value Umar Yunus' courage and loyalty in the battle. If Umar Yunus fought like a warrior, Sadeli felt he had to find another solution.

Suddenly an evil thought crept into Sadeli's mind. If Umar Yunus were killed in this battle, his dilemma would be solved. He quickly dismissed the thought. A soldier shouldn't think that way.

Sadeli wondered if Umar Yunus missed Rita. Did he long to return to her arms? Sadeli wondered why he couldn't see Rita the way Umar Yunus did.

Sadeli sighed. Humans were complicated. He suddenly felt exhausted and checked his watch. He startled when it showed twelve thirty and he quickly looked for the sun. It was high in the sky. The wind had stopped blowing. It felt as if the earth were holding its breath, terrified to see humans who were about to kill one another. Dark clouds loomed in the western sky.

"It'll be even better if it rains long and hard," Sadeli said.

Amir looked up in the same direction. "They're pretty close," he agreed.

Then they went back to waiting. They waited for the dreaded airstrike, for the bombardment of the cannons from the corvette. They waited for the lifeboat attacks. They waited and wished for the rain and storm.

"Amir, how old are you?"

Amir lifted his head. "Twenty-two, Sir."

"You were born in 1925. What do you remember from the Dutch occupation era?"

"Oh God, Sir, everything. I was born in Binjai, near Medan in North Sumatra. I went to Singapore during the Japanese occupation with my uncle who had moved there long before the war."

"Did you think of our nation's freedom when you were a kid?"

"Oh yes, Sir. I was a member of the Indonesian Boy Scouts. I was only fourteen years old at that time and I remember receiving a warning from the police not to sing *Indonesia Raya* when we marched on the street."

"You didn't like the Dutch?"

Amir laughed. "How could I, Sir? I hated them and I hold a grudge against them. They were such snobs. My father was a teacher in a plantation village. The administrators of the plantation acted as if they were kings. They violated the women. They treated the coolies like slaves. When a coolie ran away, they hunted him like he was a wild animal. When they caught him, they whipped his back to pulp."

"What about the Japanese?"

"The same thing. Even worse. We've been oppressed by other nations long enough, Sir."

"Amir, have you ever starved before?"

"Yes, I starved a lot during the Japanese occupation."

"Have you ever been sick and too poor to pay for the doctor or any medication?"

"I have, Sir."

"Were you ever without clothes?"

"Yes, Sir." Amir gave Sadeli a puzzled look.

"How did you manage to survive?"

"People helped me. Someone took pity on me."

"Amir, we revolt, we're staging this revolution now so that we won't have to depend on people's pity. Do you understand?"

"Yes, Sir."

"Before God's presence, your value as a human being is no less than that of the king of England, for example. Or Gandhi, or the president of the United States, or Stalin. You're no less than President Soekarno, Hatta, Syahrir, or any other general, and even myself. Do you know that?"

"Yes, Sir."

"That's why we're here, Amir, fighting the Dutch, who want to destroy our dignity as human beings. Lift your head high, Amir, and look anyone in this world in their eye without fear or feelings of inferiority."

"Yes, Sir."

"That way we fear no death. We're the new Indonesian men. Do you know what our revolution for independence will do for our nation?"

Amir, who had read the *Undang-Undang Dasar* 1945—the Constitution of Indonesia—

quickly answered, "Yes, Sir, we'll be a country based on *Pancasila*, the five principals of Indonesian ideology."

"What do you want from our Pancasila-based country?"

"Well, Sir, we, the common people, don't like to be oppressed or to starve. We want to live well, to be able to buy clothes, and medicine when we're sick. We like to have a house to live in, and more importantly, we want our children to have an education and develop themselves."

"That's right," said Sadeli, "education is extremely important. It will prevent our nation from continuing to live in the dark ages. We have to spread science and knowledge to as many people as possible. Only then the freedom of thinking and speech will have meaning. Don't ever forget, we are humans, not cows."

"I won't, Sir."

"Humans require more than just a full stomach. Humans need freedom for their minds and souls. Do you understand this?"

"Yes, Sir."

"Really? Explain it to me."

Amir frowned, then said, "It's like this. If someone calls something black, but I actually see it as white, then I have to be able to say: no, that's white."

"Good. You got it. Don't you ever forget that. Just remember, it doesn't matter if the one you're speaking with is someone with authority. If you disagree, you need to be brave enough to defend your opinion."

Amir was proud of himself. He was proud of joining the fight to claim his dignity as a human being, the dignity that the Dutch and Japanese had repressed all this time.

"That's what we're fighting for," Sadeli said. "In our independent country, there won't be anyone blackmailing others, or the government oppressing and leeching out the common people. There won't be any other places of political exile like Tanah Merah, Boven-Digoel, or prisons to detain people with free minds like the one in Sukamiskin. We fight so that in our country, lies won't turn into truth, cruelty won't turn into justice, slavery into freedom, suffering into prosperity, or something evil magically turn into something good."

"Yes, Sir."

"We have nothing to fear. Not even death. If we die, millions of Indonesians will continue our fight."

The sound of an airplane suddenly pierced the air. Both men sprang to their feet and looked up, peering through the gaps between the branches and the leaves as they tried to locate the plane. All of a sudden, the atmosphere turned tense. The air trembled as the sound grew closer. Suddenly Amir shouted, "There, Sir." He pointed south.

Sadeli looked in the direction Amir pointed and located an airplane heading toward the sea from the south. It was a B-26 marauder.

Sadeli imagined the crew of the Dutch corvette jumping for joy as they saw the plane coming. They must have waited for this all morning. Now they could attack and destroy his convoy.

Umar Yunus, Darwis, and Yahya also noticed the presence of the plane.

Sadeli worried about the Shalimar. He wondered if the ship had moved and was properly camouflaged. He hoped it would be invisible from the air. He managed to calm himself and think of every possible scenario. The plane circled above the sea. It was high enough to avoid any light ground artillery. It flew along the estuary, following the river. Searching. The air roared and shook as the plane made a turn to fly along another creek toward the sea.

All of a sudden, Sadeli made his decision. He would hide as long as possible. The enemy plane couldn't possibly fly indefinitely. At some point, it would run out of fuel and have to turn around.

Sadeli looked at his watch. It was a little past two in the afternoon. He wondered what the plane's airbase was. It could be Medan, Palembang, or Jakarta. Depending on the distance from the base, the radius could actually be calculated.

When the plane flew further inland to move in a bigger circle, Sadeli jumped up. He and Amir loaded the weapons and dynamite in their lifeboat. Sadeli said, "Hurry, we must pick up Syafei."

They rowed quickly across and hid the boat under the mangrove trees. Syafei helped them pull the boat deeper under the mangroves.

"Let's just get back to the ship," said Sadeli, "We must avoid the battle for as long as we can. We must also call Pak Umar Yunus back."

They waited until the airplane flew over the second time. After the plane flew away, they quickly jumped into the lifeboat, crossed the river to the bank on the opposite side, and rowed under the mangrove branches. Sometimes the branches hung low and blocked their way, forcing them to move out into the open. When the airplane approached, they had to stop and wait until it went away.

Sadeli signaled Umar Yunus; he fired two quick shots followed by two long ones.

As they continued to row, the enemy plane started to shoot during its sixth time circling the area. Starting with the estuary, it aimed at places that appeared to be good ambush spots. Further inland, they targeted places the speedboat could be hiding.

Sadeli, Syafei, and Amir pulled their lifeboat under the mangroves, jumped to the bank, and ran to find a hiding spot in the swamp among the mangrove roots. The airplane sounded like the roar of a vicious tiger jumping its prey. The air trembled violently and the helplessness it caused created fear. They sank their bodies deep into the mud.

When the enemy airplane dropped bombs about a tenth of a mile ahead of them, the earth shook. The bombs landed right on a spot of dense mangroves. The enemy must have assumed they hid their speedboat there. When the plane moved away to start a new circle, they all sighed with relief. Sadeli signaled and they quickly jumped into the boat and rowed away.

A few moments later, they heard the airplane return and they went back into hiding. This time the plane attacked the riverbank opposite them. Right after the plane left and circled far inland, they climbed into their lifeboat once more. Sadeli was happy to notice their speedboat was not where he left it. Captain Sow Chiu had moved the ship.

The three of them laughed. Then they heard the airplane attack the area where Umar Yunus lay in wait for the ambush. Shielded by the mangrove branches, they managed to keep going. They carefully looked for the speedboat.

Sadeli spotted the shallow water Captain Sow Chiu had mentioned. In the next one hundred yards, the river forked. They stopped under a mangrove tree, undecided. In the distance the enemy plane still shelled one of the waterways. Then they suddenly saw another motorboat. The Dutch corvette had sent another lifeboat to attack.

Sadeli made a quick decision. They jumped on the bank, pulled the lifeboat behind the mangrove trees, and covered it with leaves and branches right away. Each carrying a weapon, they split to find a good position.

"Don't shoot before I do," Sadeli said.

The sound of the lifeboat grew nearer. They saw it come around the bend, followed by another. A light machine gun perched on each of their bows. The tension rose as they waited and contemplated if they should let the Dutch boats pass or ambush them.

Apparently, one of the Dutch soldiers had spotted Sadeli's hidden lifeboat. The Dutch boat suddenly turned around and fired. When bullets hit the dynamite cans on the boat, one great explosion shook the air and was followed by another.

The boat was shattered. Pieces flew in every direction; nearby trees toppled as if smacked by a giant. The Dutch boat was close enough to receive part of the rain of wooden planks, iron parts, and branches.

The helmsman of the first Dutch boat steered back toward the sea, and so did the second one.

Sadeli and his men were lucky to have picked spots some distance away from where they hid the boat. Sadeli still held his fire.

A few moments later, the enemy plane came and, flying low, dropped bombs. Some landed close to where Sadeli and his men hid. "Cover your ears and lift your chest off the ground," Sadeli shouted as he demonstrated. The ground shook ferociously. Water, mud, trees, boughs, and branches flew in every direction.

They held their breath. Their bodies were as taut as a bow being drawn to the brink of snapping as the plane lifted, only to dive back down and drop bombs a second time.

The bombs tore the air once more, and smashed the earth over and over. It felt like an eternity before everything around them fell silent again and there was no more rumbling and shaking, no more airplane sound and motor noise. The explosions had ceased and the showers of bullets, bombs, branches, and leaves had stopped. Death and its demons had moved on.

Sadeli lifted his head from the ground. A little crab ran right in front of him into a hole in the mud.

He looked around the river. It was empty. The enemy's boat was out of sight. Sadeli sprang to his feet. The sky was void of the enemy plane. He was glad to still be alive. He turned around to look for Syafei and Amir. They all looked at one another, then everyone broke into a wide grin and threw their arms around each other.

"Now let's hurry back to the ship," Sadeli said.

Since their lifeboat was destroyed, they had to walk. It was an arduous trip. The mangrove-covered swamp was soft and some areas were knee-deep. They often stepped into a deep hole and it felt as if the mud was starving and tried to swallow them. Amir, who headed the line, stumbled a few times. His military training made him automatically lift his arms above his head to save his Bren. When he fell into a shoulder-deep hole, Sadeli and Syafei had to work hard to pull him up. After that, they decided to make a detour to avoid that impossible area of the swamp.

They were exhausted after fifteen minutes. Their clothes were torn and they were covered in mud from head to toe. The Bren they carried was muddy too. Sadeli ordered a five-minute break. They each were allowed to smoke one cigarette before they continued.

It took them forty-five minutes to reach the river fork where the Dutch boats had attacked them earlier. It would have taken them only a few minutes if they had their boat. They tried to spot their ship from the riverbank.

Sadeli checked his watch. It was past four. He wondered if they should swim. He formed a funnel with his hands and let out a raven cry, "Caw, caw-caw."

A few moments later, from somewhere across from where they were, another raven cry answered, "Caw – caw – caw." It was Umar Yunus. They deliberated if they should try crossing the river. The sun was low in the west. The shadows of the mangroves on the seemingly still water had grown longer.

Then they saw a boat and two rowers approach. They recognized Umar Yunus and Darwis and wondered where Yahya was. As they pulled closer, Sadeli saw Yahya lying on the floor of the boat. He was dead. He had died in the battle, sacrificing his life for freedom. There was no higher sacrifice. Yahya had given his most priced possession in this world.

Sadeli, Amir, and Syafei jumped into the boat as soon as it reached them.

"Just follow this slough," Sadeli said. "They moved the ship. It seems you fought a great battle."

"Yes," Umar Yunus said, "Yahya was shot when the Dutch lifeboat started to fire. He was hit right in his forehead. Bad luck. We managed to send them back and after that came the airstrike."

Sadeli looked at both men. They too were covered in mud and looked exhausted, but their eyes were lit with a confident fighting spirit, a soul-burning spirit of freedom.

"Yahya fought courageously," Umar Yunus said, "He was the one who ran from one spot to another."

Sadeli nodded. "Mukmin and Idrus were shot. They're on the ship now. Did you hear my signal shot?"

"Yes, and we moved right away. The trip was extremely difficult; we had to take cover a lot so the enemy plane wouldn't see us. Where's your boat?" Umar Yunus asked.

"Destroyed. The enemy hit the dynamite on board."

"I thought it was a bombing attack on our speedboat."

When they came to another fork in the river, they crossed, and when they reached the middle, a long cry filled the air: "Heeere." It came from the river, but they didn't see anything.

"Heeere," the voice called again. Then, about a hundred and ten yards away, the dense growth by the river parted and Captain Sow Chiu waved at them.

The speedboat was neatly hidden. They could only spot it when they were really close. Branches and leaves covered its entire hull. The captain had done a very good camouflage job. There was no evidence of any clearance of the trees around the ship.

They quickly boarded the ship. Sadeli rushed to check on Idrus and Mukmin. They were conscious and smiled at him. Sadeli put his hand on their foreheads.

Captain Sow Chiu said they had not reloaded some of the cargo yet. It was still hidden near the ship's initial mooring spot.

"Where are the fishermen?" Sadeli asked.

"They're hiding in the forest."

"Call them. The Dutch airplane has left and won't return. It's almost dark. We'll take turns to be on watch. We'd better load our cargo before it's really dark."

Captain Sow Chiu asked a sailor to fetch the fishermen. As if by magic, small boats appeared from the mangrove forest and gathered around the ship. The captain introduced the fishermen to Sadeli.

"Merdeka!" he shouted.

"Merdeka!" they answered. Sadeli explained who he was and said the Indonesian government was deeply grateful for their help. On behalf of the government he would give them a small token of appreciation for their services. He ended, "Now, let's continue to work a little longer and load the remaining cargo. Merdeka!"

"Merdeka!"

"Merdeka!"

Their shouts filled the forest.

Sadeli ordered Umar Yunus, Syafei, and Darwis to oversee the loading of the cargo. They placed Yahiya's body on the deck by the stern. Sadeli had decided to bury him at sea. Captain Sow Chiu ordered them to swaddle the body and weigh it with something heavy so it would sink. A plank to launch the body into the water was placed. Then, suddenly, Sadeli felt terribly tired. He sat down on the deck and leaned against a crate.

He seemed to have gone through a nightmare. It was a great miracle that they were still alive and had the ship and its cargo intact. They were lucky they could hide in a river too small for the Dutch corvette to follow.

Sadeli's thoughts drifted to Yahya. *Poor Yahya.* There was no battle without victims. If humans wanted to change their fate, they had to be brave enough and willing to sacrifice, including their own lives if it called for that.

Sadeli washed his face, hands, and feet. He also washed his mud-covered wet shoes.

When the sun set in the west and twilight dropped the curtain of night from the sky, the boats returned with the remaining cargo.

Sadeli gave the fishermen some Singapore dollars and shook their hands. He asked for their kampong's name and made a note of it. The fishermen thanked him over and over before they sailed away into the dusk. For weeks, they would talk about their heroic act in rescuing an Indonesian ship from the Dutch airplane and corvette attacks.

Sadeli asked Captain Sow Chiu to give everyone a bigger portion of good food for the night. They had decided to return to the open sea at nine that evening.

Sadeli sat alone at the bow. The tension he felt from the moment the Dutch corvette began to chase their ship had released its grip on him.

Umar Yunus suddenly showed up and took a seat next to him. Darkness started to thicken around them.

"May I smoke?" Umar Yunus asked.

"Sure, it won't alert the enemy now."

Umar Yunus put a cigarette between his lips and struck a match. The amber light of the match lit his face for a moment. When he threw the burning match into the water it looked like a small red meteor. It burned out midway. In the darkness, the burning tip of his cigarette was like a tiny red dot on a black piece of paper.

"Pak Sadeli," Umar Yunus hesitated.

"Yes?"

"I'd like to talk to you. The battle today taught me a great lesson. Yahya's sacrifice changed me. I want to keep fighting with you. I'll do anything you want me to. I now realize my mistake and transgression towards the revolution. You were right. I'll return everything I can and give it to you."

Sadeli was very happy. A warm compassion for Umar Yunus emerged within him.

Umar Yunus misunderstood Sadeli's silence and quickly added, "You can trust me. It's not just because I want to return to Singapore. I'm sure Rita will agree."

"Did you really come to your senses?" Sadeli asked.

"Just test me."

Sadeli patted Umar Yunus on the shoulder. He didn't want to rush his decision.

"Fine. I'll give you my decision after we escape this deadly trap."

They sat quietly in the dark. The sounds of nocturnal insects filled the air. Mosquitos buzzed. Every now and then they slapped themselves where they felt a mosquito sting. There were strange plopping sounds coming from the water, like things dropped into it. Amidst the nocturnal sounds, a roaring and growling sound came from afar.

It was hot. Dark clouds that had filled the sky since the afternoon predicted a torrential rain. Every so often, lightning struck and parted the dark sky. Thunder roared in waves.

"Would it be better if it rained now?" Umar Yunus asked.

"Yes," Sadeli answered.

"One thing became very clear to me when the Dutch attacked. When Yahya was shot and I felt I would die just like him, something whispered, 'Do you wish to die a traitor?' I suddenly could see myself without being clouded by self-interest. A human being cannot just work for his own needs. My happiness and Rita's happiness are closely linked to that of others."

"True, you're absolutely right." Sadeli remembered David Wayne and Inspector Hawkins. There seemed to be some eternal instinct that pushed individuals to seek and approach the like-minded ones to foster this greater understanding and respect among people. They had to pour this understanding, brotherhood, good intention, and respect toward human dignity drop by drop into the human heart.

A long crack of lightning split the sky above their heads, followed by a roaring thunder. The long-awaited storm now unleashed its force. Strong wind gushed and shook the entire mangrove forest. Waves formed on the river. Water poured from the sky.

Sadeli sprang to his feet. "Let's leave," he said.

Sadeli told Captain Sow Chiu to sail, and the captain nodded in agreement. He ordered his crew to remove all the branches and leaves that covered the ship. They had already moved Mukmin and Syafei when the rain started to fall.

The engine roared below the deck. They lifted anchor. A sailor at the bow held a rope to measure the water level. The ship moved slowly out of its hiding place on the river. It reached the fork and sailed toward the other estuary. From time to time, the sailor yelled out the water level after he checked his measurement rope. They could barely hear him in the storm. The ship moved slowly through the pitch-black darkness. Their only light source was the lightning when it struck every now and then.

They moved yard by yard. Sadeli lost track of time. He tensed as they came closer to the estuary. *Was the Dutch corvette still around? Which estuary did they patrol?*

Lightning struck and for a split-second they saw the open sea ahead of them. Then darkness wrapped around them once more.

Captain Sow Chiu turned to Sadeli, and Sadeli gave him a go signal. The captain gave an order to the engine room, and soon the engine turned faster. The ship rocked a little. They reached the estuary and sailed past it. The engine turned even faster and then they were out in the open sea. Captain Sow Chiu ordered the crew to increase the speed. Ten knots, twelve, fifteen, eighteen, twenty…and suddenly a red flame emerged from the darkness of the estuary behind them. A cannon shot was heard amidst the storm and a cannonball exploded in the sea far from the ship.

The Dutch corvette had caught them on their radar.

Captain Sow Chiu ordered an increase in speed. Twenty-two knots, twenty-five, thirty…the ship zigzagged to avoid the corvette's cannonballs.

The corvette kept firing, but missed and was slowly left far behind. Captain Sow Chiu slowed the ship to twenty-five knots. He was worried the engine would break down again.

Some time later, when the storm had passed and the sea was calmer, Sadeli ordered Umar Yunus to prepare a burial for Yahya. He wanted to give Yahya a military funeral. Everyone gathered around the launching plank where they had placed his body. Darwis, Amir, and Syafei served as the rifle party to perform the salute, while Umar Yunus acted as the commander. Captain Sow Chiu ordered a slower speed.

"In the name of the Merciful and Forgiving God," Sadeli prayed, "we, the friends you left behind, surrender you, Yahya, to the Almighty. You were still young. You fought courageously. And you left ahead of us so that this nation can have its independence and happiness. We promise to continue your fight. Dear God, please forgive our friend's sins. Dear God, please accept his soul and may he rest in peace."

Umar gave the signal. They pushed the plank into the water and performed the volley salute. Yahya's body slipped into the water and disappeared into the darkness of the sea and the night. Sadeli felt tears well up in his eyes. His voice was hoarse when he said to the captain, "Now off to Sumatra."

Chapter 9

Back in Singapore

The radio in the corner of Mai Sung's bedroom played "Traumerei." Sadeli lay on the bed and listened to the mellow violin with closed eyes. They had returned from Sumatra three days ago. He had personally delivered the sad news to Yahya's family. Umar Yunus had accepted his demotion to first lieutenant and promised to take care of the financial issue as soon as possible. Dr. Banerji had secretly tended to Mukmin and Syafei's wounds. Sadeli smiled as he remembered the doctor saying, "Actually, I have to report any firearm wound to the Singapore police. But since, according to you, this happened in Indonesian waters, this becomes an Indonesian affair, doesn't it?"

This morning, Sadeli had received a radiogram saying David Wayne's plane would return from Yogyakarta via Bukit Tinggi and was scheduled to land in Singapore tomorrow at noon. Sadeli was happy. He had sent a report to Colonel Suroso from Sumatra, and he hoped to receive his new orders through Ali Nurdin.

At the moment, his operation ran very well. The Malayan people showed strong support for the Indonesians. Sadeli hoped tomorrow additional intelligence agents would arrive to be stationed in Burma, the Philippines, Hong Kong, and Bangkok. He had also made contact with Indonesian students in India, Egypt, and even Holland. His work mounted and overwhelmed him. He would be really glad when the extra help Colonel Suroso promised finally arrived.

Sadeli was grateful to Mai Sung, who had helped him unwind. The tension and battle fatigue that seemed to almost snap his nerves had vanished. He felt content as he lay in her embrace.

***

When Umar Yunus woke up and saw Rita Lee asleep next to him, he forced himself to believe he was not dreaming. His life with Rita was a reality, and his kidnapping, the battle, and the chase by the Dutch corvette were nothing but a nightmare.

He had come home three days ago at eleven at night. When he knocked, he could hear Rita come running to the door and shout, "Johnny," with a worried yet hopeful voice. Turning the key hurriedly, she stammered, breathless, "Johnny, oh Johnny, you're back." As the door flung open, she threw herself into his arms. She laughed and cried at the same time as she pulled him into the house and sat him on the couch. "What happened? Where did you go for the whole week?" she asked and took in his tired face.

"We fought against the Dutch. We lost one of us and two were wounded."

Rita's eyes widened. "Where?" she exclaimed.

Umar Yunus then told her everything from the moment he was kidnapped. He told her he could only think of her and had tried to find a way to escape. He also told her how Yahya's death had brought him back to his senses and how bravely Yahya had fought. He ended, "After Yahya was hit, it was only Darwis and I facing death together. Rita, I realized then that if we want to live a dignified life, our actions need to warrant that. I don't think I can love you and be a coward and a traitor at the same time.

"We have to nurture our love with honor and loyalty. I want you to love me knowing that I am someone worthy of your love. I've decided to stop fooling myself and justifying my mistakes. This revelation didn't only come out of my recent combat experience, it also comes from the way you've loved me all this time.

"I've decided to return the embezzled money to Major Sadeli. Believe me, Rita, he's a good person even though he seems tough."

"Even after he kidnapped you?"

"He also demoted me to a first lieutenant."

"And now he's taking your money."

"Yes, and I still think he's a good man. The money was actually not mine, Rita. Just think, he captured me, and we were under Indonesia's jurisdiction. He could have thrown me into jail or had me executed. Instead, he allowed me to return here and work with him. Don't you think that's a miracle? At first I thought we would never see each other again. Oh, Rita, I really love you." Umar Yunus held Rita and kissed her.

Rita said, "Oh, I hate him."

"Don't. He's just doing his job. Now I know we all must do our job. We can't run away from it. Rita, do you understand now?" Umar Yunus was filled with hope.

Rita kissed him passionately on the mouth and held him tightly. "Do what you need to do," she whispered.

"Thank you for your love and trust, Rita. Your love makes me want to be a better person." Umar Yunus felt happy and at peace. He had been freed from the dark shadow of his past mistakes and violations. He had regained the pure spirit and soul of the revolution he had felt in the early months of the revolt, when everyone was ready to make sacrifices without expecting anything in return.

Umar Yunus remembered an incident during the early days of the revolution. He was driving and he hit a bike rider who came out of nowhere and crossed the road. The rider fell hard to the ground and the front wheel of his bike was severely bent, but when he wanted to give the man money for the damage and medical treatment, the biker refused. The man eyed Umar Yunus' military uniform and proudly said, "No, Pak. Never mind. We're in this fight together. Merdeka!"

Umar Yunus held Rita and buried his face between her breasts. He would do everything in his power to protect their happiness.

***

The next day, David Wayne landed in Singapore. Their flight went smoothly. Ali Nurdin had reported to Sadeli and delivered a file with new instructions from Colonel Suroso.

Sadeli now had to arrange the itinerary for the agents who had flown in from Yogyakarta. Two of them were to continue on to Manila, two others to London, another one to Cairo, and the last one to India. He had to give each of them clothing and money for the trip.

It was late at night when Sadeli finished studying the file. Colonel Suroso said the Linggarjati Treaty would be officially signed in March. The treaty would acknowledge the government of the Republic of Indonesia as the de facto government over Sumatra and Java. Signing the treaty was a bitter pill for the Dutch to swallow, but served as a tactic of both parties to buy more time.

Meanwhile, the Indonesian Republic continued its efforts in expanding the revolution. They would penetrate other islands from Java and also Singapore to trick the Dutch intelligence. Undercover agents posing as long-time Malayan residents would go to Kalimantan and Sulawesi. An official representative of the Indonesian Republic would soon be stationed in Singapore. The Indonesian intelligence had received a tip about the Dutch plan to expand their territory on Java and Sumatra. The Dutch wanted to seize the plantations in West and East Java, and East Sumatra, as well as the oil fields in South and North Sumatra. A military skirmish was bound to happen.

It was crucial to develop a financial strategy to fund the revolution domestically and internationally as quickly and comprehensively as possible. The government planned to sell the remaining opium stash the Dutch and Japanese had left behind, abroad. The drug was illegal in Indonesia except for medical purposes.

A higher frequency of flights was needed to transport the opium and other goods like gold. Singapore, Bangkok, Macao, and Manila had been chosen as trading centers. The Indonesian secret agents in those places had been instructed to make all the necessary preparations and establish networks and a mutual understanding with the related government agencies to carry out this operation smoothly. Colonel Suroso also requested plastic bombs to sabotage the Dutch's armory. He put Sadeli in charge of the operations in Singapore, Malaya, Thailand, Macao, and the Philippines.

Sadeli felt relieved after he burned the secret instruction file. He was happy the Republic of Indonesia would soon have an official representative in Singapore. Every political, propaganda, and diplomatic task would fall on his shoulders. Sadeli would be able to concentrate on the secret intelligence operations he was assigned to. He needed to meet with Wahyudi, their agent for Bangkok, before he departed.

That night, Sadeli dreamed of climbing a very high mountain. It was a tough climb. He slipped many times, but kept on climbing. When he finally reached the top and looked around, he saw a fascinating view.

First thing in the morning, Sadeli met with David Wayne and Pierre de Koonig at a seaside villa. They deliberately chose that spot for security reasons.

The three of them sat at a table under a lush pine tree by the beach with a view of clear open sea. The sun was bright and the air fresh.

"Well, we're back from your country." David Wayne buttered his bread and shaved some cheese.

"*Et vos femmes—uhh!*" Pierre de Koonig kissed his fingertips as the French did when discussing something marvelous, "*Elles sont merveilleuses. Quelle charme! Quelle beauté!* I'd risk being shot down by a Dutch airplane to know them!"

Sadeli laughed. "Don't make me miss my homeland," he said and turned to Pierre. "I'm going to ask you to fly to Indonesia again. I received new orders. Where can we get two or three more planes? At least one that can land on water, like a Catalina. Can you help? Oh dear, I forgot to ask. Will you still fly for us?" His voice was filled with hope. "Did you talk to the people there? What do you think? Did they convince you about our revolution?"

"Umm..." David threw Pierre a questioning look.

Sadeli became a little worried and was puzzled when David and Pierre burst out laughing. Both men rose. They pulled Sadeli out of his chair, embraced him and slapped his back so hard it hurt and made him think his ribs would break.

"Hey, hey, stop! Are you trying to kill me?"

David and Pierre laughed until tears rolled down their cheeks. After everyone was seated again, David said to Pierre, "He asked if we want to fly to Indonesia again."

"How dumb," Pierre said and they both laughed again.

Worried they might pound his back again, Sadeli was ready to jump up.

When they were done laughing, David said, "We will fly to Indonesia again. We want to help your revolution. You have no idea how happy we were to witness your freedom fight. We talked to a lot of people. We talked to your commander, Colonel Suroso. What a great and idealistic patriot. We talked to your ministers, political leaders, youth, and soldiers. I've never seen such true fighting spirit. I think I found what I've been looking for: the resurrection of the human spirit to foster a brotherhood in freedom and dignity.

"What an exquisitely rich country you have. When we flew over the large island of Sumatra, we saw beneath us the green forest and tall mountains, a tapestry of rice fields and rivers, with villages tucked between the greenery.

"We also flew along the southern beach of Java, over Mount Merapi, and the Borobudur temple near Yogyakarta. Then we met the people. Their fighting spirit was overwhelming, such pure idealism. Of course we will help you. I just pray you understand how to maintain the sanctity of your dream. You basically have the same spirit as the people of France when they proclaimed *liberté, fraternité, égalité*— liberty, fraternity, equality—in the Revolution on July 14, 1789. And hundreds of years later, the very slogan they shouted on the streets of Paris has become an inspiration for other nations' revolution. Tyranny and cruelty, be it by a dictator, a party, or a group, is our common enemy we must fight against, wherever it may be. Liberty must spread to every corner of the earth. No one is free as long as others are oppressed."

At that moment, Sadeli felt really close to the American and Frenchman, Inspector Hawkins and other like-minded people. There were no more cultural, racial, or religious differences among them.

He felt pulled into the current of humanity, an awareness that all humans were the same and were brothers. This was a new understanding born of the cruelty, viciousness, destruction, rivalry, and hatred of World War II that slaughtered millions of people.

"I'm so happy to have met you," Sadeli said, "after being locked in darkness by the Dutch for hundreds of years, Indonesians are now stepping out into a bright world. I thank you for sympathizing with our revolution."

"Your revolution is our revolution. Your independence is our independence. During the war, the Allied Forces proclaimed freedom to be every nation's right, but now we see our countries seem to have forgotten those promises. The United States is helping Holland to rebuild their country, which enables the Dutch to go to war in Indonesia," David said.

"And my country wants to bring imperialism back to Indochina," Pierre added.

"Now, let's go back to our task," David said. "So you need more planes?"

Sadeli nodded.

David closed his eyes, thinking. "Where's Tomahawk now, Pierre?" he asked.

Pierre shrugged. "You know him. He's probably in Antarctica or perhaps Tibet."

"Tomahawk is his nickname," David explained, "His real name is Black Hawk, he's a Native American from New Mexico. He's a very skillful and brave pilot. It will be great if we can involve him."

"The problem is how to find him. He also flies a Dakota and flies for hire anywhere in this world. His co-pilot—Dave, you remember his name?"

"Yes, Wilkens or Willikens—Bill. Last time I heard, they did a charter flight between Manila and Bangkok."

"Can we send a telegram to him in Manila?" Sadeli asked.

"Yes, we should do that. He always stays in the Manila Hotel," David answered.

"Okay, please do that. The sooner he comes, the better."

Sadeli remembered the information from Colonel Suroso about the possibility of the Dutch military invasion in mid-1947, between May and August. It was important to work as quickly as possible. "And a Catalina. Where can you get one?"

"I remember Jim Dougherty flew a Catalina. But the last time I was in Bangkok, I heard he was in Canada," Pierre said.

"A month ago in Hong Kong, I heard a Catalina did a chartered flight in China. I'll look into it when I reach Bangkok and I'll let you know."

"Alright," said Sadeli, "you two take care of the Dakota in Manila and the Catalina in Hong Kong. I'll wait for your news here. Are you flying back to Bangkok today?"

"Yes, around noon. We happen to have a load."

"Okay, but I won't see you off. I still have to prepare the cargo for your Indonesia-bound flight next week. I'll send you a telegram when it's time for you to come."

They shook hands.

"Merdeka!" Pierre and David exclaimed.

"Merdeka!" Sadeli responded.

Sadeli went to Ali Nurdin's news agency. Ali Nurdin took him to the office where they could talk privately.

Sadeli ordered Ali Nurdin to find plastic bombs to sabotage the Dutch armory. "We'll send those bombs straight to Colonel Suroso in Yogyakarta. David and Pierre will do it. I'll contact the dock and custom workers who sympathize with us."

Ali Nurdin smiled. "I think we can do that." He sounded worried when he continued, "Back in Yogyakarta, I heard the Dutch might attack as well. Can they seize Yogyakarta?"

"Well, probably. From the beginning we planned to fight using guerilla tactics. Why do you ask?"

Ali Nurdin blushed. He seemed a little embarrassed, but was unable to hold back the happiness that filled his heart and he had to share it with another person. He blurted out, "I met Nani in Yogyakarta."

"Nani?" Sadeli raised his eyebrows, not understanding.

Ali Nurdin suddenly realized that Sadeli had no idea who Nani was and told him about his unrequited love story in Jakarta during the Japanese occupation. "I met her in Yogyakarta unexpectedly," he said. "I was walking along Malioboro when I saw her across the street in front of *toko* Oen. I thought she was in Jakarta. I called her and she turned my way. I ran across the busy street and so did she. We met in the middle of Yogya's main shopping street. Her eyes were shining and erased my doubts. And so…" Ali closed his eyes as he reminisced before ending, "so we got engaged. We'll get married after we win the revolution. That was the greatest success of my Yogyakarta trip."

Sadeli laughed and congratulated Ali Nurdin. "That's further proof that we can never really know a woman. She remains an attractive and arousing mystery," he said.

"I'm so happy." Ali Nurdin beamed.

Sadeli looked at Ali Nurdin and was a little envious. He wondered why was he unable to find a woman who could evoke a deep sacred love in him and make him feel he couldn't live without her. Was he not capable of loving? Was it because he had a shallow soul? Or was he too insensitive? He knew a lot of women, but never met one who could make him want to share his life with her.

It wasn't that he disliked women. He loved to go out with women, and while he was sexually attracted to the opposite sex, his relationships had always been purely physical and only fulfilled his biological needs. He had never wanted to live with a woman and have children with her.

When he looked at his friends, like Ali Nurdin right now, whose face glowed with love, he questioned why such love never happened to him. Was it because he had been single for too long? Or because he was too revolution-crazed? Duty-crazed? He saw himself in a different light and he didn't exactly like what he saw.

Deep inside, Sadeli began to feel dissatisfied about his situation. It started with Umar Yunus and Rita, and now it was Ali Nurdin and Nani. He had always suppressed these feelings by telling himself: *You're an intelligence agent in the middle of the revolution. It's not the time to think about such things.*

It wasn't good for a revolutionary to think about the future. People could die anytime. The revolution demanded sacrifice. A fighter was better off alone. If he had to die, he wouldn't make anyone grieve over him. He could just vanish like a stone dropped into a pond. The ripples on the surface wouldn't affect other people. Then another disturbing thought surfaced. *Am I satisfied with this kind of life? To disappear from the face of the earth without leaving anything behind for other people? A child would mean an heir.* He wondered if there was any grand goal for human existence and if so, what it would be. It seemed humans existed merely to live, just like the animals and other living creatures.

There had to be a higher goal that set humans apart from other living beings. He thought about the evolution of the human, starting from the chimp and the prehistoric human who began using tools; something to hit or to dig with, a stone to throw, a lace of tree bark to tie with, leading to the use of fire. Now, eons later, humans seemed able to produce anything they could imagine, constantly reaching new levels in science, art, technology, and other fields.

The dark wild nature of humans, which was carried over from their early civilization, would not simply go away. Therefore, among the peaks of human achievements were the deep valleys of their evil and destructive nature. Cruelty, viciousness, inhumanity, war, and oppression still prevailed. The advanced technology provided humans with destructive means like the atomic bomb, and humans' destructive nature turned their own inventions into a great threat to their own safety.

Sadeli started to see concrete forms for these new thoughts. He started to see that eventually, all humans had to foster a fraternity.

Being a good nationalist alone was no longer enough. The fate of one's own country was intertwined with the fate of all other nations. To be a good nationalist, one had to be a good internationalist. An idealistic attitude might not always go well with the bitter reality of this world. Nowadays, no one was a true hero or a true villain. Life remained cruel. People had to learn to take care of themselves and their society.

"Eddy, are you tired?" Ali Nurdin's voice interrupted his thoughts.

Sadeli lifted his head and gave Ali a little smile. "No. Something suddenly occupied my mind. Ali, take good care of your love." He rose and left.

Ali Nurdin looked out of the window and watched Sadeli walk down the street until he got into a taxi. Ali admired Major Sadeli. He was a man of steel.

Syafei and Mukmin had told him about the great battle to defend the speedboat. Although he was at first puzzled why Umar Yunus was allowed to return to Singapore, he could accept Sadeli's decision after he heard about the loyalty Umar Yunus had shown in the battle.

During his time in Yogyakarta, he had the chance to visit Semarang and witness the spirit the revolutionists fought the enemy with. He was certain of Indonesia's victory. And at the end of the tunnel, Nani would be waiting for him.

Ali whistled a happy tune, thankful for having made the bold decision to leave for Singapore. It had been a bold decision since his news agency had told him they couldn't finance the trip with so much as a dime as they had no resources. He left with the $50 he had painstakingly earned and eleven pounds of silver artwork from Yogyakarta a friendly merchant had given him.

Before Ali Nurdin met Sadeli, his situation had almost overwhelmed him. He had nearly run out of funds, yet hadn't done much. And now…he looked around his office. He heard people typing, and his mind went to Nani. His future was intertwined with the future of the revolution. He would give everything for the victory of the revolution because he would be doing it for himself. The victory of the revolution would be his victory. He could even imagine a house with Nani and their children.

Chapter 10

On the Hong Kong-bound plane, Sadeli held the telegram he had received yesterday from David Wayne: *The baby is born. Come. Please hurry. Dave.*

Sadeli understood it meant Dave had found the Catalina they needed but seemed to be facing some sort of problem.

It was Sadeli's first time to Hong Kong. When his plane made a transit stop in Bangkok, he remembered Derek Scott and Sheila. He was glad he didn't have to see them again. He still couldn't forget what had happened between him and Sheila and wondered how Derek actually knew about it.

As an Easterner he was too sensitive to accept the incident as something normal. He couldn't wrap his head around the fact that Derek accepted his wife being a nymphomaniac and happily lived with the consequences. He probably would never know the story behind the two of them. There were always parts in a person's life that had to be kept private. Sadeli let out such a deep sigh, the elderly British lady next to him turned and asked, "Are you ill, Sir?"

Sadeli smiled and said, "Pardon me. I'm not ill. You will laugh at me if I tell you why I sighed so deeply."

"Ah, now you're making me curious, Sir. Please, do tell." She took off the glasses she had used to read her Graham Greene novel.

179

Sadeli almost regretted having aroused the old lady's curiosity, but he couldn't walk away now. "Well," he said, "I was thinking how difficult it is to really know a person. Everyone resembles a puzzle that hides a secret. Just when we think we know who a person really is, something happens that leaves us stunned and doubtful whether we really know that person."

"Oh, you're too young to worry about such matters," the old lady said, "Accept what life gives you with a smile."

"Yes, but people are always curious."

"I'm telling you, you're too young to bother with these issues. Believe me, leave it to the long-haired philosophers to figure things out. Where are you from?"

"Oh, forgive me. I'm Sadeli from Indonesia."

"I'm Mrs. MacDougall. My husband is a merchant in Hong Kong. Where did you say you're from? Indochina?"

"No, Indonesia."

"Pardon my ignorance," she said, "if Indonesia is not Indochina, then where is it? You look like a Filipino, or a Malayan, or perhaps a Thai."

Sadeli had no choice but to explain the history of Indonesia starting from before the Dutch occupation until the revolution era.

"Oh, then the island of Bali is part of Indonesia now," she said, "My husband and I went there in 1938. It was fabulous. We Scots used to battle the English to defend our independence. So I truly understand your fight. The ruling Labour Party in Britain will grant independence to their colonies like Burma and India. I heard that from my husband's friends in London. Perhaps the domination by the whites in Asia will end this year."

"Are you happy with the way things are going?"

"Quite. We're merchants. According to my husband, Asian countries will need products from the West for a good while. Trade will flourish. My husband thinks colonialism is an outdated practice designed to guarantee the market the sources of raw material. It's not efficient. It's too expensive, not just financially, but also morally."

"Your husband has a very interesting view. I've never heard anything like that before. If only the Dutch would learn from Mr. MacDougall."

Mrs. MacDougall laughed.

"My husband said the expenses for the soldiers, the army, the navy, and the human souls are too high for the colonizer to shoulder. A good trading relationship is much better."

"Your husband is a shrewd merchant."

"Yes, he's been working in mainland China for forty years. He only moved to Hong Kong after the war was over. During the war, he worked in the region controlled by Chiang Kai Shek. My husband said that because Chiang Kai Shek's clique is corrupt, he would eventually lose to the Communists. That's why he moved his office from Shanghai to Hong Kong."

"You've lived in China for a long time. Are the Chinese aggressive?"

"Isn't every nation?" Mrs. MacDougall continued, "Everywhere history bears the blood of people killed in wars. I myself went through two World Wars. Not to mention other wars in other countries, simply too many to mention."

"I'm sorry, that was a stupid question." Sadeli smiled and added, "But it was motivated by the position of China as the giant of Asia. People must know their neighbor as well as they can, mustn't they?"

"True. It's easy. You surely know Chinese history. They have been pushing south for centuries. In fact, the Mongolians have attacked as far as Eastern Europe. Overpopulation, limited fertile soil, extreme poverty; aren't all these great explosive forces?"

"Is there a cure?"

"Don't ask me," Mrs. MacDougall said, "I'm just a wife, a caretaker of the house. It's you, Sir, and every other leader of this new world who must solve this. You know how poverty can degrade human dignity to the level of animals? I've seen with my own eyes a father sell his thirteen-year-old daughter to a man. I know what I'm talking about because the man was Mr. MacDougall, my husband. We bought that girl. My goodness, she was so cheap. A puppy in Britain would have cost more. The girl is all grown up now and married. She lives in Shanghai.

"Have you ever seen people die of hunger? Not one or two, but thousands, tens of thousands, hundreds of thousands, and even millions? Do you know how to eliminate hunger and all kind of fears from the face of this earth? That's a job for you and people like you.

"Ten years ago, when some friends asked my husband to enter politics, he refused because he didn't want to become another failed leader, one who begins with the best of intentions but soon finds himself corrupted by power. However, you, Sir, are part of the young generation that stepped forward after World War II. Can you foster a happier and more peaceful new world?"

"Why us?" Sadeli asked.

"You're the independent countries in Asia and Africa. In the last centuries, the western countries have proven their inability to maintain peace and happiness for mankind. Can you now provide a better example? For instance, how will you solve the problems among nations? Will you, the new countries, still use the worst possible way, which is war? Or will you set a better example? Will you have a greater wisdom?"

"My, I don't know," Sadeli said, "You have such extensive knowledge that I feel I don't know anything."

"That's the beginning of wisdom," Mrs. MacDougall smiled. "You're very wise."

The flight attendance's voice filled the cabin, asking all passengers to fasten their seat belts. They were heading for turbulence.

Sadeli and Mrs. MacDougall stopped talking. A moment later, the plane went through the turbulence, churning the passengers' stomachs. Right when some of the passengers reached for the airsick bag, the plane suddenly leveled. Sadeli sighed with relief. He threw a worried look at the pale Mrs. MacDougall, who already held an airsick bag on her lap. He was afraid he wouldn't be able to hold his stomach if she vomited. It would be a disgrace to have a major of Indonesia's intelligence service throw up on a plane.

The plane leveled and the passengers started to unbuckle their seat belts. The flight attendants offered mints and refreshments. They had barely relaxed when the flight attendant asked them once again to fasten their seat belts. Apparently they were close to Hong Kong and would land soon.

Sadeli looked out the window. His seat was quite far from the wing. The blue ocean was beneath him. Some junks appeared like tiny ticks on the water. When the plane turned it was as if a screen was lifted. Little by little, the view of Hong Kong Island and Kowloon appeared. China's vastness was everywhere he looked. From up there, everything, except for the white buildings here and there, looked bluish-gray. Then the plane made another turn, and flew over a crowded harbor full of ships, junks, and motorboats. The third time it turned, the plane descended, and landed with a small bump.

Drizzle fell softly when Sadeli helped Mrs. MacDougall walk down the airplane stairs. The runway was shiny, as if it had just been freshly coated with a new layer of asphalt. A few flight attendants provided umbrellas for the passengers. Sadeli left Mrs. MacDougall in the care of one of the stewardesses.

"Don't forget to drop by," Mrs. MacDougall called after him, "I gave you our address. My husband would love to meet you."

Sadeli walked toward the immigration area. It didn't take long to get clearance. After waiting a few moments, he claimed his suitcase. The custom officers didn't ask him to open it. After a few questions about his luggage they handed him his suitcase.

Sadeli walked out of the airport and hailed a taxi. "Princess Hotel." It was where David Wayne was staying. They arrived at the destination some fifteen minutes later.

When Sadeli checked in, the front desk clerk said, "Oh, are you Mr. Sadeli?"

"Yes."

"There's a letter for you from Mr. Wayne." The clerk rummaged through a box. He took out a long envelope and handed it to Sadeli.

"Where's Mr. Wayne?"

"I don't know, Sir, but he's still staying here. Should I call his room for you, Sir?"

"Please give it a try. Thank you."

The desk clerk picked up the phone and asked the operator for David's room. After a few moments, he put down the receiver and said sadly, "No answer."

Sadeli nodded and looked at the clock on the wall. It was four in the afternoon.

The desk clerk rang a bell and handed a bellboy in a maroon uniform a key. "Room 368."

"When Mr. Wayne arrives, please tell him I'm here."

"Very well, Sir."

The bellboy carried Sadeli's suitcase and led him to the elevator. They exited on the third floor and walked down a narrow, red-carpeted corridor. The bellboy opened a room door and beckoned Sadeli.

The medium-sized room had a private bathroom and a big window. Sadeli looked out of the window and took in a busy street and layers of roofs.

Hong Kong.

He used to hear a lot about this city. It was the British's beautiful trade center in Asia, and it was the first British-ruled city that Japan attacked and took over. Hong Kong, a city where people could rocket into either wealth or poverty.

After tipping the bellboy, Sadeli lay on the bed and played back everything that had happened, like a movie on the screen of his memory.

So many things had happened since he first arrived in Singapore. In just a short time, Sadeli's experiences had amounted to what might have taken other people their entire lives to achieve.

Chapter 11

On the blank screen of his memory, the battle against the Dutch marines at the river unfolded. He heard all the explosions and whizzing bullets in the mangrove forest and again worried he would not make it out alive.

Once again he grieved for having to surrender Yahya's body to the sea. He played a tape of his childhood. The furthest he was able to reach back was when he was five. He had broken a glass and his mother scolded him. That was the first time she scolded him. It was also the only time. He could not remember her ever doing it again.

Then he recalled the battle to take over the Japanese armory. Different memories flashed through his mind. His first woman, Zainab, and the ones after her. He tried to count the women he knew and recall their faces, one by one. The images started to blur after around ten women.

Sadeli dropped off to sleep and dreamed. He drove a car in the rain along a steep and winding uphill road. The road was very slippery. Suddenly his car broke down and began to slide down the road. He stepped on the brake, but to his surprise, the brake didn't work at all, and the car slid even faster. He braked over and over, to no avail. Deep ravines gaped at him. Fear started to set in and he gasped. The car moved faster and faster. He slammed on the brake once more, and this time the car stopped right at the edge of a deep ravine.

He restarted the car. The engine turned over when he stepped on the gas pedal and resumed the climb up the mountain. When it reached the peak, Sadeli stopped the car.

The panoramic view was splendid. Terraced rice fields covered the hill slopes and stretched into the bluish-gray horizon. The ripe grain glowed like gold under the sun.

All of a sudden, he heard a woodpecker. It probably was looking for something to eat; knock-knock-knock-knock. He looked around for the bird and spotted it in a nearby tree when someone called his name, "Sadeli. Sadeli. Sadeli."

He woke up with a start. Someone was knocking on his door and calling his name. *Ugh, I fell asleep.* He jumped to his feet and answered the door. "David."

"You bloody rebel. You just sleep all day," David teased.

Sadeli was suddenly fully awake. He pulled David into the room and said, "I left as soon as I received your telegram. What happened? Did you get the Catalina? Where's Pierre? How's Derek?"

"Ho, ho, hang on. One at a time. I got the Catalina, but Jim Gantry, its pilot and owner, is nowhere to be found. I've been looking for him these past two days. Zero."

"What can I do?"

"I didn't call you here to find Jim Gantry. Instead, it's for something which I'm sure you'd be interested in."

"Weapons?"

David nodded.

"Bazooka. Machine gun. Anti-aircraft cannon. Radar. You can get everything if you agree with the price. The weapons have been paid for with the American taxpayers' money to fight the Japanese and were given to the Kuomintang. Now, the Kuomintang generals offer those weapons to anyone who's willing to pay the price."

"Where?"

"Not far from Macao's border."

"Macao," Sadeli said, "Who can we discuss the price and delivery with? Do you know these people?"

"Oh I haven't gotten that far. I think it's better if you handle it yourself. I'll just take care of the plane."

"But…" Sadeli suddenly hesitated, "isn't that illegal? I mean, are those high-ranking Kuomintang officials stealing their own weapons?"

David nodded and smiled.

"Take care of your country, Eddy," he said, "Don't let it become like this Kuomintang. In the beginning, Sun Yat-Sen's Kuomintang held fast to its idealism to dedicate themselves to the people, but now, they have become a greedy octopus that squeezes the people dry. A small yet powerful clique within the organization are making themselves richer and richer. Politicians are corrupt, as are the bureaucrats and their generals. Moral values crumble, and the people suffer. No matter how hard my country tries to help them, it won't work. The seed of their destruction was planted within them by their own leaders. One day the people will stand up against them. This happens everywhere, Eddy. If leaders only wish to fulfill their own needs, if they tell lies, get involved in promiscuity and become accustomed to a luxurious lifestyle by ignoring their people's needs, they are actually planting their own seed of doom."

"I don't mind buying their stolen weapons," Sadeli said, "What matters to me is winning the revolution. I'd even buy the weapons from Satan himself if I have to. But I agree with you. Truth and justice are more than abstract concepts. These words have a deep meaning; they are like seeds that sprout in unthinkable places. Seeds that have an amazing resilience. Tens or even hundreds of years of oppression can't kill them. Do you remember, Dave, the rebellion of the slaves in Rome led by Spartacus? The seeds of truth and justice even then lived in the soul of a slave. What do you call that?"

"Should we call it the human spirit?"

They were quiet for a moment, and then Sadeli asked, "Do you have a religion, Dave?"

"What do you mean? I was born into a Protestant family. I went to church when I was little, but I also seek God outside my church."

"The human spirit. If humans or human ambitions give life to the seeds of the abstract elements we mentioned before, wouldn't the human soul then become a part of God's own holy spirit? Wouldn't there be a godly substance within each and every one of us? A substance that, from time to time, encourages humans to do things beyond their capability?"

David Wayne looked at Sadeli and remained quiet for a few moments. Then he said, "I honestly don't know, Eddy. You may be right. The whole universe is still such a mystery. What or who was its creator? Does this universe have a limit? Or is it infinite? Are there other creatures out there on the stars in our galaxy? Are they like us in any way? Or do they have a different shape and form because they went through a different evolution in different surroundings?"

"You know, Dave, when I'm alone under a clear starry sky, I like to speculate on how big this universe is. My brain can't even imagine the speed at which light travels: 186,000-plus miles per second. This universe is extraordinarily big and shrouded in deep, complicated secrets that humans may never, ever figure out. Maybe we humans need this, so we won't stop looking, and keep on searching for the truth from generation to generation."

"That's thought-provoking," David said. "It's just we're not patient enough to find the answer in our lifetime. But you must still be tired from your flight. I shouldn't have dragged you into this kind of talk."

"No, I'm not tired at all. I want to see the city before dinner. When can we see the Catalina?"

"Tomorrow. It's in Macao."

Sadeli showered and dressed. It was around five when they stepped out of the hotel into the cool afternoon air. People, cars, and double-deckers crowded the narrow Hong Kong streets. For a few moments, Sadeli felt overwhelmed by the constant movement of people and vehicles, the vibrant colors of the shops and noises of everything rolled into one. It was as if he had fallen into a jumble of colors and sounds and ever-moving tires. It took some time before his senses were able to distinguish and separate the entities.

He took in the shops, the passersby, the restaurants with hanging duck and pork in the display windows, the rickshaws pulled by a human instead of a horse. He was fascinated by the young Chinese women who strutted in their cheongsam with flirty high side-slits that showed a glimpse of the woman's fair legs.

He smelled various pleasant food aromas and the overpowering fragrance of garlic.

They stopped a taxi to take them around the city and up into the hills where the villas were. The villas had looked like tiny dots when viewed from the plane. The view of the city and its surroundings was stunning. Sadeli said, "Hong Kong is more Chinese than Singapore, but has the British discipline."

David laughed. "The British discipline is just on the surface. The Chinese have their own lives and secrets. Besides the wealth and luxury, poverty also exists here."

David pointed at clusters of houses and shacks on the slope of a hill. They were nothing but small boxes made of crates and old board. Old tins were used to construct a roof. Paper covered the cracks to block the wind. People lived there without water, electricity, toilets, or bathrooms. The stench of human excretion, animal dung, and other filth lingered in the area, filling the nose and saturating one's senses. Here, the paupers lived on top of one another. Here, the raw and rough life was openly displayed. The source of human disgrace flowed here. Barefoot children fought over whatever was edible or usable and competed with the dogs crowding around them.

Sadeli promised silently that he would fight and work to keep such injustice from happening in his country. It was a total disgrace to have one hill display the epitome of poverty while the opposite hill glittered with overflowing luxury. "I'm sure," he said, "when my people get their independence, this kind of situation won't exist. My country's soil is extremely fertile; it's huge and very rich. Its earth holds gold, oil, coal, nickel, and iron. Its forests are vast; there's no shortage of water. Its sea is full of fish. Ah, Dave, we can create heaven on earth in my country. The chain of Indonesian islands is a beautiful and fertile garden. All this time, the Dutch have exploited our natural riches."

"I'm glad to see you happy. You do know freedom is not the only key to foster prosperity," David said solemnly.

"I do," Sadeli sighed. "You'll tell me to look at the banana republics in South America, where dictators and oligarchies terrorize and suck their people dry."

"Look also at America, my own country," David said, "We've enjoyed our independence for more than a century, but we are yet to eradicate poverty, injustice, and stupidity. Our young men and women sacrifice their lives for dreams of independence and humanity while the black people in our own country are second-class citizens. In the south, they continue to be segregated, oppressed, and marginalized. So there you go, Eddy, independence alone is not enough. It's not a guarantee for freedom from fear and hunger, for the freedom of speech and religion. You know what happened in independent Germany under Hitler, independent Italy under Mussolini, independent Russia under Stalin. There are many other examples."

"Yes." Sadeli let out another sigh. "You're evil, Dave. Everything you said made me worry about what may happen in my country after we win. I don't want to think of all the bad possibilities you mentioned." Sadeli shook his head as he tried to erase all those negative images. No Indonesian leader could possibly turn into that kind of an evildoer.

"We will foster the tradition of individual and collective freedom, and practice law-abiding citizenship. We will use our freedom responsibly. We'll foster social discipline and communal responsibility. We'll develop the tradition of honesty, truth, and justice. It'll take patience and wisdom. Dave, by nature, our society, especially on Java and Bali, still has a strong tie to old feudal tradition. The existence of leaders who lead by example means a lot.

"There is a proverb, unique to Indonesia, that says, '*Guru kencing berdiri, murid kencing berlari.*' It means, if the teacher pees while standing, an action prohibited in Islam, the student does something even worse, which is peeing while running.

"Our leaders live a humble life. They don't accumulate their own wealth. They have become accustomed to sacrificing for the people during the fight against the Dutch colonization. Just so you know, the monthly salary of our government ministers is not more than the monthly salary of a construction worker in your country."

"I'll pray you guys will be able to keep the humility you practice during this revolution all the way into your independence."

"I'm sure we will."

Their taxi stopped along the shore. They got off and Sadeli paid the fare. It was dusk and the sky turned rapidly darker. Different types of ships, boats, and junks covered in lights filled the harbor. From a distance, the sea's surface looked like a fair illuminated with red, white, yellow, green, and orange lights that lit the sky and reflected on the water.

"Let's eat." David led Sadeli into one of the many boats waiting by the stairs. Most of the boat drivers were noisy women who aggressively vied for passengers.

David and Sadeli boarded a boat taxi and David mentioned a Chinese floating restaurant.

Sadeli marveled at his surroundings. Women were engaged in all kinds of activities. Some cooked, others sewed, some breastfed their babies, others played cards. Then there were those who argued with their men, fixed odds and ends, and slept on the deck. A few boats carried couples. Their boat quickly maneuvered between the floating theaters of life.

David pointed at a brightly lit floating restaurant. Sadeli paid the boat lady. A waiter greeted them and seated them at a table on the side of the deck.

"What's so special here is that the fish is still alive and we can choose it ourselves. The snapper is really good. Do you like snapper with young bamboo shoots? What about crab and egg drop soup? Do you want rice or noodles? What do you want to drink? Beer? Whiskey? Or maybe a taste of Chinese rice wine?"

Sadeli laughed. "Do you think my stomach is a bottomless vat? Let's eat the authentic Chinese way and drink the Chinese rice wine, but just a little for me; I don't like alcohol that much."

David gave the waiter their order.

Sadeli said, "The number of people in Hong Kong is mind-blowing; they even overflow into the sea."

"Who knows whether our science will advance so much that humans can build cities on the ocean floor?" David said.

Sadeli laughed. "Like Flash Gordon?"

"You read that?"

"Yes, when I was at school, in a Dutch magazine called *De Orient*. I enjoyed his adventures as he moved from one planet to another across the galaxy. Theoretically, using the force within an atom, humans can free themselves from gravity and fly into the sky above. It's just a matter of technology."

They chatted while waiting for their food. Somehow their conversation moved to their personal lives and they felt close enough to each other for David to ask, "Are you married, Eddy?"

"No, haven't met the right one."

"Don't you like women?"

"Hmm, I love them."

"I once loved a woman. Lucy," David began his story, "Remember I told you about her in Bangkok? I was really in love with her. We were engaged, but then came the war. I went to war, and Lucy met someone else. You never experienced being heartbroken, have you? It's really, really painful. I suffered for a long time. Only after my heart started to heal could I understand and stop blaming her. I still love her. Sometimes I wonder if my endless wandering really is about hunting for the truth, or is it just me going after Lucy? Can I find another Lucy in another country? Has your revolution become my Lucy for whom I would gladly sacrifice my life?" David went silent.

Sadeli did too, as he didn't know what to say.

"Eddy, it's hard to live with an empty heart. You have to have a woman you love. A man is not complete without one."

Sadeli's recent restlessness stirred once again inside him. "I hope I'll get married someday. Hopefully she'll be pretty and rich." Sadeli tried to lighten the mood.

"Eddy," David didn't pick up Sadeli's cue, "look at the table in that corner. Isn't she beautiful? Do you like her? Now look at the dashing man next to her. They seem very happy among their guests. Watch how her eyes are full of love when she looks at her husband. Do you see that?"

Sadeli nodded.

"Well, let me tell you something, Eddy. Tomorrow noon, when her husband is at work, that lady will be in the arms of a British officer who is her lover. As for her husband, he will find another woman to make love to. They don't love each other, but they're not getting a divorce. What kind of marriage is that?"

"My view on marriage is a little old-fashioned," Sadeli said. "For me, marriage means more than just a man and a woman living together. It's also about a union of heart and mind. Sex also plays an important role in a happy marriage. I will never share my wife with another man, like…" Sadeli thought of Sheila Scott in Bangkok and he suddenly blushed. He and David looked at each other. And he knew David knew.

"Eddy, don't blame yourself about Sheila. Derek surely told you there's something wrong with her. She's a great artist, but she can't help herself when it comes to sex. She will charm any man. Derek should have told you. You were prey to her sudden attack. So were Pierre and I, and many other men. Derek knows, but he also knows it's her illness. He doesn't want to confine her or put her in an asylum. It will kill her. Derek loves her. Can you understand?"

Sadeli closed his eyes and tried to imagine being in Derek's shoes. When he opened his eyes, he said, "I'll try, Dave. I'm sorry."

"There are some hidden parts in life which simply ask for special consideration," David said.

When their food arrived, they were so hungry their conversation was limited to praise of the delicious soup and fish.

"I prefer Chinese food over famous French cuisine," David said.

"I never tried French food, but in Indonesia we also have some dishes worthy of competition. There's *sate*, different kinds of skewered grilled meat with an appropriate sauce," Sadeli explained to David, "and grilled chicken with coconut milk sauce, *rendang*, a spicy beef stew, grilled fish with sweet soy sauce, *sambal,* a hot pepper relish, *gado-gado*, or *pecel*, a cooked mixed vegetable salad with peanut dressing and *soto*, a spicy chicken or beef soup." Sadeli suddenly felt a deep longing for Indonesia and the food he just praised.

David asked, "What's your best childhood memory?"

"Waking up early on *lebaran* and being bathed by my mother. After she helped me put on my new clothes and shoes, I spent the whole day with my family and friends, eating cookies and getting money." After Sadeli explained lebaran he asked, "And what about you?"

"The kiss and hug from my mom in the morning and at night before going to bed."

"I love that too. You still remember that, don't you?"

"Yes, I was probably five or six at that time, or perhaps younger, but I remember."

"What's your worst memory?"

"Oh, I have to think about it. What's yours?"

"When my dad scolded me and I went to my mother for consolation, and she scolded me instead," Sadeli said.

"Mine is when my cat died. I cried and didn't eat the whole day."

"And what was your happiest moment?" Sadeli prodded.

"Oh, the birth of my younger sister, Pamela. I really like her. She's so cute. Here's her picture." David reached inside his pocket for his wallet and took out a picture.

Sadeli expected to see a cute and plump little girl, but the photo was nothing like that. "She's pretty," he exclaimed.

David laughed proudly. "Yes, she is. You'll like her. If she were here, she'd be thrilled to be with us. She's never been here and would love to see this place and visit your country as well. Who knows, after you win the revolution and you become a general, maybe you'll invite Pam and me to visit Indonesia." David raised his little wine cup. "To the independence of Indonesia. And Pam's visit to Indonesia."

"Merdeka!" Sadeli sipped his rice wine.

David asked, "Do you like sports?"

"Yes, swimming, tennis. You?"

"Horseback riding and fishing. When I flew over Sumatra and saw the sparkling rivers flowing down the mountain and also the lakes, I really wanted to fish there. Or hunt."

Sadeli told David what he could hunt in Sumatra, which rivaled Africa: elephants, bears, tigers, leopards, rhinos, alligators, mountain lions, and deer. He said, "Talking about tigers, when tiger season comes, those tigers roam even to the villages. They steal people's goats, monkeys, or cows. Once, I went on a road trip from Padang to Kerinci at night, and our headlights caught tigers walking down the road dozens of times. I also saw a mountain lion up a tree by the road. Do you like hunting tigers?"

"That would be really great."

"Later, after we win the revolution, you, Pierre, and I should explore Sumatra from its northern parts all the way down to the south. We'll hunt, catch fish, climb the mountain, and go camping. It'll be wonderful."

"Yes, we must do that some time." David beamed and Sadeli continued, "Don't forget the birds. We have grouse, spotted dove, and quail, delicious when fried. Then there's deer and mouse-deer."

"You make me want to go there as soon as possible." David smiled.

"I suddenly want to go home too. What do you hunt in America?"

"Oh, nothing much left. Deer, wild geese, bobcats, squirrels. Very few bears. Animals are very much protected there because people have been hunting for a long time and driven some species to extinction. It's America's extraordinary crime and idiosyncrasy. Buffalos, which in the past populated vast savannahs, are now almost extinct. Only a few of them are left in conservations. Seriously, Eddy, although my country is industrially and technologically advanced, we've been wasting our natural resources. A lot of animals are extinct and great forests are cut down. Now that it's too late, some people are beginning to raise an alarm."

"What is it like, living in your country? Does everyone really have the same chance? Can a child from a blue-collar family be the president or a general, and can a farmer's kid become a billionaire?"

David laughed. "That kind of chance still exists, but it's not as easy as people think. In the end, only the smart and hardworking ones make it, and yet, not all of them succeed. Perhaps money plays too big of a role in our society, but family values and friendships are still pretty strong. The dangerous thing about us Americans is the big trust we place in technology and industry. It's as if all human needs were just some button-click away. After the era of mechanism comes automatism, and now I heard they're doing experiments to make machines think to replace the human brain. Will all that bring happiness? I don't know."

"Ah, we have yet to deal with that kind of problem," Sadeli said. "We're still dealing with the lack of machines, technology, and industry. We are inefficient with our manpower and we waste a lot of it. Think about it: millions of our farmers spend their entire lives swinging their hoe day by day in the field or garden. And they only harvest a little more than what their family needs. If we, for example, replace their labor with a tractor, one farmer will be able to feed a number of people like in America."

"Maybe more than a thousand people," David said.

"Right, so if our farmers can be this efficient through the cooperation system, imagine how much of their labor we can transfer to other fields of production. Look at our fishermen. They only use sailboats or rowboats. Their fishing gear is also very primitive while the sea around our islands is so rich. If we can equip them with machines and modern fishing gear, their catch will be able to meet the nation's protein needs. And fish will be cheap. Another problem we have is with the becak. Not only does the job of a pedicab driver degrade human dignity, it also wastes manpower. You're lucky you don't have these problems like we do."

"I hope my country will stay alert and can keep the balance between man and machine," David said.

Sadeli put the last piece of fish into his mouth, savored it for a few moments, then sipped his rice wine. After he wiped his mouth with a napkin, he said, "Thanks, Dave, for bringing me here. As far as I remember this fish dish is the best I've ever had in a Chinese restaurant."

"Is there a better one elsewhere?"

"Oh yes. The carp *pepes* dish in West Java. You have to try this spicy banana-leaf-wrapped barbecued fish one day."

Sadeli and David bickered over paying for dinner. Sadeli ended the squabble when he said, "It's my business expense."

Once again the boat drivers vied for them. After some hesitation, they finally chose one.

The boat driver, an old man, said, "Gentlemen, you want young girls? Virgins, Mister, not expensive. Very beautiful."

Sadeli and David were too content to heed the old man's offer. They felt at peace in their awareness of a close friendship and the realization that Americans and Indonesians were not that different. Sadeli remembered Inspector Hawkins, Umar and his Malayan friends, and also Pierre the Frenchman.

David recalled his friends from different nations who fought the war against the Nazis.

"You know, Dave," Sadeli said, "the only difference between you and me is color. My eyes are brown; yours are blue. My hair is black, yours is golden blond. My skin is light brown, yours is fair."

They laughed, carefree. Friendship filled their hearts. A strong sense of brotherhood made them realize that every human breathed the same air, including the old boatman who had just offered them virgins.

If they could foster this brotherhood among mankind, the sacrifices people made during World War II would not be in vain. David sighed.

Sadeli turned to him. "Are you happy?"

David nodded.

"Me too," Sadeli said and added, "I feel like singing. Would you like to hear a song of the revolution?" Sadeli took a deep breath before breaking into "Halo-halo Bandung" with full gusto.

David clapped when Sadeli finished.

The Chinese rice wine was starting to affect Sadeli. It made him light-hearted and he happily started a repertoire of popular Indonesian love songs. He sang "Jauh di Mata," and then "Bengawan Solo," and "Saputangan," before he closed with a Batak song, "Mandegdeg."

David thought for moment, then sang "Old Man River," a popular American show tune. His voice was clear and a little heavy. He sang it with all his heart. Sadeli sang along. David threw him a puzzled look but then laughed and together they belted out the song. Heads turned at them from every boat they passed.

Chapter 12

The next morning before eight, David Wayne knocked on Sadeli's door. Sadeli was ready to go.

David said, "Let's get something to eat first."

After they ate, they took a taxi to the harbor. Sadeli bought their tickets for the ferry to Macao. They found empty seats at the bow.

Passengers started to fill the ferry. Most of them were Chinese, but people of other nationalities were there as well. The ferry horn blew three times. The crew released the ropes and the boat set sail.

Most of the passengers were ordinary people. A lot of people commuted between Macao and Hong Kong for many different reasons. Sadeli canvassed the area and tried to identify secret agents from Britain, Portugal, Communist China, or the Kuomintang.

The wealthy-looking old man in a Western suit and tie could be an agent for Communist China who disguised himself as a capitalist. The coolie in a blue outfit and rubber sandals with a big basket near him could be a Kuomintang agent who pretended to be a civilian.

A young woman leaned against the ferry's railing with her hand supporting her chin as she looked at the open sea. Her cheongsam clung to her slender body and accentuated her curves. Sadeli wondered who she could be working for, the British, Portuguese, or Dutch.

199

He had always been attracted to Hong Kong, Shanghai, Singapore, Saigon, and Macao. Before, he only read about these cities in books about international espionage, but now he experienced them himself.

The ferry had reached the open sea. The sky was clear and two small islands appeared in the distance just before the Chinese coastline. David lay on the deck chair, closed his eyes, and sunbathed in the morning sun.

Sadeli decided to give up his search for any secret agents. He followed David's example and lay back, closed his eyes and surrendered his body to the swaying movement of the ferry. He heard the engine hum and felt the ferry tremble, a movement that started from its engine down below and traveled through the stairs and walls up to the deck, went up his deck chair and into his body. He heard the wood creak and the metal parts squeak as they rubbed against each other. He picked up conversations in Mandarin, which sounded like the loud buzzing of beetles. His nostrils filled with all kinds of odors and fragrances the passengers brought with them. The scent of garlic overpowered all other smells, although at times, the fragrance of coffee and perfume interrupted it briefly. Every now and then, he was jarred by the particular sound the Chinese made: the sound of people scraping their throats and spitting. Since the Chinese in Singapore had made him accustomed to this habit he could pretty much tolerate the grating noise. With the morning breeze caressing him and the sun massaging him, Sadeli's mind slipped between sleep and wakefulness. His muscles loosened and he relaxed completely.

His subconscious surfaced and he felt he could understand himself better at a more intimate distance. He wondered if given the choice between saving himself or performing a deadly duty, what he would do. Run, or perform his duty and die?

He hesitated. In the past, he had attacked the Japanese headquarters to seize its armory and fought the Dutch marines in Sumatra's swamps, coldblooded, without asking any questions. Sadeli sighed. He couldn't come up with an answer. Suddenly the attractive body of the woman at the railing crossed his mind and evoked erotic fantasies. The thoughts aroused his passion and created a warm sensation in his groin. Suddenly he desperately wanted to hold a woman in his arms. He remembered Mai Sung.

Sadeli could no longer contain his restlessness. He turned to David and asked, "Dave, have you ever been afraid?"

David did not open his eyes but answered, "Many times. Why do you ask?"

"I suddenly can't decide what to do if I have to choose between dying while fulfilling my duty or running away to save my life."

"At least it shows you're honest with yourself. Every warrior who faces death is confronted with that choice. During the war, I was always scared when I approached the target, knowing the enemy's anti-aircraft cannons awaited me. It's not about not feeling scared. It's about learning to control fear."

"You're right. Fearless people can do everything easily."

David chuckled. "Fearless people are not brave people."

They went quiet for a moment. Then Sadeli said, "I'm hungry."

"They serve food on board. What do you want to eat?"

"Fried noodles will be great."

They rose and David showed the way to the ferry's restaurant. It was full. They spotted empty seats at a table by the window. Sadeli was happy when the woman sitting at that table was the one he had seen standing by the railing.

They greeted her and asked if they could join her. The young woman nodded and smiled a little.

"May we introduce ourselves?" Sadeli started his advances. "My name is Eddy and this is Dave." They both bowed a little in their seats.

"My name is Maria," the young woman responded in fluent English.

Sadeli observed her closely from across the table. She had a gentle face with a small, pointy nose. Her mouth was small, but her lips were full. Her eyes were not too almond-shaped, and her shoulder-length hair was wavy. She was neither pure Chinese nor pure Portuguese. She was an attractive mixture of either Portuguese and Chinese or British and Chinese blood.

After he ordered fried noodles and iced tea, Sadeli asked, "Do you live in Macao or Hong Kong, Miss Maria?"

"It's missus, not miss."

"Oh, I'm sorry." Sadeli tried hard to conceal his disappointment. "Where's your husband?"

"Oh, he passed away."

"Please, forgive me." Sadeli blushed, embarrassed. He had gotten off on the wrong foot with this pretty woman.

"Ah, never mind. My husband was beyond evil. He drowned while boating with another woman."

Sadeli and David looked at her, somewhat shocked. They weren't sure if she was serious or if she simply wanted to confuse them.

Maria gave the men a once-over and burst out laughing, as if she had just discovered something very funny. David and Sadeli laughed with her even though they had no clue what she was laughing about. They all felt as if they had known one another for a long time.

"You," Maria said to David, "I immediately know you're an American. And you," she pointed at Sadeli, "are Filipino."

David and Sadeli laughed.

"Am I right?" she asked.

"Yes, yes." They nodded as they remembered their needs for security. Maria laughed happily. "What are you up to in Macao?" she asked.

"Being tourists, sightseeing. Trying our luck at Macao's famous casino."

"And trying to get to know its beautiful ladies."

Maria laughed. "I'm a Macao citizen."

"And you're beautiful," Sadeli quickly added.

Maria threw him a meaningful look, then nodded, accepting his compliment. She was happy to be the center of their attention.

Their food arrived. Maria had ordered spring rolls. She told them about Macao while they ate.

"It's actually a dead city," she said, "That's why I go to Hong Kong once a week to visit my friends. My father wanted to return to Portugal, but my mother, a Chinese Portuguese, didn't want to. My father has passed away. There are only mother, me, and my uncle from my father's side, but he has his own family. We live off my father's stocks in his and his brother's firecracker factory."

"Oh, does Macao have many firecracker factories?"

"A lot. We produce fireworks and firecrackers for Southeast Asian countries, and we also sell to the U.S., Europe, and South America."

"What are other big industries in Macao?" Sadeli asked.

"The casino, tourists and…smuggling." Maria smiled.

David and Sadeli laughed. "What do people smuggle in Macao?"

"Oh, everything. Gold, opium, heroin, stuff like cigarettes, nylon t-shirts, and humans."

"Humans?"

"Yes. A lot of Chinese want to live in Hong Kong, but the British limit the number of people who can stay. A special organization smuggles people to Hong Kong on boats or ships."

"How come you're this young yet know so many secrets?"

"Everyone knows and lives in the midst of them."

David said, "That's great, when we need assistance with smuggling, we have Maria."

They all laughed and joked about smuggling a thousand Chinese per month to Hong Kong. With a fifty-dollar profit per person, they'd make fifty thousand dollars per month. The three of them would be very rich, live in complete luxury, and wouldn't do anything else but travel around the world.

While they talked, David rose and said, "Excuse me, I need to go to the restroom. Don't wait for me here; we'll meet up on the deck."

After paying for the food, Sadeli and Maria walked to the deck. An old Chinese couple occupied their previous seats as they walked to the bow and found a spot by the railing.

A fresh sea breeze moved the air gently. They were surrounded by fishing boats as well as various other types of boats. Mainland China's shoreline stretched along the horizon.

"What a crowded area. Is it ever quiet?" Sadeli took out a pack of cigarettes. "Do you smoke, Maria?"

She nodded and Sadeli gave her a cigarette. When the wind kept snuffing out the flame of his lighter, she laughed and lit the cigarette herself. After she took a drag, she handed it to him. "Now give me another one," she said.

Her simple act captivated Sadeli's heart. He suddenly felt very close to her.

"What is it like living in Macao, Portugal's tiny colony at the doorstep of mainland China? Don't you feel you live in an underdeveloped era trapped in the past while mankind is creating new history around you at such a fast pace?"

Maria's expression turned serious and Sadeli found her more beautiful.

Maria said, "What a beautiful way to describe how I feel. Macao has no future. It's a shipwreck in the ocean of history. I want to leave. I want to live in a forward-moving new world. Many of my friends have left already. Some went to Portugal, but don't like it there because…" She hesitated for a moment before she continued, "Dictator Salazar strangles their soul. We don't have many options. The U.S. doesn't want to take us in and neither does Australia. Portugal or its African colonies are not appealing. The lucky ones can go to Brazil. Some went there and made it as a doctor, a singer, or a handyman. We too want to live happy and free, but I'm a woman and don't have special skills. I can play piano a little, cook, and sew, something I learned in the convent. I can speak Portuguese, English, and French, and I can type. I can be a secretary. A lot of people have those skills. Who needs a secretary from Macao?" She sighed.

Sadeli felt her despair as she did not see any light in the future.

"You're still young and beautiful. From our conversation, I know you're smart. One day you'll remarry and live happily with your husband."

"Ugh." She scowled. "One of the Portuguese men in Macao will give me six or eight children and still not be satisfied," she scoffed and laughed bitterly.

"Maybe you'll meet and fall in love with a foreigner who will take you to his country."

Maria laughed; she flicked Sadeli's forehead and said, "Oh, you're a romantic. Things like that only happen in romantic novels we secretly read in the convent." She added, "It never happens in real life."

"Don't you think our fate is in God's hand?"

"Ah, now you sound like Father Alvaro, our priest."

"What do you want from life, Maria?"

"That's a strange question."

"No, it's not. Something about you made me ask."

"You're a strange person. I never met a man like you. You compliment me just like any other man, but a minute later, you ask complicated questions like I were an item you want to analyze scientifically."

"You're also a strange young woman, Maria. I never met anyone like you."

Their eyes met and locked. Each tried to understand the other better.

Sadeli looked deeply into a pair of gleaming black eyes. The pools were so deep he felt he'd drown inside them.

Maria blushed under Sadeli's gaze filled with fascination and love. Something light, like the rustle of dry leaves in the fresh morning breeze, stirred within her. Startled, she averted her eyes and fixed her wind-blown hair.

Sadeli's voice trembled a little when he said, "I have a confession to make."

She looked at him, happy, a secretive smile curving her lips.

"I'm not Filipino," he said.

"I know," she laughed.

"You know?"

"Yes. I know some Filipinos. They have a totally different English accent."

"Wow, you're very smart. You could be a police commissioner. I'm an Indonesian."

"I've read about your country. English-language newspapers in Hong Kong write a lot about the revolution there. And you're a secret agent?" she asked.

Sadeli was so surprised that Maria couldn't help but laugh. "It's a very easy guess. Right now Indonesians are revolting against the Dutch. As an Indonesian, you should be there to fight. But, you're here. Surely you can't be a tourist while your country is at war. So…"

Sadeli raised his hands.

"Don't worry," she said, "I won't report you to the Dutch Consulate in Hong Kong or Macao."

Sadeli smiled.

"I like you already, and I don't want to see you executed as a spy. Your wife and kids will cry over you in Indonesia."

Sadeli reached for Maria's hand and said, "I'm not married. No child or wife will cry over me in Indonesia."

"Well, if that's so, I'll cry over you if you get shot."

Their eyes met again. Maria looked away and blushed even more. She freed her hand and pretended to take a handkerchief from her bag. "Look," she pointed ahead, "that's Macao." A white strip of walls, ships, and junks appeared on the horizon. "Is this your first time?"

"Yes."

"How long are you staying?"

"Oh, not sure yet. It depends on my job. Three days? A week?"

"Will you come again?"

"Now I want to."

"Now?"

"Yes, now that I met you."

"Ah, you're just playing like all other men."

"You know a lot of men?"

"Uh-huh."

"Do you like them?"

"They mostly just want to find pleasure. I don't like that kind of a man."

"Do you like me?"

"Maybe."

"A little?"

Maria nodded. "But I don't know you well enough yet."

"Yes, I know. And time isn't exactly on my side. You know that my country is at war."

Then Sadeli told Maria about Indonesia's history. He started from the prehistoric era when their ancestors came down the mountains of Indochina to travel to Sumatra, Kalimantan, Java, and Sulawesi all the way to Papua and beyond. The story continued to the kingdoms in Sumatra, Java, and other islands, the construction of Borobudur and the emergence of Balinese Hindu culture, up until the arrival of the Indians, Arabs, Chinese, Spanish, British, and the Dutch. Then he told her about the battles against the Dutch, their vicious acts, and later the crimes committed by the Japanese.

"But during the hundreds of years of colonialism, my nation never gave in, Maria, not even once. Our history is full of heroes who fought against the Dutch around the country throughout the centuries. Our soil is colored by their blood and filled with the bones of those who died fighting for their freedom. And now we raise our weapons once more because the world allows the Dutch to re-colonize us. Countries that promised freedom and justice during World War II no longer seem to remember their noble pronouncements. The cannons, tanks, rifles, and the bullets the Dutch shoot at us are made in America or Britain. Why? Why don't they allow us to be free? Don't we, Indonesians, have the same rights as the Dutch, British, Americans, or Russians? But some people from those nations help us, like David Wayne, the pilot. He risks his life for us. A lot more people help us, including the Indian and British soldiers in Indonesia.

"Maria, a new awareness is on the rise, it's still tiny, but it exists; an awareness that brotherhood among mankind is more important than anything else. We, the new generation, don't wish to act as stupidly as the previous generation, which spread wars and destruction on earth. We want to create a garden of peace and happiness for humans in this small world. That's what we're fighting for."

Maria looked at him with shining eyes. "How beautiful your words are. You really are a strange man. Plant your garden quickly, Eddy. I think I'd be happy staying there. It sounds really nice the way you described it. Are you sure it won't stay a dream?"

"Oh, it's a very long journey. I dream of it now, David Wayne dreams of it, a Brit in Singapore dreams of it, and so do people in Africa, Europe, Japan, Russia, the Arab Emirates, and Latin America. Our number will grow. More and more people will want it. Ten, twenty, or fifty years from now, who knows, it'll be a really powerful force."

"Oh, I'm happy listening to you. Your eyes are gleaming!" Maria held Sadeli's hand, and Sadeli squeezed hers. They held hands firmly, as if they received some kind of power in their journey on the sea of mankind's history.

"And in the meantime?" Maria whispered.

"We have to love as much as we can," Sadeli whispered back.

Maria smiled. She took Sadeli's hand and put it against her cheek. "*C'est très charmant,*" she whispered. Her lips formed a smile and her eyes gleamed.

"*Et tu es très adorable.*"

"You speak French?" said Maria, feeling very happy.

"Oh, a little. I haven't had a chance to use it. I remembered those French words, for they suit you."

They stood in silence, holding hands and looking at the approaching city of Macao.

"I feel like I've known you for a long time," Maria said. "It's very strange."

"So do I."

"Did God bring you into my life?"

"I'm sure God put you on this ferry, this morning, so I could meet you."

They went silent for a moment.

"Eddy."

"Yes?"

"Ah, never mind."

"What did you want to ask?"

Maria was silent.

"Look at that fishing boat. It's so close to our ferry!" She tried to change the subject.

"I prefer to look at you."

"Eddy," she said, still staring at the sea.

"Yes."

"I feel really strange."

"Me too."

"Do you know how I feel?"

"Probably the same as I do."

"And what's that?"

"I never felt this feeling I have for you."

Maria nodded.

"And you hesitate because we only met an hour ago," Sadeli added.

She nodded again.

"I do too. I'm afraid this is nothing more than lust. I'm afraid I won't make you happy."

Maria was quiet.

"And how little time we have to find out."

"While we are young."

"And the whole world awaits us."

"But…"

Sadeli sighed. He wondered if he could extend his stay in Macao to get to know Maria better, if he had the right to do so. He wondered if he should go after Maria and give this seed of love the chance to grow and find its sun. His conscience said *no*. It reminded him that he was a secret agent, a major in the Republic of Indonesia's intelligence agency. His first and foremost duty was to the revolution. He had to be ready to sacrifice his life for it despite the fact that now there was a chance for him to be happy with Maria. Sadeli suddenly understood how Umar Yunus could be tempted to do what he had done. The human heart is something very complicated and humans often were unable to control it. He concluded that the world was a cruel place that could prevent love between two people from growing.

"We don't have time, Maria," he said, "but I thank God I met you today."

The ferry's engine slowed as they approached the harbor. Passengers prepared to disembark.

"So this is it?" Maria asked, "We say *au revoir* here?" Her voice quivered.

Sadeli's mind told him to say *yes* and to go find David, finish his duty in Macao as quickly as possible, then leave and never give Maria another thought. However, his heart was stronger than his mind. He looked at her, the long, wavy black hair tucked behind ears displaying red coral earrings, her gentle face, her gleaming black eyes, her disappointed expression. He took in her youthfulness and his heart prompted him to say, "No, Maria. Can we please meet again?"

Maria opened her bag and scribbled her address and phone number on a piece of paper.

"Call me," she said, "Here's my number."

The ferry slowly closed in to the dock, and lowered the gangplank.

"Hey, you two." David's voice surprised them from behind.

Sadeli turned around and suddenly felt guilty for forgetting about him for so long.

"I fell asleep," said David quickly. "Here's your bag." He handed Sadeli a small travel bag.

They got off the ferry and walked out of the harbor. Maria hailed a taxi. Before she got into the taxi, she said, "Splendid Hotel is the best here."

Sadeli and David watched her taxi drive away before they hailed another for themselves.

"A very tempting woman," David said as they drove to the hotel.

"Uh-huh," Sadeli replied.

"And you moved fast."

"There's more to it than that, Dave."

"What do you mean? You fell in love?"

Sadeli nodded.

"And now you feel you can't live without her?"

Sadeli nodded again.

"Do you have her address?"

"Yes."

"Good. Call her. Invite her to dinner, take her dancing, go sightseeing with her. Take her to bed. If you still feel this way after a couple of days, well, you should marry her."

"That's the impossible part, David."

"Impossible?"

"You know my work. I can't get married before we've won the revolution."

"Hell!" David suddenly cursed. "During the last World War, tens of thousands of people got married right before they were sent to war. Many of them never saw their wives again. You go and marry her if that's what you want."

"Ah, you're crazy, Dave. It's impossible!"

David laughed. "You think life is something we can control like building a factory? Prepare this, arrange that, finish this first and that later? You want to finish the revolution before marrying Maria? Don't be stupid. I used to think that way and you know what happened. It's very rare for life to give us the same chance twice. It's also very rare for life to give humans happiness. You have to enjoy the happiness it hands you while it lasts."

The taxi pulled over in front of the hotel. They checked in at the desk and decided to go to their respective rooms despite the fact it was only midmorning. Sadeli had barely hung up his jacket and was putting his toiletries in the bathroom when the phone rang. He ran to the bedroom to pick it up. "Hello." He couldn't keep the quiver out of his voice, nor could he hide his disappointment when he heard David's voice on the line.

"It's done. We'll go see the Catalina. Jim Gantry wants us to come see him around five. It's only ten thirty now. I don't know about you, but I'm going to sleep. Have fun." David laughed as he hung up.

Sadeli put down the receiver. He fingered the note in his pocket with Maria's phone number then abruptly asked the operator to call her.

The phone rang, but no one picked up. He imagined the phone to be located in a big and empty room. After it rang several more times and he almost gave up, someone picked up and a woman said in

Portuguese, "Hello, this is the residence of Dona de Abburizi. Who's speaking?"

Sadeli answered in English and told her he would like to speak with Dona Maria.

"Oh, wait a moment, I'll get her."

Sadeli heard the woman call, "Mariaa! Mariaaa!" He heard Maria answer from afar then the clacking sound of shoes on the floor. Happiness wrapped his heart when he heard Maria's melodious voice on the line.

"Maria speaking."

"It's Eddy."

"Oh, Eddy." Her voice echoed the happiness he felt when she answered the phone.

They were silent for a moment, each waiting for the other to say something.

Sadeli felt like he could hear Maria's heartbeat through the phone; it traveled through the wire into his ear. "I'm free till five. Can I come over?"

"Oh, that's wonderful. Come quick. Just grab a taxi. I'll be waiting."

"*A bientot*," Sadeli said and hung up.

He was jubilant. He grabbed his jacket and rushed out of his room and into the street. A few taxis were waiting. Sadeli went to the closest one and gave Maria's address to the driver.

"Yes, Sir." The driver opened the taxi's door for Sadeli.

After a short, fifteen-minute ride, the taxi turned into a narrow street and stopped in front of a house with white walls.

Sadeli paid the taxi and walked to the front door. It had a sun carving in the center with Portuguese writing above it: *Casa del Sol.* House of the sun. How beautiful. It suited Maria perfectly; she was the sun he had found on the ferry.

Sadeli pressed a button and he heard light running steps approaching. The door opened, and Maria stood in front of him. She welcomed him with a wide smile, and her happy face glowed like the sun.

"Maria."

"Eddy," Maria whispered. She reached for Sadeli and pulled him in.

"Welcome to my house. You must meet my mother first. She is a little under the weather and in her bedroom. I thought you wouldn't call. I've been waiting."

Maria held Sadeli's hand as she walked him through the big house furnished with antique furniture and paintings on the walls.

Maria stopped in front of a portrait of a good-looking man with a moustache, sharp eyes, and broad forehead. "My late father," Maria said, "Now let's meet my mother."

Maria walked ahead of him, climbing a broad staircase, crossing a carpeted landing, and then stopping in front of a door. She knocked and called, "Mother."

A soft voice answered.

Maria opened the door and pulled Sadeli into the room.

An old Chinese woman sat on a rocking chair by the window. The sun rays lit her gentle face when she turned toward them. Sadeli noticed how beautiful she still was and looked into a pair of very calm eyes.

"Maria, who is this young man?" the old woman asked in Chinese.

Maria told her mother about meeting Sadeli on the ferry and said he was a general.

"No, no," Sadeli interrupted in Chinese, "not a general. I'm only a major."

Maria and her mother turned to him, shocked. Maria even stopped talking and dropped her jaw. Sadeli laughed and said, "Is my Chinese that awful?"

Maria and her mother laughed. They were happy.

"Oh, you made Mother laugh. That's great," Maria said.

"Come, you two, sit near me." Maria's mother pointed at the low chairs by the window and said, "Well, young man, tell me about your country."

Maria protested right away, "Don't take too long, Eddy, I want to take you to see the city."

Once again Sadeli told the history of Indonesia, about the fight for independence, about the suffering during the Dutch and Japanese occupations, and about the ongoing revolution. When he finished, Maria's mother looked at him for a moment. Then she looked at Maria and seemed to want to say something, but didn't. She simply sighed and said, "Maria, take him to see the city."

Maria kissed her mother on the cheek. Sadeli rose and shook her hand. Then the two of them left the room.

"She likes you," Maria said, happy.

They went down the stairs.

"Let me show you around the house first," she said. They went from one room to another until they finally reached the backyard.

Sadeli was stunned. He didn't expect the backyard to connect to the beach. He held his breath when he noticed the backyard was beautifully modeled after a Japanese garden. A small pavilion with a tiled roof stood hidden among the pine trees. Near him was a small pond with big corals.

Maria grabbed his hand and led him to the pavilion. She stopped in front of the door and looked at Sadeli for a moment. Then she opened the door to a medium-sized studio. Near the window was a workshop with a half-done painting. There were paintings on the wall. Some were finished and some were not. The paintings were neither completely naturalistic nor true abstracts. The colors were bold and so was the composition.

One big painting showed a naked couple. The man stood on his head, while the woman in front of him bent so her head was close to the man's head on the ground.

"Are they that bad?" Maria whispered.

It brought Sadeli back to reality. "No, no," he quickly said, "I didn't know you're a painter." He seemed to look at Maria with a new pair of eyes, searching for other secrets inside her. He said, "I like the colors you use and your bold composition. It's just I don't understand that one. What are you trying to say?"

Maria smiled at him. Then she suddenly pulled him into her arms, held him and kissed him on the mouth. When she let go, she whispered, "This is what I'm trying to say. When a woman loves a man, she will do anything to be with him, including join his upside-down world."

"Maria…"

She grabbed his hand and showed him around the studio to look at other paintings. She stopped in front of a door and looked at Sadeli. She suddenly blushed and looked down. Her hand turned the doorknob. When the door opened, she said quietly, "My bedroom."

It was a medium-sized bedroom and, unlike the studio, it was neatly arranged. A vase of white roses sat on the dressing table by the window. Everything in the room was white: the furniture, the wardrobe, the ruffled curtain, the pillowcases and bedding. Everything looked clean and beautiful and evoked a new understanding bearing its own question in Sadeli's heart. The studio had shown him an unexpected side of Maria, and this bedroom showed him yet another side of her. Both sides attracted and pleased him. He somehow felt familiar with the elements and had been looking for them and now he found them in her. A gentle and warm feeling embraced his heart. He looked at Maria. Their eyes locked. For a long time he looked deep into her black and radiant eyes.

Sadeli slowly pulled Maria closer and kissed her on the mouth. Then he whispered, "I love you."

Maria held him close and with a rather hoarse voice she said, "Let's go and see the city."

They held hands as they walked out of the house, and they held hands during the entire rickshaw trip around the city, and as they climbed a hill to see an old church, all the way until they sat down in a small restaurant by the sea.

Their table was under a lush, big, old pine tree. The sun was shining bright and the sea breeze was blowing steadily. In the distance, junks and fishing boats appeared like white and black dots on the grey ocean.

Inside the restaurant, a gramophone played a popular romantic Portuguese folksong about losing and finding love, about unfaithful love. The female singer's voice was extremely beautiful and sad at the same time.

"Do you like this song?" Maria asked Sadeli. He nodded.

"It reflects our Portuguese soul," she said. "We grieve in happiness. Our heart is stronger than our brain. We're passionate in joy and sadness."

They ordered a bottle of wine and a Portuguese fish dish.

"Maria, you're a woman with many talents. Do you also play a musical instrument?"

"Piano and guitar, but not that well."

"Do you sing?"

"A little."

"You're being modest."

"No, I'm telling the truth. And you, do you like music?"

"I love it. I also play piano a little, and I'm proud of my voice." Sadeli pretended to sing.

"Oh, then you have to play sometime at my house. My mother really loves music and singing. It would make her happy if you asked her to sing." Maria added, "I'll tell my friends you're a famous radio singer in Indonesia, and you just came here to visit. Oh, they'll be so jealous."

"Hush, hush, hold it right there," Sadeli protested, "My voice isn't good enough to be heard by everyone in Macao. I'm embarrassed."

"Now you're being modest."

"No, really."

They looked at each other, smiled, and then laughed and held each other's hand tighter.

Their food arrived and Maria asked, "Is it good, Eddy?"

"Yes."

"Add more ketchup. You're using too little."

Sadeli added more ketchup to his plate.

"Is it good now?"

"Hmm, yes. Is this an authentic Portuguese dish?"

"Yes."

"Do you like to cook, Maria?"

"Now that I dislike the most."

"Hmm."

"Would you be happy if I were a good cook?"

"Ah, in my country, a woman can only marry after she has learned to cook."

Their eyes met. They smiled, and held each other's hand tighter.

"What's the food like in your country, Eddy?"

"It's really spicy. The main ingredients are coconut milk and red chili. You can add meat, fish, vegetables, or anything else to that combination. There are other spices, of course."

"Oh, it sounds delicious."

"Will you try my cooking?" Sadeli asked.

"Are you a good cook?"

"Just for one dish, *sate,* either beef or chicken. The meat is cubed, skewered, then barbequed on charcoal. The sauce is a combination of finely ground peanut, salt, chili, a little shallot, sweet soy sauce, and a little lime." Sadeli suddenly craved sate.

"Come and cook that at my house," Maria said.

"I'll be embarrassed if it doesn't come out right."

"Please, Eddy, you must," Maria pleaded.

Sadeli smiled. "Fine, but don't blame me if it doesn't taste good."

Maria looked at him.

"I can't stop thinking about what I would have missed if I hadn't taken that ferry to Macao this morning," Sadeli whispered.

"And I almost didn't go back to Macao this morning. A friend asked me to go see a new film today, but something told me to board that ferry."

"Are you religious, Maria?"

"Not really. I'm Catholic."

"I'm Muslim and just like you, I'm not exactly a devout one, but I really thank God for arranging our meeting today."

Sadeli and Maria tightened their grip on each other's hand. A fresh ocean breeze caressed the calm South China Sea. As they sat in the shade of the lush pine, their love grew rapidly. Each gaze made them say, "I love you, darling," and every locking gaze turned into a passionate embrace. The pressure of their hands reflected the beat of fervent longing. The world around them, including the melancholic

Portuguese folksong, slowly dissolved. Soon there was nothing else but the two of them wrapped up in their love.

***

Sadeli was back in his hotel room before five. His body felt light and his heart was high up in seventh heaven, among the shining stars and thousands of moons. He heard the angels' beautiful singing. He still could taste the sweet kiss Maria placed on his lips when they parted in front of her house.

He whistled as he showered. Gone were all of his fatigue and doubts. He took his meeting Maria as a good sign and continued to whistle as he got dressed.

There was a knock on his door and Sadeli let David in. "Well, someone is really happy today." David smiled.

Sadeli grabbed David by the arm and pulled him into the room, slapping him on the shoulders, almost skipping.

"Hey, hey, are you drunk?"

"No, no, I'm in love," Sadeli broke into a song, "And I am loved. And oh, she's so pretty." He finally stood still in the middle of the room.

"Maria?" David asked.

"Yes." Sadeli nodded.

"Congratulations." David shook Sadeli's hand.

Sadeli put on his jacket and said, "I'm not too sure this is good for her. You know what I do. We still have to face great battles against the Dutch."

"Don't think about that. Grab happiness when it pops up. Don't wait."

"Let's go," Sadeli said.

They walked to the street and David hailed a taxi.

"Jim lives a little outside the city," David said.

During the taxi ride, Sadeli told David about his day with Maria.

"One day, you must come to see her paintings. Ah right, I have to make sate one of these nights." Sadeli then told David about his promise to make sate for Maria.

Their taxi slowed in front of a villa surrounded by high walls covered with purple bougainvillea and entered the engraved iron gate. They drove through a rather untended garden then stopped right in front of the main door.

An old, stooped Chinese maid opened the door and welcomed them. She said something in Chinese, but Sadeli couldn't understand her accent.

David and Sadeli exchanged glances, shrugged, and followed the maid into the house. She knocked on a closed door, then opened it without waiting for any answer. Sadeli and David entered the room and were surprised to see a man lying in bed.

"Jim Gantry?" David asked softly.

"Have a seat." Jim waved, smiling.

Sadeli and David took a seat on the chairs by the bed.

"I'm really sorry," Jim said, "My dysentery relapsed two weeks ago. And now the doctor ordered bed rest. I can't fly the Catalina for you. I'll just sell it as is. Check it out. It's docked near the Soo Chow Company's warehouse. You know how much it's worth. Settle it with my representative in Hong Kong. Good luck."

Jim Gantry closed his eyes. He looked exhausted with his sunken cheeks and pale complexion.

David and Sadeli looked at each other. Sadeli was disappointed, for he was hoping to see a fit and healthy pilot who would help Indonesia seize its independence. Instead, in front of him now was one seriously ill pilot. David gave Sadeli a signal to leave the room.

David put his hand on Jim's shoulder and said, "Get well quickly, Jim. You'll soon hear from us."

Then David and Sadeli left.

"Let's go and check the plane." David hailed a taxi and added, "Don't forget, we have a seven o'clock appointment with two beautiful ladies tonight."

Sadeli quickly registered what David meant: they were to meet the agents who would sell them the Kuomintang's weapons.

Sadeli and David spotted the Catalina as soon as the taxi stopped by the Soo Chow Company warehouse. A Portuguese man who stood on the dock approached them.

"Mr. David Wayne and Mr. Sadeli?" He extended his hand. "My name is Oliveira. Jim Gantry asked me to show you the Catalina. Mr. Gantry said you're allowed to take it for a spin."

Oliveira led them to a small motorboat at the dock. He started the engine and Sadeli released the rope. Oliveira skillfully maneuvered the boat alongside the Catalina and fastened the rope to the plane. He signaled David and Sadeli to board the plane while he released the ropes that tied the Catalina to the buoys.

"I'll come back as soon as you land," he said and he moved back to the dock.

David closed the Catalina's door. The cabin was a little dirty and messy. David checked the fuselage by knocking at some parts every now and then. As he sat on the pilot seat, he signaled for Sadeli to put on his seatbelt. Then David checked the instruments, tried the pedal and the steering wheel, then started the engine.

At first the engine sounded rough and David frowned. Then it improved, sounding better. Even Sadeli, who was not a pilot, could tell the difference. David seemed content now. He turned to Sadeli and gave a thumbs-up before they departed. The Catalina moved slowly between the scattered ships toward the open water.

After checking the wind direction, David pushed the accelerator harder and they moved faster. He checked the speedometer before he gently pulled up the steering wheel. The Catalina's nose went up a bit and suddenly they were off the water.

David smiled. The Catalina climbed and circled above the sea until it reached 500 feet, 1000 feet, 3,000 feet. Macao, the Chinese mainland, and the ocean sprawled beneath them.

After they circled Macao twice, David signaled he was about to land. Sadeli admired David's landing skills. He barely felt the plane touch the water. They slowly taxied to the plane's initial location. David turned the engine off and Sadeli opened the door.

Oliveira tied the buoys' ropes to the tail of the plane before he moved his motorboat to the plane's door. "She is wonderful, isn't she?"

David nodded. The motorboat returned them to the dock. They declined Oliveira's offer to take them back to the hotel.

"Eddy," David said as they walked along the beach, "we can use the Catalina. It's still in good condition. We just need to fix its steering mechanism first; it wasn't that smooth. The engine is still fine. Since Jim is sick, I'll fly it. Let Pierre fly the Dakota…ah, no, I need Pierre in the Catalina because he's highly experienced. We'll find someone else for the Dakota. To make the flight you want, the Catalina needs to land on lakes and rivers, and that requires lots of experience. Let me take care of the Catalina."

David checked his watch. It was past six.

"They'll pick us up at a restaurant exactly at seven. It's up to you, Eddy, whether or not I should join your negotiation with them."

"I think you should, Dave. Who knows, maybe they'll talk about transporting the weapons."

They took a rickshaw to the agreed-upon restaurant. Dave chose a table by the door.

"I have a good feeling about this operation," Sadeli said and drank his cold beer.

"Hmm. We shouldn't rely too much on premonition in our line of work. What actually is a hunch?"

"Ah, something we don't have a logical explanation for, but it holds some truth," Sadeli said. "I mean, we never know. The fact is that every human has many dimensions. Some we don't understand, because we don't know how to find out about it."

"In our line of work, it's better to just stick to logic," David said.

"That's what differentiates you, a man from the civilization of technology, from me, a product of a society that stands with one foot deep within the old tradition while the other one is eager to step into the modern world. We can't detach ourselves from the outside world, the world we can touch and see. Yet, for my people, there is another world full of powers that interfere with our daily life. I'm not sure we have to get rid of it completely. There's something interesting within it that makes us fantasize and dream."

David smiled. "We too have that kind of world, but it stays in the children storybooks," he said.

At seven o'clock, a small Chinese man dressed in black and wearing thick glasses came to their table and said to David, "Ah, Mister, you want to see the lotus flowers?"

"If they are white, yes." David looked at him closely.

"Come. The car is outside," he said.

At the port, the messenger led them to a motorboat, which soon took them to a twenty-ton yacht.

They climbed the yacht's stairs. The messenger yelled out something in Chinese that Sadeli couldn't make out. A crewmember met them and took them into the saloon. A fat and tall Chinese man dressed in white welcomed them.

"Mr. Sadeli and Mr. Wayne? I'm General Kang's deputy. My name is Colonel Hua. We can talk freely here."

"As you know, Colonel Hua, we need weapons like bazookas and radio interception devices. I'm sure you know exactly what we need, Colonel."

The colonel smiled. "Before we talk about our trade, what would you like to drink, gentlemen? General Kang hasn't used this yacht for a while, so we only have modest provisions to entertain our guests. I can only offer you tea or hot coffee."

"Tea, please," Sadeli and David said almost simultaneously.

Colonel Hua clapped and a shipmate came. Colonel Hua told the sailor to make some tea.

"Tell me, Major Sadeli," Colonel Hua said, "what's happening in your country now? How are my fellow Chinese doing there?"

Sadeli hesitated for a moment. He wondered if he should tell the colonel about the clashes between the republicans and some of the Chinese. It might displease the colonel and jeopardize their chance to buy the weapons. Still, Sadeli decided to tell him the truth. "The Chinese in Indonesia are indeed a problem for us," he calmly said,

"Most of them never joined the Indonesian national movement for freedom; only some of them did. In fact, many Chinese preferred to work with the Dutch. Even now, most of them live with a wait-and-see attitude. We even suspect that the majority of them prefer the Dutch recolonize us because it means they'll regain their position as the middleman in trading all around Indonesia. But that is impossible. In the future, this position will go to Indonesian merchants since they occupy the bigger ratio of the population."

"However, your government has no policy to drive the Chinese immigrants out of your country?" the colonel asked.

"Oh, absolutely not. We know that more than two million Chinese and most of their descendants will live in Indonesia for generations to come. In fact, my government proposes assimilation so the Chinese will blend in and really become Indonesians. But this is difficult."

"Yes, we know," Colonel Hua said, "What I think I need is your guarantee of not using these weapons against the Chinese in Indonesia."

"Ah, we don't consider them the enemy. Unless," Sadeli hesitated for a moment before he added, "unless they join the Dutch and fight against us. In that case, we'll use every single weapon we have access to. You're in the military, you surely understand."

Colonel Hua rose and pulled a map from a drawer.

"This is the map of Southern China." He traced a river before stopping at one point. "Gentlemen, you fly approximately sixty miles inland from the estuary and land here. I'll be waiting. Of course, that's after we have agreed on the price," he said with a smile.

"Forgive me, maybe it's not my place to ask," Sadeli interrupted, "why is your general selling these weapons?"

Colonel Hua smiled and said, "We have a surplus. The war against the Japanese is over. These weapons are not well documented, so whoever has them, owns them. And also, perhaps my general thinks it's better to sell them to you than to let them fall into the hands of those Communists. Or maybe because my general wants to help another Asian nation seize their independence. Who really knows why?"

"You think the Communists will get this far south?" Sadeli was a little surprised. He didn't think the Communists in China were that powerful.

Again, the colonel smiled. "Mao Zedong is a great leader," he said, "and the Communists have such remarkable discipline and devotion. We are no match for them."

"You speak so frankly," Sadeli said.

"We have to be realistic. Chinese are very realistic," Colonel Hua said, smiling.

"Well, let's talk about the price then," Sadeli said.

During the next thirty minutes, they negotiated the price, pickup, payment, and security procedures.

***

It was around ten in the evening when Sadeli and David were back at their hotel. Sadeli said, "Tomorrow I'm going back to Singapore to take care of the financial matters and the flight to Sumatra for the Catalina. You stay here to take care of that plane. I'll be back in a few days."

When he reached his room, Sadeli called Maria.

"It's Eddy, Maria. I'm glad you're not yet asleep."

"Oh, Eddy, I did wish you'd call," she said.

"Maria, we have to redo all of our plans. I have to return to Singapore tomorrow morning. But I'll be back here in two or three days."

"Oh." Her voice echoed her disappointment.

"Maria, I have to leave early in the morning. I'd like to see you."

"Now?"

"Yes."

"Come, Eddy," she said softly, "I'll wait for you at the front door."

Sadeli rushed down to the street and hailed a taxi.

Maria opened the door even before he knocked. She pulled him inside and said, "I'm so happy you're here." She hugged him and their lips met.

Maria pressed herself against him. He felt her lips, her breasts, her stomach, and her thighs. She whispered, "Mother's asleep, let's go to my pavilion."

On the sofa in Maria's studio, they held each other, kissed, talked for a few moments, and went back to hugging. When their breathing was calmer, she asked, "Why do you have to leave so suddenly, Eddy?"

"It's a normal thing in my job," he said, "You know we're at war."

"Oh Eddy, I'm worried."

"About what, Maria?"

"When you leave in the morning, I fear I'll lose you. Maybe you won't come back again."

"Maria…"

They hugged and kissed again.

He whispered, "Oh, my love." The fire that had burned steadily in his underbelly now flared as if stoked by a strong wind. The flame burned higher and higher. Sadeli rose and took Maria's hand. As they hugged and kissed, they moved into her bedroom and undressed each other between whispers and kisses.

The world around them faded away and disappeared. Their reality was nothing but their bodies and their passion-ridden five senses. On her all-white bed, he kissed her hair, her brow, her eyes, her nose, her lips, her cheeks, her chin, her neck, her breasts, down to her stomach and bellybutton. She wiggled, and her fingers pulled his hair and encouraged his head to go further and further down. She moaned as she moved, "Come, come my love, oohh, now love, yes, yes." Her lips met his once more. The wild storm of passion took them higher and higher. They both moaned and whispered, "Now we're one," and the storm took them to a new height, and finally the volcano erupted, sending fire and blinding red light into the air before darkness fell.

And when the storm cleared, the wind calmed, and their breathing eased, Maria's fingers caressed Sadeli's face, traced his eyebrows, lips, cheeks. She whispered, "*Je t'aime, je t'adore.* I love you, I adore you." And Sadeli murmured those words back to her.

After a while, Sadeli opened his eyes and whispered, "Can we get married tomorrow before I leave?"

"Do you really want to?" Maria's eyes were filled with joy. "Oh, Eddy." She held him close, tears running down her cheeks.

"Why are you crying?" Sadeli asked.

"I'm so happy."

Sadeli said, "We have to be practical now, Maria. I'm a Muslim and you're a Catholic. Can we get married at the city hall here?"

"Oh yes, and mother surely would want us to have a Catholic wedding ceremony in the church."

"Oh right, I almost forgot your mother." Sadeli, embarrassed, smiled. "I must propose tomorrow. Will that sadden your mother?" he asked, worried.

Maria laughed a little. "No, mother is a wise old lady."

"If I'm gone, Maria, ah…" Sadeli fumbled.

"What is it, Eddy?"

"Hmm, I mean, Maria…" He couldn't finish his sentence.

Maria looked at him, worried.

"The thing is, Maria," he started again, "I mean, if I'm gone and you know you're…" He looked at her like he was asking for pity.

Maria smiled and said, "You mean if I'm pregnant?"

"Yes, yes," he said quickly, "Please take good care of our child."

Maria squealed a little, laughed, and hugged him. "Do you want a girl or a boy?"

"A girl as pretty as you are," Sadeli said and continued, "And when I'm gone, I want you to keep painting, Maria."

"Why?"

"I saw your paintings and now I know how deep your feelings can be. You can become a really good painter, Maria."

"Eddy, you encouraged me. I'll keep on painting."

And like millions of other couples in love, they soon talked about the many dreams and things they would like to do someday.

Chapter 13

Sadeli did not feel like talking to any of the other passengers on the flight from Hong Kong to Singapore. He purposely looked for an empty row of seats. His mind was filled with what happened between him and Maria in Macao. They got married in the city hall with David Wayne and a few of Maria's family members as witnesses. Maria's mother cried as she hugged him.

Sadeli remembered the moment he asked for her blessing. The old woman had taken a good long look at him and said, "A Chinese proverb says, *Take your time when you want to do something new in life.* Are you sure about what you and Maria are going to do?"

"Yes. I have fallen in love for the first time in my life and it is with Maria. I'm old enough to know what I want."

"Hmm," the old woman had said, "age does not guarantee that a person knows himself. Maria is my only child. Are you taking her away right now?"

"Oh, no, my country is still at war. Of course I want to take her to live there once peace returns to Indonesia."

"I also would like to visit your country. I've heard so much about it. Some of my friends have been there. Once, Maria's father planned to go there, but then World War II broke out." Her eyes searched for Sadeli's once more. "Can you provide a living for Maria?"

"I'm sure I can. She is willing to live a modest life. I'm not rich and neither is my family. In Indonesia, I'm an officer in the military."

"What do you mean?"

"Well, someone in the military can't be rich. We have to live from our salary. My career in the military is what awaits her. Unless, after the war, I feel I can be more useful outside the military."

"I don't know how much a military officer in Indonesia makes," Maria's mother said and added, "I hope you don't mind Maria receiving financial support from me. It's actually her right, her inheritance from her father. When I die, she will inherit all of my wealth. She can easily live off her inheritance. You have to think through whether these different circumstances between you and Maria will work and won't cause any trouble later. I say this without any intention to look down on your position, either as an Indonesian military officer or as a man."

Maria's mother's honest remarks had stunned Sadeli. He realized how poor he, and everyone who fought for Indonesia's independence, was. Yet, their dreams of independence were so rich. He wanted to tell Maria's mother about it, and without much thought, he said spontaneously, "I have to admit I'm a poor man, and I don't know how long I'll stay one. All Indonesians are poor. Our president, generals, and ministers are all poor. The Dutch exploited us for more than three hundred years, but the promises of our revolution are filled with improvements for our life and our honor. No amount of wealth can ever measure our freedom and honor. I don't have anything to offer Maria right now other than my love for her."

Maria's mother had looked at him and smiled. "I appreciate your honesty and modesty, but love alone is not enough to live on in this world. Everyone in love always says they can live off their love, but humans also have to eat, need shelter, and money to live. Living in extreme poverty can ruin love. You don't believe this now, and neither does Maria. Indeed, young people in love have their own way of thinking.

"I'm old now, and I've seen a lot in this life. As a mother, my only concern is Maria's happiness. To tell you the truth, I'm very worried. It isn't that I don't like you. Your life and Maria's are worlds apart. Will you two be able to overcome the differences? I don't know. I don't want to ruin Maria's happiness by withholding my blessing. So with fear in my heart, I give you my blessing, and I pray the two of you can be happy for as long as you live. I'm worried you will go to war again."

Sadeli kissed the old woman's hand. As if tired from talking, she closed her eyes and he quietly stepped out of the room.

Maria stood waiting outside the bedroom; filled with joy, beauty, and passion, she was radiant like the sun. She hugged him and asked, "What did Mother say?" She kissed him passionately when he said her mother had given her blessing.

"And now I'm married to Maria," Sadeli said to himself, his focus returning to the present flight to Singapore. He still had trouble believing that everything starting from the ferry ride from Hong Kong to Macao, to meeting Maria onboard, going to her house, the passionate lovemaking in her bedroom, and ending with their wedding was not just a dream, something that had happened only in his imagination. However, the wedding band on his ring finger was evidence he indeed had married Maria.

He had to leave for Hong Kong right after the wedding and there had been no time to consummate their marriage through their passion. With tears streaming down her face, Maria said goodbye at the door of her house. She didn't try to hold him back because they had made a promise.

Sadeli couldn't find the words to soothe her. He held her tightly and kissed her on the lips before he whispered, "I'll come back to you, Maria. Wait for me."

Maria tried with all her might to hold back her tears. She wanted to keep up a front because her mother was there. When her mother predicted this would happen; she had said she would bear it.

Sadeli sighed. He wondered what Maria would be doing now. His conscience began to bother him. Thoughts tumbled through his mind. *Was it right to marry her? Have I been pushed by lust, and am I being selfish? Am I fair to her?* He knew that in a revolution, anyone, especially a soldier like him, should not count his days. Duty and obligation could lead him to death anytime. What rights did he have to make Maria love and marry him, only to leave her the next moment? There were no guarantees when he would return to Macao. Perhaps a new instruction awaited him in Singapore, ordering him to return to Java or Sumatra. There was no telling if he would be sent back to the battlefield.

Sadeli knew there was a chance for all of that to happen. Based on the report he had received, the Dutch were in fact preparing a military move toward the Republic of Indonesia. However, the Linggarjati agreement of November 15, 1946, which was soon followed by a de facto acknowledgment from the United States, Britain, Australia, Thailand, India, Syria, and Iran, had strengthened Indonesia's position.

If the Dutch attacked the Indonesian territory, the established network overseas would be able to carry on the fight for their independence internationally. They had secured networks with London, New York, Washington, the Middle East, Australia, and Southeast Asia.

I've done a lot, he tried to console himself as he still felt guilty about pursuing his own happiness with Maria. Sadeli remembered how he used to see life in a simple way: it was either black or white, good versus evil. A knight was someone pure, honorable, bold, and muscular, willing to sacrifice his life at any time for justice and truth.

As it turned out, life was not as simple as that. Some responsibilities were difficult to fulfill. Following a truth blindly could create damage that turned into inevitable disaster. He was glad he had reconsidered his decision regarding Umar Yunus.

People could say bad things about him and Maria if they wanted to badmouth him. Even the truth was not always absolute. It could have sides and versions, and everyone might say his or her side represented the whole truth.

Sadeli sighed once more. The revolution had taught him many life lessons. With a hint of melancholy, he admitted he not only had changed, but was still changing. He hoped to be able to hold fast to the essential truths that had guided his mind and shaped his life.

Everything necessary to make Indonesians happy and live properly was available in their homeland. All they needed now were good leaders who would devote themselves to the people, who would lead the people to work and improve their lives.

Sadeli remembered what Inspector Hawkins had said back in Singapore. Using Napoleon and Genghis Khan as examples, Hawkins had pointed out that every revolution claimed victims among its own figures and supporters.

Throughout the entire human history, there had not been any single pure ideology people had been able to retain all the time. In the end, power always corrupted the powerful. Scandals plagued every government throughout history. Humans, with all their desires and lust, were complex, and power placed a person in situations of irresistible temptation. Power enabled a person to do everything, take everything without fear of anyone.

Sadeli wondered if Indonesians would be able to avoid this fate.

Tired of thinking about all the complicated issues humans were faced with, Sadeli fell asleep.

The flight attendant woke him up when the plane was about to land at the Singapore airport.

Ali Nurdin waited for him outside the customs gate. "I have important news from Yogyakarta," he said.

"Tell me your news later at the hotel," Sadeli said, then asked, "But how's everything here? Good?"

***

In the hotel room, Ali told Sadeli about the coded telegrams he had received from Yogyakarta. One instructed Sadeli to carry on with the attempt to acquire weapons from the Kuomintang general. A more pressing one ordered Sadeli to buy radio interceptors and transport them immediately to Indonesia, some to Bukit Tinggi and the rest to Yogyakarta.

Sadeli understood what those two telegrams meant. The military commanders in Yogyakarta believed the Dutch would conduct a military offensive. A report about the greatly increased activities of the Dutch naval fleet and air force since May confirmed this.

Another telegram introduced Patnaik, an Indian who wished to help the revolution. He would fly his own plane to Indonesia and transport medicines. India would also send fabric to Indonesia.

Egypt would send a representative named Monem to Indonesia. Sadeli had to contact Patnaik and Monem when they stopped in Singapore en route to Yogyakarta and take care of their safety.

Sadeli was happy his country had expanded its foreign network. Indonesian students and sailors who traveled to India, Egypt, and other Arab countries as well as Western Europe, Australia, and the United States, contributed greatly to introducing their nation's revolution for freedom. Now the result of their efforts began to show.

"Ali," Sadeli said, "we'll buy the radio equipment first and transport it on the Catalina, which David will fly. He's preparing the plane in Macao and he'll be ready in a couple of days. You go on that Catalina to Yogyakarta. This first flight also tests the routes that the Catalina can fly, Hong Kong, Bangkok, Singapore, Lake Singkarak, then along the west coast of Sumatra. Where's the map?"

Ali Nurdin produced a map from his bag and laid it out on the table.

Sadeli drew a straight line from Lake Singkarak passing Mount Kerinci to the west coast of Sumatra, then another straight line to the south coast of Java, and an eastward turn toward the Maguwo airport outside Yogyakarta. He said, "We need to notify Bukit Tinggi and Yogyakarta, so they can prepare everything necessary for this flight."

During the next week, Sadeli and Ali Nurdin worked hard. They also asked Inspector Hawkins to help arrange the security of the operation. The inspector told them to notify Indonesia to be on full alert. He had heard from sources he wouldn't name that the Dutch would attempt a military approach.

Then they received a telegram from David Wayne. The Catalina was ready and he was waiting for orders to fly to Singapore. Sadeli immediately sent a telegram telling David to leave right away.

"The sooner the radio equipment arrives in Indonesia, the better," Sadeli said. "And you should get ready to leave at any time," he added.

Ali Nurdin looked at Sadeli, a little hesitant.

Sadeli asked, "What is it?"

Ali Nurdin looked away as if he were a little embarrassed, then he turned back to Sadeli and said, "There's something I want to tell you; it's very personal. I'm a little uncomfortable, but I need to ask you a favor."

"Don't worry. Go ahead; we're revolution brothers." Sadeli tried to put Ali at ease.

"I don't know if you'll change your opinion about me after you hear my story," Ali Nurdin said and added, "You always put your duty above anything else."

"Is that what you think of me?" Sadeli smiled.

"Yes, and I really respect you for that. You seem to be capable of setting aside every personal feeling and need and devote your entire body and soul to the revolution."

Sadeli grinned and said, "You're wrong. I'm just an ordinary human being. I'm not any different from you." Sadeli wondered if he should tell Ali Nurdin about meeting Maria and his sudden wedding. Perhaps Ali Nurdin's respect for him would go down a peg or two after that.

Sadeli drew a bead on Ali Nurdin. He was rather thin, dark skinned, and had curly hair. He had a gentle face, with eyes that showed his sensitivity. After working with Ali for a few months, he had grown to respect the man. Even though they had not had opportunities to have a casual discussion, Sadeli considered Ali Nurdin a relentless fellow patriot who never refused any task assigned to him. He thought, *Maybe this is the time to get to know this co-worker better,* and said, "Go ahead, tell me what's going on, my friend. Who else can you pour your heart out to but me? There isn't anyone else but the two of us here."

Ali Nurdin held Sadeli's eyes. He broke into a smile when he said, "Nani sent me a letter from Yogyakarta." He halted before he laughed a little and continued, "I'm sorry for such an abrupt beginning. As a journalist, I should have done better. Here's the thing, there's a change in our wedding plans. I've been thinking all this time and decided that we should just get married during this revolution. Only God knows how long we'll live. Shouldn't we fill our lives with love as long as He's giving us a chance to live? When you told me to go with the Catalina, I felt like it was a sign from God for me to marry Nani when I reach Yogyakarta. The favor I was going to ask you is to allow me to bring Nani with me to Singapore. Of course only if there's space on the Catalina." Ali's eyes were filled with hope.

"Marry her, Ali. Marry your Nani. During a revolution and war, God only gives us happiness in increments. We can die tomorrow, who knows? I'll write Colonel Suroso to let Nani get on the plane if at all possible."

Sadeli wondered if he would have given Ali the same answer if he hadn't married Maria back in Macao. Now, he wanted to share and spread the happiness he felt with everyone. It was important for him to have other people be as happy as he was. At that moment, he felt really close to Ali Nurdin.

"Oh, thank you. I feel at ease now," Ali said.

"I'm happy I could help," Sadeli said and added, "The final goal of our revolution is not only to gain freedom for our country and nation, but also to make all Indonesians happy and change our backward society into a newly developed one."

"I truly agree." Ali beamed and continued, "That was my dream too when I first joined *Surya Wirawan*—the Indonesian nationalist youth movement—before World War II."

"Oh, you are a member of Surya Wirawan? Me too. Which chapter are you?"

"Medan, back when I studied there."

Sadeli felt even closer to Ali Nurdin now.

"But," Ali said, "I don't think it's easy for us to change our society."

"Why?" asked Sadeli.

"I became a journalist during the Dutch occupation and worked through most of the Japanese one. I've seen with my own eyes how the people with power behave. They often don't do as they say."

Sadeli remembered Inspector Hawkins' words.

Ali continued, "And, it's not like Lord Acton said, that power tends to corrupt and absolute power corrupts absolutely. Our own culture stands in the way. Our own feudal values are a huge obstacle to changing our society into a developed and open society."

"What do you mean? Give me some examples."

"One thing I've paid attention to since the Dutch occupation, is Indonesians' behavior towards power, especially, sorry Sir, don't take this personally, among the Javanese. They consider power as a gift from the Supreme Being, and those in power were bestowed with *wahyu cakraningrat*. The Javanese expect those in power to always say and do the right thing, and believe that everyone should obey the ruler or the king. How can we develop healthy democratic values within that kind of mindset, when people blindly obey everything a ruler says? Another behavior is our tendency to bend to nature because we feel guilty if we try to control it and change situations to accommodate our needs."

"I agree with your first opinion. It's indeed a mental attitude we need to get rid of, and it may not be easy. However, I somewhat disagree with your second opinion. Perhaps going with nature is one of our traditions we should keep. Why can't people live peacefully with nature instead of destroying it?"

"You misunderstood me. I didn't mean that. Of course humans shouldn't destroy nature. What I meant by bending or accepting nature is resigning to fate. We have an abundance of natural resources. Why don't people in our country, except for a small area in Kalimantan, mine the gold, silver, and diamonds like they do in the U.S., India, Ceylon, Burma, and other places? People mine gold in Mandailing, but they only do it when the price of rubber falls. Why don't our people make use of our country's natural resources? Indonesians must change their behavior and learn to make use of these resources to improve their lives. Attitudes like resigning to fate, to God's will, to God's power, must change. We have to convince Indonesians that their fate is in their own hands."

Sadeli asked, "Are you sure we all can stay united and devote ourselves to our nation after we seize our independence?"

Ali Nurdin held Sadeli's eyes and said, "As a journalist, I've seen too many weaknesses in our leaders. They will corrupt. I think we should always be alert. History has shown us humans can either turn into animals or be people who put the greater needs of mankind above their personal interests. So to answer your question, it can go either way. The chance is fifty-fifty."

"You're very realistic. Hopefully our people and leaders will learn from history. I hope all the sacrifices our nation, especially our youth, made will not be in vain."

"I hope so too. We are actually a nation of gentle people who obey their leaders and rulers. It would be a shame if, after all their sacrifices our leaders simply forget the promise of this revolution."

"Well, let's get back to our present reality," Sadeli said, "You better get some sleep. If David arrives tomorrow, we may have to work through the night to load the cargo on the Catalina. I'll talk to Inspector Hawkins and our leaders about the flight's safety details. Perhaps the Catalina should land outside the Singapore waters and we'll have to load the radio equipment using a boat. We have a hard day ahead of us."

***

The next day, after he talked to Inspector Hawkins, Sadeli told Ali Nurdin to rent a boat and have it ready on the west coast of Johor.

Sadeli pointed at a spot on the map. "David will land here, outside the Singapore waters at one a.m. Right after we load the cargo on the Catalina, you will head to Lake Singkarak. Tonight, we'll go together to the boat and wait at sea."

Ali Nurdin and Sadeli hurried to finish the necessary preparations.

At midnight, both of them left the Johor coast on a boat that headed for the calm open sea. The sky was filled with dark clouds. Only a few stars were out.

"Everything will be fine as long as it doesn't rain and the wind won't come up." Ali Nurdin worried as he looked at the sky.

Sadeli asked, "Do you think there are any Indonesians sleeping soundly on the other side of this sea tonight? What would they be dreaming about? What's on the mind of the soldiers on watch on the front lines and in the camps? What would the wives or parents who are waiting for them at home be thinking?"

"Surely each of them dreams of our independence day," Ali said, "just like we are on this boat. Who would have guessed we'd be here now with a Chinese crew of eight waiting for a Catalina piloted by an American and his French partner?"

"Right. Before the war, I never dreamed of being a soldier," Sadeli said. "I thought I would spent the rest of my life as a teacher."

"Don't you find it strange that people of other nations help us with our revolution? On this night alone, we have Chinese, an American, and a Frenchman working with us. And the laborers in Australia have been helping us since our declaration of independence. In fact, even some Dutch sympathize with our revolution."

"I think that's the very nature of human freedom. People in this world will always support a fight for freedom. Sure, some help us because we pay them. There have been mercenaries throughout human history, but not everyone wants to sell their soul for money."

"I hope this revolution will really awaken our people from their centuries-long slumber," Ali said. "You know what impresses me the most from our historic heritage on Java? It's not the Borobudur, but the Hindu temples on Dieng plateau. I've been there once for a vacation. After I saw those temples, I realized that Indonesians are actually capable of building something as long as they believe in themselves. If our ancestors could build those temples at the cold top of the mountains, I'm sure our people can do whatever other nations do."

"I'm glad you like the Dieng temples. I like them too. When I was younger, I went there to visit my uncle who was a regent's assistant in Wonosobo."

Ali said, "I also admire magnificent Lake Toba in Sumatra and Bukit Barisan with its valleys, lakes, and rivers." He suddenly longed to return to Sumatra. They were quiet for a few moments and kept an ear to the ground for the sound of an airplane, but they heard nothing other than the night breeze sigh, and the small waves lap against the boat as they rocked them gently. Sadeli tried to check his watch in the darkness but he couldn't see anything. Ali Nurdin turned on his small flashlight and pointed it at Sadeli's watch for a second. It was almost one in the morning.

"I hope David won't be late." Sadeli sounded worried.

"I remember our talk in your hotel room about how Indonesian people need to change," said Ali Nurdin, breaking the silence.

"Yes?" said Sadeli.

"Who is brave enough to change our people?" said Ali Nurdin. "I really want to do it. When we're done with the revolution, I want to write as many books and brochures as I can or even publish a newspaper or magazine. A lot of our nation's behaviors and mindsets need changing. And we can only do this by introducing new mindsets and behaviors. Modern education needs to reach even the most remote villages. Teachers must hold an important role after the revolution, and so must writers and artists, because we have to develop new Indonesians and build a new Indonesian culture."

"Do you want to do away with all of our old culture?"

"No," Ali Nurdin answered quickly, "I don't accept everything from the Western culture readily. We must keep quite a lot of customs from our original culture because it holds values that make our life happy, like enjoying a tight, loving family bond, the respect and love we have for our parents, good moral values, harmony in society, and helping one another. However, I want to declare war against conservative, narrow-minded, and reactive religious behaviors shown by leaders and devotees of any religion. I want to see Indonesians carry out their religious activities using their free will and with a good and profound understanding of their beliefs so they won't be misled. And I want to fight against superstitions that still control the souls of many people. This includes the superstition toward the hallowed ones. It is common to believe that when a person rules, he becomes sacred and can't do wrong. This is nonsense. Every human being is the same. When all the people are given the same quality education and everyone receives the same amount of information, they'll throw out their existing superstitions and conservativeness. That's how we're going to foster a democratic society in Indonesia."

Sadeli chuckled. "You're so enthusiastic, Ali," he said, "Although I do agree with your opinions, I don't think it'll be that easy to change our society and culture, especially the Javanese. Many Javanese became doctors or lawyers, and even studied in Holland, but when they returned to Indonesia, they were once again caged within that old Javanese cultural framework with all of its restrictive behaviors. Perhaps it takes a few generations to replace these old cultural behaviors. Let's hope the unity we're forging through a collective sacrifice within the revolution will be strong enough to overcome difficult times that may come up later after we win this fight. And what's more important is…"

Sadeli stopped midsentence and looked up, listening. Ali Nurdin and the rest of the crew followed suit. The sea breeze carried a buzzing sound like that coming from a black bee. It came and went softly, and then returned, louder and closer this time, only to slowly disappear again. Then the distinct sound of an airplane engine came toward them.

"Send the signal," Sadeli said.

Ali Nurdin picked up a big flashlight from the deck. He aimed it at the now-loud airplane sound and flashed the signal: one long, one short, another long one, and ending with another short one. He turned the flashlight off and waited. The dark sky was only filled with the engine sound, which came closer and closer.

Ali Nurdin repeated his light signal: long, short, long, short and waited in the dark. Then suddenly, a red light crossed the dark evening sky, long, short, long, short.

"David Wayne!" Sadeli let out a relieved sigh. "Turn on the lights at the hull and stern, and the ones on the sides of the boat as well," he ordered.

They didn't see the Catalina descend and land, but a few moments later, the plane moved toward them on the water.

"Turn off the lights," Sadeli said.

For a moment, darkness enveloped the boat. After their eyes adjusted to the darkness, they saw the Catalina was very close.

The Catalina's door swung open. Pierre de Koonig poked his head out and said, "You there, Eddy?"

"Yes, get ready for loading."

The crew lowered a large rubber boat onto the water and they loaded it with crates containing radio equipment.

Sadeli handed Ali Nurdin a small bag containing the report for Lieutenant Colonel Salamun, the head of intelligence in Bukit Tinggi, and another one for Colonel Suroso. "Get on the plane with this first batch of cargo," he said, "I'll come with the final batch. Tell Pierre and David I want to have a word with them."

Ali Nurdin jumped into the rubber boat. Soon, Sadeli saw him get on the Catalina.

Sadeli headed towards the Catalina on the rubber boat with the last load of crates. Pierre pulled him up and held him so tightly that he pretended to choke and said, "You, hungry French bear, don't kill me." Pierre let go of him and laughed.

"Dave is in the cockpit," Pierre said.

Sadeli walked towards the front of the plane and entered the cockpit. "Welcome to Singapore." Sadeli shook David's hand. "How was the flight?"

"Wonderful. Did you bring extra gas?"

"On the boat. Pierre and Ali are taking care of it."

"Are you happy?"

Sadeli smiled. David's question hinted about Maria. He nodded and said, "I owe you forever for bringing me to Macao."

David patted Sadeli on the shoulder and pulled him into the copilot's chair. He opened a map and pointed to a spot on it.

"We're here now," he said, "and after we've refueled, we'll take off. If everything goes right, we'll reach Lake Singkarak before dawn." He refolded the map.

"Don't worry, Sadeli, this is a good plane. Colonel Hua wants to meet you in Macao as soon as possible. He said you have to hurry if you still want the bazookas and other weapons. The situation in China is deeply concerning. He wants to take you to their secret storage place so you can check the weapons yourself."

"You think it's safe for me to go there?"

"It's probably safer than going to Indonesia now, Eddy." David laughed.

David handed Sadeli a small envelope. "Here's the address to contact Colonel Hua in Macao. And here," David took out another envelope from his pocket, "is a letter from Maria."

Sadeli took a few envelopes from his pocket and handed them to David and said, "One of these has a letter that explains your current flight to my boss. You like him, right? He's a bit quiet but he'll listen to you carefully. Just ask him for whatever you need. And this one is for Captain Matias. He'll introduce you to sweet ladies if you want him to, and he can introduce you to anyone you want to meet in Yogyakarta: students, soldiers, officers, and even President Soekarno. He does nothing but go in and out of the presidential palace." Sadeli abruptly stopped when Pierre poked his head into the cockpit and gave a thumbs-up.

"Goodbye, Captain Wayne." Sadeli rose and shook David's hand. "Have a good flight." He gave David a pat on the shoulder before heading outside.

Ali Nurdin stood by the door.

Sadeli shook his hand and said, "Have a good trip. Congratulations to you and Nani."

"Thank you, Sir. Thanks for everything."

They closed the plane's door. Sadeli jumped into the rubber boat and the crew immediately rowed back to the boat.

David turned on the Catalina's engines one by one. When Sadeli stood on the deck of the boat, the plane started to move slowly into the darkness. He imagined David, Pierre, and Ali Nurdin waving to him.

The sound of the engine grew louder as the plane turned toward the open sea and moved across the water. It moved faster and faster, then took off and disappeared into the darkness. Only the sound of the engine connected its passengers with Sadeli, who still stood on the deck. For a moment Sadeli felt lonely, as if he was left behind. He wanted to be on that airplane, flying through the night toward Sumatra, toward his country and his people who were fighting for their lives.

Sadeli sighed and ordered the crew to take him back to shore. He had a letter from Maria. Once again, his heart turned warm and happy. He would leave for Macao the day after tomorrow to negotiate a weapons deal with Colonel Hua, and see Maria. Warmth filled his entire being as he thought of her.

Chapter 14

Ali Nurdin woke up with a start. The roaring sound of the Catalina's engine filled his ears. Two hours had passed since they left Singkarak Lake, and now they were flying way off the coast, heading to the southern coast of Java. They hoped to make it to Maguwo airport after dark. The Dutch fighter jets stopped patrolling after dusk.

Two days ago, they had landed safely on Lake Singkarak. Everything had gone smoothly; the surface of the lake was as still as a pond. They were welcomed by Lieutenant Colonel Salamun and other community leaders who, they were told, had stayed up the whole night waiting for them by the lake.

It was more like a party than a simple welcoming. They were escorted to a government guesthouse where a crowd was already waiting. In his entire life, Ali Nurdin had never received that kind of welcome and respect. Everyone came to shake his hand and ask him questions. Finally they asked him to deliver a speech.

Ali Nurdin was stunned. He wasn't used to speaking in front of many people. After his effort to refuse was proven in vain, he finally gave in. His voice trembled when he spoke. "Ladies and gentlemen, let me introduce myself. I'm only a journalist. I help Major Sadeli in Singapore. The pilot is Captain David Wayne, an American pilot who sympathizes with our revolution for freedom, and his friend is Pierre de Koonig, a Frenchman. Please stand, gentlemen."

The crowd clapped while David and Pierre stood, blushing.

"We are no bloody heroes." David laughed.

"What did he say?" someone asked.

"Viva to our freedom," Ali Nurdin said and smiled. He suddenly felt good and happy. He continued with the story about their flight through the night and told the crowd that a lot of people abroad supported Indonesia's fight for independence. He said, "Especially the people of Malaya feel that Indonesia's fight for independence is theirs as well."

The crowd cheered and clapped.

When the welcome ceremony was over, they led Ali Nurdin and the two pilots to Bukit Tinggi to meet and dine with the governor.

***

Two hours ago they had departed from Lake Singkarak and continued their flight with a rather full airplane. There were five military officers, including three soldiers, an officer from the navy and another from the air force. There were also three members of the KNIP or *Komite Nasional Indonesia Pusat*— the Central Indonesian National Committee, an equivalent to a legislative body appointed to assist the president of the newly independent Indonesia. One was from Masyumi, a major Islamic political party, another from PNI or *Partai Nasional Indonesia*, the Indonesian National Party, and the other from PSI or *Partai Sosialis Indonesia*, the Socialist Party of Indonesia.

The three army officers guarded a few small, yet sturdy and heavy chests. Ali Nurdin knew they contained gold from the National Bank and it was all for their revolution.

Ali Nurdin rose, stretched, and walked toward the officers. He had been introduced to them earlier. He said, "Major, how's the situation in Sumatra?"

"Pretty calm, except in North Sumatra. The Dutch tried to infiltrate the area south of Medan. They tried to reclaim the oil mines there."

"But there's no great battle so far?"

"No. They're still testing our defense."

"Abroad, we heard the Dutch may conduct a military aggression offensive in July," Ali Nurdin said.

"We're ready. Sumatra is so large. We'll see how long they can last playing tag."

"I think their strategy is to claim Java first," said Ali Nurdin, "If they succeed in conquering well-populated Java, they'll have a strong footing to expand their power all over Indonesia once more. They seem to want to apply the VOC's old tactics and strategies. They will try to divide and conquer again."

"That's true," the major said, "I was sent to Yogyakarta to prepare for every possibility so we can establish a great coordination of commands in Java and Sumatra."

"Hopefully, this modern radio equipment," Ali Nurdin pointed at the chests in the back part of the Catalina, "will make the task easier."

The major smiled at him.

Ali Nurdin left him to sit next to the leader of Masyumi, a member of KNIP.

"How are you doing, Mr. Abdullah? Cold?"

Abdullah nodded. "It's pretty cold," he said as he tried to control the chattering of his teeth. The Catalina flew at a high altitude.

"I'll get some hot coffee," said Ali Nurdin. He then got up and headed toward the back of the plane. He returned with a thermos of hot coffee and cups. "Anyone else wants some?" Ali passed the thermos and cups then went back to his seat next to Abdullah. He asked, "How long did you stay in Bukit Tinggi?"

"The KNIP in Yogyakarta sent me there as a Masyumi representative four months ago to explain the Linggarjati agreement to the parties, the people, the government, and the army. The committee also sent a delegate from the PNI and the PSI."

"How did the people of Sumatra react?"

"Quite well, although no one was happy to hear about the Linggarjati agreement. Everyone thought it was an unsatisfying compromise for us as well as for the Dutch. The Communists already started to oppose it, and so did the left wing within PNI. The left socialists in Amir Syarifuddin's group are also against it. If we're not careful this Linggarjati agreement can tear us apart."

"We heard abroad that the Dutch will conduct a military action against us," Ali Nurdin said.

"That could actually benefit us. If the Dutch attack, we can preserve our unity." Abdullah smiled.

Abdullah's answers upset Ali. He wondered if Sadeli was aware of the condition. He said, "The situation in Indonesia is not as good as I thought abroad."

Before he had the chance to carry on with the conversation, David Wayne's voice boomed through the speakers, "Please put on your seatbelts, we're going through turbulence."

Soon, the plane shook violently. The passengers looked at one another. Abdullah turned pale. He looked like he was about to vomit, but he struggled not to. The air force officer couldn't hold it any longer and quickly grabbed an airsick bag. Abdullah then lost control and reached for a bag also. The rest of the passengers tried to avert their eyes.

Some fifteen minutes later, the plane broke free from the turbulence and David's voice came over the speakers, "We passed the turbulence, you may take off your seatbelts."

Ali Nurdin rose and headed toward the cockpit. He poked his head in and asked, "Do you want some hot coffee?"

Pierre pointed at a thermos on the floor underneath his seat. David wore the radio headset and couldn't hear Ali Nurdin.

Pierre asked, "How's everyone back there?"

"Okay."

David noticed Ali's presence at the door. He turned his head and raised his left thumb. Ali Nurdin replied with the same gesture, then closed the door and went back to the cabin. Everyone seemed tired. They sat listlessly in their chairs and had closed their eyes.

Ali Nurdin returned to his seat in the very last row. It was uncomfortable, and he stood up again, took a thick blanket, spread it near the chests, and lay down. An officer followed suit, using his backpack for a pillow. Soon, other passengers did the same thing.

Ali Nurdin smiled and took a small book out of his jacket pocket: *The Iliad* by Homer, a war story by a Greek poet. Humans had not changed since prehistoric times. They killed and battled one another for wanting to seize someone else's land, for women, for pride and arrogance, for greed and envy. In Greek tragedy, everything seemed inevitable for humans as everyone had to carry out his or her predetermined role. It was no different from the present. Mussolini was followed by Hitler in Western Europe, Stalin in the Soviet Union, General Tojo in Japan, the Americans, and Chiang Kai Shek in China. They were all involved in great wars of the world. In fact, the modern wars surpassed the magnitude of the war Homer had written about. The atomic bombs that were dropped on Hiroshima and Nagasaki made it seem that gods participated in human wars.

War now raged through Indonesia. The Dutch seemed to lose their power and tried to recolonize Indonesia. However, no one on the face of the earth could convince the Indonesians not to fight against it.

Ali Nurdin looked up from his book. He glanced around and wondered what his fellow passengers were thinking of at the moment.

Abdullah leaned against the side of the plane. The cold of the panel eased the headache that had come on when the plane entered the turbulence. He recalled saying goodbye to his wife before he left Sumatra. They had been married for fifteen years and had eight children. Since he became a member of the KNIP, and the organization moved from Jakarta to Yogyakarta, he had not been home for two years. During that time, he met a woman.

Sundari was at ease in public. She was fluent in Dutch and English, and was also active in *Laskar Wanita Indonesia*, the Indonesian Female Warriors.

Abdullah was really attracted to Sundari and he knew she felt the same way. When he returned to his wife in Sumatra, he realized the big difference between Siti Aisyah, his wife, and Sundari in Yogyakarta. Aisyah was a village woman who was not fluent in Dutch, let alone English. She did not have any social graces and was unattractive. It would be hard to bring her along to a social function if one day he managed to secure some high-ranking position or became a minister. He never dreamed that his current position as a party member would lead to the opportunity to be one of the high-ranking officials of the country. In fact, if Natsir, the current Minister of Communication, became Prime Minister one day, there would be a big chance for him to become a cabinet member. Abdullah was one of the KNIP members who came from Sumatra, and Sumatra played an important role in the Republic of Indonesia.

The image of Sundari danced through his mind—her sweet face, her olive skin, and her shiny black eyes. "I have to marry her," he told himself, and drowned in warm dreams about him and Sundari. His fantasies charged ahead of the roaring engines of the Catalina, to a house on Cemara Street, in Yogyakarta.

***

Iryshad, a representative of the PSI in the KNIP, was younger than Abdullah. He was tall, a bit stout, and had a strong countenance. He was thirty-five. He didn't finish his education at the medical school in Jakarta. Instead, he joined the Indonesian national movement for independence before World War II. He started by joining the *Pendidikan Nasional Indonesia*, the Indonesian National Education Party, one of the earliest political parties in Indonesia under the leadership of Hatta and Syahrir, which aimed for the country's independence through self-reliance. He was a Syahrir disciple. Syahrir was an idealist with a fighting spirit.

Irsyad was happy to be on the Catalina. He thought of the flight as a part of the revolution and he wanted to experience every aspect of it. He wanted to feel all the misery, the pain, the sorrow, all the death, hope, and dreams, all the passion and love all Indonesians felt in this revolution, either as a society or an individual.

Ever since he had joined the revolution, Irsyad had kept a diary in which he had recorded his feelings, his fears, and his dreams;

everything his senses could pick up from his surroundings. In his opinion, Indonesians needed to help one another through the use of the cooperation system. They needed to have a just distribution of profits among all members of society and put in place organized, government-controlled activities geared toward public economic welfare. He believed that for the nation's welfare, natural resources should be used under government supervision. He knew that in order to establish an even and just nation, the law should apply to everyone without exception, and every citizen should have the same rights and obligations. Those were the dreams of Irsyad and his friends.

In the meantime, education should reach all layers of society. A becak driver's child, as long as he or she had the brain or talent and put it to work, should have the chance to become a doctor or an engineer, a president or a minister, a general or an admiral, a writer or an artist. They needed to foster this kind of climate so Indonesians could develop their talents in their jobs and any field of creativity, knowledge, and modern technology. Feudal relationships and behaviors, conservatism, superstitions, inferiority, fear, underdevelopment, poverty, stupidity, all these negative traits would be replaced by clear thinking and rational behavior of an open-minded society that would face everything without being obscured by irrational prejudice. That was Irsyad's dream.

His friends always challenged him about that because to create the society of his dreams, he was willing to keep his party in power for a decade or two to lay the foundation for such a society. They asked, "How can you keep your party ruling for that long while we have decided to run this country as a democracy, which means we have to conduct a general election?"

Irsyad would explain that it was impossible to have the democratic lifestyle they wanted because most Indonesians were not equipped with the knowledge and skills to live in a democratic society. He said, "We're still shackled in feudal ties and this will influence people's choice in the election. They won't think of their own needs."

His friends argued, "However, we must not veer from the foundation of our struggle, which is to create a people-focused socialist society. We have to be smart and find ways to reach our goals within the existing framework of our culture."

Irsyad replied that it wouldn't work with the current conditions. Unless they eradicated the current conservative, feudal society, all they would get was the continuation of a feudal society. His friends said, "If the party wants to keep ruling after the revolution is over, we have to seize power. We might be successful, but we will definitely encounter dangerous opposition from all other political groups. The Islamic and the nationalist parties as well as other parties will turn against us. It would be exceptionally hard to fight the Communists. Perhaps this would cause a bigger problem, maybe a huge catastrophe that will destroy our unity. In fact, perhaps our very independence will perish."

Faced by these kinds of possibilities, Irsyad went silent. He was very much aware of these difficulties. It was not easy to develop a nation, and it wasn't something that could be done in a day or a year.

Still, this didn't dampen his spirit to keep on fighting. He once said that looking ahead into the next fifty or seventy-five years, he was thrilled with the improvements this nation could possibly achieve, yet the first twenty-five years would be most vexing.

Irsyad looked at Ali Nurdin and smiled. Ali Nurdin smiled back at him.

***

Karel Sinantang, the leader of the PNI North Sumatra chapter and a member of the KNIP, couldn't stop thinking about the development plans he would like to propose to the central government. He didn't want to wait until the revolution was over. He always told his fellow party members and friends that Java, with its huge population and limited natural resources, needed to send its people to other islands. Whereas Sumatra had an abundant natural wealth but not enough human resources to exploit it. "That's why," he said, "cooperation between Java and Sumatra is a logical step to take. We can start development projects without having to wait for the revolution to be over."

Leaning against the Catalina's wall, he took out his notebook and wrote down the thoughts that popped into his head. At the top of his list was the power plant project of the Asahan River. They should use the waterfall of Lake Toba for a power plant. He dreamed that the areas around the Asahan River, surrounding the waterfall all the way to Medan, would become a big industrial complex. With the power they generated, they would be able to mine the aluminum ore on the east coast of North Sumatra and also the tin in Biliton and Bangka. They could build various factories.

Karel dreamed of becoming some sort of industrial development king of Indonesia. He wanted to make Indonesia the pride of Asian nations for its industrial advancement. In his dream he envisioned highways and railroads along the island of Sumatra, while a network of air and naval transportation spread like a spider web and covered the whole country from north to south, east to west. *If the government develops the Indonesian entrepreneurs, we can develop Indonesia into a major Asian country just within a short time. Our people are meticulous and skillful workers. They are easy to train and we are rich in natural resources. All there's left to do is to combine the human resource, natural wealth, and modern technology.*

He gradually grew tired of thinking about which industrial project to develop first. His mind drifted to a woman in Solo whom he had visited before he was sent to Sumatra. And suddenly he forgot all about his projects. He put his notebook in his shirt pocket, closed his eyes, stretched his legs, and decided to go to Solo as soon as he reached Yogyakarta.

***

Ali Nurdin woke up with a start. He looked around; his fellow travelers were still sleeping. Abdullah let out a soft snore and the officers were sound asleep on the plane's floor. Ali Nurdin got up and

251

looked outside the window. It was overcast. He checked his watch; it was after 5 p.m. He walked to the cockpit. Pierre de Koonig turned to him.

Ali asked, "Is everything fine?"

Pierre nodded.

David Wayne turned around and said, "Give me a cigarette."

Ali Nurdin took a pack of Camels from his pocket, lit one, and handed it to David.

"To the north over there," David pointed, "is the coast of Java." He checked his watch. "We'll land at Maguwo in two hours. I hope they'll be ready with the runway lights."

"Don't worry. We informed them already," Ali Nurdin said. "Major Sadeli took care of it."

"How are our passengers in the back?"

"They're asleep."

"A plane at three o'clock," Pierre suddenly yelled, cutting David off.

David and Ali looked to the right. Far away from them, like a small black dot, was a plane.

"Is it the Dutch fighter jet?" Ali Nurdin was anxious.

"All passengers, fasten your seat belts," David ordered and repeated, "All passengers, fasten your seat belts."

Ali Nurdin left the cockpit and made sure everyone put on his or her seat belts.

"What is it? What's going on?"

Ali explained, "We saw a plane far away. It's most likely a Dutch plane." As soon as he seated himself and fastened his seat belt, the Catalina dove.

The plane's movement jolted all the passengers. Everyone turned pale and was shocked. Ali Nurdin silently prayed, asking God to save them. Abdullah did the same while Karel Sinantang quickly made the sign of the cross.

When the Catalina entered a thick cloud, David pulled the plane back up and kept it flying inside the cloud. The thick cloud blocked the sunlight. It felt as if they flew inside a giant pillow of cotton. Everyone anxiously tried to pick up the sound of the enemy's plane.

Suddenly David's voice came over the speakers, "I'm sorry, gentlemen, for the sudden dive. We had to get into this cloud to hide from the unknown plane. We have to treat all the planes in this area as if they were Dutch. I'm not sure if the plane saw us, but it's better for us to take cover immediately. So, don't worry if we make another sudden move, just stay calm. Thank you."

David's calm tone took the edge off everyone's anxiety. Ali Nurdin envied David for maintaining his composure during such a tense situation. He figured it must be the result of David's training and experience during World War II.

The men exchanged glances and feeble smiles as they tried to encourage each other.

A few moments later, the Catalina flew out of the cloud and twilight flooded the cabin through the windows. Ali Nurdin checked his watch. It was just past five thirty. Hopefully the enemy had not spotted them and had flown away. He was just about to sigh with relief when the Catalina suddenly made another dive into a big cumulus cloud and David's calm voice said, "The enemy is attacking," and flaming red bullets parted the sky like lightning but missed as the Catalina once again disappeared into the cloud bank.

Abdullah prayed out loud. Karel Sinantang made the sign of the cross numerous times. Irsyad sat down, all tense. Everyone's anxiety changed into terrible fear. They felt death was ready to grab them by the neck.

Ali Nurdin thought of Nani and worried, *Is this the end of my life? Would Nani be just waiting in vain in Yogyakarta?* He was saddened.

Ali checked his watch. They had been flying inside this cloud for five minutes. *Please, God, let this cloud be a very long and thick one.* He looked out the window and noticed the cloud started to thin. Then, suddenly, before they reached the open sky, David made another deep dive. The plane went faster and faster as if it were an arrow aimed at the surface of the sea.

Ali Nurdin was shocked. He thought they were shot down and on their way to crash into the sea. *Oh God, we're done.* He closed his eyes and was overcome by a horrible fear as he waited for death to come.

Ali quickly opened his eyes when he heard the roaring of a plane outside. Through the window, he saw the Dutch fighter jet swoop in. The Catalina continued to dive even faster. He couldn't help but look for sea level. Fear gathered in the pit of his stomach as he watched the sea getting closer and closer. They could crash into it at anytime and drown, or their plane could crash and burn before exploding, thus delivering them to their deaths. He suddenly remembered his mother and wondered what she was doing at the moment.

When he was absolutely sure they would crash and he would be able to touch the water when he reached out the window, David pulled up the steering wheel. The plane squeaked and creaked. Then, painstakingly slow, with the help of everyone's prayer, the Catalina lifted its nose little by little before it flew adjacent to the water. Everyone looked at one another, relieved, yet still full of fear and anxiety.

"I'm sorry, gentlemen, we had to dive to avoid the attack from the Dutch jet," David said calmly and continued to fly low above the water.

Everyone pressed their faces to the windows, and looked for the jet that had attacked them earlier. The sun began to sink into the western horizon and darkness fell quickly.

"There's no sight of the enemy jet," David said over the speakers. "We'll fly higher soon. I hope you're all fine."

A few moments later, the plane started to climb toward the stars that began to show in the quickly darkened sky. Way below them, the sea looked like a strip of gray-black paint.

Ali Nurdin took off his seatbelt and stood. He staggered a bit. Suddenly his whole body, his muscles and joints, were all tense and painful. His voice cracked when he said, "We made it, thanks to our skillful pilot."

Everyone looked at him and tried to smile.

"Alhamdulillah, praise God!" Abdullah said.

Everyone looked as if they had just woken up from a nightmare.

Ali Nurdin walked to the cockpit. Pierre de Koonig turned to him with a wide smile and asked, "Everything good back there? We were faster than the Dutch boy, weren't we?"

"I've never been that terrified in my whole life," Ali said.

"We were scared too." David smiled and added, "I'm scared every time the battle starts. Every time I see the enemy's plane come attacking or when we start attacking, I'm scared. Everyone is afraid to leave this world."

Ali said, "Thank you, Dave, you saved our lives."

"And mine too," David said. "We have to hide this plane in a very safe place right after we land because the Dutch fighter jet will surely look for it in the morning."

Ali said, "I'll remember to tell Colonel Suroso."

In the darkness of night, David Wayne changed the course of the flight, over the south coast of Java heading to the Maguwo airport in Yogyakarta.

Chapter 15

Ali Nurdin held Nani's hand as they sat on a sidewalk in Kaliurang, a small mountain city near Yogyakarta. It was the second day after David Wayne had skillfully landed the Catalina at the Maguwo airport guided only by the emergency runway lights.

Ali had used the first day after the landing to report to his office, meet Colonel Suroso, and see Nani's parents to ask for their blessing. They were to marry in two days. Today, his office had lent him a car and he took Nani to Kaliurang.

They took a walk holding hands and chatted happily. There wasn't much more they could do; someone was always passing by.

Ali told Nani about all his experiences since he arrived in Singapore. He told her about Major Sadeli, and shared the story of the attack by the Dutch fighter jet numerous times. Every time he told her the story, she held his hand tightly and, if no one was around, hugged and kissed him passionately before she quickly let go. Everything Nani did made Ali happy.

"Nani," he said, "I don't know how many times I have said this since I came back. War has no justice for anyone. I'm sure of this, but need you to know this too. As long as there's war, there's always a chance something can happen to me."

257

"Hush," Nani put her hand over his mouth, "Don't talk like this. You're challenging fate. Just think of our happiness. No one knows what tomorrow can bring. I have stopped wondering."

They rose and continued their walk. At the top of a small hill, they inhaled the fresh air. They were surrounded by pine trees, flowers, grass, flying birds, and a running creek. A patchwork of rice fields sprawled far below.

Ali said, "Being here with you, Nani, the war and revolution seem far away. It almost feels we could plan our future."

"Yes," she said, "Tell me about your plans for our future."

"I dream we will have our own house, a car, and…" He glanced at her and smiled.

"And what?" she asked.

"And three kids," he said.

"Hush." Nani blushed and squeezed his hand.

"Hey, you're so pretty with those blushing cheeks," he said, then suddenly screamed in pain, "Ouch." Nani had pinched his thigh hard.

He grabbed her and lay her down on the grass. She tried to free herself but he closed his arms tightly around her. They kissed and rolled on the grass. They breathed heavily as they sank deeper into their passion. He held her breast and felt her nipple harden between his fingers. Ali was amazed by the passion Nani showed under the open sky. Their eyes met and they smiled. He let go of her and rolled over. When Nani's hand accidentally touched him, he started to have an erection. He sat up and tidied his clothes.

He said, "Nani, I can't wait for the day after tomorrow."

She smiled lovingly and said, "Go on with the story of our future."

"Oh right, I really want to be stationed overseas so I can expand my knowledge and skills as a journalist. I'd like us to live in either Europe or America for two or three years. Then we'll return to Indonesia and I'll dedicate my life to being a journalist. If possible, I'd like to publish my own newspaper. Being a journalist for a news agency is quite exciting and it's a good way to gain some experience, but I feel I can only develop myself into a real journalist if I work at a newspaper.

"I'll make my newspaper a vehicle to educate our people so they will know their rights as free citizens. I won't let them get fooled by people who claim to be leaders. The Indonesian press should defend the people against power abuse and work together to foster a democratic society. My newspaper should become a window and a door to the outside world so our people will be able to follow every development and advancement made by other nations in various fields of science, technology, industry, et cetera. In short, I want to turn the newspaper into a tool for modernizing the Indonesian people and society."

"I support your dreams, Ali," she said, "I'm proud of you. I'll help you as your wife."

"And you, my darling," he said, "what about you, what do you want to do after we win this revolution?"

Nani thought for a moment before she said, "I want to do something in education for women. Indonesian women need to free themselves from their disadvantaged position and be able to work with Indonesian men as equals."

"I think it's as important for Indonesian women to better themselves as it is for the men. Tell me about your experience working for the Red Cross."

"I was once sent to the battlefield outside Magelang. During the first week, my friends and I had to nurse the wounded soldiers. It was heartbreaking to see such young bodies ruined by bullets or shrapnel of shells or cannonballs. Some had lost their feet, others had their stomachs or eyes destroyed. At first I thought I wouldn't be able to stand it, but I became used to seeing disfigured bodies. It evoked an intense hatred and anger towards the enemy within me. I kept wondering, why did they come from the other end of the world just to spread death and destruction among our people? I was amazed that the vicious attacks didn't scare our soldiers. In fact, it spurred their fighting spirit. But…" She went silent.

"What is it, Nan?" Ali encouraged her.

"I don't know if what I feel is right, but I feel all this is too cruel. I never thought our own youth could be as cruel as I witnessed. We retaliated against the enemy with the same cruelty they treated us with. Some of the enemy's soldiers were captured, then brutally stabbed and chopped up." She was silent again.

Ali hugged her. "I understand, Nan. I used to be on duty at the Bekasi battlefield. I saw what you saw. I once witnessed Doctor Soebandrio, our Secretary General of the Information Ministry, saw off a soldier's shell-destroyed leg when he was an army medic. He had to amputate the man's leg to save his life. It was devastating to see a young man lose his leg. I felt a raging anger for the enemy who had done it to him. War is cruel; it involves killing and destroying many people's belongings. It's important we don't fight to oppress another nation. We are not a bloodthirsty people who wish to kill the Dutch. We fight to defend the freedom we have proclaimed. We fight to defend our independence from the attack and recolonization by the Dutch. I'm sure we fight with justice on our side."

"I know. But every time I see a soldier or an ordinary man covered in blood from an attack, my body trembles and my heart cries."

They were quiet for a few moments. Then, Ali said, "I have to tell you about Colonel Suroso, Major Sadeli's commander.

"Back in Singapore, I imagined he was tall and fit like Gatotkaca. But he turned out to be completely different. He is slender, of average height, with a kind expression and a pair of bright eyes. He is a very composed person. According to his aide, he is a pious and devout Muslim. He never misses any single prayer time, and he even prays in his office. He is soft-spoken, and he's the head of the intelligence agency. Later, after we get married, you have to meet him and thank him. He promised me a seat for you on the Catalina so you can come with me to Singapore."

"Oh!" Nani hugged him, "You didn't tell me you'll take me to Singapore."

"You thought I would leave you here right after we got married and let you wait for God knows how long?" he asked.

"Yes, and I'm willing to do so," she said.

Ali hugged and kissed her, and their passion ignited once more. He whispered, "Oh, Nan, Nan, you really do love me. I actually wanted to tell you the news after we got married."

They let go of each other and looked at each other, their eyes filled with love and happiness.

Ali checked his watch and was startled. He pulled Nani back into his arms and said, "We have to return to Yogya, Nan. I still have to go to the palace to deliver a package from Major Sadeli, a few Arrow shirts for Bung Karno. I never thought Bung Karno would remember to order Arrow shirts from abroad during the revolution. He sure likes fancy clothes. I also have to meet Colonel Suroso again.

"There's something Colonel Suroso said that I want to share with you. He said the world had changed after World War II. The world's power axis has changed too. If Britain once ruled the world through its many colonies, then now, the superpower countries are Soviet Russia and the United States. Russia wants to expand the Communists' power around the globe. On the other hand, the United States will oppose that attempt and won't support any colonization. The Labour Party in Britain will change its own politics regarding colonization. It will be impossible for the Dutch to mobilize help to recolonize Indonesia. As long as our people keep on fighting relentlessly, we will surely win. That's what Colonel Suroso said, and I agree. The sacrifices you witnessed, Nan, won't be for nothing."

In the car, Nani asked if Ali could drive her to Magelang the next day. She still had some of her clothes there. Ali agreed. On their way back Nani never stopped singing. Her voice was sweet and delightful. Ali Nurdin felt so light it was as if he could defy gravity and fly all the way up to the sky.

***

261

On the same day Nani and Ali Nurdin went for an outing to Kaliurang, Sadeli woke up in Maria's bedroom in Macao. He opened his eyes and instantly remembered where he was. He turned to his side and he stared with wonder at Maria's naked body. She was asleep with her back turned to him. The young woman's beautiful body enticed Sadeli to reach for her. Still half asleep, she turned to him. Her red lips were slightly parted and her black hair covered half her face.

He pressed his body to hers and kissed her face, her eyes, brows, cheeks, chin, and lips before he went down to her neck, her left breast and then her right one. She moaned in delight and he felt her nipple harden inside his mouth. She hugged him and tightened her hug as she whispered, "Eddy, Eddy." And then they repeated what they had done a few times the night before, repeated what a man and a woman had done since God created them, yet it always felt new every time they did it, just like this time.

Sadeli had left for Macao after the Catalina flew from Singapore to Sumatra in the dead of night a few days before. During the two days in Macao, he had handled the weapon transaction with Colonel Hua. All the preparations were done and he just had to wait for David Wayne's return with news from Yogyakarta. He now had the time to enjoy his marriage and to enjoy Maria, the young woman who never ceased to evoke his passion and joy.

Maria's mother had made peace with him. She was pleased to see Maria happy and said to him, "Protect Maria. That's all I ask from you."

The second day Sadeli was in Macao, Maria started to paint a portrait of him. "Too bad you don't have your uniform with you, Eddy," she said, "I want to paint you as an Indonesian major."

"I have a picture of me in that uniform," he said, and gave her a picture of him with his army buddies.

"Hmm, you look different in uniform. You seem fiercer," she teased and continued, "For now, let me paint you shirtless all the way to your stomach."

That morning, after they got up, showered, and had breakfast, she asked him to take off his shirt again and pose for the painting. "Don't sulk, Eddy. It'll take at least a week for your portrait to be done. And that is if you stop pulling me back to bed," she teased.

He smiled at her, lovingly, and said, "If I have my way, you'll never finish my portrait."

Someone knocked on the door.

"That's Mother," she said. "She surely understands us." She threw a glance at Sadeli and laughed. Then said, "Come on in, Mother."

Maria's mother pushed the door open and stepped into the room. She looked at the two of them and laughed. "Good morning. I want to take you both for a ride. We didn't take Eddy to see the firecracker and firework factory," she said.

"Oh mother, you're being silly. What's so interesting about the factory for him?" Maria said.

"Ah, let him decide for himself if he likes it or not." Maria's mother looked at Sadeli and said, "Don't you let your wife decide what you like or don't like, young man."

"Well, Maria," Sadeli said, "Mother is on my side now. Of course I'd love to see the factory. I only burned some firecrackers and fireworks when I was little. I really want to see how they are made."

"Alright," Maria smiled, "We'll leave in half an hour. I want to work a little longer on my painting."

Maria's mother waved and closed the door as she left the room.

Maria chuckled and said, "I'm happy she's taking you to the factory. It means she really accepts you as her son-in-law and as a son."

Thus Sadeli went to the factory and saw how firecrackers and fireworks were made. From the factory, they visited the ruins of an old Portuguese church on a hill downtown. There was nothing left but the stone staircase and walls.

When they sat on the top of the staircase, they had a view of the surrounding sea and mainland China. Maria's mother pointed at the faraway land mass and said, "My family came from there. You know, Eddy, when I married Maria's father, I got myself a Portuguese family at another corner of the earth. And after you married Maria, my family got a new member from yet another part of the earth. But actually it's not something new to us Chinese. China is a huge family.

It consists of so many tribes with different languages. Without the Chinese characters, they would not have been able to understand one another during these thousands of years.

"There are good things we can learn from the Chinese culture. It's the oldest culture in the history of mankind. Confucius and many other thinkers expressed so many wise thoughts about humans and life. Maria's father used to talk to me about Socrates and Aristotle, and I always replied with sayings from Confucius. At first he didn't believe any Chinese would be able to have such profound thinking, and he thought I stole those sayings from the books of Greek philosophers. It was really funny." The old woman smiled as she reminisced about her late husband.

"In your opinion, Mother, what can we learn from the Chinese culture?"

"I'm sure there are some lessons to be learned," the old woman said, "The Chinese survived for thousands of years from one dynasty to another. Look how the Ming dynasty survived for hundreds of years because of its strong family bond. Strong families make a strong society. Just like any other nation, the Chinese showed some cruelty and viciousness in their history, but still, a strong family bond saved their culture for thousands of years."

"Other than that?" Sadeli asked.

"The ethic of working hard. The Chinese have to work very hard on their own land if they want to make it because nature in China is harsh and difficult to deal with. Snow falls in the winter, and the flood in summertime can destroy fields and wash away cattle. The wars throughout history have made the Chinese use everything they can to survive. They are used to distress and are used to hard work."

"In my country, nature is a lot kinder to our people," Sadeli said, "There are two opinions about Indonesians' work ethic. One says Indonesians tend to be lazy because nature grows all kinds of plants without any help or work from a human. Millions of coconut trees grow by themselves along the shores, and dense forests full of natural resources are waiting to be harvested. The climate and nature there don't encourage people to work hard.

"On the other hand, some think Indonesians are hardworking people. The farmers and fishermen have a tough life and they have to endure difficult challenges from nature. Perhaps both opinions contain some truth.

"In my opinion, my people are more talented in arts. The nature in Indonesia encourages people to be artists. In every village, people play music, sing, dance, carve, weave, knit, and make jewelry from gold and silver. They carve houses and make statues. They turn paddy stems and bamboo into flutes, and goat and sheep skin into drums.

"West Java has a musical instrument called *angklung*, and it sounds lovely. *Gamelan* in Java and Bali is an orchestra with complicated notes and rhythm. If the world were just like it was two thousand years ago, with no international trade, no modern industries that need raw materials like oil, tin, iron, and rubber, no ship and airplane, and no radio, perhaps Indonesians would be very happy to keep on playing music, singing, dancing, and making beautiful things. Now, this artist nation has to compete with the tough merchants from Japan, China, Europe, and America, and they have to deal with nations with modern industries that are thirsty for the resources our soil has. Who will win this battle, the artist nation or the merchant ones?" Sadeli asked.

"Oh," Maria said, "You have an attractive way to illustrate your nation and others with modern industries. But is a battle, a confrontation, necessary?"

"Can't the artist nation develop entrepreneurial skills?" Maria's mother asked.

"Right now your artist nation has turned into a soldier nation, so it can change itself," Maria said.

Sadeli smiled. "The change from artist to soldier seems easier than from artist to entrepreneur or administrator because an artist and a soldier have a lot in common. Soldiers live and fight motivated by their emotions, feelings, and spirit, just like artists are inspired by their creativity, which is closely related to feelings."

"This is something new," Maria said, amazed, and continued, "I never heard anyone compare soldiers to artists."

Sadeli said, "People just forget, but they have a lot in common. A soldier with a true cause is willing to bear hunger, rain, thirst, and other misfortunes to achieve the goal he is fighting for. The same goes for an artist. Remember how Gauguin lived in poverty to stay faithful to his art. When he did so and succeeded, the world gave its acknowledgment and he reaped the fruit of his persistence."

"You speak so convincingly." Maria laughed.

Sadeli said, "Look at me. I love music. When I'm no longer in the military after the revolution, I'll perhaps be a musician or a composer. Many songs and music often pop into my mind and ask me to play them, but I never obey. I don't know if I'm going to be a good musician or composer, but I feel something inside pulls me in that direction. Or if it's not music, I want to be an architect, creating buildings and forms. I'm interested in doing that."

"If you're no longer in the military, why not?" Maria's mother said.

"I studied to be a teacher," Sadeli said, "I obeyed my parents, and my father wanted me to be a teacher. He sent me to a teaching school. So if I want to be an architect, for example, I have to study that. Go back to school again."

"There's nothing wrong with that," Maria's mother said, "Everyone can pick up something new to learn anytime."

"That's true, but we can't decide anything right now," Sadeli said, "We still have to wait."

And suddenly, the three of them sensed how fragile the present was. Sadeli felt the joy and passion that engulfed him and Maria could vanish any second. A telegram from Colonel Suroso ordering him to return to Indonesia could erase all the brightness in Maria's eyes and the warmth of her embrace. Maria also realized that.

Maria's mother, an old woman rich in life experience and wisdom, felt sad as she looked at the fragile joints of her daughter and son-in-law's happiness. She knew there was nothing she could do and remained silent.

She looked at her daughter. Maria's face seemed to glow in a bright, gentle light, the glow of happiness. Suddenly the old woman shared in her daughter's happiness. Perhaps this kind of happiness would vanish in an instant, but Maria had had the chance to experience it, no matter how brief.

She said, "Ah, don't think too much about what tomorrow might bring. We have to be happy and content with the pieces of happiness God gives us. That's what life is. It's not about having something forever, but about experiencing it piece by piece. A piece of happiness at one time, and a piece of sorrow at another. Life alternates."

Sadeli and Maria smiled. Maria's mother looked away to hide her tears.

"Let's go home," she said.

***

The weather was nice and the main street between Magelang and Yogyakarta was empty. Ali Nurdin and Nani felt the car move slowly even though they went down the same street before; it was the one with potholes and checkpoints every now and then. They didn't have any problem with the checkpoints because aside from the fact that a car with *PRESS* written in big letters on its windshield received special treatment from the guards, the special identification card Colonel Suroso had given them also enabled them to pass with ease.

A few miles outside Magelang, two soldiers asked for a ride. They were headed to a guard post some three miles away.

Ali Nurdin and Nani let them in the car. The soldiers were very young. Ali guessed they couldn't be older than nineteen. He asked, "Are you with the *Tentara Pelajar*, a military unit of students?"

They nodded.

"What's your plan after the revolution?" Ali asked. "Staying in the military?"

"Oh no," one of them said, "I want to go back to school. I want to be an engineer."

"I want to be an agriculture expert," said the other.

"Good," Ali said, "Our country needs experts in those fields and many others."

"Which battlefield were you deployed to?" Nani asked.

"Semarang," the two of them answered in unison.

Ali Nurdin glanced at the old Japanese rifles in their hands. They were very old compared to the modern ones used by the Dutch soldiers. *How unfair.* He looked at the young men's faces and their eyes lit with fighting spirit and thought, *Our enemy doesn't have the same motivation we have in this fight, so even though their weapons are better, they will lose. They don't know what they are fighting for, and they want to reinstate an outdated system of colonization.*

"How much longer will the revolution last?" one of the soldiers asked.

"It's hard to say," Ali said, "The Dutch won't give up just like that, even though both sides signed the Linggarjati Agreement. The agreement is not satisfying for us either."

At that moment, they suddenly heard the roar of a jet. The two soldiers yelled, "Look out. The enemy's jet."

Ali quickly stepped on the brake and pulled over immediately.

The two soldiers jumped out even before the car came to a halt. They bent over and ran, then jumped into a ditch alongside the street.

Ali opened the car door, pulled Nani out, and ran toward the ditch where the soldiers hid. The roaring sound of the jet was terrifying. It shook the air, seeming to slash the sky. Suddenly, Ali felt Nani stumble a little, but she still ran following his lead. The bent-over run on the street chased by bullets from the machine gun of the swooping jet felt like eternity. When they reached the ditch they threw themselves on the ground.

Nani's body fell on top of his. When he turned to her, his world shattered. It was as if thunder roared and lightning split his mind open. He stopped breathing as Nani fell to the ground, blood all over her chest.

The two soldiers crawled to them. "She's shot," they said. One of them took a small bag from his backpack and said, "There's a bandage and sulfate powder inside, Sir. Cover the wound and let the doctor at the hospital treat it later."

Ali Nurdin automatically held out his hand. Numb, he took off Nani's shirt, which was torn by the bullets at the side. The blood still oozed from the bullet holes in the side of her body. He spread the sulfate powder on the bandage and covered the wound with it. All his happy dreams were shattered by the fire from a Dutch machine gun. Nani was drenched in blood, unconscious. Her face grew paler under the sun as she wheezed for breath while lying in the dry ditch.

"Please help me carry her to the car," Ali Nurdin said.

"Not so fast, Sir. The jet may return and they'll shoot at anything, a car, carriage, people, anything they see on the street."

Ali snapped, "I'm not afraid of them. She needs to go to the hospital right away. I want to take her to a hospital in Yogyakarta."

"But…" The two soldiers stopped arguing when they saw Ali Nurdin's face, and they immediately helped him carry Nani to the car and laid her gently on the back seat. Ali Nurdin got behind the wheel and started the engine.

The two soldiers jumped back into the ditch. "He's crazy." They frowned when they saw the car move.

Ali Nurdin drove without thinking. His brain only gave one order he repeated over and over, *to a hospital in Yogya, to a hospital in Yogya*; his tears started to stream down his cheeks all the way to the end of his nose before they dropped onto his lips and went further down his chin and neck.

He stopped at every checkpoint, but whenever the guards peered in and saw his face and Nani lying on the backseat, they waved him on and told him to keep going.

When he arrived a few hours later at a hospital in Yogyakarta, the staff rushed Nani to surgery. A doctor who knew Nani immediately asked to contact her parents. They came quickly and waited outside the operating theatre with Ali until the doctor came out and said, "There's hope. We need blood."

Ali said, "Take mine, Doctor."

The nurse checked Nani's parents and Ali's blood. They had a match with both his and Nani's mother's blood.

Ali said, "Mine first." He turned to Nani's parents. "It's my fault. Forgive me."

"It's not your fault. Don't blame yourself," Nani's father said and continued, "Our life is in God's hand. Let's pray she'll make it."

The three of them bowed their heads in prayer and Nani's mother burst into tears.

The doctor came and said, "The bullet went completely through. It broke two of her ribs. She's still unconscious, but breathing well now. Come with me."

They followed the doctor in silence. Nani lay with her eyes closed. Her parents and Ali Nurdin came closer. Her mother wanted to hug her, but the doctor wouldn't let her.

"Don't disturb her," he whispered, "Let her sleep. Don't stay long. You better go home first."

Ali Nurdin took Nani's parents home. When they asked him to come in, he said he had to meet Colonel Suroso. On his way to the colonel's office his mind gradually started to function again. Questions raced through his mind. What happened? Why did the Dutch jet strike? Was it true that the Dutch were attacking at every front, conducting a military aggression?

He pulled up in front of the colonel's office and went right in. The colonel's aide said the colonel had been looking for him.

"What happened?" Ali Nurdin asked.

"The Dutch launched their military aggression, Sir. You should go in right away. Colonel Suroso needs to see you."

Colonel Suroso immediately noticed something was wrong when he looked at Ali Nurdin. "What's wrong?" he asked as he moved toward Ali.

"On the way back from Magelang, a Dutch jet attacked us." Ali struggled not to let his voice crack. He continued, "We jumped out of the car, but Nani was shot. She's in the hospital now, badly injured." Ali fought back his tears and ended, "She was still unconscious when I left her."

Colonel Suroso held Ali's shoulder and led him to the desk. "I'm sorry. Sit down; try to calm yourself. We have to be strong."

"I don't understand why this has to happen to her. What did she do wrong? How has she sinned? What's exactly going on?"

"The Dutch launched the military offensive we've long expected. We were ready and right now, our troops are fighting them everywhere. Can you leave tonight on the Catalina?"

Once again, the twist of fate threw Ali off balance. If the Dutch jet had not attacked earlier, he would have taken Nani with him and they both would be leaving for Singapore on the Catalina. Now the colonel asked him to fly back, and leave Nani at the hospital while she was still unconscious. *Can I leave her like that? Should I not be at her side until she's recovered?* He was about to refuse, when suddenly another thought crossed his mind. This was a revolution, a war: If he wanted to get revenge for what happened to Nani, he should keep fighting. In fact, he should fight harder than ever.

"Alright, Colonel," Ali said, "but this time I'd like to leave as an agent, not a volunteer like I did before. I don't care what rank you give me. I'll continue my work as a journalist, it's a very good cover, but now I want to fight as an enlisted man."

Colonel Suroso looked at him and said, "Very well. We'll commission you as a lieutenant. I'll take care of all the paperwork. It will be done before you leave. However, I hope you won't see our fight as a means to implement your personal revenge. I don't want our men to see every enemy soldier as their personal adversary to destroy. A soldier must fight according to a planned strategy and tactic and must only do what his command says. There is no room for personal vindication."

The colonel offered his hand and said, "I pray Nani will get well soon and you can get married as soon as possible. Surrender yourself to the Almighty. Safe travel. My aide will give you the letters for Major Sadeli."

Ali Nurdin shook Colonel Suroso's hand. "So long, Colonel. Please keep me informed of Nani's condition."

Colonel Suroso nodded and Ali Nurdin left the room.

Later that evening, David Wayne successfully took off from Maguwo airport in the darkness of night and raced to Lake Singkarak.

They needed to pick up cargo that had to be transported abroad to fund the revolution.

As the Catalina moved through the dark evening sky, loneliness overtook Ali Nurdin once again. The few officers on board were asleep and populated their respective dreams.

Ali Nurdin recalled the moment of the car heading to the Maguwo airport, where David and Pierre shook his hand and slapped him on the shoulder, saying, "Be strong, my friend." He had no idea how they knew about his tragedy. Perhaps Colonel Suroso had told them.

The pilots' sympathy helped Ali Nurdin a lot. He reasoned that millions of people were victimized during the previous World War. An untold number of Indonesians were victims of the Dutch army. He had no right to ask God for an exception for himself and the people he loved. Still, his heart was reluctant to accept that reality.

In the darkness of the Catalina's cabin, his memory played back the shooting incident he and Nani were in when the Dutch jet bombarded them.

He tried not to recall Nani's sweet face turned pale with trembling lips and closing eyelids, quivering as if they were the broken wings of a butterfly dropped to the grass. Tears blurred the image.

Ali Nurdin finally gave in. Tears ran down his cheeks as he cried over Nani, over his love, over his happiness the enemy bullets had destroyed. He cried over the fragility of human life.

The dream of his life was shattered by a man-made bullet on a street on the outskirts of Magelang. "There's no use to think about the future," he said to himself. And suddenly a cold feeling sneaked into his heart. A cold voice said he would never see Nani again. She would die. He too wouldn't survive this revolution. He would die before they became victors. He wouldn't live to see his nation seize their independence. He wouldn't live to enjoy what the flag of freedom would bring them. He would die before that, somewhere, sometime.

Ali felt at peace. He felt it was only natural to accept this fate. In fact, he was happy to follow Nani to the other side.

The Catalina roared through the quiet evening sky. The engine sound was rhythmic and the weather was nice. In the cockpit, David and Pierre relaxed. Pierre hummed a French love song about longing for a lover.

Oh pretty girl from Paris,
your eyes shine like stars in the sky.

Chapter 16

December 1948

Nearly a year and a half after the momentous events first unfolded, Sadeli had a rare quiet moment to reflect on all that had happened in Indonesia, beginning with the first Dutch military aggression on July 21, 1947, which they referred to as a *Politionele Actie*. Six months later, on January 17, 1948, the Republic of Indonesia and the Netherlands signed the Renville Agreement on board a US naval fleet that happened to be docked in Jakarta Bay.

Major Sadeli reported to his superiors that, based on information from his British sources in Singapore, the Allied Forces left some 62,000 weapons to the Dutch. This was proof that, despite their declared refusal to meddle in the dispute between the Netherlands and Indonesia, the Allied Forces did supply the Dutch with weapons.

In August 1948, Muso, one of the Indonesian Communist leaders who had stayed in Russia for a while, arrived in Java. He built the Communist force not only within the *Partai Komunis Indonesia*—the Indonesian Communist Party—but also among the youth, farmers, and the army.

The clash between the Communists and non-Communist groups and parties escalated. The Communists harshly criticized the politics supported by Soekarno and Hatta.

Meanwhile, the Dutch kept violating the articles of the Renville Agreement while accusing Indonesia of doing the same thing.

On September 18, 1948, the Communist rebellion broke out in Madiun. The Siliwangi Division that had moved into remote areas after the Renville Agreement was then deployed to Madiun and the rebellion was contained.

For a few weeks, Muso succeeded in avoiding capture, but in the end, he was shot dead by the military troops that pursued him.

Not long after the crackdown on the Communist rebellion in Madiun, Sadeli and the Indonesian intelligence agency received information that the Dutch were prepared to launch the second military attack. The news they gathered clearly showed that this time the Dutch intended to occupy the entire island of Java and capture the leaders of the Indonesian Republic. The Dutch would utilize all their weapons, in addition to those the Allied Forces had left them.

Prior to December 19, 1948, the Netherlands and Indonesia were preparing themselves for a new battle that might determine the fate of the Indonesians, whether they would become an independent people, or be colonized once more.

During the second military aggression, which began on December 19, 1948, casualties fell all over the battlefields in Java, Sumatra, Bali, Kalimantan, and Sulawesi. Thousands of Indonesian youth were captured, tortured, and imprisoned by the Dutch. Some of the Indians in the British Allied Forces units deserted their command and joined the Indonesian army.

All Indonesian people lived in extreme poverty. The Dutch destroyed and burned the villages and impounded the rice harvest. The people were shot at and captured, but Sadeli was proud of how they endured all the misery and made sacrifices with great patience.

The Dutch then tried to divide Indonesia into independent states and found some Indonesians who were willing to cooperate.

Indonesia had yet to recover from the wounds and damages of the Madiun rebellion, but the people's fighting spirit and flame of freedom never burned any brighter. Abroad, the preparation to carry on the fight had been completed, and Sadeli, though proud of the revolution's progress, steeled himself for the challenges still to come.

After Ali Nurdin reached Singapore, he delivered the cargo and the documents to Sadeli, and told Sadeli what had happened to Nani. He was touched when he saw Sadeli's expression change and tears fill his eyes. Ali noticed Sadeli's hand tremble when he squeezed his shoulder. All Sadeli could utter was, "Dear Allah."

Ali Nurdin reported that he now was an official agent of the intelligence, for he no longer wished to be only partially involved in the fight and merely help Sadeli as a civilian.

"I want to destroy our enemy with my own hands!" Ali Nurdin said. Something in his voice made Sadeli look deep into his eyes.

Two months later, a month too late, Ali Nurdin received letters from Colonel Suroso and Nani's father with the news of Nani's death at the hospital a week after he had left Yogyakarta. Ali received the news calmly. He already knew. He had known since the night he spent in the dark cabin of the Singapore-bound Catalina. He had known since then and already accepted it.

After receiving the news of Nani's death, Ali Nurdin tirelessly presented various ideas to attack the Dutch outside Indonesia. He read about the attack of the Italian frogmen against the British naval fleet at the port of Alexandria, Egypt, in World War II, which succeeded in sinking part of the British fleet. He planned a strategy to attack the Dutch ships that stopped in Singapore on their way to Indonesia. He had learned to use explosives from Sadeli and trained himself to use diving gear.

Sadeli rejected his plan. He said, "You have an excellent plan. Unfortunately, we can't implement it as we will then challenge the British in Singapore. They will shut down our propaganda and intelligence headquarters, and Indonesia's international relations in Asia will suffer."

Ali Nurdin understood Sadeli's reason and accepted his decision.

Sadeli's plan to acquire bazookas from the Kuomintang army through Colonel Hua failed. The Chinese colonel never showed up again in Macao. Later, Sadeli heard rumors about the colonel's death in some incident. Sadeli understood such an incident could just happen to anyone in China, especially to an army officer.

He couldn't find another contact and shifted his attention to the Philippines to obtain weapons. After the war in the Pacific was over, the Japanese as well as the American troops left many weapons behind in that country.

Sadeli never had the chance to tell Ali Nurdin about his marriage with Maria. He often wanted to, but something held him back whenever he saw Ali Nurdin's grief-stricken face. He worried the happy news would cause Ali to grieve even more.

Ali Nurdin had changed a lot. The man was a lot quieter now; he worked tirelessly, and had become a lot thinner. The bubbling excitement of the revolution he used to show had vanished from his face. He talked more calmly now and only when necessary. It was as if he had been through a test. He had passed the test but also lost all his effusive idealism and the romanticism of the battle he fought. He had turned from a man who fought in the revolution into a weapon of the revolution. Sadeli took a deep breath. He regretted the changes he noticed in Ali Nurdin.

***

On December 18, 1948, Major Sadeli, Ali Nurdin, David Wayne, and Pierre de Koonig left Lake Singkarak for Singapore. When they flew over the Jambi area along the Batanghari River, the left engine suddenly sputtered. The left propeller stopped, came on again, and then came to a complete stop. David landed the aircraft smoothly on the water before Sadeli and Ali Nurdin had the chance to be afraid that the Catalina would crash.

Once they landed, Pierre emerged from the cockpit. David steered the plane toward the river. Sadeli and Pierre took out the rubber boat and rowed to the bank to tie the plane to a big tree. Some of the lush branches of the tree leaned close over the water and partly covered the Catalina.

"Make sure the entire plane is covered with branches and leaves," Pierre said to Sadeli and Ali Nurdin, "I don't know whether this is a small or a big problem. It might just be a clogged fuel pipe."

Sadeli and Ali Nurdin quickly cut branches to cover the plane. David joined them to help.

It was around three in the afternoon. It was hot and the river flowed lazily. Forest sounds came from both sides of the river. They heard cormorants calling. Sadeli noticed dark clouds begin to fill the sky. He said, "Hopefully, it won't start pouring."

However, the clouds grew darker and the wind blew stronger. At first the treetops started to sway, then the trees shook. Thunder rolled and it suddenly poured hard.

They quickly went inside the plane.

David said, "We didn't have time for a thorough check. Pierre checked the fuel pipe and it didn't seem clogged. We need to recheck the engine. Looks like we can't continue our flight today."

They checked their watches. It was almost four.

"How long will the rain last?" Pierre asked.

"Can't tell," Ali Nurdin said, "It can be quick or last for days."

"Hopefully this one will end soon," David said. "Are the ropes strong enough to hold the plane? I'm afraid the river will flood."

"As long as the flood doesn't send a big log down from upstream, we're fine." Pierre's statement actually increased their worry.

They looked at one another and began to feel their anxiety rise. Since David made the emergency landing, Sadeli had not worried much. He thought it was just a small malfunction that could be fixed in no time and they would continue their journey. He had done flights like this more than ten times within the last year and a half, and they always went well. He thought the problem with the engine was a regular, minor one. With a skilled pilot and engineer like David and Pierre, he was sure the problem would be fixed quickly.

However, David and Pierre's comments made him worry. What if there was a flash flood upstream? What if the storm uprooted trees, caused them to tumble into the river, and then hit the Catalina as it came along the stream? The plane might suffer such severe damage that it could never fly again. What would they do with the gold and opium they carried on board and had to sell abroad to fund the revolution? And what about them? Would their lives end here, on the riverbank in an unknown jungle that was not even on the map? It would be unfair to have to die not from the enemy's attack but from either a broken or loose screw in an airplane engine. It didn't seem right to die anywhere else but on the battlefield.

Sadeli thought of Maria. Who would give her the news of his death? He had not told anyone about their marriage. He suddenly realized she might never know that he died in the Sumatra jungle. How long would she wait in vain? He wondered if she would think that he had left her for another woman. Or would she assume, after a while, that he had died?

Sadeli reasoned with himself that David and Pierre knew about Maria. If they made it, they would surely tell her. The thought relieved him until he argued, "How do you know both of them will make it? They are clearly in the same situation you are." He wondered if he should tell Ali Nurdin about his marriage now and give him Maria's address, but Ali Nurdin was also in the same boat. The thought of Maria waiting in vain saddened him deeply.

"Hey, brooding won't do anyone any good." Pierre's voice startled him. "Let's play some bridge while waiting for the rain to stop."

They sat on the plane's floor. Pierre shuffled the cards. David lit a Tarumartani, a cigar from Yogyakarta he liked a lot. "It's better than a Cuban cigar," he said.

"We have canned food and enough water, and there's even more outside," Pierre said and looked out the Catalina's window. "No one's hurt, so why should we be sad? Play your radio, Eddy!"

Sadeli turned the radio on and music filled the cabin with Minangkabau songs played by *Radio Republik Indonsia*, in Bukit Tinggi.

Outside, the rain continued to pour.

"This reminds me of the time de Gaulle ordered an attack on a French colony in Africa. Our plane, a British cargo carrier, had to do an emergency landing in the middle of the desert. It was a lot worse than our situation now. The Germans were still strong in Africa at that time. They still controlled the air space. Our broken plane was beyond repair. The wheel's axle broke during landing. Our water supply was extremely low. According to the map, the nearest water was at least two weeks away on foot. Imagine, two weeks of walking. If we stayed put, there was a big chance the German jet patrol would find and attack us. The fourteen of us decided to die walking. After two days, water and food were gone. We had accepted our fate to die in the damned desert, when suddenly a group of North African Arabs who were fleeing the Germans found us. Since then, I never give up, no matter how terrible the situation is," Pierre said.

Sadeli and Ali Nurdin looked at him and smiled.

The rain kept pouring far into the night. They felt the water level rise, but still deemed it safe to spend the night in the plane.

Ali Nurdin snored lightly, and Pierre leaned against a crate with his mouth open.

"I'm sorry for this accident," David said to Sadeli.

"Ah, no need for an apology. In fact, you saved us from a terrible crash. This sort of thing is inevitable. If it has to happen, it happens."

"Okay, thanks. I'm glad you think that way," David said and added, "Don't worry, Eddy, Pierre will get us out of this. He's a skilled engineer."

"Yes, I'm glad he's with us."

"You know, Eddy," David said, "I didn't tell you this, but I'm really glad you brought me to Indonesia. Now I feel useful. I had nowhere to go after the war. I just wandered around. Going home to America didn't seem appealing. My experience during World War II pushed me to look for the answer to questions that had been disturbing me. The war caused such a catastrophic level of damage across Europe. I took part in it. And then the Pacific too, although it was more against the military for this one, except of course for the atomic bombs on Hiroshima and Nagasaki. The cruelty inflicted by humans on other humans was beyond inhumane.

"I've always asked myself why humans have to kill and torture one another with such brutality that even beasts can't compete with it. I've seen how other nations live, cultures that are different from mine.

Why can't humans coexist in peace? I really respect your revolution for independence. I remember that when the Americans revolted against the British, they wished to be independent too."

"I'm glad you found us," Sadeli said, "Whether we will leave here alive or dead, this revolution will carry on."

They went quiet. Sadeli fell asleep with David's soft voice singing in the background.

I need a lot of loving, you need a lot of loving,
the world needs a lot of loving....

***

As soon as it was bright enough, early the next morning Pierre and David started to work on the engine.

Sadeli ordered Ali Nurdin to stay while he went to scout their surroundings. There were fairly tall hills approximately two miles to the north. Based on the map, there was no village within sixty-two miles of where they were.

The jungle was filled bird and monkey sounds. The soil was wet and steamy due to last night's rain. Water still dripped from the leaves and branches. Sunlight slipped through gaps between the dense foliage and tumbled onto the forest floor. From a small clearing on top of a hill, Sadeli had a view of his surroundings. The jungle stretched as far as he could see.

Oh Allah, he thought, and suddenly felt forsaken in the vast jungle. People could easily vanish without leaving a trace here, just the way it was in the desert Pierre told him about the night before.

Sadeli hurried down the hill. He got lost a few times, and when he reached the riverbank it was close to ten in the morning.

As soon as he arrived, Ali Nurdin yelled, "The Dutch attacked!"

Sadeli quickly jumped into the rubber boat and hurried back to the plane. Once he was on board, Pierre, David, and Ali Nurdin surrounded him.

"Radio Australia just broadcast the news that the Dutch troops attacked Maguwo airport in Yogyakarta this morning, at the break of dawn. They occupied the airport and entered Yogyakarta."

"Oh Allah," Sadeli said, "They finally conducted their military offensive."

"Well, this means war," David said.

"And here we are, useless," Sadeli said.

"We can fix the engine. It just takes some time," Pierre said.

The hum of an airplane engine suddenly filled the air. They tensed and quickly jumped into the rubber boat and rowed to the bank. The airplane sound grew louder.

"It's the Dutch air patrol," Sadeli said. "The first thing they do is of course cut off the air contact between Java, Sumatra, and other countries. I hope they won't spot our plane."

David said, "Hopefully the leaves and branches camouflage the Catalina well enough and they won't see it from the air."

The sound of the enemy's plane moved away then disappeared. Pierre shouted, "Come on, let's get back to the plane. I don't want to die a sitting duck for the Dutch jet."

While Pierre and David worked on the engine, Sadeli and Ali Nurdin were on guard, listening for approaching enemy planes.

Although Sadeli wanted to know the update about the Dutch military aggression, he didn't dare to turn on the radio. He did not want to miss the enemy's jet that could fly by any second.

David said, "Eddy, once we're done fixing the engine, we really have to decide when we'll take off. Obviously, we can't leave at night. I don't trust this river. Go and check how safe this river is for our takeoff. We shouldn't take off too late in the day because there's a significant chance we'll meet the Dutch jet. This Catalina is no Mustang fighter jet."

Sadeli told Ali Nurdin to come along to check the river.

When they returned about an hour later, Pierre and David greeted them with wide grins.

"Done." Pierre waved at the plane.

Sadeli and Ali Nurdin helped Pierre remove the Catalina's camouflage. Then Pierre gave David a thumbs-up. David turned on the ignition. The propeller moved slowly and then slightly faster, the engine sputtered, stalled, and then caught on. The propeller moved faster and smoke came out of the engine. Then the engine engaged fully and sounded just right.

They laughed and Sadeli felt like jumping up and down for joy. They shook hands, hugged, and slapped one another on the back. David turned the engine off. Sadeli said, "Let's turn the radio on and get the latest update."

The Australian Radio stated that President Soekarno and Vice President Hatta, along with Sutan Syahrir, had been captured by the Dutch during the morning attack in Yogyakarta. The Dutch only met a weak resistance and occupied the palace in Malioboro easily. The white flag was raised at the palace when the Dutch entered the vicinity. The Australian broadcast reported the Republic's army withdrew and avoided confrontation.

Ali Nurdin and Sadeli looked at each other, while Pierre and David looked at the two of them.

"That's Dutch propaganda," Sadeli said firmly and continued, "Bung Karno promised he would lead the people's army himself when the Dutch attacked. He said he would lead the guerilla war against the Dutch. Try the Bukit Tinggi Radio. I can't believe he surrendered."

The Bukit Tinggi Radio confirmed the Dutch attacks in many places, but it also broadcast the formation of the Emergency Government of the Republic of Indonesia led by Sjafruddin Prawiranegara as the Minister of Finance and Mohammad Natsir as Minister of Information.

"Ah, this means Soekarno and Hatta were indeed captured," Sadeli said and explained, "According to the plan, the Emergency Government will take over when Soekarno and Hatta are no longer able to lead." The Bukit Tinggi Radio announced the establishment of the Java Command under the leadership of Colonel Nasution. "Why didn't they escape?" Sadeli wondered out loud.

"He'll fight," Ali Nurdin said.

Sadeli thought of Colonel Suroso and wondered where he would be now. He felt an urgency to return to Singapore. There he could patch the interrupted connections. They had to intensify the fight overseas now. But first, they needed to get out of this jungle.

At five fifteen they got rid of all the leaves and branches that covered the plane. David turned the engine on. They deflated the rubber boat, put it back inside the plane, and released the ropes that secured the plane. Then the Catalina roared and moved along the river, picked up speed and went even faster before David pulled up the steering wheel. They lifted off the water and flew low over the jungle. Half an hour later, when the dusk set in, David flew the plane higher. Then night fell and enveloped the Catalina with darkness.

Meanwhile, far below them the ocean cradled the islands of the Indonesian archipelago where millions of people faced the killing of their fathers, sons, daughters, husbands, fiancés, friends, and mothers, as well as the destruction the Dutch military action spread all over Indonesia. However, no one, including Sadeli and Ali Nurdin, was afraid.

That night, Sadeli and Ali Nurdin sat in the darkness of the Catalina's cabin knowing they had to keep fighting. At the end of that fight waited lovers, their nation's independence, and joy of the freedom the Indonesian nation had dreamed of ever since the first time the Dutch colonizer set foot on Indonesian soil.

***

They parted ways at the Singapore airport. David and Pierre wanted to stay for a while to check out the plane more thoroughly.

After dropping Ali Nurdin at his place, Sadeli went on to his apartment. He hesitated at his apartment door. He sensed someone was inside his apartment. He wondered if it was Amah, the housemaid, or a Dutch intelligence agent with orders to kill or kidnap him.

His instinct and training as an agent spiked instantly. His blood rushed as he took his key from his pocket. He slowly inserted it into the keyhole, then quickly pushed the door open and scanned the whole living room. It was empty.

He stood by the door, hid behind the wall, and scrutinized his surroundings. There was no one. He listened intently and tried to pick up any sound. He closed the door gently and walked to his bedroom. He stopped in front of the door.

Surrounded by a dead silence, he told himself it was impossible for a Dutch agent to be here. They could not have known he would arrive in Singapore that night.

After calming himself he opened the bedroom door and stopped in his tracks; his eyes bored through the dim light and fixed on the bed. A woman lay there, sleeping soundly. He eased closer, before he suddenly exclaimed, "Maria!" and quickly jumped onto the bed. "Maria, Maria, Maria. You, oh, darling, when did you get here?" He showered her with kisses.

Maria woke up slowly, then jerked up and threw her arms around Sadeli. Holding him tightly, she whispered, "Eddy, Eddy, thank God you're here."

"Hey," Sadeli suddenly said after they hugged and kissed, "why are you here? What happened in Macao?"

"Oh, everything's fine there. Mother's healthy as always."

"Well, then why are you here? When did you arrive?"

"Ah, one by one," she said. "I arrived this afternoon. Why I'm here? Isn't it obvious? To be with my husband. Aren't you happy?" she teased.

"Oh I'm really happy you're here, but don't you know the Dutch attacked Indonesia and we're now at war with them? You better stay with your mother until the war is over. It's safer for you in Macao."

She smiled and said gently, "That's exactly why I came, Eddy. Because you're now at war against the Dutch."

"Uh, I get it," Sadeli said, "You want to join and fight the war?"

She chuckled. "Are there no traditions in your country that allow the women to fight alongside their men?"

"Oh sure, there are a lot of them," Sadeli said.

"Well, we have that as well. Both the Chinese and the Portuguese have such tradition. A wife stands by her husband in war, even at the battlefield. That's why I came here. And Mother approved. In fact, when I told her I had to fly to Singapore after hearing the news on the radio about the Dutch aggression in Indonesia, she quickly agreed."

Sadeli looked at Maria. Wonder, amazement, worry, and then pride in his wife merged with such a great joy it almost made him explode. He held her and whispered, "Oh, I really, really love you, Maria. I'm proud of you, my wife. Yes, stay here. The two of us will be together. I'm sure your presence is a sign that we'll win this war."

When their bodies and souls met and unified, Sadeli felt all his doubt dissolve in Maria's warm, loving embrace. He had witnessed the power of love from a woman to a man. And with such power, he felt he could do anything. He loved Maria as much as he loved the freedom for his people. And this power, he was certain, would defeat the Dutch imperialists.

***

Epilogue

The Dutch conducted their second military offensive between December 19, 1948 and January 5, 1949. Even though they held Soekarno, Hatta, and Sutan Syahrir captive, the blow didn't break the fighting spirit of the Indonesian army and the revolutionists. Battles against the Dutch broke out all over the country. And the Dutch's attempt to divide and conquer the Indonesians through the formation of States failed. Internationally, the Republic of Indonesia's revolution gained great sympathy from many countries, and the United Nations Security Council ordered the Netherlands to obey the restoration of the Government of Republic Indonesia in Yogyakarta.

The Emergency Government of the Republic of Indonesia succeeded in carrying the leadership torch for the fight for independence. On May 7, 1949, Indonesia and the Netherlands signed the Roem-van Roijen Agreement. Soekarno and Hatta returned to Yogyakarta.

Then on December 27, 1949, at 9:15 a.m. in a ceremony at the royal residence of the former Dutch Governor General in Jakarta, the Dutch officially acknowledged the sovereign Republic of Indonesia.

***

Notes

Chapter 1

Pandan mat*:* Mat made from the woven leaves of the pandanus tree.

Pak: Abbreviation of Bapak, meaning father, a respectful term of address for an older man or one who holds a position of authority or command.

Chapter 2

Melayu: A term referring to the indigenous Indonesian and Malaysian people.

Cheongsam: A tightly fitting, long, straight dress with a high side slit.

Genjumin: A Japanese term for the native people of Southeast Asia.

Bung: Term of endearment for a leader, e.g. "Bung Karno" for President Soekarno. Also jovial term of address for a man of the speaker's age, similar to "Bro" or "Buddy."

Inlander: The Dutch word for "native."

Romushas: Indonesian forced laborers during the Japanese occupation in World War II.

Heihos: Indonesian paramilitary soldiers in service to the Japanese.

Chapter 3

Hongi tochten: Expeditions/raids by the Dutch warships of the VOC (Dutch East India Company).

Cultuurstelsel: The Dutch "cultivation system," by which colonies were required to devote a portion of their crops to export.

Kuli kontrak: Indonesians forced by the Dutch to work as indentured servants.

Chapter 4

Becak: Type of Indonesian pedicab in which the driver sits behind the passenger.

Chapter 5

Merdeka: "Independent" or "free" in the Indonesian and Malay languages, the word served as a battle cry during the independence movement.

Chapter 6

Klongs: In Thailand, a canal used for transportation and drainage.

Ramwong: A slow, circular Thai folk dance.

Chapter 8

Indonesia Raya: Indonesia's national anthem.

Pancasila: The "five principals" of Indonesia's official political philosophy, which are belief in God, humanity, unity, democracy, and social justice.

Tanah Merah: An infamous Dutch prison camp in Papua.

Boven-Digoel: A Dutch prison camp for exiled Indonesian nationalists and Communists in New Guinea (now Papua).

Sukamiskin: A prison near Bandung, Java.

Chapter 9

Malioboro: The main shopping street in Yogyakarta.

Chapter 11

Lebaran: The Indonesian name for the Muslim holiday of Eid al-Fitr, one of Indonesia's major national holidays.

Chapter 13

Wahyu cakraningrat: The blessing given to leaders for ruling the country.

Chapter 14

VOC: "Vereenigde Oost-Indische Compagnie" – Dutch East India Company

About the Author

Mochtar Lubis is one of the most well-respected names in Indonesian literature. Born on March 7, 1922 in Padang, he was also a world-renowned journalist who was a feisty crusader for the freedom of the press and an unwavering believer in universal humanism, truth, and justice. His career in journalism predates Indonesian independence. Fluent in several languages, he monitored the Allied Forces' radio broadcasts overseas and translated them into Japanese. Shortly after Indonesia's independence, he worked as foreign affairs editor of Antara, the Indonesian National News Agency, from 1945 to 1952. He published the first English-language newspaper in Indonesia, the *Times of Indonesia*, in 1952 and was a war correspondent with the United Nations during the Korean War. He is primarily remembered as the editor of *Indonesia Raya*, a daily newspaper that never shied away from voicing balanced criticism of the current government and exposing the ugly truth of corruption and misconduct. His uncompromising and unrelenting journalistic principles led to his numerous imprisonments under the presidencies of both Soekarno and Soeharto, and the banning of the newspaper six times in total. As a journalist, Lubis was also active in the International Press Institute and the Press Foundation of Asia.

Lubis is additionally recognized as one of the greatest literary figures Indonesia has ever produced. He wrote *Senja di Jakarta,* possibly his best-known work in the Western world, during his house arrest under the Soekarno government. The work was originally published in the UK as *Twilight in Jakarta* by Hutchinson & Co. in 1963, and is considered the first-ever Indonesian novel translated into English. From the English translation, the novel was then translated into Dutch, Malay, Italian, Spanish, and Korean prior to being released in Bahasa Indonesia in 1970. Since then it has also been translated into Japanese. *Jalan Tak Ada Ujung*, another of his famous novels, delves into fear and courage during the Indonesian revolution and is considered by many to be his best work. The novel won a national literary award in 1952 and was translated into English as *A Road with No End* in 1968 by A.H. Johns and into Mandarin in 1988.

Lubis also founded a cultural and literary monthly, *Horison*, in 1966 and served as its editor for 36 years.

Lubis' endeavors as a journalist and novelist earned him several prestigious international awards. He was the first Indonesian—and remains one of only three—to have received the esteemed Philippine Ramon Magsaysay Award for Journalism and Literature, in 1958. In 2000, the International Press Institute honored him in its list of 50 World Press Freedom Heroes of the past 50 years.

Mochtar Lubis passed away on July 2, 2004 in Jakarta after battling Alzheimer's disease for a number of years.

About the Translator

Stefanny Irawan was born in Jember, Indonesia, on October 20, 1980. Her love of language and story started in preschool when her mother read her storybooks and comics and introduced her to the alphabets. While her kindergarten peers were just learning to read, she was way ahead of them and was in fact chosen to read the protocol aloud in the Monday flag ceremony. Her parents nourished, perhaps unknowingly, her love for words and literature through subscriptions to children's and teenage magazines and the crosswords books she found lying around the house. Then she started to write poems and stories. Her first published work was a short story in *Kawanku*, an Indonesian teen magazine, when she was still in middle school. She studied English Literature as her major at Petra Christian University, where she further forged her fondness for literature, written expressions, and theatre. She graduated cum laude in 2004 and soon found her prose published in regional and national newspapers such as *Koran Tempo, Media Indonesia*, and the now-defunct lifestyle magazine, *A+*. In 2006, Gramedia Pustaka Utama (GPU) published her first short story collection, *Tidak Ada Kelinci di Bulan!* (*No Bunny on the Moon!*). Her works are also found in several anthologies such as *Jurnal Prosa 4: Yang Jelita yang Cerita* (Metafor, 2004), *Rahasia Bulan* (GPU, 2006), *Menagerie 7* (Lontar Foundation, 2009), and *Un Soir du Paris* (GPU, 2010). Her short story, *Hari Ketika Kau Mati—The Day You Die—*

was chosen for Anugerah Sastra Pena Kencana's *20 Cerpen Indonesia Terbaik 2009* (*20 Best Indonesian Short Stories in 2009*). Before translating for Dalang Publishing, she translated books for GPU, including the well-known classic from Gaston Leroux, *The Phantom of The Opera* (GPU, 2011). *Daughters of Papua* (Dalang, 2014) was her debut in translating from Indonesian to English.

She is currently an adjunct lecturer in the English Department at Petra Christian University, where she teaches creative writing, literature and theatre classes, and serves as the Managing Director of Petra Little Theatre. She is a Fulbright scholar with a Master's Degree in Arts Management from State University of New York (SUNY) at Buffalo.

*More Storytellers from
Dalang Publishing*

Only a Girl
Lian Gouw

Three generations of Chinese women struggle for identity against a political backdrop of the World Depression, World War II, and the Indonesian Revolution. Nanna, the matriarch of the family, strives to preserve the family's traditional Chinese values while her children are eager to assimilate into Dutch colonial society. Carolien, Nanna's youngest daughter, is fixated on the advantages to be gained by adopting a western lifestyle. Jenny's western upbringing puts her at a disadvantage in the new independent Indonesian, where Dutch culture is no longer revered. The unique ways in which Nanna, Carolien, and Jenny face their own challenges reveal the complexity of Chinese society in Indonesia between 1930 and 1952.

Price: $17.95
Paperback: 298 pages
ISBN: 978-0-9836273-7-1

My Name is Mata Hari
Remy Sylado
Translated from the Indonesian by Dewi Anggraeni

My Name is Mata Hari tells the story of Margaretha Geertruida Zelle, a young Dutch woman married to an older military officer assigned to the Dutch East Indies. Claiming her mother's Javanese ancestry, she changed her name to Mata Hari, Malay for "eye of the day."

As Mata Hari, she danced on stages across Europe and the Middle East, and took many high-ranking military and government officials as her lovers. Convicted of espionage during World War I, she said at the end of her tumultuous life, "I am a genuine courtesan. And I am a dancer in the true sense."

Price: $17.95
Paperback: 334 pages
ISBN: 978-0-9836273-0-2

Potions and Paper Cranes
Lan Fang
Translated from the Indonesian by Elisabet Titik Murtisari

In Lan Fang's award-winning novel, Sulis is a young woman selling potions in Surabaya's harbor district. She meets Sujono, a day laborer with dreams of becoming a freedom fighter, and whose passion for Matsumi, a geisha called to Java by a Japanese general, is destined to ruin all of them. Each tells the story of their lives during the Japanese occupation of Java and Indonesia's transition from a Dutch colony to an independent republic.

Price: $17.95
Paperback: 252 pages
ISBN: 978-0-9836273-3-3

Kei
Erni Aladjai
Translated from the Indonesian by Nurhayat Indriyatno Mohamed

At the end of Suharto's New Order, the Kei people hold on to their traditions as they flee the violence that divides Muslim from Christian and destroys the villages. Namria, a Muslim girl, works as a volunteer in a refugee camp when she meets Sala, a young Protestant man. Grounded in the islander's belief of "We drink from the same spring and eat from the same land, the land of Kei," the two fall in love amid the chaos that will soon separate them.

Price: $17.95
Paperback: 224 pages
ISBN: 978-0-9836273-6-4

Daughters of Papua
Anindita Siswanto Thayf
Translated from the Indonesian by Stefanny Irawan

Seven-year-old Leksi lives in modern-day Papua with her grandmother Mabel and her mother, Mace. Pum, an old dog of unknown ancestory, and Kwee, a pig, along with Leksi, look back at the past as they face an uncertain future. In *Daughters of Papua,* the present is marked by a contentious election, with the gold company that wants to rob Papuans of their heritage the only winner.

Price: $17.95
Paperback: 224 pages
ISBN: 978-0-9836273-9-5

The Red Bekisar
Ahmad Tohari
Translated from the Indonesian by Nurhayat Indriyatno Mohamed

The *bekisar* is a fine crossbreed between jungle fowl and domestic chicken that adorns the houses of the wealthy. Lasi, whose father was a Japanese soldier, fair skinned and beautiful, is such an acquisition for a rich man in Jakarta. She is born in a village where the main source of income is tapping coconut palms for their rich sap, or nira. Her life takes an unexpected turn when she is betrayed by her husband and flees to Jakarta. She meets Mrs. Lanting, procuress for men in high government and social circles, who sells her to the rich Handarbeni. Lasi enjoys the new splendor as a much-desired ornament, but is alarmed when she discovers the marriage is a sham. Kanjat, a childhood friend, is now grown into a man. Lasi and Kanjat rediscover their affection for each other. Their bond is the village, its people and traditions. They struggle to free Lasi from a net of power, corruption, and deceit.

Price: $17.95
Paperback: 294 pages
ISBN: 978-0-9836273-2-6